ny White

Tony White is the author of cult novel ROAD RAGE! and a leading figure in the literary underground and the Brit Art gang. He has had journalism published in a wide variety of titles (including the TLS, Wired and The Big Issue) as well as editing the review section of a leading modern art magazine. He frequently gives performances of his fiction – as often in clubs, art galleries, or performance art venues (including a disused toilet) as in traditional bookshop settings – as well as co-ordinating readings at the ICA and cult venues. He is also publisher of the critically acclaimed samizdat imprint Piece of Paper Press, and literary editor of The Idler magazine.

Also by Tony White

Road Rage!
Low Life Books

britpulp!

edited by
TONY WHITE

SCEPTRE

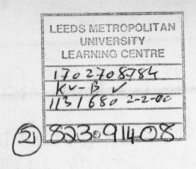
Introduction and collection Copyright © 1999 Tony White

For the copyright on individual stories see page vii

First published in 1999 by Hodder and Stoughton
A division of Hodder Headline PLC
A Sceptre Paperback

The right of the contributors to be identified as the Authors
of the Work has been asserted by them in accordance with the
Copyright, Designs and Patents Act 1988.

10 9 8 7 6 5 4 3 2 1

British Library C.I.P.
A CIP catalogue record for this title
is available from the British Library.

ISBN 0340 738936

Typeset by Palimpsest Book Production Limited,
Polmont, Stirlingshire
Printed and bound in Great Britain by
Caledonian International Book Manufacturing Ltd, Glasgow

Hodder and Stoughton
A division of Hodder Headline PLC
338 Euston Road
London NW1 3BH

For James, my son (when he's old enough to read it).

Acknowledgements

'The Spencer Inheritance' © Michael Moorcock 1998, (previously published in The Edge Magazine)

'Eddie' © The estate of Edward Lewis 1974, taken from the novel *Jack Carter's Law*

'Author's Notes' © Richard Allen 1970–73

'The Man Who Took Down the Great Pitpat' copyright © Victor Headley 1999

'The Long Drive-by' © Nicholas Blincoe 1999

'Falada' © Catherine Johnson 1999

'Signal' © Roy A. Bayfield 1999

'Shifa' © Steve Aylett 1999

'Jail Bait' © Stella Duffy 1999

'In the Box' © Simon Lewis 1999

'Know Your Enemy' © J.J. Connolly 1999

'Kitchen Sink' © Jane Graham 1999

'Promise' © Karline Smith 1999

'Taxi Driver: a strange tale from Endland (sic)' © Tim Etchells 1999

'Sex Kick' © Stewart Home 1999

'Stupid' © Jenny Knight 1999

'Bernadette' © Billy Childish 1999

'The Sprawl' © Darren Francis 1999

'Different Skies' © China Miéville 1999

'The Last Good War' © Steve Beard 1999

'A0' © Tony White (Translations by Elke Heinemann) 1997

'Riding Bareback (Jack's last words)' © The Estate of Jack Trevor Story, taken from the novel *Shabby Weddings*

With Thanks ...

Untold thanks to Sarah Such for having the vision to spot the potential of this project, for tireless support throughout its execution, and without whom ... etc. Ditto to Neil Taylor, *and* for taking up the reins, and to everyone at Sceptre for their enthusiasm and hard work, especially Sarah Ballard. Special thanks to all of the contributors for being so damned good at what they do and such a pleasure and an inspiration to work with, and especially to (in alphabetical order) Steve Beard, Nicholas Blincoe, Stewart Home, and Michael Moorcock, whose input, support and suggestions above and beyond the call of duty have been more than invaluable. Not forgetting Steve Pope and everyone at X Press, who have been my link with Victor Headley in Africa; George Marshall at S.T. Publishing for the Richard Allen permissions; Roderick Dymott and Sue Herbert at Allison & Busby for Ted Lewis's 'Eddie'; the various agents; James Pyman, and all of the friends who've listened to me banging on about this for the past year.

Contents

Introduction

Confessions of an Editor

My intention with this collection is to map territories and trajectories between the literary underground and mainstream popular fiction, by presenting – for the first time – rare, or never-before-published material from some of the late greats (Jack Trevor Story, Richard Allen, and Ted Lewis), and the literary giant Michael Moorcock, together with new stories by some of the freshest, most influential writers around.

From the outset the project has generated enormous excitement, and garnered support from everyone that I've approached. Perhaps this is because there is a generation of writers emerging who, like myself, remember the days when you could walk into your local, perhaps provincial, W.H. Smith's and be confronted by wall-to-wall pulp fiction. Your eyes would be drawn along the shelves and encounter the latest in Richard Allen's million-selling series of 'youthsploitation' 'Skinhead' novels, the biker novels of Peter Cave or Mick Norman, Sven Hassel's WWII epics, and the beginnings of Michael Moorcock's genre-defying 'multiverse' experiments. A moral questioning of the post-war 'sexual revolution' was played out on those heaving shelves too, and mapped in the 'Confessions' novels of Christopher Wood, and also in the parallel London crime scene of gangsters, porn-millionaires and bent cops described by Ted Lewis in his 'Carter' novels. And even if the 'Confessions' novels have now been consigned to a seventies-kitsch half-life and the libidinal gun play of Sven Hassel has been diverted into the shoot-'em-up computer game, the influence of these classic pulp paperbacks has never been more keenly felt than it is today, with much of the most innovative fiction drawing on the energy of pulp and genre writing.

Amongst the 'factory' writers of the sixties and seventies, the late James Moffat, pseudonymous writer of those 'Richard Allen' novels, seems now to be generally considered paradigmatic. Certainly, his reputation as a fast worker ensured that his publishers at New English Library threw him novel ideas and deadlines measured in days rather than the usual months or years. Moffat is a legend, reputed never to have re-read or re-written anything he wrote, and alleged to have measured the time it took to write a book in bottles. What is certain is his perceived influence on some of the most exciting contemporary writers: Nicholas Blincoe, Stewart Home and Victor Headley all had their debut novels compared with the street imperatives of Richard Allen's furious narratives. Recognising this, and with the co-operation of George Marshall at S.T. Publishing, I've been able to compile for the first time all of the 'Author's Notes' that prefaced most of the volumes in his 'Skinhead' series. It seems a timely move to throw the spotlight back on the author rather than his output. I hope you will agree that these give a truer picture, both of the man and of his novels, than any excerpted chapter could have achieved.

Mainstream publishing today is a world away from the heady heyday of the New English Library, when the likes of Jim Moffat could bang a novel out on any given subject. Contemporary themes, whether they be 'youth cults' or anything else, are no longer exploited as, or even before, they become news. Witness the recent spate of club-inspired writing that has dominated the paperback sales charts over the past few years. Rather than exploiting a trend or an era-defining movement like the late-eighties' ecstasy culture as it was happening, there has effectively been a seven- to ten-year gap, during which time the culture has been assimilated and re-packaged as nostalgia or personal reminiscence. During the nineties it has largely been left to smaller independent publishers to exploit the hunger for the output of the more action-minded and culturally astute producers of contemporary fiction. The X Press was formed in order to print Victor Headley's ground-breaking and hugely successful novel *Yardie*, after it was turned down by publisher after publisher who couldn't see the market. Scottish publisher S.T. Publishing acquired the rights to all of the Richard Allen 'Skinhead' books, bringing them out in a series of anthologies which haven't stopped selling to a new generation of readers. Stewart Home's early novels, such as *Defiant Pose* and *Red London* were published by Peter Owen and Scottish underground/political imprint A.K. Press respectively. Headley and Home were among the first to re-appropriate the vitality of pulp writers like James Moffat; as Steve Beard wrote in *iD* magazine, Home sampled 'the speed and aggression to make the link with Blake and Burroughs', while Headley used 'a few riffs to draw a map of the Black Atlantic in London'. I'm very pleased that they are both represented in the pages which follow. Victor Headley's story, 'The Man Who Took Down the Great Pitpat', is an extract from his forthcoming novel, *The Best Man*, which promises to be his best since *Yardie*, and Stewart Home is represented by his new novella, 'Sex Kick'.

britpulp! is not an attempt to define a generation of writers; after all, the stories collected here span some thirty years. It should also become apparent fairly quickly that this is not a themed anthology. While the reader may be forgiven for assuming that 'pulp' is synonymous with sex and violence, and indeed authors like Stewart Home have confessed to using these devices in order to 'keep the readers happy', there is a lot more on offer here than the shagging 'n' fighting story. Admittedly there's a *fair* amount of what might be euphemistically called 'action', though it could be said today that the laughably gratuitous sex scene is more the province of what LeRoi Jones, in his introduction to the seminal 1963 US anthology *The Moderns* (Mayflower-Dell) calls 'serious middlebrow establishment fiction', so-called quality literature. Reading the stories which follow, you may agree with my assertion that they are in fact jammed with gratuitous *storytelling*, and that it is the plot-lines which are brutal and break-neck.

Michael Moorcock kicks it all off with a new Jerry Cornelius story entitled 'The Spencer Inheritance'. Jerry Cornelius started life in the sixties as a kind of anti-James Bond character, but he quickly mutated into one of the most enduring characters in science fiction. I'm glad he's back, and very proud to be able to include him in this collection, a sentiment that also applies to the final story, 'Riding Bareback', by the late Jack Trevor Story, author, famously, of *The Trouble with Harry*. This is the first mass-market publication of an extract from Jack Trevor Story's final novel *Shabby Weddings*, and they are effectively his last words; 'Riding Bareback' was finished only minutes before he died. That we are privileged enough to share those moments is due entirely to Mike Moorcock's support for this collection.

Between Moorcock and Story, then, you will find as much diversity in voice, genre, style and subject matter as there might be in any good bookshop's fiction section. There's the truly classic 'Eddie', from Ted Lewis's novel *Jack Carter's Law*. There's also perhaps a contemporary counterpart to Ted Lewis in J.J. Connolly's tale of cocaine-trading gangsters, 'Know Your Enemy'. When I approached Stella Duffy to contribute to the collection, she was unsure whether there had ever been any authentic female voices in pulp — but with Duffy's wannabe young offenders in 'Jail Bait', as well as Catherine Johnson's teenage horse-killer, Jenny Knight's surreal, Jacuzzi-bound fantasy, and Karline Smith's hexed basketball star it's safe to say that there are now!

Steve Beard's science fiction, 'The Last Good War', continues the heritage heresies explored in his novel *Digital Leatherette*, the result of his pre-punk encounter with Ballard and Moorcock, while the likes of international cult author Billy Childish and Jane Graham are fulfilling a similar function to Christopher Wood in the literary landscape of today, but with the crucial difference that the bitter, romantic, and occasionally comical 'confessions' of these two authors are for real. Even Darren Francis's 'The

Sprawl' reads like a more sombre 'confessions from the music industry'.

From the fractured precision of Tim Etchells' fragmentary short stories to Nicholas Blincoe's 'The Long Drive-by', Simon Lewis's 'In the Box', the understated horror of Roy A. Bayfield and China Miéville, and the ballistic wisecracks of Steve Aylett, all of the writers brought together between these covers were either responsible for defining, or have re-captured, the energy and excitement of pulp fiction at its best. The result is *britpulp!*, I hope you enjoy it.

Tony White, December 1998

Michael Moorcock

'THE SPENCER INHERITANCE'
A JERRY CORNELIUS STORY

Michael Moorcock edited *Tarzan Adventures* at the age of seventeen, writing for *Eagle* and *Bible Story Weekly* before joining the Sexton Blake Library at nineteen, where he wrote *Caribbean Crisis* for the series, published under the house name of Desmond Reid. Later, as editor of *New Worlds*, he worked for the famous Gold brothers, publishers of Hank Janson. His only Janson was a short story – 'The Girl who Shot Sultry Kane' – published in *Golden Nugget*. He also completed one of James Moffat's 'Hilary Brand' novels, but can't remember which one. As a teenager and a young man he knew most of the great pulp writers, including Steve Francis (the original Hank Janson), a founder of *New Worlds*, which became one of the most influential literary magazines of its day. Moorcock's most recent stories are 'Cheering for the Rockets' and 'The Camus Referendum' (both Jerry Cornelius) and 'London Bone' (in *New Worlds*, USA). His novel *Mother London* is being reprinted by Scribners UK, who will also be publishing his new London novel, *King of the City*.

ONE

'Leave Me Alone'

'I mean, once or twice I've heard people say to me that you know Diana's out to destroy the monarchy ... Why would I want to destroy something that is my childrens' future?'

Diana, Princess of Wales,
TV interview, November 1995

'Oh, cool! This—' With all his old enthusiasm, Shakey Mo bit into his footlong, '—is what I *call* a hot dog.' His bearded lips winked with mustard, ketchup and gelatinous cucumber.

'Things are looking up.'

Close enough in the cramped confines of the Ford Flamefang Mk IV to suffer the worst of Mo's fallout, Jerry Cornelius still felt a surge of affection for his little pard. Mo was back on form, an MK-55 on his hip and righteous mayhem in his eyes. He was all relish again. Mounting the ruins of the St John's Wood Wottaburger, their armoured half-track rounded a tank-trap, bounced over a speed-bump and turned erratically into Abbey Road. 'Bugger.' Mo's dog had gone all over the place.

'It's chaos out there.'

Major Nye fixed a pale and amiable blue eye on the middle distance. Neat grey hairs ran like furrows across his tanned old scalp. His sinewy body had been so long in the sun it was half

3

mummified. They were heading for Hampstead where they hoped to liaise with some allies and carry on up the MI to liberate holy relics in the name of their dead liege, who had died reluctantly at Lavender Hill. The old soldier's steering was light and flexible, but sometimes it threatened to overturn them. Glancing back across his shoulder he voiced all their thoughts.

'This is going to be a good war, what?'

'At least we got a chance to lay some mines this time.' Colonel Hira brushed a scarlet crumb from his chocolate fatigues and adjusted his yellow turban. Only Hira wore the official uniform of the UPS. The United Patriotic Squadrons (of The Blessed Diana) (Armoured Vehicles' Division) were famous for their eccentric but influential style, their elaborate flags. 'Those Caroline bastards will think twice before taking their holidays in Dorset again.'

A saccharine tear graced Bishop Beesley's flurried cheek. Seemingly independent, like toon characters, his fingers grazed at random over his face. From time to time he drew the tips to his lips and tasted them. 'Surely this is no time for cynicism?' His wobbling mitre gave clerical emphasis to his plea. 'We are experiencing the influence of the world will. We are helpless before a massive new mythology being created around us and of which we could almost be part. This is the race-mind expressing itself.' His massive jowls drooped with sincerity. 'Can't we share a little common sentiment?' He squeezed at his right eye to taste another tear. 'Our sweet patroness died for our right to plant those mines.'

'And so her effing siblings could spray us with AIDS virus in the name of preserving national unity.' This was Mo's chief grievance. He was afraid he would turn out positive and everyone would think he was an effing fudge-packer like Jerry and the rest of them half-tuned pianos. 'Don't go forgetting that.' He added, a little mysteriously, 'Private money blows us up. Public money patches us up. Only an idiot of a capitalist would want to change that status quo. This is an old-fashioned civil war. A class war.'

Major Nye disagreed. 'We're learning to live in a world without poles.'

'Anti-semitic bastards.' Mo frowned down at his weapon. 'They deserved all they got.'

'Are we there yet?' The cramped cab was making Jerry claustrophobic. 'I think I'm going to be sick.'

TWO

'Our grief is so deep ...'

'... when people are dying they're much more open and more vulnerable, and much more real than other people. And I appreciate that.'

As above.

The convoy managed to get as far as Swiss Cottage before a half-dozen of the latest 10x10 extrasampled Morris Wolverines came surfing over the rubble towards them.

The hulls of the pocket landcruisers shone like pewter. The style leaders in all sides of the conflict, their streamlining was pure 1940s futurist. Their firepower, from the single pointed muzzle of a Niecke 450 LS, was the classiest ordnance available. Those laser-shells could go up your arse and take out a particular pile if they wanted to. It was just that kind of aggressive precision styling which people were looking for these days.

'But can it last, Mr C?' Shakey Mo was taking the opportunity to retouch some of their burned paint. The fresh cerise against the camouflage gave the car the look of a drunk in the last stages of cirrhosis. Mo ignored the approaching squadron until almost the final moment. Then, nonchalant, he swung into his gunnery perch, pulled the safety lid down behind him, settled himself into the orange innertube he used to ease his lower back, flipped a few toggles, swung his twin Lewises from side to side with the heel of his hand to check their readiness, pushed up the sights, tested the belts, and put his thumbs to the firing button. A precise and antique burst. The rubble between their Ford and the rank of savvy Morrises suddenly erupted and clouds billowed. A wall of debris rose for at least twenty feet, then began to settle in simple geometric patterns.

'Here's some we laid earlier, pards!'

Mo began to cackle and shriek.

Following this precedent, ash rained across Kelmscott and all the Morris memorials. Ancient PreRaphaelites were torn apart for scrap, their bones ground for colour, their blood feeding the sand. It became the fashion to dig up poets and painters and own a piece of them. No grave was safe. Everyone now knew that such gorgeous paint was wasted in the cement of heritage. Heritage parks.

'Cementaries?' Jerry did his best with his associations. Why was it wrong to resist their well-meaning intentions?

What secrets could they possibly learn? Nothing which would embarrass me, of course, for I am dead. But secrets of the fields and hedges, eh? Yes, I've found them. It's easy with my eyes. Or was. Secrets in old stones, weakened by the carving of their own runes and the casting of dissipate magic. Desolate churches standing on cold ground which once raced with energy. Why is there such a cooling of this deconsecrated earth? Has the ether been leeched of its goodness by swaggering corporate capital, easing and wheezing its fat bodies through the corridors of privilege, the ratholes of power. Help me, help me, help me. Are you incapable of ordinary human emotion?

Or has that been simulated, too? Or stimulated you by its very nearness. Yet somewhere I can still hear your despairing leitmotifs. Messages addressed to limbo. Your yearning for oblivion. You sang such lovely, unrepeatable songs. You sank such puritan hopes.

But you were never held to account.

Blameless,
  you were blemished
only
in the minds
of the impure
Of the impure, I said,
but not the unworthy.
For this is Babylon,
  where we live.
Babylon,
  where we live.
This is Babylon, said
  mr big.
What, mr b?
Did you speak?
Only inside, these days,
  mrs c,
for I am dead and my
loyalties are to the dead
I no longer have desire
to commune with the living
  Only you
  mrs c.
  Only good
  old mrs
  c.

Murdering the opposition
  It is a last
  resort.
  He came up
  that morning
  He said
  From Scunthorpe
  or was it Skegness.

You know, don't
you?
The last resort.

Don't blame me
You're on
your own
in this one
I said
Nobody
calls on
me
for a report.

Oh, good Lord.
Sweet Lord.
Let me go.
There's work to be done, yet:
You don't know
the meaning
of pain,
she looked over my head
she looked over my head
the whole time she spoke
Her eyes and voice were
in the distance.
You may never know it,
she said.
You could die
and never know it.
And that's my prayer.
Loud enough for you, Jerry?
Loud enough?
she asked.
There's an aesthetic

in loudness itself.
Or so we think.
Can you hear me, Jerry?
Jerry?
An anaesthetic?
    he said.
Oh, this turning multiverse
    is in reverse
And whirling chaos sounds
    familiar patterns
in the shifting
    round
Yet still,
    they take the essence from
    our common ground
    They take our public
    spirit
    from
    our common ground.
We become subject
    to chills and bronchial
    seizures
Now we are paying that price
    Given that prize
    Severed those ties
    Those hampering
        second thoughts
    Those night rides
        down to where
    the conscience still pipes
    a piccolo
    still finds a little resonance
    among the ailing reeds.
    Some unrooted truth
        left to die

down there.
Can you hear it?
Loyal to the end.
Loyal to your well-being.
Wanting nothing else.
Can you hear it?
Still piping a
hopeful note
or two.
All for you.

'You must be
   fucking
   desperate,'
she said.

The SciFi Channel
   Our ministers are proud
      to announce the
   restoration of the English
      car industry
   Record sales of light
      armoured vehicles
   has made this a boom year
      for our
   auto-makers.
      Bonuses all round,
      says Toney Flair
   our golden age PM.
      Let's give ourselves
      A pat
      on the back.

The domestic arms trade
   has stimulated the

domestic car trade
The economy
has never been
stronger.

We are killing
two bards
with one
stone.

Look at America.
That's their
lifeblood,
right?
You
know
what
I
mean?

You
know what I mean?
I mean
what
have
I
done?
I mean
why?
I mean
you
know
why?
I mean
you know.

Came out of the West
Out of the grey West
Where the sea runs
And my blood is at ease.
And this is where I rest.

THREE

Was Diana Murdered?

International crime syndicates are cheating Princess Diana's memorial fund with pirate versions of Elton John's 'Candle in the Wind' . . . Illegal copies of the song, performed at the Princess's funeral, are undercut by up to £2.50 and have been found in Italy, Hong Kong, Singapore and Paraguay. Profits will fund the drugs and arms trade.

Daily Bulletin, Majorca, 26 September 1997

'Gun carriages.' Major Nye lowered puzzled glasses. 'Dozens of them. Piled across Fitzjohns Avenue. Where on earth are they getting them?'

Behind their battered Ford the smoking aluminium of the Morrises fused and seethed, buckling into complex parodies of Paolozzi sculptures. Abandoning his Lewises, Mo had used a musical strategy aimed at their attackers' over-refined navigational circuits. A few Gene Vincent singles in the right registers and the enemy had auto-destructed.

'It used to be glamorous, dying in a crash. But the nineties did with auto-death what Oasis did with the Beatles. They took an idiom to its dullest place. This wasn't suicide. It wasn't even assassination. It was ritual murder. How can they confuse the three? It was the triumph of the lowest common denominator. The public aren't fools. Don't you think we all sensed it?'

Finchley's trees had gone for fuel. Its leafy authority removed, the Avenue had the air of an exposed anthill. Ankle-deep in sawdust, people clustered around the stumps, holding branches and leaves as if through osmosis they might somehow restore their cover. They had no spiritual leadership. As Jerry & co rumbled past, waving, playing snatches of patriotic music and distributing leprous bars of recovered Toblerone, they lifted their rustling limbs in dazed salute.

'These places are nothing without their foliage.' Mo lit his last Sherman's. The deadly oils released their aromatic smoke into the cab. Everyone but Jerry took an appreciative sniff. Jerry was still having trouble with his convulsions.

He had developed a range of allergies with symptoms so unusual they had not yet hit the catalogues. This made him a valuable target for drug company goons, always on the lookout for the clinically exceptional. New diseases needed new cures. But he was not prepared to sell his blood-rights just to anyone. There were ethical considerations. This was, after all, the cusp of a millennium. There were matters of public interest to consider. The Golden Age of corporate piracy was gone. We were all developing appropriate pieties.

Mournfully Bishop Beesley saw that he was on his last Mars Megapak. Yet compulsively he continued to eat. Rhythmically, the chocolate disappeared into his mouth, leaving only the faintest trails. They slipped like blood down his troubled jowls.

'Seen anything from the old baroness at all?'

Mo scarcely heard him. He was buried in some distant song.

'You made
the Age
of the
Predatory Lad.
It paid you
well.

13

'What price victory now, Mr C?'
'Eh?'
Jerry was still preoccupied with his physical feelings.
He lifted his legs and howled.

FOUR

Das War Diana

'I'm not a political animal but I think the biggest disease
this world suffers from in this day and age is the disease of
people feeling unloved.'

As above

Hampstead Heath was a chaos of churned mud and tortured
metal given exotic beauty by the movement of evening sunlight
through lazy grey smoke. In the silence a few bustling ravens
cawed. Hunched on blasted trees they seemed profoundly uneasy.
Perhaps the character of the feast upset their sense of the natural
order. They were old, conservative birds who still saw some kind
of virtue in harmony.

The house the team occupied had a wonderful view all the way
across the main battlefield. Its back wall had received two precise
hits from an LB7. The body of the soldier who had been hiding
behind the wall was now under the rubble. Only his feet remained
exposed. Mo had already removed the boots and was polishing
them appreciatively with the previous owner's Cherry Blossom.
He held them up to the shifty light. 'Look at the quality of that
leather. The bastards.'

He was upset. He had been convinced that the boots would
fit him.

'You turn people into fiction you get shocked when they die real deaths.' Little Trixibell Brunner, never less than smart, had agreed to meet them here with the remains of her squadron.

'Bastards!' Clinging vaguely, her mother drooled viciously at her side. Lady Brunner was having some trouble staying alive.

Trixi lifted disapproving lips. 'Mum!'

The infusions weren't working any more. Uncomfortably wired, Lady B muttered and buzzed to herself, every so often fixing her bleak eyes upon some imagined threat. Maybe Death himself.

Jerry was trembling as usual. His mouth opened and closed rapidly. Lady Brunner smiled suddenly to herself, as if recalling her old power. 'Eh?' She began to cackle.

Trixi let out a sigh of irritated piety. 'Mother!'

Until a month ago Trixi had been Toney Flair's Chief Consorte and tipped for the premiership when her leader and paramour took the Big Step, which he had promised to do if he had not brought the nations of Britain to peace by the end of the year. He would join his predecessors in US exile. It was the kind of example the British people now habitually demanded.

Trixi, growing disapproving of Toney's policies, had uttered some significant leaks before siding with the Dianistas whom she had condemned as upstart pretenders a week earlier. But at heart, she told them, she was still a Flairite. She was hoping her actions would bring Toney and his deputy Danny to their senses. Until the Rift of Peckham they had supported the Dianist cause. She would still be a keen Dianista if those twin fools, the Earls of Spencer and of Marks, claiming Welsh heritage, hadn't allied themselves with the Black Stuarts and thus brought anarchy to Scotland. Rather than listen to all these heresies, her mother had stood in a corner putting pieces of Kleenex into her ears. One of her last acts in power was to make them both Knights of St Michael.

A shadow darkened the garden.

Jerry was compelled to go outside and look up. Limping over low was the old *Princess of Essex*, her gold, black and fumed oak finish showing the scars of recent combat.

Mo joined him. He gazed approvingly at the ship. 'She always had style, didn't she?' he said reverently.

Jerry blinked uncertainly. 'Style?'

'Class.' Mo nodded slowly, confirming his own wise judgement.

'Class.' Jerry's attention was wandering again. He had found a faded *Hola!* and began to leaf through it. *'Which?'* For the last couple of centuries Britain had seen her monarchs identify their fortunes first with the aristocracy, then with the upper middle class, then with the middle class and ultimately with the petite bourgeoisie, depending who had the most power. No doubt they would soon appear on the screen adopting the costumes and language of *EastEnders*. They were so adaptable they'd be virtually invisible by the middle of the century. 'Style? Where?'

'Essex.' Mo pointed.

As if in response, The Princess shimmied girlishly in the air.

FIVE

Dodi's Psychiatrist Tells All

Those of us who met Diana can vouch for it, and the rest of us know it's true: She brought magic into all our lives and we loved her for it. She'll always be what she wanted to be – the Queen of our Hearts.

'Diana, Queen of Our Hearts', *News of the World*, Special Souvenir Photo Album, September 1997

'It was then,' Major Nye told Trixi Brunner, 'that I realised a lifetime ambition and bought myself a good quality telescope with the object of fulfilling those two fundamental human needs — to spy on my neighbours and to look at the stars. But Simla seems a long time ago. I often wonder why they resented us so. After all, they didn't have a nation until we made them one. It was either us or some native Bismark. Much better we should get the blame.'

'I believe they used to call that paternalism.' Trixi could not help liking this sweet old soldier.

'Quite right.' Major Nye squared his jaw approvingly.

His nasty locks bouncing, Mo swung round on the swivel gunseat. 'Can I ask you a personal question?'

Trixi adopted that open and agreeable expression which had become so fashionable just before the outbreak of armed hostilities. 'Of course,' she said brightly.

'How much time do you spend actually making up?'

'Not that long.' She smiled as if she took a joke against her. 'It gets easier with practice.'

'But about how long?'

'Why do you ask?'

'It would take me hours.'

'Hardly half-an-hour.' She softened.

'What about retouches?'

'I really don't know. Say another half-hour or so.'

'What about clothes? I mean, you're always very nicely turned out.'

'You mean getting dressed?'

'And deciding what to wear and everything. Say you change two or three times a day.'

'Well, it's not that long. You get used to it.'

'An hour? Two hours?'

'Some days I hardly get out of my shirt and jeans.'

'How long is a break in St Tropez?'

'What do you mean? For me? A couple of weeks at a stretch at best.'

'And how much time do you spend working for others?'

Trixi frowned. 'What do you mean "others"?'

'Well, you know, lepers and all that.'

'That's hardly work,' said Trixie. 'But it does involve turning up and posing.'

Major Nye patted her gentle shoulder. 'The public is very generous in its approval of the rich,' he said.

'It's the poor they can't stand,' said Mo. 'What I want to know is how many big-eyed children will starve to death just because Kim the Stump got all the photo-opportunities? Why isn't there more fucking anger? There's only so much charity to go round!'

'And nothing like enough justice.' Major Nye turned his chair towards the car's tiny microwave. 'Anyone fancy a cup of tea?'

He peered through one of the observation slits. A gentle mist was rolling over the picturesque ruins of Highgate. Marx's monument had sustained some ironic shelling. You could see all the way across the cemetery to Tufnell Park and beyond it to Camden, Somers Town, Soho and the Thames. It was a quiet morning. The gunfire was distant, lazy.

'Do you think it's safe to lower our armour?'

SIX

Now You Belong To Heaven

Then, amazingly, the masses who had prayed and sung the hymns, wept deeply as the service floated over London, began to applaud ... Once the hearse had passed, each and every one of us went home alone.

Leslie Thomas, *News of the World*, 7 September 1997

Something in Jerry was reviving. He flipped through the latest auto catalogues. He felt a twitch where his genitals might be.

Rover Revenges, Jaguar Snarlers, Austin Attackers, Morris Wolverines, Hillman Hunters and Riley Reliants all sported the latest tasty fashions in firepower. Their rounded carapaces and tapering guns gave them the appearance of mobile phones crossed with surgical instruments. They were loaded with features. They were being exported everywhere. It made you proud to be British again. This was, after all, what you did best.

But the politics of fashion was once again giving way to the politics of precedent. Jerry felt his stomach turn over. Was there any easy way of getting out of the past?

SEVEN

Diana's Smile Lit Up Wembley

The world is mourning Princess Diana – but nowhere are the tears falling more relentlessly than in Bosnia ... She met limbless victims of the landmines ... but she did much more than add another victim to her global crusade ... She made a despairing people smile again.

News of the World, 7 September 1997

'Thirty years and all these fuckers will be footnotes!' Mo stood knee-deep in rubble running his fingers over the keyboard of a Compaq he had found. The screen had beeped and razzled but had eventually given him the Net. Taking a swig from his gemini, he lit himself a reefer and flipped his way through *The Sunday Times*. 'Do they only exist on Sundays?'

'For Sundays.' Jerry was frowning down at a drop of machine oil which had fallen on to his cuff and was being absorbed into the linen. 'Do they exist for Sundays or do they appear any other days?' He was still having a little trouble with existence.

'We shouldn't have left him alone in the prozac vault.' Trixi Brunner brushed white powder from her perfect pants. 'You only need one a day.'

'I was looking for extra balance,' Jerry explained. He smiled sweetly through his wrinkling flesh. 'This isn't right, is it?'

Major Nye shook his head and pointed. Across the heaped bricks and slabs of broken concrete came a group of irregulars. They wore bandannas and fatigues clearly influenced by *Apocalypse Now*. This made them dangerous enemies and flakey friends. Virtual Nam had taken them over. Jerry sized them up. Those people always went for the flashiest ordnance. He had never seen so many customised Burberrys and pre-bloodstained Berber flak jackets.

They had stopped, and in the accents of Staines and Haywards Heath were calling a familiar challenge: 'For or Against!'

They were Dianistas. But not necessarily of the same division.

Mo cupped his hands and shouted: 'For!'

Major Nye looked around vaguely, as if for a ball.

With lowered weapons, the group began to advance.

Major Nye thought he recognised one of their number.

'Mrs Persson?'

Carefully he checked his watches.

EIGHT

Princes Teach Charles To Love Again

Princess Diana was named yesterday as the most inspirational figure for Britain's gay community. *The Pink Paper*, a gay newspaper, said a poll of its readers placed Diana way ahead of people such as 19th-century playwright Oscar Wilde who was jailed for being homosexual or tennis star Martina Navratilova.

Daily Bulletin, 26 September 1997

'You never get a free ride, Mr C. Sooner or later the bill turns up. As with our own blessed Madonna for instance. All that unearned approval! Phew! Makes you think, eh?'

'I was his valet, you know.' 'Flash' Gordon's lips formed soft, unhappy words. He was an interpreter attached to the Sloane Square squadron. His raincoat was secure to the neck and padlocked. They had found him in some provincial prison. 'Up there. He was a gent through and through but not exactly an intellectual. She was twice as bright as he and she wasn't any Andrea Dworkin, either. I "wore the bonnet" as we say in Tannochbrae. Some days you could go mad with boredom. Being a flunkey is a lot more taxing than people think. At least, it was for me.'

'Weren't you afraid they'd find out about your past?' Mo noted several old acquaintances amongst the newcomers, not all of them yuppies.

'Well I was a victim too you know.' Flash understood best how to comfort himself.

Una Persson, stylish as ever in her military coat and dark, divided pants, straddled the fire, warming her hands. Her pale oval face, framed by a brunette pageboy, brooded into the middle distance. 'Don't buy any of that cheap American shit,' she told Major Nye. 'Their tanks fall apart as soon as their own crappy guns start firing. Get a French one, if you can. Here's a picture,' she reached into her jacket, 'from *Interavia*. All the specifications are there. Oh, and nothing Chinese.'

'What's wrong with Chinese?' asked Jerry. He lay beside the fire, staring curiously at her boot.

'Don't start that,' she said firmly.

But she answered him, addressing Mo. 'It's totally naff these days. Jerry never could keep in step.'

'No free lunches,' said Jerry proudly, as if remembering a lesson.

'No free lunches.' Una Persson unslung her MK-50 and gave the firing mechanism her intense attention. 'Only what you can steal.'

NINE

Sign Your Name In Our Book Of Condolence

As Mr Blair's voice echoes into silence, Elton John gives his biggest ever performance. He opens with the first words – 'Goodbye England's Rose' – of his rewritten version of one of Diana's favourite songs, 'Candle in the Wind'. Billions around the world sing with him and remember the 'loveliness we've lost'. In Hyde Park, many watching on giant videos weep uncontrollably.

News of the World, 7 September 1997

'It's not the speed that kills you, it's what's in the speed, right?'

Sagely Shakey Mo contemplated his adulterated stash. 'You want to do something about that nose, Mr C.'

Jerry dabbed at his face with the wet kleenex Trixi had given him. For a few moments he had bled spontaneously from all orifices.

'Better now?' Bishop B looked up from the month-old *Mirror* he had found. It was his first chance to read one of his own columns, 'God the Pal'. He was getting along famously with the newcomers.

They understood all about Christian Relativism, Consumer Faith and Fast Track Salvation. They had read his *Choice In Faith* and other pamphlets. They were considering tempting him to transfer and become their padre. Trixi was even now involved in negotiations with her opposite number. They used the *can* as their unit of currency.

Not having the stomach to finish them off, the Dianistas had brought a few of their better-looking prisoners with them. The allies now stood shoulder to shoulder, staring down at the foxhole they had filled with the cringing youngsters.

Mo felt about inside his coat and came out with a small, clear glass medicine bottle whose top had been carefully sealed with wax.

'See that?' He brandished the vial at the baffled prisoners. 'See that? You know what that is? Do you? You fucking wouldn't know, would you? That, my dirty little republican friends, is one of *her* tears.' With his other hand he unslung his weapon.

As they heard his safeties click off, the half-starved boys and girls began to move anxiously in the trench, as if they might escape the inevitable.

'She fucking wept for you, you fuckers.' Mo's eyes shone with reciprocal salt. 'You fucking don't deserve this. But *she* understood compassion, even if you don't.'

The big multifire MKO made deep, throaty noises as it sent explosive shells neatly into each tender body. They arced, twitched, were still. Nobody had had to spend much energy on it. It was a ritual everyone had come to understand.

Mo slung the smoking gun on to his back again.

'You want to search them?' He winked at Trixi. 'I haven't touched the pockets.'

His visionary eyes looked away into the distance. Killing always heightened his sense of time.

Bishop Beesley murmured over the corpses while Trixi slipped into the trench and collected what she wanted. 'It was a culture of self-deception,' he said.

Trixi pulled herself up through the clay. 'Isn't that the definition of a culture?'

Apologising for the effect of the cold weather, Bishop Beesley urinated discreetly into the pit.

Jerry turned away. He was asking himself a novel question. Was everything going too far?

TEN

Reflexivity

Last Sunday a light went out that illuminated the world. Nothing would turn it back on. The death of Princess Di, the fairytale princess, the human royal, left us all totally stunned.

I am not a Johnny-come-lately to sing the praises of our magical princess. Unlike many others who now describe her in such glowing terms but certainly did not during her life, I have again and again expressed my love for Diana.

When I got some readers' letters knocking her I was saddened. I wonder how they and all the grey men who put her down feel now? The people have spoken.

Michael Winner, *News of the World*, 7 September 1997

'Islands within islands, that's the British for you.' The Hon. Trixibell had long since given up on her race. It was her one regret that she had not been born a Continental. Her mother still shuddered if the word was mentioned.

Their convoy had broken through to the MI. Although heavily pitted and badly repaired, the motorway was still navigable. It left them more exposed, but it had been a while since any kind of aircraft had been over. Several friendly and unfriendly airforces

were abroad, on hire to Continental corporations. It was th...
way to raise enough money to pay for the quality of artillery ...
demanded.

'We have had to learn,' PM Flair had announced over the radio,
'that we only have so many options. Economics is, after all, the root
of most warfare. We can have guns and butter, but we can't have
aircraft carriers *and* the latest laser-scopes. It makes sense, really.
Only you, the warriors in this great cause, can decide what you
need most. And if you tell us what you need, *we will listen.* I
guarantee that. Unfortunately, I am not responsible for the failings
of my predecessors, who set up the supply systems and who were
as unrighteous as I am righteous. But we'll soon have the engine
overhauled and back on the road, as it were, before Christmas. I
have long preached the gospel of personal responsibility. So you
may rest assured that I will keep this promise or take the Big Step
in the attempt. Thank you. God bless.'

There were seven weeks left to go. By now the people's PM
would probably be praying for a miracle. Ladbroke's and the Stock
Exchange were setting all kinds of unhelpful odds.

Jerry himself had not ruled out Divine Intervention. Surely
something was in control?

'It's not that long since you were collateral yourself, Mr C.' Mo
attempted to revive his friend's self-respect. 'Remember when your
corpse was the hottest commodity on the market?'

'Long ago.' The old assassin contemplated his own silver age.
'Far away. Obsolete ikons. Failed providers. Lost servers. Scarcely
an elegy, Miss Scarlett. Hardly worth blacking up for. Government
by lowest common denominator. A true market government. Poets
have been mourning this century ever since it began. Anyway, how
would I remember? I was dead.'

'As good as.' Una Persson settled a slim, perfect reefer into her
holder and fished her Meredith from her top pocket. Her elegant
brown bob swung to the rhythm of the half-track's rolling motion
and Jerry had a flash, a memory of passion. But it hurt him too
much to hang on to it. He let it go. Bile rose into his mouth

over the purple Liberty's bag. Something
le him, mirroring the social fractures in the
ng without his guidelines. This disintegration
n for many years and was now accelerating as
edicted. Was he the only one who had planned
all the others lost their nerve in the end? He stared
around him, trying to smile.

'Either stop that,' said Una, 'or pass me your bag.'

'Here we go!'

Ignoring the twisted and buckled signs which sought to misdirect them, they turned towards Long Buckby and their ideal. At some time in the past couple of years a vast caravan of traffic had come this way, flattening the borders and turning the slip-road into a crude highway, reminding Jerry of the deep reindeer paths he had once followed in Lapland, when he had still thought he could find his father.

He had found only an abandoned meteorological post, with some photographs of his mother when she had been in the chorus. Her confident eyes, meeting Jerry's across half a century, had made him weep.

A relatively unblemished sign ahead read:

WELCOME TO THE SHERWOOD EXPERIENCE
Sheriff of Nottingham Security Posts Next 3 Miles.
No admittance without Merry Man guide.
ROBIN HOOD'S FOREST
and FUEDAL FUEDING VR
(one-price family ticket value)

'I told you we were near Nottingham.' Mo sniffed. 'There's nothing like that smell anywhere else in the world. God it makes you hungry!'

'Takes you back a bit, eh?' said Major Nye. 'Now this, of course, is where an off-road vehicle proves herself.' The delicate veins on his hands quivered and tensed as he found his gears.

'Isn't it still relatively unspoiled?' Trixibell tried to take the bib from her mother, who clung to it, glaring and mumbling. Lady Brunner's lunchtime pap was caked all over her face and chest. 'The heartland of England. Where our most potent legends were nurtured.'

'That's crap, dear,' said Una. 'The only thing nurtured around here is two thousand years of ignorance and prejudice.'

'So she's right,' Colonel Hira rubbed softly at his buttocks. 'The heartland of England.'

'Fucking tories,' said Mo.

'Right on!' Colonel Hira's chubby fist jabbed the air.

'Haven't you forgotten how fucking concerned, caring and multi-cultural the conservatives really were, colonel?' The Hon. Trixibell was furious. 'One more crack like that and you'll be whistling "Mammy".'

'I thought you were with the other lot.' Major Nye was puzzled.

Trixi made an edgy gesture. She hated argument. It was so hard to tell who really had the power these days.

'That doesn't mean I can't see all sides.'

Laughing, Jerry coughed something up.

As best they could, the others shifted away from him.

It was getting crowded in the steel-plated cab. The heat was unseasonal. What was going wrong with the weather?

'Greenhouse!' Jerry was reading his phlegm. 'We have to get back to Kew. Kew.'

'Kew?' Mo cheered up. He had always tried to avoid the Midlands.

'Queue?' Trixi shook a vehement head. 'Queue? Never again.'

'Kew,' said Jerry. 'Kew. Kew.'

'You should get that looked at.' From the shadows under the instrument panel Bishop Beesley surfaced. 'You could infect us all.'

Everyone was staring at him. They had believed him gone off with the renegades.

He adjusted his mitre, shrugged his cassock straight and took a firm grip on his crook. 'There were small, unsettled differences,' he explained. 'In the end I could not in conscience take another appointment. My place is with you.'

'But you've wolfed the supplies,' said Mo.

'There was hardly anything left.' The bishop was all reassurance. 'Hardly a bite. Not a sniff. I wish I could tell you otherwise. A little jam would have been welcome, but no. These are harsh conditions and the Church must find the resources to meet them. I suggest that we pick up our holy charge and proceed directly to Coventry where negotiations are already in progress. They're well-known to have enormous stockpiles.' His mouth foamed with anticipatory juices. 'Rowntrees. Cadbury's. Terry's. Everything. Warehouses worthy of Joseph!'

'Coventry's the soft option.' Mo found the butt of his Monteverdi. Contemptuously he stuck it into his mouth. 'You want chocs, Bishop, we should go to York. It's the obvious place. They always make the highest bids on this stuff.'

'Stuff?' Bishop Beesley was outraged. 'Is that any way to speak of such holy remains? The Church's motives, Mr Collier, if not yours, are of the highest. Coventry is much closer. Moreover the bishop there is well-disposed towards us. Did you hear what the Bishop of York had to say. Idolatory he says! Step into the 21st century, divine colleague, I say. But when all the dust settles, security is our chief concern. As I am sure it's yours. We should never forget that ours is above all a profoundly spiritual quest.'

'Oh, for God's sake! Oh, Christ!'

Accidentally, Trixi had put her hand into Jerry's jerking crotch. Jerry's lips gave an odd spasm. 'Come again?'

ELEVEN

Prince Harry To Meet The Spice Girls

Earlier, just outside London, the hearse had to stop before it joined the motorway so police could take away blooms from the windscreen. The flowers made a poignant mound on the hard shoulder. Once inside the Althorp estate Diana was laid to rest quietly and privately on an island set in a lake. Her day was over.

News of the World 7 September 1997

There were now some forty armoured cars, in various states of repair, and about a hundred mixed troops on rickshaws, mopeds, bicycles, motorbikes, invalid carriages and milkfloats. Fifteen horsemen wore the tattered uniforms of the Household Cavalry. They were spread out for almost thirty miles, with Jerry & co. in the lead, creeping along the A428 to relieve the besieged manor of Althorp. The radio message had described a good-sized army of combined Reformed Monarchists, Conservative Republicans, Stuarts, Tudors, Carolines, Guillomites, New Harovians and Original Royalists, all united in their apostasy, their perverse willingness to diss the Madonna Herself. Camping around the walls like old queens.

'You hard girls. It's a conspiracy, isn't it?' Shakey Mo passed Trixi's dusted reefer back to her. 'I call you The Cuntry. You are the country, aren't you? You're running it, really. The old girl network. Your mum's their role model. Our Madonna's their goddess. A monstrous constituency. A vast regiment!'

'Keep mum.' Jerry giggled into his bag. 'Keep it dark. Under your hat. Close to your face.'

Baroness Brunner began to cackle again. It was high-pitched. Some kind of alarm. Her hideous old eyes glared vacantly into his. 'It's all in the cards, lad. All in the tea-leaves. Cards and tea-leaves made up my entire cabinet for a while. That way I could control the future.'

'Wonky.' Jerry twitched again. 'It's going all wonky.'

'I warned the wonkers.' The old baroness sighed. Her work was over. She had no more energy. 'Where am I? Can I say wonkers?

29

I told them it would go wonky. You can't say I was wrong.' Independent of her words, her teeth began to clack slowly and rhythmically. She drew a scented silk cushion to her face. In vivid threads, the cushion bore the standing image of the Blessed Diana, with a magnificent halo radiating from around her blonde curls, her arms stretched as if to hug the world in love, flanked by choirs of celebratory angels. There was some sort of Latin inscription, evidently embroidered by an illiterate hand.

Jerry watched her breaking up. She was in worse shape than he was. She had spent far too much energy trying to get her predictions to come true. It made a shadow of you in no time. It had been the death of Mussolini and Hitler. That's what made most presidents and prime ministers old before their time. Memory was the first thing to go. Which was embarrassing when you couldn't remember which secrets to keep.

Jerry sighed. There wasn't a lot of doubt. Things were starting to wind down again.

He shivered and drew up the collar of his mossy black car coat.

TWELVE

Two Billion Broken Hearts

We think Diana was killed through drunken driving . . . We think. I think. But we do not know. I do not know. Every newspaper and news organisation, with the exception of the more excitable elements of the Arab media, has decided it was an easily explained crash. Lurid theories about her death abound on the Internet but that is the domain of students in anoraks – desperate like the fundamentalist Muslims, to pin something on the Satans of the Western security services and their imperialist masters. Yet people who read serious newspapers and watch serious television programmes still have their doubts. Perhaps in this uncertain world they need to find a perpetrator, they cannot accept that the most popular woman of her time was wiped out with her playboy lover in an ordinary car crash after a night at the Ritz.

Chris Blackhurst, *The Observer*, 19 October 1997

'Are you sure it's not a lookalike or a wannabe?' Sucking a purloined lolly, Trixi stared critically up at the slowly circling corpse. 'And he could be pretending to be dead.'

The swollen head, the eyes popping, the ears flaring, stared back at her as if in outrage at her scepticism. Oddly, the silver paper crown his executioners had placed on his head gave the Old Contender a touch of dignity.

'We're going to have to burn him.' Major Nye came up with his clipboard. He was counting corpses. 'Before his followers get hold of him. He's worth an army in that state.' He paused to cast a contemplative and sympathetic eye over his former monarch. 'Poor old boy. Poor old boy.'

The rest of the besiegers were either dead, dying or sharing a common gibbet. By and large the century hadn't started well for the Monarchists. It looked like the Dianistas were soon going to be in full control of the accounts.

'Good riddance, the foul, two-timing bastard.' Mo had sat down comfortably in the grass with his back against the tree. He was cleaning his piece with a Q-tip. 'First he betrays his wife, then his mother, then his lover. He makes Richard the Third seem like Saint Joan.'

'He struck me as quite a decent, well-meaning sort of chap.' Major Nye glanced mildly at his board.

'I don't think we want to hear any more of that sort of talk, do we, Major?' Trixi had the moral high ground well sorted.

'He gave her a lovely funeral,' said Bishop Beesley. 'That huge wreath on the hearse with "MARM" picked out in her favourite flowers. It made the Krays seem cheap. A proper people's send-off.'

'The man was a monster.' Trixi firmly held her spin. 'The Prince of Evil. The Demon King. That's all you need to remember.'

'But what of the Web?' Una came walking through with a scalp-pole she had liberated from the Shire Protection Association. 'Can you control that, too?'

'Like a spider.' Trixi's words were set in saliva. She tasted her own bile as if it were wine.

In a moment they would achieve the culmination of all she had ever dreamed.

'They're getting a raft ready to go to the island,' said Una. 'I knew you'd want to be there at the moment they dug her up.'

Trixi quivered. 'You realise this will give us power over the whole fucking world, don't you?'

'It goes round and round.' Una put her scalps into Jerry's willing right hand. 'Hold on to those for a bit. And come with me.'

They stumbled over the ruins of the manor, over the remains of tents and makeshift defences. Crows were flapping down in waves. Parts of the battlefield were thick with heaving black feathers. It had been impossible in the end to save either the attackers or the defenders. But the island, by general consent, had not been badly shelled.

They arrived at the lakeside. A raft of logs and oil-cans was ready for them.

'Good Lord.' Bishop Beesley gestured with a distasteful Crunchie. 'That water's filthy. Thank heavens we don't have to swim across. There's all kinds of horrors down there. What do people do? Sacrifice animals?'

'It's our duty to take her out of all this.' Mo picked up a long pole and frowned.

'Clearly the family no longer has the resources.' Stepping on to the swaying boards, Trixi Brunner assumed that familiar air of pious concern. 'So we must shoulder the burden now. Until we can get her into safe hands.'

'You're still sending her to Coventry.'

'That's all changed.' Bishop Beesley chuckled at his own misunderstanding. 'I thought it was the Godiva headquarters. She almost went to Brussels. But we've had a lovely offer from Liverpool.'

'Which we're not going to take.' Trixi's sniff seemed to make him shrink. 'Ten times her boxed weight in generic Liquorice Allsorts? That's pathetic! You're thinking too parochially, Bishop. Don't you realise we have a world market here?'

'She's right.' Una began to pole them out over the water. 'America. Russia. China. Wherever there's money. And the Saudis would buy her for other reasons. It's a seller's market.'

'Russell Stover. Hersheys.' Convinced, the bishop had begun to make a list. 'Pierrot Gormand. My Honeys Tastes a Lot of Lickeys.' Thoughtfully he popped the last of his Uncle Ben's Mint Balls into his mouth. 'Sarah Lee. Knotts Berry Farm. Smuckers. America. Land of Sugar. Land of Honey. Land of Sweetness. Land of Money.' His sigh was vast and anticipated contentment.

'Syrup?'

THIRTEEN

We'll Win World Cup
For Diana

... The Royal Family often seem to behave in ways which could actually be called unpatriotic, and their denial of Diana, the world's sweetheart, was the biggest betrayal of all. But then, what can you expect from a bunch of Greeks and Germans ...

Her brave, bright, brash life will forever cast a giant shadow over the sickly bunch of bullies who call themselves our ruling house.

We'll always remember her, coming home for the last time to us, free at last — the People's Princess, not the Windsors'.

... We'll never forget her. And neither will they.

Julie Burchill, *News of the World*, 7 September 1997

'We might have guessed the yellow press would be here first.' Trixi had the air of one who was glad she had anticipated the right make-up for an unexpected situation.

She glared furiously down into the empty grave.

'Who are you calling yellow?' Frank Cornelius brushed dark earth from his cords. 'Anyway, I wasn't here first, obviously.' His features had a blighted look, as if he had suffered severely from greenfly.

'But you know who was, don't you?' Una Persson poked impatiently at him with her long-barrelled Navy Colt. She had chosen it because the brass and cherrywood went best with her coat, but it was a bugger to load. 'That earth's still fresh. And the coffin looks recently opened.'

Bishop Beesley was shattered. He sat on the edge of the empty grave licking the wrapping of his last Rolo.

'This is sacrilege.' Mo paced about and gestured. 'I mean, it's inconceivable.'

As usual at times like these, Jerry had risen to the occasion.

'I think we're going to have to torture you for a bit,' he told his brother. 'To get the information we need.'

'That won't be necessary, Jer'.' Frank's smile was unsure.

'Yes it will,' said Jerry.

'It was all legit.' Frank spoke rapidly. 'The upkeep of the site was tremendously draining, as you can imagine. After the old earl went down outside South Africa House at the battle of Trafalgar Square, there was a bit of a hiatus. The surviving family has responsibilities to its living members, after all. They brought a 'copter down while you were shelling the house. She'll be in Switzerland in an hour or two. Procter and Gamble have acquired the cloning rights. This is democracy in action. Think of it — soon, anyone who can afford one gets one! Charities will snap them up. Live! Oh, Jerry, this is what we've dreamed of! Of course, she doesn't actually belong to the people any more. She's a corporate property. It's Princess Diana™ from now on. A dually-controlled subsidiary, People's Princess (Kiev) PLC, own all the copyrights and stuff. But there'll be more than enough of her to go round. Charity gets a percentage of those rights, too. PP are a company with compassion. Their chairman's a notorious wet.'

'I wish you'd tell us all this after we've tortured you,' said Jerry.

Frank sank to his knees.

'Sorry,' he said.

'*You're* fucking sorry.' Mo unhitched his big shooter, unsnapping the safeties, going to Narrow Ribbon Fire and pulling the trigger in one fluid, chattering movement which cut Frank's head from his body. It bounced into the grave and rested in the desecrated mud, looking up at them with mildly disappointed eyes. A groan came out of the torso as it slumped on to the stone. Blood soaked the granite.

'Loose cannon.' Mo seemed to be apologising.

Jerry was getting pissed off. He rounded on Trixibell. 'I told you this was strictly cash. I should have got it from you up front. And now this little bastard's robbed me of my one consolation.'

But Trixi had been thinking.

'Wait here. Come with me, Mo.'

She began to tramp through the mud towards their raft. She boarded it and Mo poled his way to the shore.

While Una Persson did something with the grave, Jerry squatted and watched the Hon. Trixi.

She and Mo walked up the shore to where they had parked their Ford Flamefang.

Una came to stand beside Jerry and she too studied Trixi and Mo, watched as they dragged old Baroness B. from the cab. Trixi's mother made peculiar stabbing motions at the air, but otherwise did not resist. Her teeth were half out of her mouth and her wig was askew but the worst was the noise which came from her mouth, that grating whine which people would do anything to stop. In her heyday, men and women of honour had agreed to appalling compromises just so that they might not hear her utter that sound again.

Even after Trixi had stuffed her mother's moth-eaten wig into the rattling mouth, the old girl kept it up all the way back to the island.

Jerry was beginning to realise that his recovery was temporary. He reached for his purple bag and looked on while Trixi and the rest bundled the noisy old woman into the coffin and tacked the lid back on. There were some unpleasant scratching noises for a bit and then they knew peace at last.

'It's a pity we didn't keep one of those gun carriages.' Mo was polishing the top.

'They won't know the difference in Coventry.' Trixi pushed Jerry towards their car. 'Check the raft. Have a root around. We'll need all the bunjee cords we can get for this one. Once we get to the car she'll have to go on the roof.'

'I'm not sure of the wisdom of deceiving the Church.' Bishop Beesley fingered himself in unusual places. 'Where does devotion end and sacrilege begin?'

'Don't be ridiculous.' Trixi started to haul the coffin back through the mud towards the waiting raft. At the waterside Jerry and Una took it over from her.

She paused, catching her breath. 'Nobody can go further than the great British public. Besides, Mum's an authentic relic in her own right. Surely she's well worth a lorryfull of Smarties? It'll be the muscle we need to get us out of trouble. And if she's still alive when they open the box, they've got an authentic miracle. Who loses? A deal's a deal, vicar. Any port in a storm. Isn't modern life all about responding appropriately to swiftly changing situations? And isn't the Church all about modern life?'

'Besides,' Mo gestured in the direction of the real world, 'we haven't got much choice. We're going to have to buy petrol.'

'Well,' said the bishop, 'we'd better not tell the men.'

'We'll divvy up after Coventry, say.'

This began a fresh round of intense bargaining.

'There is another alternative ...' Nobody was listening to Mo. He shrugged and stepped down towards the raft.

'But I understood I would receive part of my share in confectionery.' Bishop Beesley was close to panic.

At a signal from Una, Jerry helped Mo aboard, then loosed the mooring rope. He and Mo began to pole rhythmically through the detritus towards the bank.

It was some minutes before Trixi and the Bishop noticed what was happening, and by then Mo and Una were loading the coffin on to the roof while Jerry got the Ford's engine going.

'Now Church and State will have time to establish a deeper and more meaningful relationship.' Una opened her *Diana of the Crossways* and began comparing it to her charts. 'Someone has to preside over the last rites of that unsatisfactory century.'

After his brief flurry of energy, Jerry was winding down again. 'It suited me.'

Major Nye's face appeared at the window slit. He was puffing a little. 'Hope you don't mean to leave me behind, old boy.'

'Can't afford to, Major.' Una's spirits were lifting. 'We need you to drive. Climb aboard.'

As Major Nye's legs swung in, Jerry shifted to let the old man into the seat. The others settled where they could. The cab had not been cleaned and the smell of vomit was atrocious. From overhead on the roof there came a faint, rhythmic thumping which was drowned as Major Nye put the car into gear and Mo took his place in the gunnery saddle.

Their followers limping behind, they set off towards Coventry, singing patriotic songs and celebrating the anticipated resolution.

'All in all,' Jerry sank back on to his sacks and rolled himself a punishing reefer, 'it's been a tasty episode. But it won't go down too well in the provinces. I'm beginning to believe this has been a poor career move. Market forces abhor the unique.'

What would I know? I say. What would I know? I am dead and a friend of the dead.

We get no respect these days.

Note: Parts of this story have already appeared in *The Observer, Evening Standard, News of the World, OK!, Hola!, Die Aktuelle, Hello!, Pronto, Globe, Daily Bulletin, National Enquirer* and elsewhere.

Ted Lewis

'EDDIE'

Ted Lewis was born in Manchester in 1940. After four years at Hull Art School, he worked in London, first in advertising, then as an animation specialist in television and films (including The Beatles' *Yellow Submarine*). His first novel was published in 1965. He went on to write nine books including, famously, *Get Carter* (Allison & Busby), which was made into a film starring Michael Caine. 'Eddie' is an extract from the novel *Jack Carter's Law*, which is currently out of print. Ted Lewis died in 1982.

Walter's house is a very nice house. Just as nice as Gerald and Les's. It's on Millionaires Row in Hampstead along with all those other businessmen's nice houses. Only unlike all the other houses it isn't lit up like Blackpool Illuminations. There's not a light on, not even a porch light to illuminate the slowly drifting snowflakes. The whole house is dead and you don't have to get out of the car to know that the occupants have gone away. It has that feel about it.

'Well, that's one less way to Jimmy Swann,' I say, lighting up a cigarette. In the passenger seat next to me Peter takes a packet of cheroots out of the pocket of his leather coat.

'They may be coming back,' he says. 'They may just be out for the afternoon.'

I shake my head.

'Walter's got three kids. After what's happened today he's sorted them and his Mrs out of it. Just playing safe, just in case.'

'If that's the case then Eddie'll have done the same,' Peter says, lighting a cheroot.

'I don't know. Eddie lives different to Walter. He still lives in the Buildings, in the flat his old mother used to have. Like a palace inside, so I hear, but still the Buildings. He likes the security of his old surroundings.'

'Yes, but if he knows we're getting on to him his living room and two bedrooms won't seem all that appealing.'

'But he doesn't know yet, does he? I mean, Walter's the one with the head, the forward-looking one. It'd be just like Walter to slide out of it in the hope that if everything's blown then he'll know about it when he's called on to identify Eddie.'

'So we go and see if Eddie's at home, then?'

I switch on the ignition and let out the handbrake and the car begins to slip away from the kerb and I say to Peter:

'If we are in luck, and Eddie is at home, you take your lead from me, right? I don't want your enthusiasm for your work cocking up the whole operation. I mean, if it did, I'd just as soon see to you as I'd see to Eddie or anybody else.'

'Jack,' he says, 'you've got such a wonderful way of putting things. Did you know that?'

'I always was good at English,' I tell him. 'Or so my old English teacher used to say.'

We drive along in silence for a while and then Peter says:

'Incidentally, I don't give two fucks about what's behind all this, the ins and outs, but I would like to know, in your opinion, who's going to come out of it best.'

'Why, so that if it's the Colemans you can do a little pirouette and end up facing the other way?'

'I always face the other way. Or hadn't you noticed?'

'I only notice things that are likely to affect me.'

Peter rolls down the window and throws the cheroot out.

'But do you see what I mean?' he says. 'I came to Gerald and Les for finance. That's all I'm interested in. This little tickle I presented to them could see me in the sun for the rest of my life.'

'In that case I should keep doing your banking with Gerald and Les. That way you might even get to go on the job.'

Peter doesn't answer that and when I make my next right turn I catch a quick glance at his face. It's set like some old boiler who's concentrating on her bingo card. I shake my head and look at my watch. It's ten minutes to six.

It takes us another half an hour to get to Eddie's. I park the car in a side street and Peter and I walk back to the corner and look up at the Buildings on the other side of the road. They look like reject plans for Colditz. Real artisan's dwellings and I bet Eddie's still paying the same rent his dear old mother used to pay. And with his money he prefers to stay there. We look at the Buildings for a minute or two more and then I say to Peter:

'What have you got with you?'

'What I've always got,' he says. 'My quiet little peashooter.'

'You haven't got your shotgun stuffed up your shirt?'

'No,' he says. 'Unfortunately I said goodbye to that this afternoon.'

'Thank Christ for that,' I say.

'You'd be well out of it by now if I hadn't brought it along.'

'If you say so,' I say, beginning to cross the road.

'Too bloody right you would,' Peter says, following after me.

We get to the other side and go through the arch that opens into the courtyard that's formed by the four interior walls of the Buildings. Apart from tracks of footprints round the sides the large central area of snow is pure and unbroken and under the lights from the landings the whole scene looks like something from an old British picture.

'Eddie lives on the top floor,' I say to Peter. 'You'd think that seeing as he chooses to stay here he'd at least have bothered to move down a bit.'

We walk round the inside of the courtyard until we come to the foot of the flight of stone stairs that leads up to the landings. Everything is very quiet, it being the tea-time hour. We get to the third landing without seeing anybody. Eddie's flat is the third one along on the right as you stop off the stairs. We walk along the landing and stop outside the front door. There is a small panel of frosted glass set in the door and through it there is the faint glow of light from deep inside. I look at Peter and he looks at me. I step forward and have a look at the lock. It's a Yale so that doesn't take long and when I've finished the door opens half an inch without making any noise at all. We wait and listen for a few minutes and from inside I can hear the sound of someone talking on the 'phone beyond a closed door. I can't tell who it is or what they're saying but at least there's somebody at home we can talk to.

I push the door open so there's room enough for Peter to go through and when he's done that I follow him and close and lock the door behind us. We're in a small square unlit hall. Including the front door there is a door in each of the four walls. One of the doors is open about an inch and this is where the light and the voice are coming from. I walk the couple of steps it takes to get to the door and I have a look to see what I can see through the crack.

Eddie's been very considerate because he's placed himself precisely where I can see him. He's standing over by the window with his back to the room, looking out at the falling snowflakes. The 'phone's pressed to his ear and whoever he's talking to is doing all the talking at the moment because Eddie's just making the occasional grunt of agreement. He's wearing the waistcoat and trousers to a very nice dove-grey pinstripe suit and on his feet he's wearing a pair of tartan carpet slippers.

I push the door open very very slowly. Eddie continues nodding and grunting so without making a sound I move into the room and Peter follows me. When we're both in, Eddie puts the receiver down on the cradle which is perched on the window sill and scratches his head and shoves his hands in his pockets and continues to look out of the window until in the blackness he registers our reflections instead of the snowflakes. Then he spins round and catches the phone with his right hand and sends it crashing and tinkling to the floor. He looks from side to side like a rubbish defender looking for someone to play the ball to, then chooses a direction and begins to bluster through the furniture in the direction of the kitchenette but I take off at a tangent and cut him off and at the same time Peter pulls a chair directly in front of the door we've just come through and sits down in it and takes out a cheroot and lights it up. Eddie now is forced to forget his instincts and pulls himself up short to try and rationalize the situation. He knows there's nothing he can say, because if there was we wouldn't be there. There's no way out for him, but he can't prevent the cogs in his brain turning and turning just in case he can come up with something. So I light up a cigarette and look round the place and wait for Eddie to reach his logical conclusion.

The place is done out like a miniature brothel. Everything that is possible to have a pattern on it is patterned: the suite, the curtains, the wallpaper, the carpet, the cushions. One wall consists of rose tinted panelled mirrors and yet in the middle of those panels is set an electric fire and round this fire there is even an inlaid pattern of roses. In fact all the patterns are floral (but never the same one twice) and the whole effect makes the ramrod stripes of Eddie's beautiful suiting seem quite spectacularly out of place, like a graph superimposed over a flower study. And then there are the ornaments. There are a couple of shelves on the wall where the window is that are brimfull of miniature liqueur and spirit bottles. Then there are three whole shelves on a bookcase that are stacked with mementos of holidays abroad, like pot sombreros or ash-trays set in basket-weave or little figures of donkeys in sombreros with little bambinos leading them or cellophane encased dolls in national costume, or models of famous pieces of architecture with tiny barometers set in relevant positions to the design. And then there are the reproductions; Picasso's Clown, Tretchikoff's the Tear, the wild horses in the surf.

I throw my spent match in a waste bin with a floral pattern which is set in a mock wrought-iron receptacle and I say:

'I always thought it quiet round here, Eddie, until I saw the inside of this place.'

By this time Eddie has reached the macaroni stage and his face has gone as slack as a melting waxwork and the only thing that stops him sinking to his knees on the carpet is the unconscious awareness of the knife edges in his trousers. His mouth is wide open like the mouth of a fish with a hook inside it but he's not going to be able to control his lips so that he can form any words. His face is the colour of vanilla ice cream and beads of oily sweat are slowly following the downward pattern of his expression. Inside he must be wishing he'd worshipped a little more fastidiously at the shrine of the God he's now praying to.

'Well,' I say. 'Eddie.'

Eddie's hands move briefly as though somebody's pulling the strings and I walk over to him and flip the top of my cigarette packet and offer him a cigarette but all that happens is that his mouth falls open a little bit wider. So I take hold of one of his hands and insert a cigarette between the fore- and middle fingers and lift his arm and hold his hand so that the cigarette is near his lips and he automatically does the rest himself. I light the cigarette for him and he manages to inhale and while he's doing that I draw well back and hit him as hard as I can just below his breast bone. The punch makes him stagger backwards rather than fall over immediately but he's got to fall over sometime and when he does it's across a low table next to the colour telly, upending the little wrought-iron magazine holder and scattering the telly papers all over the place. I give him a few minutes to get his breath back and to pass the time I watch the cigarette I gave him burn a hole in the centre of one of the flowers in the pattern on the carpet.

When Eddie's got himself back together I say to him:

'As you know, we haven't the time to play mulberry bushes. All we want to know is what's happening, from beginning to end. That's all we want, Eddie, and I think you know that shooting shit won't help your position one little bit.'

Eddie drags himself up off the floor and supports himself on the back of an easy chair and exercises his lungs for a couple of minutes. Then he looks up at me and says:

'What's going to happen to me?'

'I don't know, Eddie,' I tell him.

He looks down at the back of the chair again and nods his head.

'Yes,' he says.

I sit down in the opposite armchair and say:

'Tell us first, Eddie. You never know, depending on what kind of fairy tale it is there might just be a happy ending.'

Eddie stays the way he is for a minute then works his way round to the front of the chair and eases himself down into it. Then he sees the cigarette lying on the floor burning its way through the carpet and he bends over and picks it up and flicks the ash into an ash-tray and takes a drag. Then he passes his hand through his hair and is about to speak, but before he can, I say:

'First, Eddie. The wife. The kids. Where are they?'

'They're out of it,' he says. 'They're away. That I'm not telling you.'

'It's not important right now,' I tell him. 'Just didn't want us to be interrupted once you got into full flow.'

Eddie takes another drag on his cigarette.

'It wasn't my idea,' he says.

I don't make any comment on his statement so there's no alternative but for him to go on. 'I mean, I said to Wally, we're all right as we are, aren't we? What's wrong with the set-up we already have? This idea is going to bring us nothing but fucking strife. But Wally just rubbed his hands together and said he'd been looking forward to a set-up like this for years.'

Eddie puts the cigarette out in the ash-tray. He looks at me and then at Peter and then back to me.

'What was the idea, Eddie?' I say to him.

'Well, it wasn't even Wally's idea, was it? I mean, if it hadn't been served up to him he'd never have thought of it by himself, would he? I mean, be fair. Would he?'

'So whose idea was it?'

Eddie makes sure he's not looking into my eyes when he says:

'Hume.'

Eddie might be avoiding my eyes but I can certainly feel Peter's boring into the back of my neck when the word drops into the silence of the room.

'See, Hume comes round to see Wally one day about this bullion job we put out over in Bromley. He comes steaming in with his usual spiel about how he's fitted up somebody who wasn't even on the job and how to save himself ten out of twenty this somebody's going to stand up and point at me and Wally. Of course, Wally tells Hume to piss off and go and play in the next street. I mean, the thing is that this somebody's a geezer called Danny Ross and Wally did Danny a great big favour once and Danny's soft as shit and he'd do thirty rather than

47

point at me and Wally and Wally tells Hume as much. Hume doesn't like it, understandably enough, so he takes his pleasure by saying that if Danny's such an old mucker of ours we'll enjoy seeing him do a twenty-five for this and a couple of others Hume will fit him in on, not to mention Danny's old lady who he'll do for harbouring and receiving and being an accessory and all that rubbish. So Walter says all right, all right, how much? Hume calms down and then he asks us how much we fenced it for. I mean, he sat there and fucking asked us. So Walter tells him half of what we got for it and Hume says in that case ten grand'll see Danny at home with his wife and kiddies until the next time. Wally says five and they finally fix a figure. And with that Hume trolleys off. For a while Wally's blazing and all for putting a bomb outside Hume's front door but I cool him off and he lets the matter drop. Then a month or so later Hume comes back and says to us how'd we like to have him as a permanent partner? Wally says Fucking lovely, it'll only cost us fifty grand a year at Hume's rates, why doesn't he start today? Hume wears it all and when Wally's finished he says Let's not be silly, you could even afford that if you had Gerald and Les's patch as well and Wally says Yes, you can afford anything when you're dead. Hume shakes his head a few times and then puts us this proposition; first, that he'd heard he could get Finbow's job if Finbow was out of it. And that would be a step in the right direction but Gerald and Les would still be there, Finbow or not. So, he says, supposing somebody blew the whistle on Gerald and Les? Supposing it could be guaranteed that somebody would be out of the country the day the trial ended, with a new name on his passport and free passage to anywhere he wants to go with his family and ten thousand quid out of the police fund? Plus, of course, whatever me and Wally'd want to chip in, which could make the offer much more attractive. And he says with him in West End Central and Gerald and Les and you out of the way he'd look after us the way Finbow looked after you lot. And we'd be doing twice the business, what with the shops and the clubs and the places and all those things.'

'Yes,' I say to him. 'I know about those things, Eddie.'

'Look, Jack, for Christ's sake, do me a favour, will you?' He slides off the chair and sinks to the floor and puts his hands on my knees. 'Christ, I didn't . . .'

I take his hands away.

'Sit down and finish the story,' I say to him. 'There's time for all that afterwards.' Eddie shakes his head and a tear flicks from his eye on to the carpet but he back-pedals on his knees and finds the chair and slides back into it.

'I told Wally he'd be barmy to think of it but Wally shut me up and asked Hume if he'd worked out how to do it yet. Hume said he'd let us know and he went away. He comes back a week later and tells us he's done some sniffing and he's found out from someone in the Fraud Squad that Mallory's behind some dodgy companies that are just about to make the headlines and even Mallory won't be able to avoid getting five to seven. So he promises Mallory some friendship if he can figure a way to blow Finbow and put it on Gerald and Les. And he does. He comes up with the pictures and Jimmy Swann. Wally's over the moon about it, especially as Hume says he's already put it to the top brass and they're prepared to let him play it his way and also finance Jimmy. And from then on there's no stopping Wally. He can't wait for the action to start.'

'What held him back last night?'

'Hume wanted him to keep buttoned up. But today when Wally heard about you getting to the Abbots he decided to have his fun and join in. You know what Wally's like.'

'Yes, I know what Wally's like,' I say. I light another cigarette. 'But Hume saw me last night. He could have had me then. Jimmy needn't even have signed his statement.'

'Hume fixed Finbow but he doesn't want anybody to know on account of being next in line. So he's worked it that some-one else does the lifting and he's prepared to come in with any further names and evidence for the glory later on; that's why so many names are still walking around enjoying the fresh air. But after today Hume will have to start pulling them in right away.'

Eddie stops talking. I don't say anything for a while. Eventually I say:

'So where's Jimmy Swann?'

Eddie shakes his head.

'Only Hume knows that.'

I look at him.

'We could do a deal with Hume. We could tell him where to get at Gerald and Les and make the takeover nice and smooth in return for being left out of it and carrying on as we are.'

'That's right,' Eddie says. 'Wally's always wanted you on the firm, Jack. It'd work out perfect.'

'And you could still get the finance for your tickle,' I say to Peter.

'Spot on,' he says. 'You got it in one.'

'Except that if we were to do what you've just said we'd both be on twenty-fives whatever this chancer's trying to tell us.'

'You wouldn't,' Eddie says. 'I guarantee it. I can phone Hume and do a deal right now.'

'Do you believe what Eddie says?' I ask Peter. Peter shrugs.

'What's the alternative?' he says. 'We're on a definite loser the other way.'

'And what if I say I'm going to play this the way I set out to play it?'

Peter looks me in the face and is quite motionless. This is where he has to decide what to do and until he's done that he is very careful not to do anything which will cause me to react. He looks beyond me at Eddie and then back to me and he's just about to speak when there is a slight movement behind me and I whirl around just in time to see Eddie disappearing round the corner of the L-shaped room, the part that leads to the kitchenette. I rush after him but there is a lot of furniture in the way and before I'm at the corner of the 'L' the kitchenette door has slammed. Peter is already on his feet and I shout at him to open the door behind the chair he was sitting in and get into the hall. I make it to the kitchenette door and yank it open but of course Eddie is no longer in the kitchenette because through its other door, the one that leads into the hall, I can see Eddie scrambling at the lock handle of the outside door. I hurry across the kitchenette but I'm never going to make it because now Eddie has got the outside door open and the only thing that's going to stop him is Peter but the outside door slams as Peter appears in the hall. I get into the hall a second after Peter and already he's twisting the lock handle. He's gripping his shooter in his free hand.

'Whatever you do, you cunt, don't shoot,' I tell him as I follow him through the door. We turn left but there's no sign of Eddie; he's already legging it down the stairs. We rush along the landing and Peter calls Eddie's name as we go, as if that's going to make him stop for a moment's reflection. I make it to the top of the stairs first and start going down them two at a time but when I get to the second landing I'm still no closer to Eddie because he's already out of sight and on the second flight of stairs but when I get to the top of them I stop short when I see what's on the third step down: one of Eddie's tartan slippers is lying there, sole upwards, and I look beyond the slipper to the foot of the stone staircase and see the still figure of Eddie lying there, arms outstretched, face down, his head at a completely wrong angle to the rest of his body.

Peter pulls up sharp too and we both stand there at the top of the stairs looking down at Eddie's body. Then I turn to Peter and take hold of him by his neck and with all the angry force in my body I push him backwards until the balcony wall stops us going any farther. The shooter slips out of Peter's fingers and with both hands he tries to loosen my grip on his neck but there's no way he's going to be able to manage that. I keep pressing until he's leaning out over the empty courtyard and with my free hand I hit him several times across the face.

'I should let you drop,' I tell him. 'I should let you drop right now.'

I hit him again and step back and then I pick up his shooter and point it at him.

'Or shall I shoot your fucking knee caps off? Shall I do that instead?'

Peter pushes himself away from the balcony wall and looks at me the way Eddie had looked at me when I'd first walked into his living room.

'Jack . . .' he says.

'Shut it,' I tell him. 'Another word and I'll do it.'

Then I put his shooter in my pocket and turn away from him and begin to walk down the stairs, picking up Eddie's slipper on the way. When I get to Eddie I bend over him and turn him face upwards but there are no miracles for Eddie this Christmas. His dead eyes reflect the naked light bulb in the stairwell's ceiling.

Peter makes his way down to the bottom of the steps and leans against the wall, supporting himself on the handrail. I look up at him.

'All right, you fucking egg,' I tell him. 'Get hold of the legs.'

I put the slipper back on Eddie's foot and then I take hold of him underneath his armpits and look up at Peter again and he moves and gets hold of the legs and as we lift, some change slips out of Eddie's trouser pocket and the coins make a tinkling sound as they hit the stone floor.

We get Eddie to the bottom of the stairs that open into the courtyard. The snow is still falling and the courtyard is still empty. We carry Eddie away from the light on the staircase and into the shadow of the balcony above and then we put Eddie down.

'Right,' I say to Peter. 'Now you go and fetch the car and back it in the courtyard entrance and open up the boot. I know you're going to do exactly that because you don't want to wake up every night for the rest of your life wondering if tonight's the night I'm going to appear at the end of your bedstead. Do you?'

I hand him the car keys. He doesn't answer. He looks at me for a moment and turns away and hurries across to the courtyard entrance and disappears round the corner. Then I take hold of Eddie again and under cover of the balcony I drag him round to the arch and wait for Peter. I look at my watch and decide to give him two minutes. If he's not back by then the only thing I can do is leave Eddie where he is and take one of the few remaining chances I have left.

But within the allowed time there is the sound of the car backing into the archway. I grab Eddie again and start pulling him through the snow and I hear Peter get out of the car and unlock the boot and by that time I have got Eddie to the rear of the car. Peter takes Eddie's legs again and we lift Eddie into the boot and close the lid. Then I tell Peter to drive the car back to where it was before and wait and I go back up to Eddie's flat and put the furniture back the way it was and get rid of the cigarette ends and then I pick up the address book that Eddie had been writing in and slip it in my pocket. After I've done that I put the flat black case on the settee and flip the catches and open the lid and my eyes are greeted with the beautifully symmetrical pattern of ranks of wads of nice crisp notes. At a quick guess I would say there is twenty thousand worth at least. I look into the case for a minute or two and then I get up and find Eddie's bedroom and slide open one of the doors on the built-in wardrobe. I take out one of Eddie's overcoats and a pair of his shoes and as I'm doing that I notice that on the top shelf there is a stack of brightly wrapped Christmas presents out of sight and of reach, all ready for Eddie to deliver to wherever his wife and kids are spending Christmas.

I shut up the wardrobe and then I switch out all the lights and close all the doors and go out of the flat.

When I get back to where Peter is I throw the coat and the shoes in the back seat and tell him to drive to a place I know beyond Liverpool Street. Peter does as he's told and sets off without saying anything. His face looks even pastier under the sodium street lighting and his mouth is set in a light thin line and it's not because he's been affected by Eddie's death because normally he'd be making the most of the funny side of it. I sit there in silence myself and let him sweat for a while.

The place I'm thinking of is about half a mile off Liverpool Street itself. This place used to be a block of insurance offices and for the last few weeks it's been in the process of being demolished. I passed it by a few days ago and its cellars and their interlocking passages are now wide open to the weather. It takes us about quarter of an hour to get there and when we arrive I tell Peter to drive down a side street that would have been boundaried by one of the walls of the demolished building. We park at the far corner of the site away from any lights, and I tell Peter to wait in the car while I go and take a look around. I walk on to the site and over to the edge of one of the sunken corridors and drop down into it. Now I'm out of sight and I take out my keyring and play the small torch along the corridor until I come to a pile of plastic rubble sacks lying on the floor next to a narrow cupboard set in a tiled wall. I climb out of the corridor and go back to the car and tell Peter to get out and open up the boot and we carry Eddie back to the corridor and I get down in it and Peter lowers Eddie down on to my shoulders and I carry him to where the cupboard is and tug one of the plastic sacks over his feet and legs and one over his head and his torso and prop him up in the cupboard and close the door on him. Unless they decide to take out the cupboard in the morning he'll be safe there till after Christmas.

I climb out of the corridor. Peter is still standing on the edge and he waits for me to walk past him and falls into step behind me. When we get back to the car I get in the driving seat and Peter gets in the other side and when he's closed the door I say to him:

'The only reason you're not propped up next to Eddie is because I couldn't carry the two of you on my own.' He takes out one of his cheroots and tries to find his lighter.

'So you know what you're doing for Christmas, don't you?' I say to him.

He manages to light his cheroot but it takes him two or three goes. He blows the smoke out and says:

'I was right,' he says. 'You know I was only talking sense back there.'

'Yes and look where your sense got us.'

He's quiet for a while.

'So what now?' he says at last.

'You're the one with all the bright ideas,' I tell him. 'I was hoping you'd tell me.'

Richard Allen

'AUTHOR'S NOTES'

'Richard Allen' was one of the pseudonyms used by James Moffat (others included James Ferrier, Trudi Maxwell; the list goes on). As 'Richard Allen' he wrote eighteen 'youthsploitation' novels, the most famous of which are *Skinhead* and *Suedehead*. These notes first appeared as introductions to the New English Library editions of the novels, often in response to press criticism or fan mail. They are presented here in their original form: any inconsistencies are the author's own and have been left uncorrected. *The Complete Richard Allen*, comprising all eighteen of his novels, is published in a six-volume set (S.T. Publishing). Another Moffat volume, *Satan's Slaves*, originally published under the pseudonym 'James Taylor', was recently re-published by CodeX, and re-attributed to 'Richard Allen'. James Moffat died in 1993 aged seventy-one.

FOREWORD

Demonstration is an ugly word today. And demonstrators are automatically associated with militant student bodies or those 'foreign' elements pandering to Maoist-Communist slogan-chanting malcontents. Within a decade, the peaceful right of protest has drastically become an issue with the British public. Liberals tend to downgrade the disruptive effect of violent demonstration. Right-wing advocates simply shrug and criticise the leniency shown by Courts to those 'caught in the act'. But to the working man with his long traditions of fair play, Britain is Britain and to hell with the world generally, abhors the very word 'demonstrate' nowadays.

Unlike 'skinhead' violence which is apparently the vicious outlet for lower-class status-seeking, demonstrators are a unique creation of a Cold War-'Bomb' fascination. From simple beginnings – the right of youth to refuse parental guidance and become fodder for global slaughter – the demonstration now encompasses every form of protest imaginable. Let a body take exception to any facet of national life and there *must* be a demo!

No sane individual would refute youth's right to protest. Regardless of generation or era, youth has always rebelled against established authority – either parental or legal. Yet never quite like today's mass parades and anti-police hysteria.

Law-abiding citizens deplore the senseless cry of 'Pigs', those needless injuries, the inhumane treatment of innocent police-horses, the deliberate destruction of property that follow so-called 'peaceful demonstration'.

Elements are at work under cover of legitimate organisations to disrupt essential services; to encourage working men to consider employers as bloody-minded bastards incapable of understanding lower-class problems; to foment a desire for total anarchy. Scotland Yard's 'Special Branch' have the names and backgrounds of dozens of known 'terrorists' engaged in undermining anything even remotely approaching a peace-purpose demo. These same professional demonstrators can be hired by other militant units to encourage strikers, to supply the much needed 'backbone' for paid political disturbances, to support any cause no matter how tenuous, how just or unjust; how disastrous for Britain as a whole.

There is an awful lot to be said for that ancient British sense of justice that these people can be allowed their freedom. The very slogans they shout suggest an alliance with Iron Curtain diplomats, or at the least with communist ideologies. One does not have to wonder very long to arrive at a conclusion concerning their monetary support. Nor does one have to think hard about their fate if they tried those self-same tactics in a strict communist state. The insults, the destruction of property, the empty-headed denial of a man's right to express his opinion would not be tolerated for a split-second in Russia, China, Cuba or North Vietnam. It speaks highly of a capitalistic democratic system that pays social security benefits and grants to those seemingly dedicated to the complete overthrow of that which feeds and nurtures these vipers.

The majority of British youth are against violent demos. The preponderance of students believe that study is their grant-given duty. Unfortunately, democracy permits militants and those debased power-seekers to infiltrate and control aspects of community life – be it a student council, a shop steward's committee, a political party. Their weapons are words, oratory, fear, brute force when all else fails. Twisted facts, plausible arguments, uninhibited sexuality – these are the thin edges of their wedge. Pot and disregard for set standards are the broader knife-thrust. Abuse of social security, claims of police brutality, infiltration of news media are the final involvements.

Awareness is the only alternative to their insidious sneak attacks. To be forewarned still holds true. But apathy and whispers that all is well can bring Britain – and, indeed, the Western world – to its knees. It is up to youth – those intelligent searchers after a better Earth – to fulfil their bright-eyed, zestful promise to make this a much better land for you, and them to live in.

The challenge is theirs – youth's. Either they elect to stay within a democratic framework or utterly destroy what has taken centuries to construct; and with it the dreams of lost generations of teenagers who have sacrificed life itself for a cause they believed would endure all outside attacks.

Richard Allen
Gloucestershire, 1970

AUTHOR'S NOTE

In the interests of sanity let no one be under the mistaken impression that the writer sympathises with anti-social behaviour, cultism or violence for the sake of violence. That Joe Hawkins – 'hero' of *Skinhead* – should have aroused a national following and made the paperback a best seller is, indeed, gratifying to an author.

Any author worth his salt takes a fictional character and skilfully blends him into factual situations so that the reader is almost convinced the hero lives and what he is doing is in keeping with how it is logically assumed he would act under a given set of circumstances. *Skinhead* looked at the cult, took note of everything the average skinhead did in the course of his anti-social duties and faithfully represented Joe Hawkins as the epitome of society's menace. At no time did I attempt to glorify Joe Hawkins.

Suedehead, like *Skinhead*, is an attempt to show a specific section of the community in action. Both are maladies of our permissive society which has, rightly or wrongly, encouraged the growth of off-beat cults within a framework peopled by law-abiding, decent, sometimes dull citizens. Youth has always had its fling but never more blatantly, more unconcerned with adverse publicity than today. In fact, it is my opinion that leniency in courtrooms catering to fads by mercenary-minded rag-trade merchants, a soft-pedalling attitude by politicians who look for teenage votes to save their seats and an overwhelming pandering by the news media are the real contributing factors of this instantaneous explosion which now places the nation as a whole in jeopardy. Britain cannot survive long in a climate of anarchy. Every man, woman and child must draw strength from a democratic, wholesome ideal – and those who attend to unfruitful, undemocratic, irrational pursuits only do so at the risk of losing those precious freedoms which this country has valued for countless centuries.

If this portrayal of a menace is used as an excuse to uphold deviousness then I surrender to the wiles of culpability. And having said that, I trust that the readers have enjoyed the story and will find some sane outlet for their various energies other than those Joe Hawkins enjoys.

Richard Allen
Gloucestershire, 1972.

AUTHOR'S NOTE

Judging by the popularity of the paperbacks, SKINHEAD and SUEDEHEAD, the pundits are totally wrong when they state that teenage cultism is fading away. It would appear, from the response to SUEDEHEAD, that skinheads are like old soldiers – they are forever there in the wings.

After two books featuring Joe Hawkins, it was my intention to let the character rest for an indeterminate period of time. The readers, however, have decided otherwise. Letters from the book-buying public make it patently clear that Joe is an established favourite. Almost without exception, the letters request – no, *insist*

– on another Joe book. Whilst it is exceedingly gratifying for an author to find his works included in the top ten paperbacks of the year, it poses certain problems to meet the demands.

Joe, we remember, found himself confronted with a four-year prison sentence in SUEDEHEAD. That seemed, to me, to put paid to his activities for quite a while. But Joe Hawkins is a resourceful character. An old adage mentions not being able to keep a good man down. The same holds true for the Joes of this world. Bad pennies, like good men, have a habit of turning up at an alarming speed.

In years to come, Joe Hawkins will probably be quoted as an example of this era we have named 'the permissive age'. If so, then the author can count on more than sales success. With that thought in mind, I wish to thank all of those who have spread the gospel and taken the trouble to write. It is for you that SKINHEAD ESCAPES is specially written.

Richard Allen
Gloucester, 1972.

AUTHOR'S NOTE

Some people have criticised parts of my previous books dealing with the skinhead problem and, I believe, some teachers have suggested that they are less than helpful.

What is the criterion of right or wrong? Surely the readers of SKINHEAD and SUEDEHEAD are equally entitled to express choice!

From many letters received, I have reached one conclusion – the teachers are out of touch with their pupils. Morality is not just a platform issue. It is a living part of this great experience we call growing old. Teenagers, today, are not governed by middle-age thinking. Nor do they fail to see through hypocrisy. Regardless of what those in power like to believe, the days of the whitewash and the brainwash have gone forever.

The place to challenge teenage rights is in the clubroom, a

discotheque, a football special. Face-to-face talking, without the strictures of classroom or courtroom. Old fashioned attitudes and a 'thou shalt not' bigotry only confirm teenage views that speaking to adults is a complete waste of precious time. And the young find time a very valuable possession. Don't misunderstand me. I am not in the business of telling authority how to conduct itself. I am speaking as an individual with experience in dealing with the teenage mind. Far be it for me to instruct educationalists and others in what book should, or should not, be placed on the selected examination list. I do, however, believe that modern writers of stature are more important in the beginning than the classical masters.

In the final judgement it is up to the individual. The voting age has been lowered. Authority admits that young people are reaching 'thinking age' much earlier than ever before. So, to my fans, read on. Enjoy the freedoms of self-determination. Decide for yourselves. Nobody is twisting your arm to buy my book, but nobody should decide for you what is, or is not, your scene ...

Richard Allen
Devon, 1972.

AUTHOR'S NOTE

At the time of writing this there is a wave of speculation regarding the contents of certain books. And not without reason. Whilst deploring censorship of any sort I must admit to a horror of 'open' publishing. That is to say, categorically, the type of production currently available in the United States and some Continental countries.

Some British magazines have reached, in my humble opinion, the limit of what should be regarded as 'decency licence'.

Yet, those who would demand controls on what we, the public, read, seem bent on denying us all the opportunity of learning about life as it is lived in the raw.

The case for objectionable or non-objectionable material is

bound to fall flat when confronted by a need to portray events, social phenomena and fads in their true light. How can anyone condemn the skinhead books when, according to the letters received from countless thousand fans, the consensus of opinion is that they – and they alone – present skinheads, suedeheads, boot boys and now smooths as they really are?

Where would their value be if every 'terrace terror' spoke and acted like an undergraduate of a theological college?

Providing that the characters are a slice of life there can be no complaint. Providing that those who call themselves skinheads, smooths, what-have-you, recognise themselves and write acclaiming the portrayals then I for one, consider that all efforts have been worthwhile and that this book – plus the others in the series – are, in a small way, representative of our modern society and a source of reference for future students of our violent era.

To those who have written – thanks. Your letters are always a tonic.

Richard Allen
Devon, November, 1972.

AUTHOR'S NOTE

It has happened again! Joe's popularity has necessitated yet another book recalling those days when he roamed the East End as a free-agent.

Regardless of all that befalls Joe Hawkins, his fans insist that he continues to entertain them in paperback format. Even although Joe is confined behind bars on a life sentence, the clamour is too great to be denied.

So – SKINHEAD IN TROUBLE.

Here are the missing parts that SKINHEAD, SUEDEHEAD and SKINHEAD ESCAPES did not provide. This is Joe's torment, his 'inside' story set against the frustrating backdrop of top security prison life. This is Joe with the wraps off. Joe is facing his greatest challenge.

Richard Allen
Devon.

AUTHOR'S NOTE

A skinhead book without Joe Hawkins seems to me to be going against the grain, but I feel the moment has come to introduce my readers to another character, Roy Baird, and given time, Roy will rank in popularity alongside the redoubtable Mr Hawkins.

To all those who have taken the bother to send letters to me, and there are many, I dedicate this book. That includes the boys and girls in Hull, Manchester, Renfrewshire, Chester, Ashford, Gillingham, Bristol, Exeter, Newcastle, Bradford, Southampton, Gloucester, Wolverhampton, and just about every district in London. To those who selected me as a subject for school examinations, I hope you get top marks.

Richard Allen
Devon.

AUTHOR'S NOTES

Smoothies, as a book, should do much to heal the rift between various factions of the skinhead cult. Between those who cling to the original beliefs and those who have progressed beyond that first flush of revolutionary individualism.

Perhaps 'individualism' is the wrong choice of word. Skinheads invariably follow patterns laid down by 'members' long since married, long since abdicating their right to belong.

One is tempted to paraphrase the world's best seller by stating that skinhead begat suedehead which begat boot boys which now begat smoothies.

If this is so then the family tree is one of marvellous ingenuity, of widely varying contrasts. During the suedehead period aggro for the sake of kicks almost totally vanished. Along came the boot boys with football mania and a return to the days of senseless violence. They were — and, in some areas, still are — terrace terrors.

Nothing more, nothing less. The skinhead love of football had been vanquished and they sought only to destroy, maim, disrupt by force of numbers.

Not so the smoothies. Former loyalties remain but they have a distinctive formation. A higher echelon structure. In terms of skinheadism the smooth is an upper class snob. An elite character. A 'black sheep' with the purities of a petty criminal when compared to the hardened no conscience crook.

There are those in disagreement with this evaluation, no doubt. Just as some found my pen-picture of a suedehead very much against their regional definition of this cult. But, all in all, I believe the majority of my readers will back the 'scene' I paint on a printed page canvas.

It is for them that I say – what next?

The opposite of smooth is rough. Do we then return to the skinhead era or do we progress down a path towards self-determination and a loose grouping of mates holding vaguely similar viewpoints without the necessity of banding together in gangs, mobs, crowds bent on numerically superior aggro?

That is for each to determine. The Smooth is an evolutionary forward step. A crawling from the slime advancement. Regardless of the reasoning behind this change, the 'movement' has, at last, a chance for survival within the permissive society. The opportunity for all skinhead descendants to mould into a single unit exists. All it takes is the will and the desire to forget old differences, old aggravations. The image does not gleam brighter by senseless violence or the tearing-apart of railway carriages.

As Joe Hawkins would have said: 'We were born on a football pitch and that's where we belong'.

And even Joe – from his cell – would have to admit that time does change everything, and everybody!

Richard Allen
Devonshire.

Victor Headley

'THE MAN WHO TOOK DOWN THE
GREAT PITPAT'

Victor Headley is the author of the best selling novel *Yardie* (Pan), and three other novels, *Excess*, *Yush!* and *Fetish* (X Press). This story is an excerpt from his forthcoming novel, *The Best Man*.

I waited for what seemed like an hour at least. Apart from a couch against the back wall, and a metal file cabinet under the window, the desk was the only furniture. Through the open door, for a good forty minutes, I watched uniformed and plain clothes police pass by, listened to bits of conversation. I wasn't really worried about my fate, it's the uncertainty I didn't like. Just as I was getting fed up with waiting, a short and plump woman constable in uniform stopped and looked at me, asked me if I wanted a drink. I was surprised, that was a first! I said I would. Maybe she had mercy on me because my arm was in a sling, anyway she brought me a coke and disappeared. From time to time I could catch the crackling of a radio communication in the office next door. There was a lot going on apparently. Then, when I was starting to think I would spend the day like that, a man came in and stopped by the desk. He just looked at me for a few seconds, without a word. Medium height, round-faced with a dark brown complexion and a low haircut, he wore a light green suit, white shirt with no tie. I couldn't rightly say I knew his face but there was something familiar about him. He was clean shaven but for a short, well groomed moustache. His eyes fixed me, brown and hard but with no animosity.

'Lewis!' he called, not too loud, but right away the big constable who had shackled me earlier came on in.

'Take off the cuffs,' the man in the suit told him, which he did before going out again.

'I'm Detective Sergeant Roy Glenford,' the man told me.

It didn't ring a bell with me, but I said, 'Good morning, sah.'

Might as well be polite, as courtesy might well play in my favour if this was the man who had my fate in his hands. I expected him to sit at the desk and start asking me questions, but he quickly browsed through some of the papers scattered there, took a pen out of his inside jacket pocket, made a few scribbles on some of the sheets, then left without a word. I didn't even think of running out of the station; it happened to some of my friends, but I had checked the layout coming in and it was clear that I wouldn't make it to the entrance. I felt a little better without the handcuffs, and more dignified too. The painting on the wall behind the desk showed a solitary silhouette atop a misty mountain top with reddish clouds behind. I spent a few more minutes checking it out. There was a kind of sadness in there, to me anyway . . .

I heard his voice giving instructions to someone, before the detective came back into the office. He pushed the door closed and sat at the desk this time. For a couple of minutes he was making notes in a pad he'd taken out of one of the desk drawers, scribbling finely line after line, stopping once in a while to search his brain it seemed. Eventually, he leaned back in the comfortable leather armchair, tapping his pen against his chin. I could see he was looking my way but not really seeing me, considering some other problem. He nodded to himself, then asked me directly:

'Your name?'

'Carlton Nash.'

'Hmm.'

He made a sound like he reflected about the sound of my name, the way he seemed absorbed! I had been 'interviewed' by police before, so I expected more questions, in the rough mould like usually. But this man didn't seem in a hurry. I watched him cock his head slightly towards the door, picking up on some crackling phrases over the radio.

'You're on a murder charge, right?'

Out of balance, I took it in. It was a question that just begged a 'yes' on my part, but it wasn't the way I saw it.

'I just get out of the hospital today. I don't get charge with not'ing yet Sah.'

That little rectification made the detective smile.

'Yes, ... not yet.'

I knew, all the time I laid in the hospital, that I would have to face the police sooner or later. It would have been easier to die on that street corner, in a way, but my only regret was not being charged for Lookman's murder. Detective Glenford picked up his pad and started leafing through it, methodically. Twice he looked up at me for a brief moment, his face expressing nothing much. I didn't really like the way he stared. My arm was itchy bad!

'Tell me; where did you get the gun from?'

He wasn't looking at me, he was asking it like any other question, matter-of-factly.

I had known that moment would come, but I repeated the same thing I had given to the first policeman who came to the hospital to interrogate me.

'I found it.'

That made the detective look up from his pad. He sounded jokey.

'You people are really lucky, you know. I have never found a gun yet in my life. And I'm a policeman!' He chuckled.

It seemed to amuse him, genuinely. It didn't amuse me somehow. I was starting to wonder why he didn't behave like the other policemen I had come across previously. He asked:

'Tell me ... Cartlon; this gun, you found it before or after the elections?'

He was waiting for an answer from me, knowing I knew it was a trick question anyway; if I said before, he'd ask why I hadn't given it in at the amnesty, if after, why did I keep it? I had his eyes into mine. There was no joke in them.

'I found it that same day,' I said simply.

There was no cockiness in my tone, the policeman didn't take it bad. He even nodded, still checking something in the handwritten notes on the page in front of him.

'OK,' he said, putting the pad down on the desk. 'Let me see if I get the story right ...'

His back against the chair, the man adjusted his shirt collar before telling me:

'Your don cut up your sister, you find a gun ... and go out to shoot him.'

He paused, but not to await any confirmation on my part.

'Then, on the way to revenge, you get ambushed by two gunmen, probably hired by your don ... They shoot you down, but you manage to kill at least one before collapsing badly wounded.'

'The dyamm man makin' it sound like a newspaper article!' I was thinking. All the same, fancy talk or not, that was the living truth!

'That is exactly what happened, Sah. God knows!'

'Look; let's leave God out of this,' the detective pointed out, then, 'Anyway ... so now; your don is still alive, you too but you have a murder charge to face ... Tell me Carlton: who's the winner?'

I didn't answer that, but he must have read the anger in my stare. There was a rather long silence between us, a few bursts of crackling on the radio next door. Detective Glenford sighed heavily, leaned forward from his vantage spot. His elbow perched on the edge of the desk, he asked me:

'You think I'm your enemy, don't you?'

It didn't seem to matter to him that I kept not answering most of his questions.

'And you think the next man across the border is your enemy too, right?'

I kept quiet. Quietly he asked me:

'So ... how many men you killed before that?'

No policeman had ever asked me such a question. But this one was serious; he was real relaxed about it, like someone who's discussing a bet at the tracks or something.

'Carlton,' he said. 'I'm going to ask you one question, and I'd just like you to answer me truthfully.'

He paused, while across the desk, his inscrutable eyes weighed me out. What kind of policeman was this one, with his games.

'Have you ever killed a man?' he asked, very serious.

I looked at him blankly. But he went on.

'Tell me if you have ever taken a man's life while you look into his eyes, at close quarters, I mean ... Have you?'

The face of the man leaning comfortably in the leather chair was intense but calm, his tone almost detached. He gave me half a minute during which I realised I would never answer that question. He knew.

'It takes nothing to do it with this though!' he said then, pointing casually with his index finger to the grey muzzle on the table near the ashtray.

'OK Carlton,' he said, after looking away to the window which was open on the rumours of the town, the still free and their daily runnings.

'You don't know me, but I know you,' he stopped, visibly, that didn't sound like good news, but he explained.

'Oh, not just you, but almost every street man across the areas. I have a lot of information.'

From the corridor came two solid knocks and the door pushed half-open. Detective Glenford made a little beckoning sign with his left hand and sturdy uniformed policeman stepped to the desk. He only threw me a brief glance, but it was one of those that let you remember that when a policeman has seen you once, it's for ever. He whispered something close to his 'boss', waited for a reaction. All this time since the knocks, Detective Glenford had been observing me with that indefinable meditative look he had, and it was starting to annoy me. I didn't like it. He glanced briefly at the big police and nodded twice. The other one moved out swiftly.

'So, Carlton Nash, Carlton Nash ...' Detective Glenford squinted, like the name had to bring up something from his memory. It did ...

'Yes, Carlton Nash, aka Skid, or Skidder ... born ... '59, no ... '60, involved in sectarian violence between areas since quitting secondary school aged fifteen, became driver to ex-area leader Jingles, then his right hand man. Operates a small-scale ganja operation, distribution, mostly. Don't smoke ... five arrests, no convictions.'

Spelt out in that impersonal tone, this could have been the eight o'clock news, but it wasn't: it was me, my life! And how the hell did he get to know me so well?! I have always been pretty straight-faced, but I must have shown some surprise that morning.

'Information, Carlton. Information is power.' He smiled, not really a happy smile, but a smile. I knew he would soon get serious.

'This is my job here; I want you to understand this. The thinking is this; you must know your enemy well if you want to defeat him. That's why my job is to know everything I can about you, all of you,' he declared. Then he got up and went to peep through the window, came back having satisfied his curiosity. He sat and played with the key ring he hadn't let go of since coming in.

'I was born and bred in Kingston,' he started, 'Papine. Left the island at fifteen to follow high school in the States, California ... only came back to spend summer holidays at home. I started studying to become an attorney, became a policeman instead ... Life's funny, eh?!'

Yes, it was funny, but I couldn't help him with that.

'You know why I decided to come back home, Carlton?'

He was looking at me but I had nothing to say.

'I came back here to see if what I have learned could help ...'cause I don't want to see what happened in the States happen here.'

That sounded serious. I was starting to feel didgy about all this talk. 'Let's get done with this,' I was thinking, 'Send me to court for murder and done!' But Detective Roy Glenford was never a man to rush unnecessarily, I was to learn this. I must have looked bored. I heard him ask:

'You know what else I know about you, Carlton?'

He was leaning back in his chair.

'You are not involved with drugs ... am I right, sah?'

'It's true,' I answered simply, impressed in a way.

Then the detective dropped:

'You know why Jingles died?'

I would have to have been a very cold, very dead-inside man for my face not to show something. The man knew he had got through to me now. He told me:

'Jingles died because he didn't want to play ball ... because he didn't like the drug business, and he didn't want his people to be dealing with it.'

The detective let it sink in before adding:

'Him refusing to get Bertie killed was just an excuse; they were gonna kill him anyway ...'

There was a hard stare between me and Detective Glenford. Right now he wasn't no policeman to me anymore, he was talking about my family.

'Come on Carlton; who had the most to gain from Jingle's death? ... Think.'

That kind of meditation was getting painful to prolong.

'You're mad, right? I'm gonna tell you something even stronger: Jingles was dead the day he started to have peace talk with the other side.'

There was a silence.

'Certain people didn't want to hear about another peace treaty, that's not good for their business. And Jingles had already done a lot for the first one, he was a big man.'

Thinking about Jingles had never been a pleasant thing to do any day of the year since he had gone. Next I heard Detective Glenford ask me, very normally:

'You want to know who set up Jingles?'

I kept alternating between looking at him and the calendar

behind him. Who the hell was this man anyway? My eyes were into the policeman's own, waiting. But he was a player, a man who loved to toy with feelings, other people's feelings.

'Tell me something, Carlton,' he squinted at me. 'You was driving on that arms shipment job, wasn't you?'

I didn't expect that. He pushed on as I stared blankly.

'I'm pretty sure it was you ... Anyway, the reason I ask you: you ever find out who gave away the play?'

No one ever had, as far as I knew. So what was he talking about. Then it got worse.

'We'll get back to that later ...' he said, before switching scene.

'Tell me if you remember; on the night Jingles died, who was driving him on the mission?'

I knew that, but I wasn't prepared to discuss it with him, whatever he knew already. He told me:

'Lookman was driving, wasn't he?'

'It wasn't Lookman,' I said simply, like I cared to prove him wrong for once, him and his know-it-all attitude.

'It wasn't him,' he frowned, like caught out. 'You sure?'

I wasn't revealing anything he didn't know, I felt, so I said:

'The driver died.'

There was a reflective silence, then the man said:

'Hm hm,' shaking his head slowly.

He gave it fifteen seconds of suspense before declaring calmly:

'I wasn't on the scene, but ... I reached just after they had taken the bodies away ... and I can tell you this, there was blood on all the seats, except the driver's.'

He waited for the implications to rise up in my mind, then he laid it all out.

'Lookman was driving Jingles that night, he switched with the other guy, I forgot his name, at some point. That way he was making sure the ambush would work.'

The man had shaken me right there. What was he saying? Then he threw me down, thumped me inside.

'And it wasn't an undercover police squad neither ...'

A pause, two still eyes on me.

'The contract was given to some gunmen from the next side. That's why you couldn't drive that night: you might have got lucky again and saved Jingles.'

I was retracing and crisscrossing the allegations this man was handing me against what I knew as facts. He must have followed my inner reasoning, for Detective Glenford said casually:

'The police had no reason to want Jingles dead; on the contrary, you follow me?'

I saw him shaking his head with what looked like sadness, or maybe frustration.

'You want to know why I'm telling you all this, instead of giving you up to my colleagues down the corridor?'

He waited, seeing I was still turning around in my head what he'd just told me.

'I'm telling you that you and all the others putting your lives on the line out there don't know what the hell is going on.'

I said nothing.

'It's not about area, or party anymore; all this is done with, you must know ...' he paused.

'It's about drugs and guns, lots of guns ...'

I didn't take the stare personally. The man in the suit asked me:

'You know how many police officers got shot and killed on duty last year, Carlton?'

I didn't.

'Thirty two,' he told me. Waited for it to impress my conscience.

'So the police must change too, and that is where I come in. My job here is to organise the "counter-attack", as I call it.'

If he was trying to scare me, he'd wear himself out. But he explained patiently.

'So, the mission I've been given is to form a unit totally independent from the politics, totally clean ... Like the Incorruptibles, you've seen the movie?'

I had. I nodded, wondering what I was doing talking cinema with that policeman now!

'I'm gonna organise a strikeforce that's gonna cut down the trade in Jamaica before it even spreads,' he declared confidently.

From what I had seen happening on the street, it was going to take a lot of work. But I said nothing. He went on:

'I have been back over a year now, things are moving fast and I'm almost ready to start operating. With intelligence back up, I've got good men, real tough and dedicated fighters.'

That man sounded serious about his work. That surely meant more pressure out there for guilties and innocents alike.

Then, as I delved in my mind on darker days to come, Detective Glenford said, very straight faced:

'Look; I've got an idea: I'd like you to work for me.'

I thought I had heard wrong at first, but he was waiting for my reaction to the 'idea'. I let him have it up front.

'Yuh better send me straight to Gun Court, sah; I'm not no informer!'

Detective Glenford shook his head.

'That's not what I'm talking about . . .' He gave me one of those long, drilling-through stares of his, then switched to another side, as usual with him.

'Tell me something, Carlton . . .' he paused to watch me with what looked like a glint of amused anticipation.

'Suppose I let you out.' I must have seemed interested.

'Suppose I let you go free,' he said to me.

I knew he wouldn't do it, but I had nothing to lose supposing, just to go along with him.

'. . . Drop everything . . . I let you back out on the street; what are you going to do?'

I thought about it for a full minute. The policeman waited. I would have liked to answer something positive, but I just couldn't. He knew. He said:

'You've got three options, basically.'

He spelt them.

'You leave the island and try your luck in another country. It might work.'

I waited for the other two.

'You go back to your area, shoot it out with Lookman and, if you stay lucky, you could become the new don.'

I kept my eyes in his.

'But for how long?'

He raised his eyebrows, waited before continuing, but I had nothing I cared to say.

'Or you're really unlucky and some guy from the other side sees you somewhere and gets himself a name and a lump sum for your life.'

My face reflected my perplexity. Detective Glenford flashed the wicked semi-grin of a flattering, crooked car salesman.

'You're a big man now, you've got a rep,' he said, then added with mock respeck, 'You're the man who took down the great Pitpat.'

Nicholas Blincoe

'THE LONG DRIVE-BY'

Nicholas Blincoe's debut novel, *Acid Casuals*, was published by Serpent's Tail in 1995 and described by the *Daily Telegraph* as the 'best debut crime novel of the year ... blackly comic and highly inventive'. A second novel, *Jello Salad* (Serpent's Tail), cemented his reputation for cool and stylish thriller writing. His last novel, *Manchester Slingback* (Picador), won the Silver Dagger award for crime fiction in 1998. A new novel, *The Dope Priest*, is published by Sceptre. Nicholas Blincoe lives in London where he also writes for television.

Being a Francophile doesn't make me a jerk. The truth is, I always was on the gauche side. Sitting beneath a plane tree in the public square of a town between Paris and Bordeaux, smoking a *Gitane* and reading *L'étranger*, how cool do I think I look? The last time I was here, sitting in this exact same position, I was seventeen years old and hitching my way through France. Now, twenty years on, I've got a rental sitting in the town carpark. Also, *L'étranger* is in French. Last time around I was reading the English translation.

So, what happened twenty years ago, and why do I need to recreate it so nearly exactly?

I arrived on the autoroute from Paris where I had been sleeping rough. I was wearing a dark suit, similar only in its shade to the one I am wearing now. That suit came from a charity shop, this one very clearly didn't. I picked up my ride in a Paris suburb, twenty minutes walk from the last Metro station. Three hours later, I was set down here, in this very town.

The driver was nervy. His car was luxurious and power-steered, so easy to drive it couldn't sop-up his nervous energy. He tried conversation but we had so little vocabulary between us, my travel Scrabble bag of words soon emptied and so did his. The journey ended with him saying *au revoir*. I said, Yes.

We could share a much wider ranging conversation now, if we were to meet again. And it would largely be thanks to Albert Camus. *L'étranger* is a good first read if you are trying to read

French. Take my tip. The language is straightforward; Camus has no time for metaphors or any other booby-trap dragged into fiction by slumming poets. Even better, if you are not French, Camus has the advantage of being not wholly French either. Especially in *L'étranger*. True, he focuses on what happens on the *inside*, as French writers tend to do. But despite his focus, Camus keeps the stuff of the interior to an absolute minimum. On its publication, the lean style was viewed as the authentic voice of the existential vacuum; or so I was told by this French guy. He was something of a book expert, so I wasn't going to call him on his information.

What I will say, the existential interpretation does absolutely nothing for me. Looking in the windows of an empty bookshop, maybe you would see a sign of the emptiness at the heart of the human condition. Or you might see a sign that says, *'En vacance, 3 août – 2 septembre'*.

Did I mention that it's August? There are signs all over the town explaining that the shopkeepers are away.

But back to Albert Camus, who is the reason I am here at all, in France, during my lone summer holiday. The best word for Camus, I think, is *americain*. To me, the word describes a series of transatlantic conjunctions. Like be-bop and red wine. Harley Davidsons and Bikini Girls. Negroes and striped jerseys. *Gitanes* and Lucky Strike. Crime and *Noire*. And Camus's compatriots on this mid-atlantic plateau are writers like Raymond Chandler, Chester Himes, Jim Thompson, Charles Willeford, Patricia Highsmith; but only if they're read in *un esprit americain*, as hard-boiled as the egg in a *salade niçoise*. The strange thing is, I'm not sure either the French or Americans are capable of understanding the space they've created together. I think you need to be an outsider to really dig it, poised between one place and the other. In Coventry, say. Unless you happen to be on your summer holiday.

Twenty years ago, sprawled on a public bench in my charity shop suit and reading *The Outsider*, I imagined that I looked like Jean Paul Belmondo, the poster boy for all us *americains*. I can feel a blush rising, now, as I remember. At thiry-seven, with a face that has creased and hardened through age, nicotine and, even, a measure of living, I still look nothing like Jean Paul Belmondo. I look like . . . what? The man climbing out of the taxi on the corner, the man replacing the telephone receiver at the other end of the bar, the man unhooking his wife's coat from the hat stand in the restaurant. The kind of man everyone sees everyday without ever registering. But even they can be made to seem dark, dangerous, romantic . . .

So, my French guy, the antiquarian book expert, has left on his annual holiday. I walked past his shop a few hours ago and read the note he had taped to the inside of the glass door, the date in September when he will re-open. He gave the numbers that jaunty look the French always use when they handwrite a date or a figure or a telephone number, with up-strokes and tics and squiggles so the horizontals flex off their line. I know he still owns the shop because he signed the note just below his return date. Also, it is his name on the shop sign, *Guy France – Bouquiniste*. I couldn't make any sense out of the sign then, not realising that Guy France was his name rather than a redundant description of his nationality and gender. I didn't know the word for an antiquarian bookseller, either. I could see the books racked on the shelves, floor to ceiling, just the other side of the window.

The shop was different then. There seemed to be much more stock, a more cluttered feel. There certainly wasn't space for a central table, like he has now, displaying special books, bargains, whatever.

Back then, when I first found Guy's shop, I had just finished a chapter and decided to go walking. It was getting dark, too dark to read but too early to go to a café and eat. I wandered into one of the streets that led off the square, recognised the name of the bookshop and decided to take a look. Guy was cashing up when I entered and he didn't look up until I spoke. I told him in simple French, that I wanted this book and held up *The Outsider*.

'*Mais en français, s'il vous plaît.*'

He was surprised to see me again, but one of the few things he had managed to make me understand, as we raced down the autoroute in his swish car, was that he had a copy in his library, and he showed me a plastic bag with the name of his shop on it. Pointing to his own chest as he said, '*Moi, Guy France.*'

And I said, '*Je sais.*'

Why did I ask for the Camus book? Partly because I wanted to say something charming and that's not easy when you have the vocabulary of a three-year-old. But also because I knew I would finish my copy within thirty minutes of re-opening it. And then I would miss it. Buying the French version was a possible way of extending the experience. I had already guessed it would make a good book for a beginner.

Guy smiled and said, Yes. He had a copy. He stepped to one side and pointed to the glass case behind his cash register. The book was propped upright, in the centre of the middle shelf. The price tag said a little over five hundred pounds, if I've got that right. Understanding the French currency as poorly as the French language, I tended to translate everything into pounds as I was looking at it. So maybe my calculation was wrong, or my memory of it. But it was a lot of money.

Guy said, 'It is a first edition, when there was a war and not so much the paper for books. Also, Albert Camus, he writes his name to a friend, as his thanks for a *jolie* evening.'

I said, 'It's too expensive.'

He nodded. 'I understand.'

I stayed with Guy until he left for his August break, three weeks later, during which time I learnt French and played hard-to-get. I know he was glad to say good-bye. After his success as a pedagogue and his failure as a pederast he was utterly exhausted. I had done nothing to deserve a present and I didn't get one. Certainly not, and despite all my many hints, a rare first edition of *L'étranger*.

I wanted to spend the night in my old bedroom in the apartment above the shop, but Guy has turned it into a small office. I can't say I blame him. If he has fewer rooms to choose from, I'm sure he'll have more success when he invites his pick-ups into his bed.

He has made other minor changes, too, but fortunately he never changed his locks.

His own room has been re-decorated and re-papered. It makes quite a difference. The style is clean and fresh but Guy is clearly an oldish man now. The colour scheme betrays him. His bed is made, folded at the bottom army-style, holding tight as a bungee rope across a roof rack. I practically have to do a press-up to prise enough room for myself beneath the bedsheets. Sleeping in a strange bed, I don't expect to fall asleep immediately. I read for three hours, finishing *L'étranger* and the French translation of Charles Willeford's *High Priest of California*. The Charles Willeford book was waiting for me on his bedside table, almost as though I was expected.

One thing I did, before I even looked at the upstairs rooms, I slipped into his shop to check if the glass cabinet was really empty. I expected it to be. The last thing I saw him do, before he left for his vacation twenty years ago, was to take the most valuable of his books and lock them in his safe. The safe was in the wardrobe of my room – now his office. He wasn't worried that I was watching, counting off the books as he stacked them one-by-one inside the safe with his old army pistol and his small but valuable collection of fountain pens. He knew I could never open the safe. How would I know that he kept the key in the pocket of his old dress uniform, zipped inside a protective bag, hanging in the wardrobe of his room? He never realised how thoroughly I got to know all his secret ways. I was very discreet.

I could hardly expect to find the same signed, first edition copy of *L'étranger* in his safe. It might have been nice, at least to have held it one last time, but I don't really care. As I leave town at six in the morning, the road is zebra-striped, the tarmac white between the black shadows of the plane trees lining the route. It's beautiful and calming. I feel calm. Up ahead, there's a hitchhiker. Maybe an

Arab but he could just as easily be a tanned English boy, hitching through France. I slow down. Driving an English hire car, I'm on the same side as him as I crawl to the kerbside. My left arm hangs out the window, Guy France's French army pistol feeling heavy in my hand. The car is still moving as I bring it up and fire, so it is technically a drive-by shooting. The beginning of my long drive-by.

Catherine Johnson

'FALADA'

Catherine Johnson lives in London. She has had four novels published, including *Landlocked* (Pont) and *Other Colours* (Women's Press). She likes getting up early and glaciers.

When someone is dead they don't move. Sounds obvious I know, but when someone doesn't move they're there for you. Which is more than you can say about most people.

When I was fifteen I had this horse – well, pony really – we kept him under the railway arches down Spitalfields. Cruel, some people said, but I reckon they was just jealous. Sherry. I know, sounds more like a girl's name, but that was his name. Lovely chestnut colour, sort of orange, with a white flash – blaze – down his face.

Sometimes, of an evening, I'd hop over the fence after the arches was shut and sit in his stable in the dark. I could talk to him see. Put my arms around his neck and tell him everything. All the rubbish between me and Keeley Foreman and the rubbish at school. Everything. And Sherry would like, rest his head in my arms. One whole ton of horse's head just resting there in my arms. You can always tell real love off of an animal.

When I first started going with Gavin we used to go over the arches to snog and that. It was quiet and after dark there was never anyone around. Well, Nadine's dad's guard dog, Major, this really dumb ridgeback. He'd had a stroke and slobbered all the time out of one corner of his mouth – like this – couldn't stop it see. Anyway, we was up there one time in the corner of Sherry's box, standing up, had to because of the shit. Anyway, Gavin's going at me and I open my eyes and Sherry is like staring at me, looking right at me with his big horse eyes. And I just went cold, right.

I had to get Gavin off of me and he's not pleased at all, to put it mild, and he's shouting and that and I'm going be quiet be quiet and Sherry's sort of pawing at the ground scraping through the shavings at the concrete making this really awful squeaky noise. And Nadine's Archie and her dad's trotter Sultan are doing that rumbling horse breathing and Major's barking. So I try telling him, Gavin, about the horse and that of course I really do love him, but maybe next time we should do it over his mum's while she's gone up Lakeside. And Gavin looks at me like I'm mad and then he looks at Sherry and punches him, punches the horse in the jaw. Seeing Gavin with a bleeding hand just makes me laugh, but it makes him mad and he jumps the stable door and I thought he'd gone home. But he comes back in two minutes with a lump of paving stone from the roadworks down Sturridge Row. And Gavin clocks him – Sherry – right on the forehead.

So of course I'm mad then. I'm shouting at him and Sherry kicks out at him. And I have never seen Gavin move so fast in all of his life. Gone, over the gate out the yard over the fields and into the lane. Last I saw of him he was running through the tunnel to Commercial Road. I stopped following him then and went back to Sherry. I look over the door and Sherry was lying down on his side breathing fast little dog-pant breaths. I was panting too, from the running, so at first I couldn't really tell what was what. Gavin couldn't have done this. I flicked back Sherry's forelock – that's the long bit of mane over his forehead – like a fringe. There was blood, not loads of it, like when you scrape your knee. It didn't look too bad. Then I remembered. Gavin had hit him on the poll. A blow there can kill. Nadine's dad told me that when he was loading up Sultan to take to a show in Essex. He told me about a horse's head weighing a ton too.

Sherry's body was sort of trembling. I thought I should get a vet, but the nearest one was Mr Aboaba in the Bethnal Green Road and he only does dogs and cats and small mammals. I lay down beside Sherry and put my arms round him. I told him it was going to be all right.

This was when it happened. Sherry spoke. You can laugh, I know, it's not something I go on about so you can take it or leave it. All I know is what I know.

So Sherry goes to me. And this is funny because when he speaks he speaks in exactly the sort of voice you'd expect. Sort of deep and rumbly. Anyway, he goes to me, Dionne, I am dying. And I just crack then, I just crack, I'm crying and crying, I reckon I'm mad. And I'm holding this horse's head and it's speaking. He says I've got to take him home. So then I go to him how the hell can I lug a horse's body all the way down Wentworth Street and up in the lift and then get it through into our flat, and have Mum going on about the smell. And he says, Sherry says, all serious, in fact completely serious. 'You must cut off my head.'

Well I can laugh now but then I just cried more.

I cried until Sherry was cold and it was dark.

Sherry never said nothing more til about midnight. I've got one of those light-up watches so I could check. The tears had just about stopped and I was trying to think about what to do. I'd convinced myself I was just a bit hysterical, like when Stacey downstairs swore she'd seen Michael Jackson walking down Fashion Street at eight in the morning. I'd moved the horse off of me and I was about to go.

Then he started up again.

He wanted me to cut off his head. I told him I didn't think I could do it. He told me Nadine's dad had a chain saw in the shed with the feed and I should go and get it and put his head in a sack. I told him, I said, where the hell did he think I was going to get a sack at this time of night and he just said 'Cut off my head' again in that deep low voice.

By this time I was a bit scared so I got the saw and it took me ages to figure it out because I'd never used one up to then, nor since. Sherry helped, told me what to do and that, he'd watched Nadine's dad, I couldn't have done it without him.

I was worried about the mess mostly. And about cutting Sherry who I would say was my best friend. It was a total nightmare getting him back over the flats too. I got a sack, like he said, one of those paper ones the feed comes in, but I never liked lifting his head into it, what with the blood and bits and that. I had to keep saying to myself, reminding myself, it was Sherry – my Sherry – and I suppose it was the least I could do.

It was the best move. Even all the bother of making sure the sack didn't get piss on it off of the floor of the lift. Sherry was right. But Sherry is always right, except for the lottery or the pools; if you ask him anything like that he just shuts up. He knew when Mum died – to the minute – and how many GCSE's I'd get, which was three: Religious Studies, English and Computing. He knew I should've packed Gavin in ages ago. I keep Sherry out on the balcony so he doesn't hardly smell at all. He did want me to start calling him Falada, he says it's what you call talking horses. But he's always been Sherry to me, and I can't start calling him something totally different now, just cause he's a head.

Roy A. Bayfield

'SIGNAL'

Roy A. Bayfield has written and performed his own work in a variety of settings, and his writing has been published in a number of small presses and horror/fantasy zines.

I remember when my father was learning Morse code. He would sit in front of the valve radio with its sheet of green names gleaming dully, having tuned into some distant outpost. He would listen intently for hours to the short/long bleeps, his brow furrowing at the occasional snarl of static. His HB pencil flying all the while across the backs of old music manuscript sheets as he furiously decoded the signal.

One day he was riding home from work on a bus that had a squeaky wheel-bearing. As it accelerated away from the bus-stop, it emitted a stream of irregular squeals. After a while he realised that, unconsciously, he was translating these as Morse. As language. But he would never say what words had come . . .

We are the decoders. Our brains assemble reality from the seething . . . *No, bollocks, this isn't enough.* If I am to leave any kind of meaningful record, if I am to excuse my actions at all, I will simply have to tell the story. One more example perhaps, and then we shall begin.

Have you ever stopped in a street, in any street in a town, and thought about how many words there are in your field of vision? If you had total recall, if you could look at that scene as if it were a photograph, imagine the sheer amount of verbiage you would read. Probably enough to fill a couple of pages of a novel, or perhaps a small volume of concrete poetry. A silent cacophony, like COME

PRAY EQUIPMENT BOOTS TELFORD A4123 BULLY'S
NIGHT OF INTERIORS STARRING VIVA STOP SALE
SALE SALE LUNCHTIME SHOWCASE £299.99 BANK AT
LAST RING ROAD STARS FUCK TIME ASSOCIATED
GREAT BRITISH DIVERSION GPO193 MANDERS GOT
WAS THIS LOUSY HEALTH WARNING FULL PROMISE
RELOCATED BOYS STATION endlessly, endlessly in your
eyes. What is it telling us, this enormous sentence? What is it
trying to make us do?

The first time it happened I came round with my head full of the
sound of a gigantic lead bell. I was run through with euphoria, the
insides of my eyes blazing with the afterimage of a million white
cellophane Christmas trees all interlocking . . .

I was lying flat on my stomach in wet grass, my face pressed
against the ground and my arms stretched out in front of me. I
rolled over, shivering and laughing, and lay for a bit looking up
at the sky.

Within minutes I began to feel the wintry thrill draining
away.

I realised that I had no idea where I was or what I had been
doing. I got to my feet unsteadily. My hands were blue with dirt
and covered in tiny scratches. The fingernails were long and filthy,
except the middle one of each hand, which seemed to have been
crudely chewed away. I was wearing a dark coat I didn't remember
seeing before.

Looking around, I saw that I was standing on a grass and
bramble bank next to a railway line. The bank fell away from
the track to a row of terrace back gardens. There was a familiar
mechanical hissing from the silver rail; looking along the track
I could see the yellow snout of an approaching 125. I was still
clambering down the bank when the train smashed past, the wind
from it pushing me back. In that moment, appalled, I realised
what I had been doing lying by the track; how I had cut my nails
so crudely.

I was too exhausted to be shocked. I began to pick my way through the head-high cow parsley, heading towards a bridge a quarter of a mile down the line. An old man wearing a vest was looking at me over the back of his fence. What's the matter, I thought, haven't you ever seen anyone cutting their nails before?

It was reassuring to find this residue of humour in myself. I had begun to think about the chilling possibilities of mental breakdown. I assumed I had been on some sort of formidable binge, except that I felt more than usually healthy. I tried to focus on the immediate past. All I could recall were confused fragments: unknown stations, a field with soil made of oily rust, a man with a large red moustache shouting at me while he ate a chicken leg. Watching a bee dying on a wet road.

The last normal, coherent thing I could remember was being in my back garden. It wasn't much of a garden really, just a strip of land where builders refurbishing the terrace had thrown the rotting window frames and old plaster. After work I used to go out there and plink at beer cans with a wildly inaccurate air pistol. I had been walking down the path to add a marrowfat peas tin to the target, and had noticed a scrap of paper in amongst the weed-grown rubble. It looked like the page from a book, and, mildly curious, I had picked it up to see if it would give me any clues about the previous inhabitants.

My memory was extremely clear here, as if something of overwhelming importance had been about to happen, so that my mind had focused very clearly on the moment.

I read the first sentences on the page, 'as he had never seen on her face in his waking hours, and say, "But of course, you know it isn't really the apple. It's the ..."'

That was the abrupt end of my coherent memories. It was as if I had been flipped over into a different kind of time, the ambiguous period that had just ended.

I reached the bridge, where the passage of kids had scoured a runnel of bare earth leading up to a gap in the fence. The bridge gave me quite a good view of an expanse of red-brick semis, but

I hadn't a clue where I was. My mind was offering up all kinds of embarrassing possibilities to describe my actions during the fugue. I was particularly worried about my job. I had only worked at the gallery for eight months, and it seemed unlikely that I'd been into work for several weeks.

I fished out my wallet. Not surprisingly it contained no cash, but there was – joy! – a familiar looking credit card. I began to make immediate plans. Some high buildings on the horizon seemed to indicate where the centre of town was. It must be a large place; there would be a station. Once there I would know where I was, be able to get back home.

Nervous breakdown brought on through overwork, I thought. Temporary nervous breakdown. The magic words made the problem seem more manageable. These were things that actually happened, that happened to other people anyway.

The strong impression I had that it was *reading a word* that had sent me into this weird state was surely a retrospective delusion.

The walk into town took about half an hour. In my tramp-like state, I wasn't stared at; I was actively not stared at. It was like living in another world. All I wanted to do was get home.

It turned out that I was in Peterborough, of all places. In the station I found the sanctuary of the toilets. By going through all my pockets I gathered enough change to buy a disposable toothbrush and shaving kit. By the time I had finished using this, and thrown away the awful coat, I looked no worse than the average art student. I ventured back out into Peterborough for a brief foray to the cash machine, feasted on a brace of hamburgers, then got on the train back to Stoke.

Feeling like a character in a story, I peered surreptitiously at the date on the newspaper which the man sitting next to me was reading. I had been incommunicado from myself for over three weeks.

As the train took me home, I pondered this latest development in my existence, trying to make sense of it. Try as I might, I couldn't see how reading a word on a scrap of paper could give me amnesia for three weeks.

I was a feckless character, I suppose. I had drifted disaffectedly through college and various jobs on the margins of culture. I had never had a job or a girlfriend for more than a year, and I had lived in six or seven different towns around the UK. I had no ambition. 'I eat whatever is put in front of me' was my motto.

A bearded man in a suit sat down opposite me. He was writing feverishly in a leather-bound notepad, obviously trying to meet some deadline to do with his job. As I got off the train, I glanced over his shoulder to see what he was writing. '9-12 departed 6 mins late. Chick & Mayo sandwich q. good! Intersected with Pride of Scotland at Bletchley. Engine change Reading.'

I went into work in my best suit, having groomed myself extensively. There were all the usual jokes from the attendants, 'Have a nice holiday then?', that kind of thing. The interview with the boss was more embarrassing than painful.

'Why didn't you ring in? There are procedures we have to follow. We can't help you if you don't let us know what's going on. As it is, I shall have to give you your first verbal warning. If you hadn't been here more than six months we would have sacked you ...'

'So where were you then?'

Mick broached the question the following night in the Albion.

'Oh, you know, out and about.'

'Look, I know it's boring, but if you're in any kind of trouble, we can always help out ...'

'No, it's OK, really. I just had a bit of woman trouble, you know. Left over from before I moved here. Nothing a couple of pints won't cure. What're you having?'

It happened again six weeks later. I can almost see the word; it's like having something on the tip of your tongue. Of course, I had looked for the previous scrap of paper, but I couldn't find it. I must have taken it with me.

The gallery was hosting an exhibition which consisted of six enormous cromalin prints mounted along one of the gallery walls, with a fountain playing in a long stainless steel trough in the middle of the floor. The photographs looked like delicate, sketchy Jackson Pollock-type abstracts at first, but on closer inspection were revealed to be life-sized reproductions of graffiti-covered WC cubicle doors. The words and drawings on the doors were the main focus of interest, the practical literature of a certain type of gay encounter, wild fantasies and matter-of-fact pleas for contact. Captions indicated where each door had come from, service stations and municipal toilets from all over the country.

The exhibition was due to open that evening, and I was taking the opportunity to look at the show properly before the punters arrived. I became absorbed in the texts, and must have been reading for over twenty minutes. Some of the writers seemed to have items on more than one door, and I was trying to trace them from place to place when I read the word, written in marker pen, nestling somewhere in the webs of desire, HERE 4–30 SATURDAY I AM A MIDDLE AGED PROFESSIONAL WITH GOLDEN HAIR ON MY CHEST, LEAVE ...

And six weeks later I came back to myself, on all fours behind an advertising hoarding, weeping uncontrollably as I stared at a tiny parcel wrapped around again and again with black tape, wrapped incredibly tightly as if to prevent its ever being opened again.

I simply gave up this time. I was horrified that it should have happened again, so dramatically. I felt as though I had been pulled open, that I was a gaping wound and everything was falling out of me. It turned out that I was in Whitby, so I sent the gallery a postcard of resignation and caught a train to London.

James was aghast when I turned up at his flat.

'Christ almighty, what have you been doing?'

'I don't know, I don't know. Look, can I stay here for a couple of days?'

Luckily James had been on his own when I called round. I had a bath and borrowed some of his clothes. After a cup of tea I began to feel a bit more human. I managed to persuade him that I had neither gone insane nor commited some crime, though for all I knew I'd done both.

Although I was exhausted, I found it very hard to sleep in James's spare room. My mind was racing with possibilities.

Once again, a number of incoherent images came when I contemplated the gap period. A naked boy lying on a hillside with a sprig of fir in his mouth. An enormous black tanker ship. My hands scrabbling in the earth, burying small bottles filled with milky fluid.

I had no idea whether these had actually occurred, or whether they were merely fevered images conjured up by my brain to fill the gap in my experience.

I hung around James's flat, eating, drinking, playing tapes. In the evenings we might go to the pub opposite, but I was a pretty poor conversationalist. I was trying desperately to read as little as possible; averting my eyes from the free newspapers that dropped onto the mat, covering the sleeves of cassettes with my hand as I got the tapes out, looking at the wall while the TV was on.

The dreams seemed to have more reality than the dull days in the flat. I would sleep till noon, watching them unfold. One recurring dream was a cheap spy mystery, a convoluted plot involving sleeper agents who were activated by code words which reached them through a variety of bizarre methods. Mostly though I dreamt of performing a series of stoical murders in the service of something which I could only envisage as a cross between a church (in both senses of the word) and a gigantic, undersea creature.

Throughout the dreams there was a feeling of giant space, of exponentially increasing freedom. The dream protagonist was a monster of purpose. I began to contrast the feeling of power and will I glimpsed in the dreams with my own feckless existence.

James came back one evening to find me giggling over a six-pack in the front room.

'What's up?'

'Nothing. Listen, sorry I've been such a git over the past few weeks. I think I just needed to get sorted, you know.'

'Don't worry about it. I'm glad you're a bit more cheerful though.'

That night I took him out for a curry with my waning credit card. The next day, as soon as he was at work, I got down the big dictionary from his bookshelf and started flicking through the pages, like a man playing Russian roulette, my eye scanning through the sheets of words until

Now I'm sitting on bare planks in this room on the south coast. Some of the planks have been torn up and burned in the fire. I write this by the light that comes through a hole ripped in the corner of the marine ply which covers the window. The wood was nailed over all the windows in this street when it was condemned.

The people I have begun to think of as 'us' moved in during the summer, making a whole street of squatters. It is as if the street is no longer a part of Brighton, as if it has become a self-contained township of the lost.

I haven't gone out since I came round in this place, the best part of a year since I was in James's flat. The squatters come and go, sporting dirt as personal ornamentation. They seem to regard me with some measure of awe. I suppose I look like some extreme prototype of their ilk. Matted hair cascades across my own ragged clothing. I have a mummified hand in my pocket, and a tiny grey flesh ear pinned as an earring to my own.

One woman comes around quite often. She frightens me and excites me at the same time. She has the word KALI carved into her shoulder in big ragged scars and, most disturbing of all, has one armpit shaved and another bushy with hair. She brings me food, vegetarian junk food of various kinds. And drink; cider and strong lager.

I'm just hanging around really, waiting. I think next time I'll go over completely, give 'myself' up totally to the great and terrible freedoms.

Steve Aylett

'SHIFA'

Steve Aylett was born in 1967 and is the author of *The Crime Studio*, *Slaughtermatic* and *The Inflatable Volunteer* (Orion), and *Toxicology* (Four Walls Eight Windows, US).

Before Beerlight got really bad it was a city of strangers. Few people knew each other well enough to get seriously mad. But as with all cultures at all times, there was a subculture which anticipated a trend. This is what the cops, amid the jostling of press-conferences on the precinct steps, termed a 'rogue social element'. Communication was a cult to which, when the cultural histories were written, everyone would claim they had belonged from the beginning.

One of the forces to bring it into the mainstream was Doctor Albert Shifa. Author of *Know the Futility and Do It Anyway*, he specialised in aggression therapy. He advised angry men to strike pillows and other soft furnishings all innocent and unawares until the fury subsided. Learning thus that rage could be taken out on targets irrelevant to its cause, most of his patients went on rampages more randomly destructive than the Basra Road bombing.

Though troubled, the Doctor persevered until he had occasion to treat the hitman Brute Parker, one of the fiercest bastards in the state. Parker thought he wanted to calm down some after a painful affair with the judgment angel Aggie Swan. As Parker lay on the couch, wound tight as a deepsea service cable, Doctor Shifa told him there was no need to take out the old graphic equaliser at the nearest and dearest opportunity. 'No call to decline into murder and ridicule, Brute.'

'It's me who is lookin' into the guns, Albert Shifa.'

'Sure it is, I'm sure. You ever take off them aviator shades Brute?'

'In my dreams. But there's flyin' camels there too, so it don't seem too likely.'

'Flying camels, crikey. That's as much and a little more than I can absorb today, Brute. I'd like you to try some relaxation and containment techniques. Take this piggy bank home with you. It's like a swear box except in this case you put a dollar in every time you want to shoot someone.'

'This will save me enough for ammo.'

'No, Brute – you miss my point.'

'You think I'm dumb.'

'Easy, tiger – I'm just trying to set you straight.'

'No, you're workin' an angle. What else, I gotta wear sew-on mittens?'

'That's right – sit up, breathe deep—'

'I'm gonna kill.'

'Count to ten, Brute, give yourself pause—'

Parker did count to ten, yelling each number at a louder volume, advancing on the Doctor, shuddering to beat the band, fists like wrecking balls, veins bulging like inner tubes, backing him into a corner until at ten the explosion of multiphonic bellowing heard from the Doctor's office made it known that Parker was a troubled man.

Following scenes of patient-straddled chest-pushing gurney rides and stand-clear heartshock, the Doctor awoke in a state of trussed-up mummydom, and sensing that he had a visitor, turned his eyes painfully to the side.

'Hello Albert Shifa. I have brought grapes in a bag.'

'Parker,' snaffled Shifa, muting his alarm, 'er you shouldn't be here. The police—'

'I have come here to thank you for my treatment Albert Shifa. You made me mad and I beat you all to pudding. This is as it should be, simple and direct. Never again will I take out my anger on those innocent of its cause. God bless you Albert Shifa.' And he walked out, taking the grapes with him.

And so Shifa developed his direct action theory. Why take it out on pillows when the real cause was out there? No longer was his office a blizzard of feathers and injustice. Pop Joey conferred a lead safe upon Gilly Charmers from a height of forty-seven feet. Teddy Beltway shot the life out of Clinton Marks Deal in what he described as his 'own small way'. Gilbert Wham gave Chad Viagra an upward view of the bay. Hammy Roadstud dispensed so many bullets he started selling advertising space on the casings. Ban Saliva even used 'doctor's orders' as a defence when arrested for feeding pasta to the chef responsible. Rain was washing away tears and sidewalk brains, and it was Doctor Shifa who found himself in the perjury room with the cod-eye a real possibility. His defence attorney was Harpoon Specter, whose back was still healing from the slapping it received after his last case – defending Parker. Out of superstition Harpoon hadn't washed or changed his clothes since. Every gesture of this unshaven bum corrupted the air.

His closing argument was a weeping sore of mitigation. 'Murderous rampage? Easy for them to say. We've all felt that gun eruption coming up like a sneeze. Don't deny it. Add to that the knowledge that liberty is seldom reasonable and never innocent. Why take a chance? So we put the unearthly boot in, of course we do. Al Shifa told them to do it? By what authority? Haven't they minds of their own? Well let's suppose, for argument's sake, that they haven't. What's left but raw bloody violence? And let's face it, they're a dab hand. Gilbert Wham once conducted an interesting rampage in which he punched anyone who'd stand still for it – and several who wouldn't. Yet by his own testimony today we've heard how Al here turned him around. Chad Viagra knifed Gilbert, Gilbert drowned Chad, and there for them the matter ended. You might even say that Chad exhibited somewhat of a victim psychology. And that random violence, thoughtless and unfocussed, is mere masking behaviour. Excuses which leave us idle? Occam's Razor – the simpler the truth, the more painful it is to swallow. We must, according to Cicero, study each thing in the most perfect example we have of it. Let us take the man in the street. Besieged from all sides by violence and the splintered systems of authority. His eyes are bulging, his face is weird, his pants are the colour of clouded jade. He sweats like a bastard. Yells torrents of abuse at small, skittering dogs. Smothers himself with lard. And yes, if wronged, he kills. What do we expect, after all? We are forever and impossibly surprised. Look at the 2K bug – even when a disaster makes an appointment we're not prepared. And we call ourselves the masters of our planet. Yes, ours is the seething diamond mine of the stars. What are we but knots of oxygen?'

'Speak for yourself, Mr Specter,' spat the judge, exasperated. 'I don't know if you've gone batshit crazy or if my grasp of our beautiful language has turned all to pus but for God's sake stick to the shocking facts – the retinal bars of my migraine are giving me ideas about you.'

'Thank you your honour. The question before you is a simple one, ladies and gentlemen of the jury. In suggesting that these poor morons kill the objects of their rage rather than an innocent bystander or even some stuffed effigy, did the Doctor offend? This government has taken the law into its own hands – very well, then let the punishment fit the crime. Instruct by your example, and see if this doesn't leave you satisfied. The denizens of Beerlight are desperate. Why should their desperation be quiet?'

'For peace,' said the judge.

The jury decided the Doctor was guilty as hell. But someone in authority had taken Specter's words to heart. At the killing hour, twenty grim spectators gathered to watch the electrocution of a pillow.

Stella Duffy

'JAIL BAIT'

Stella Duffy has written two novels, *Singling Out the Couples* and *Eating Cake*, published by Sceptre, and three crime novels, *Calendar Girl*, *Wavewalker* and *Beneath the Blonde*, published by Serpent's Tail. She has written thirteen short stories, a one-woman show for herself, a musical cabaret, *Close to You*, and the script for Gay Sweatshop's dance/theatre piece *The Hand*. She is also a performer and writer with the comedy company Spontaneous Combustion, and recently toured Britain with *Lifegame* for Improbable Theatre. Stella lives in South London, purely because it annoys North Londoners.

Jill's telling me the girl unit at Holloway is the coolest thing she's ever heard of. Special and new-made and all shiny and clean. And just for us. It was on the radio – I didn't hear it, I don't listen to that kind of radio, don't listen to any kind of radio, got enough voices of my own to listen to, tell the truth – but Jill heard about it and she told me and we thought it was just so fucking cool. It's not got any of the old bitches in it, sad old slags and the slappers who've been around forever anyway and don't know where else to be, except just this side of North London, downwind of Hampstead, turn back if you get to Arsenal, you've gone too far. You've always got to go too far.

Getting our first tattoos together. Real tattoos, paid for and sterile and everything. Watching the man painting on her skin, soft flesh raised into hoarse red welts, wiping away the blood and adding new colour, pretty yellow and blue and deep red darker than her blood. Then my turn and Jill said it wouldn't hurt, didn't hurt her, did it? She wasn't whimpering for fuck's sake. So I took off my bra, lay down, heart shape over heart space. But it did hurt. Too fucking much. I made him stop even though she said I couldn't. Made him give up halfway through. He said I must have a low pain threshold. Maybe I do. I also have a tattoo of a broken heart.

Sitting in Jill's bedroom – also kitchen, lounge, bathroom, the lot – sitting on the floor, leaning against her knees, hoping if I wait here long enough she might stroke my head again, play with my hair. She doesn't. We're sitting there and then she says how fucking crap the end of daylight saving is, how she can't stand it and now the bloody sun's coming in waking her at eight in the morning and then it's dark by four, dark before the day's even started and too damn cold and what the fuck are we supposed to do for Christmas dinner anyway? I thought it was a big leap from the end of October to the full stuffed turkey, flaming Christmas pudding, but you could see what she meant. Then she said we should go to Holloway. For the festive season. And I'm like fuck me but you're a mad cunt, madder than I am, and Jill says that's just not possible, just not possible. But she's not making a whole lot of sense either, she can't mean it, that place fucking stinks and anyway last time we tried that shit she got to Holloway, I ended up in bloody Stile, two weeks out of my mind in boredom valley and then luckily just about loopy enough to get shunted off to community care hole. Left there in a halfway house to nowhere, easily influenced, just keep the mad fucker on the medication and she'll be good as gold, good as Goldilocks, steal your fucking porridge you stupid great cunts and what do you mean I can't see her, I have to see her, who else is there? Then fuck you bitch and now what's the problem, you've got another eye haven't you? Oh Christ and such a lot of fucking blood and God I hope it's not mine, there's nothing like an institutionalised period to start the day, end the day, start the week – more radio fucking shite – and then the quiet and the sweet icecream and jellies, temazepam baby I am, will be, ever be, hush now good girl.

Anyway, anyway, the point being that the last time we tried to come in from the cold they tore us apart and broke my heart and Jill came tumbling after. But apparently . . . Holloway's got this new young offenders' unit and the radio lady from the North thinks that's shit, thinks all the money will go there, showcase for the dangerous young ones, too much of a good thing and what about the poor little girls in the frozen North, where will all their good money go? Stay down here baby, warm in the soft South where it always has been, did you not notice it's why we moved here too? So – it's the end of October. We just have to do it well enough, big but not too big, within the next couple of weeks, then the least it'll be is remand and maybe even a few months more to get us all the way into spring, fever of the recently freed.

But we have to do it right. Too big and we'll not see summer soon enough. Too small and it's crap cell night, maybe a caution, and worse than that the possibility of another fucking year fucking the carers. So whoring's out because that's always leading back to some foster daddy, let me hold you and make it all better baby, oh yes please do, that's just what I need. And shoplifting's good for the clothes, or the dinner, or even just the sheer fucking thrill of being bad in the shining light of security cameras and in the face of Henry Stupid, the thick cunt who stands at the door pretending to be a security guard, biceps for brains and a dick the size of my clit, but shoplifting won't get us Christmas crackers with plastic scissors inside. And housebreaking is possible but Jill's still terrified of dogs and gets tinnitus with too much loud noise – or a too hard smack on the head – and if we want them to get us it would have to be dog or alarm and what's the point of the pointless break-in if you get away with it? Indeed.

First break-in. We were thirteen, fourteen at the most. Maybe Jill was already fourteen. Fast shared a gram of speed and running around the town, new town with walkways turned into airplane runways, ready to fucking take off there was so much of the too-much energy spilling round my veins. Then Jill says we should use the excess and do a job. She's been watching daytime re-runs of The Sweeney, *it takes me a minute to work out what she's talking about. There's a place on the corner, a flat above the closed off licence, the woman who lives there works every day, gets the bus first thing and isn't back until dark. She'll be safely at the office. It's easy to get in. No dog, no alarm, she's probably not even thirty yet that woman, no money for any good security shit. Good guess, no security at all, but she's got a great place. Easy in through the back window and it's nice in there. Just bedroom and lounge, kitchen and bathroom. And all of it girlie soft and warm, too much pink, but it'll do us. We eat bacon and eggs — Jill can't eat much, but speed's never really affected my appetite, I'm weird like that. I can just soak those drugs right up. She does me a big breakfast — half a packet of bacon, three eggs just how I like them, yolk running all over the bacon, bright yellow into the setting fat, geography rivulets on the plate. Bacon's a bit too salty, smoked back, but good anyway. I chew the rind and walk through the little flat. We think about a place like this, maybe Jill and I could get a place together, share it. The woman's got chocolates in her fridge, Creme Eggs too, we take the telly into the bedroom and get into bed, sheets quite clean, must have been changed only a few days ago and no fucking or period stains, maybe she's got a washing machine, easier that way to wash your sheets whenever you want to. We eat chocolate and watch Richard and Judy, laugh at the phone-in moan-in, but then it's too comfortable and warm and we fall asleep and we've got problems of our own. It's dark, the only light is from the telly, the woman's walked in and guess who's sleeping in her bed and she's off on one and screaming at us, hitting at us and I don't know what the fuck she's so pissed off for, we didn't take anything. Jill can't believe she's hitting her and I can't believe she's hitting Jill, can't she see how stupid that is? She's fucking lucky we fell asleep, we were going to take loads of shit and we didn't so what's the fucking problem? What is your fucking problem you stupid fucking ignorant bitch? Big dry cleaning bill I expect. Hard work getting all that blood off the pretty pink duvet in your basic home washing machine. The woman moved out weekend after that. Squatters moved in. Bet they didn't keep it as nice as she did.*

Jill rolls a joint, mostly tobacco, thin rub of hash into it, then special treat for the goodest of good girls, sprinkling of coke across the top — she worked last night in the city boy street, sweet rich boys paying in kind. Kind city boy forced to hand over cash too when Jill explained what was going to happen when she stopped twisting his balls and the blood flooded back in and then out again when she used the blade hidden in her other hand. Fifty quid, just like that. Scared city boy pissing in his own wind. But driving home anyway. Whimpering back to his girlfriend and just an especially difficult day in the money markets darling, I'm a bit tired, maybe

I'll have a little lie down. No you bitch, don't fucking touch me there, I didn't mean that kind of a lie down, for fuck's sake, is that all you bloody women ever think about? Jill and I lie back and dream of Holloway, special shared room and painted walls and breakfast and lunch and dinner and hide out in the house of girlies until summer comes around. I'm wondering, just briefly, if Jill's got this completely right, if it's all going to be so fucking lovely, I mean the point is, it is a house of detention right? But she's sure it must be great because otherwise why would the Tory bitch on the radio be so fucking concerned and anyway, even if it's just like the same old place, no new paint job or anything, if it isn't for the old ones, if it's just for us, then think of how it will be, no old lady smells and no mad mothers crying for their fostered babies and the following, always following because we're always the little ones. We'll be big girls, just us, our very own home from home. Which, when the home you're homing from is ten foot square of peeling damp and the screams of the dozy cunt next door who will keep welcoming him into her bed and then getting surprised when he lets his fist into her face as well, if that's home and Jack Frost is on his way, then maybe anything's better. Or maybe I just wanted Jill to stroke my hair again. Like she did. Just the once. Soft stroking like she meant it, not absent action like I might have been the cat or her own head in need of a good itch. Anyway, anyway, the hash is spreading my mind all over the fucking place, it's chocolate spread brain, and then because neither of us smokes tobacco if we can help it, we're getting a nicotine rush too and I'm just starting to refocus when the pretty little truth drug kicks in on top of all that and my poor bitch of a brain doesn't know what to do. Mouth opens and closes and doesn't know if it should laugh or talk and starts to say words, any will do, but tobacco dries my lips and nothing comes out just a goo gah of bollocks and pretty soon Jill thinks I'm really funny, really fucking funny and I so want her not to laugh at me, I want that hand to stroke my head not point fucking laughing at me.

* * *

First time laughing, too stoned, new to us, first time laughing so much, giggling stoned laughter and it won't go away and I've peed my pants and Jill and me both just laughing even more at that, sticky ammonia turning cold in my jeans. She's trying to cut out a line of speed to sharpen me up, take the edge off the giggle, but her hand's shaking so much and I'm laughing so much I blow it all over the table. Stopped me laughing though.

Nothing to stop her laughing at me now and I'm not wasting good drugs on her sense of humour this time. So I'm fucked off and hate her. Hate her hard. Worried by the hate, it's the one that scares me, and I really don't like to hate Jill, but she is so not going to stop laughing, she's having far too good a fucking time and I think maybe I need to leave now, go out for a walk, get away from the laughing bitch because I might just have to smack her fucking big mouth if she doesn't stop, and I've never hit Jill before, though she's hit me loads of times and I don't know if I could hit her, not really, but right now I might just slam my fist so far into that laughing gob of hers it'll come out her cunt next time she sees it. I don't like being this angry. Worries me. Don't like it at all. And then – bliss, sweet rapture, and praise the gifts of the virgin who'd hate to see me harm a hair on the beloved's head, I've slammed pissed off hands hard into my pocket and there's a couple of jellies in there with the condoms and the polo mints. I know, but it only sounds like an odd combination at first. You figure. And then maybe I can just about do this. The jellies and the coke and the hash? I don't know if it's a great combination, it's not quite the real thing, but fuck it I might as well anyway because daylight saving has all gone and it's dark at four thirty now and so we're not going anywhere, right? Wrong.

Jill stops laughing and pulls me out of the door with her. I don't need a coat she says, even though it's bloody freezing, shit sleety rain far too early in the year and slashing at my face, but she tells me not to worry, there's a nice warm BMW parked just around the corner and we can put the heater on full and move in for half an hour or so. Jill can't drive but she knows everything else there is to know about cars. How to get through the electric locking system. How to turn off the alarm without a key. How to start the motor. Jill fucked a mechanic for a few months last year, stole his knowledge and fucked off with his new set of tools too. Left his dick, not the best of his tools. And it's a nice car, big and easy to drive. At least it is until Jill starts trying to direct me, over there, that right turn, no not this, the next one, shit you've missed it, U-turn, here, yes of course you can, you fucking well can, don't talk shit, you fucking well can. Fucking well can't. Coke, hash and jellies, power steering power steered from the passenger seat. Straight into an oncoming Nissan. We barely move, the BMW takes the swipe with a fat and solid crunch – side impact bars, air bags as standard, there's something about these company cars that makes even facing the wrong way in rush hour not seem so bad. The tinny little Japanese spins out and then back into the line of traffic, driver looks as if he thinks it might be all right. He's facing the right way. His neck isn't broken. Chassis is though. I'm dazed and Jill's pulling at my hand, grabs me out of my seat and we're running fast, down a couple of dark streets, through a pathway, old lady shrinking against the wall, holding her trolley to her like a shield, thanking God we weren't interested. A couple of people chase at first, but they don't really care. Much more concerned about the guy in the Nissan than the couple of girls who've pinched some rich git's car. God knows he'll have enough insurance. I bet Nissan Man's only third party, he looks like a local. Want to tell Jill, but she'll hate me for worrying, looking back. Jill doesn't look back. Quick turn left, no idea of exactly where we're headed but we know there's a canal along here somewhere, no-one comes to a canal at dusk. Not unless they're running too. Into an overgrown estate and thanking winter now, glad of early sunset. I'm fretting about fingerprints but Jill is so sure that's irrelevant, bloke'll get his car back and don't the cops have better to think about than that and who the fuck knows where we live anyway? No-one. No-one but Jill. We find the canal and follow the line down towards town, brighter lights and I really am freezing now, coke rush long gone, just a headache from too many drugs and the adrenaline mix, temples throbbing, I'm thinking maybe we're headed home, maybe we can leave it for tonight, back to Jill's and a bag of chips, vinegar and grease on my hands until the morning, but Jill sees me shivering and my goose-pimpled skin takes her ahead to the turkey. She wants us safe and warm for Christmas. Tucked up cosy and waiting for Santa. Inside.

First Christmas alone. The mother and father have gone away. Packed their car with a DNA-variegation of children and driven to their cousins in the North. And I will not go with them. I will not go to the happy family and play the good child. We have been fighting for weeks and then she said it, the mother, OK, don't come, we'll take the others. You stay here. By yourself. That's fine. She turned the electricity off as she left and removed the key card. Christmas morning listening to the one radio in the house that had batteries and boiling milk for hot Weetabix, grateful for the gas stove. I'm eleven, Jill's twelve and a half. She knocks on the door, shivering in pyjamas and dressing gown. Her lot are still asleep and can she watch telly at my place, she knows we have too many kids here for them to attempt the sort of TV rules they have at her house. No TV. Jill can't believe it, is shocked — all alone? Stunned — they've really left you all alone? And so fucking excited. Stays all morning. By eleven we've finished the Baileys and started on the Tia Maria. Weetabix with hot milk and whisky. Her gran swears by whisky to keep you well, milk to line the stomach, makes Jill a hot toddy every night in winter. Jill says it will stop us getting sick. It doesn't, but we're not bothered. Morecambe and Wise are probably on telly now, it doesn't matter. Queen's message comes and goes and Jill still isn't going home, she's having too much fun and I do think, I really do, that maybe her gran will be worried, but then the thought passes and anyway, she won't know to find Jill here, thinks my lot are all away. They are. Early evening and there's Advocaat and some cheery cherry brandy and Jill thinks we should set fire to a pudding. But we haven't got a Christmas pudding, so it's the last of the Weetabix and a third of a bottle goes on top, because there's alcohol in Christmas pudding too, isn't there? So it can't matter how much we throw on. Can't matter until the lit Weetabix flies up to the greasy nets and we've left the gas on to heat the place and there's a lot of flame, lot of fire and we run out to the balcony, Jill screaming, nylon dressing gowns glowing in the night wind. Hospital, new homes, new parents, Jill's gran can't cope and she joins me in care limbo.

Until that Christmas Jill had only been my best friend. After that she was my only friend.

We're out now, so we may as well stay out. We may as well make it happen tonight. That's Jill's plan. Along the canal for a bit, past a couple of girls out working. Not looking for work, actually working. Jill gives a few pointers to the one giving a blow job. 'Slower love, slower. The gentle gobble's what the bloke's after, aren't you mate?' Punter and girl look up, Jill's smiling, as much as you can smile with your gob wide open miming the mouthing. The girl slows down, the punter nods relief and grins, winks at Jill. The kid's probably only about fourteen, no fucking idea yet. 'That's it love. You've got him now. He's happy now. Well done love, that's it, keep on, good girl.' The bloke's smiling, eyes closed, pants down. Jill reaches for his wallet, poking out of his trouser pocket, grabs a twenty for herself and pushes another into the girl's bra top. Poor bitch must be freezing. All the while Jill's sweet talking the pair of them through it. 'Now you've got it, good girl, that's the way. Soft and slow. See love, there's some things your mum'll never teach you.' He's grinning and moaning to himself and the girl's sucking and slobbering for all she's worth, eyes wide and delighted. We walk on, maybe ten yards and once we're almost at the bridge Jill shouts out, 'That's it! Good girl. You're doing a great job, great job. Soft and slow and get them going and now——' The girl looks up, mouth full, the punter opens his smiling eyes, grateful inquisitive looks towards the pair of us from both of them, 'Now bite the fucker off!' Jill screams with delight, girl chokes with laughter, man freaks, cock shrivels, nothing to blow. God knows why they do it, men are a fuck of a lot braver than us. I'd never trust anything that tender to the teeth of a stranger. We run off and Jill can't get over herself, fucking delighted she is. Twenty quid richer too.

✵　　✵　　✵

First trick. Jill's idea. We've both done it, Jill figures we might as well start getting paid for it. Jill figures. I'm fifteen, she's sixteen. Legal. Real. I'm nervous about it though so she tells me to watch her, see how she goes and if she can do it, then so can I. A fuck's a fuck, right? And I can just stop with a blow job if I really want to. I don't know. Seems to me your actual fuck — eyes closed, all noise and panting — is a damn sight less personal than having some stranger's dick in my mouth. Anyway, she's street-cornering herself and I'm stopping in the dark part, under the arches, watching her and these lads come up. It's a stag party. They want her for the groom. What'll she do for twenty quid? We didn't know much about market forces at the time. She offered the lot. Quite a show, best man got a hand job, bride's little brother got a blow job and then Jill's feeling a bit knackered so she calls me out of the corner and asks the groom how does he fancy me and her together? This is all out in the fucking street, mind. Anyway, course he does. So I'm there right and Jill reckons it'll be fine and then we're fooling about and now the groom's got his dick out and Jill reckons I should do him, get it over with, at least she's there with me. So I turn to do him and then I see it's all of them that are waiting. Not just the groom and this wasn't the deal and Jill's saying no, this wasn't the deal, but that's not the fucking point, right? The best man's not quite so drunk now. She did half a dozen of them and I did six of the others. This was not voluntary. Except when they left the little brother ran back and gave us another twenty each. So it wasn't really rape either. Was it? We got better at it after that. More fucking careful anyway.

So I'm thinking about that girl and how I'm so bloody happy to be running round in winter with Jill and not on my knees by the canal and we're coming back up to Holloway Road now and Jill says that's auspicious. It's a sign. Yeah, it's a fucking road sign. Not what she means. And there's lights and cars and a few drunks and some young people in groups, pissed and laughing on their way out for the night, and Jill's speeding now, really fucking speeding, God knows what on. Cold and potential and the twenty quid in her pocket I guess. And she's looking all around and thinking who can we do? What can we do? Then she sees it, other side of the road, furniture shop. And in the window, a bloody fairy tale bed. Really fairy tale. A four poster straight out of Sleeping Beauty. All over girlie shit and frills and pretty embroidered roses, wide curtains with white flounces and I can't believe that Jill even thinks that looks like anything, but she's just completely taken with it, and they've done some special lighting on it too, it's all soft and golden, glowing in the cold street. And the cover turned down and a silk nightie laid out just waiting for the Princess to float in and sleep forever, no night dancing to wear out her shoes, no hidden pea to bruise her delicate skin. Perfect. And Jill's got a rubbish bin and it just goes right through the window, before I can say not to, before I can even ask what the fuck she's doing and the glass only takes two hits and then it shatters, glass mountain collapses with sparkling prisms all around us, glitter snow on the ground and the ringing of alarm bells. And Jill just takes her time, gives me her clothes, one by one, like I'm the fucking palace maid and I fold them up and put them on the ground because what else can I do and then she's naked and she climbs in through the broken window, glass under her feet but that doesn't matter and I help her put on the nightie and she just gets into bed. Climbs into the bed. I plump up the pillows and tuck her in and kiss her goodnight, pull the curtains around her. I'd turn out the lights but they're flashing blue.

First night in the girl place. It's OK. Really it is. Lots better than I've been in before, that's for sure. It's really not bad. The lady on the radio was right. I mean it is Holloway, but it is pretty flash too. Jill doesn't know though. It all took ages working out what had happened, if they were going to do her or section her. I was easy, accomplice, best friend, no nutter me. Not now. Only then they figured same for her — she was bad, not mad this time. True too. She's not mad. Pissed off, but not mad. Jill turned twenty while we were on remand, they reckoned she's too old for this. Too late for it to do her any good. Fucked her off no end. I didn't think it would be all right being here without her. But it's not that bad. Not as bad as I thought anyway.

Simon Lewis

'IN THE BOX'

Careful love. Don't get it everywhere. I'm not being funny, it's just I've had the interior re-upholstered. Got the whole lot replaced. Even the floor carpets. My wife said not to bother, a lot of expense for nothing. Go off in the caravan for a long weekend, that's what she said. Get it out of your system. It's clean as you like, it's all in your head. She didn't understand.

You alright? You look a bit pale. Here, open the window, get some fresh pollution down your neck. That better? Right. Make yourself comfortable. What's that gunk you're drinking? That's like a strawberry milkshake, is it, but flat? Full of chemicals I bet.

Charlie, I've picked up outside the club, I'm going to Hackney.

Cunt. Excuse my Anglo Saxon. Not you, the crackly voice on the radio. My controller. You know what he told me? Told me to sound my aspirants. Thinks he's superior to all of us, the ones on the streets, thinks we're scum. He was trying to show me up. Thinks just because I've driven a minicab for twelve years, I don't know what an aspirant is. Well the jokes on him, cause I do. It's a 'Haytch' sound. Haytch. Haytch. I'll haytch him if he carries on.

Good night was it? I hope you don't mind me saying so, you look like you haven't been long on this planet. Your eyes are popping out of your skull. They look like dinner plates. You've been taking those lovey dovey pills. Oh, it doesn't bother me. I get all sorts in here. Careful with the drink love. Don't spill the milk. Not on my new upholstery.

I scrubbed, I hoovered, had it cleaned professionally the lot. But there's some stains that never go. So I thought, enough, I'll rip the whole lot out and put in new. Start over. You'd have thought my insurance would have covered something like that happening. But would it? Would it bollocks.

Oi, watch it mate. You see that? Nearly took the wing mirror off. Idiot. There's some nutters on the roads this time of night, I tell you.

You want to hear why I had to change it? The upholstery. This'll get you. It's four in the morning right, it's raining, I've been working eight hours straight, I've just necked half a thermos of cold coffee and my haemorrhoids are humming. Excuse the medical detail but I'm painting a picture. I'm called out to a house in Dulwich. Nice area, Dulwich, you don't get the flotsam you get round here. I park up in the drive of this big house and take in the baubles on top of the gatepost and the Range Rover. The place is all dark, and I wonder if I've got the wrong place, when the door opens and this bloke walks out carrying this box. He's quite a pale guy, I'd say late thirties, with a shiny bald head and knobbly hands, and he's holding this box all out in front of him. It's about the size of a hat box, this by this. All wrapped up in pretty wrapping paper, gold and red stripes, and with a big red ribbon around it, tied in a bow at the top.

Well he gets in the front and slips the box carefully onto his lap. Now I notice that he's got hair growing out of his ears. Now I'm a little hirsute in that area myself. But I trim every other week. Not that I'm going to make any assumptions. I keep an open mind. I mean, so what if Mr Posh Box is a little lax in the personal grooming department? Oh, and also he's got dirty fingernails, and a couple of little dark spots on his shirt and he's breathing quite .hard. He gives me an address in Eltham. His voice is a bit shaky, and I get the impression that he's a little on edge.

I see he hasn't done his seat belt up, so I ask him to clunk click.

I'm not being funny, but if people ride in the front I like them to be protected. You've got yours on, yeah? Good. No don't take it off, what are you doing? Put it back on. That's right, the metal bit slots in there. You having a bit of difficulty? Alright, leave it. Wait till we stop at some lights, easier to do it then. You need to get to bed, I reckon.

Well Hairy Ears tries to pull the belt around himself but the box gets in the way. He gives the belt a jerk, then lets it snap back into the holder. He could have got it in, but it's not like I want to make an issue of it. I mean, if he doesn't want to wear it, that's his prerogative.

I tool the car out of the drive. That's what people do with cars in books. They don't execute a manoeuvre, they tool. So I tool the car out the gravel drive, and I turn to the guy, I'm a chatty bloke, I don't know if you've noticed, I turn to the guy and I say, 'Nice pad. Yours?' 'No,' he says. 'A mates?' I ask. 'My business partner,' he says. So now, naturally, I ask him what his business is. 'Kitchenware,' he tells me. 'It must be a profitable partnership,' I say, meaning that he seems to be doing alright, from what I've seen of his partner's house. Maybe he doesn't understand me right, because at this he gives a short, dry laugh. 'It was,' he says. 'It really was.' I ask him politely to elaborate on his use of the past tense. He explains that he and his partner had to separate. I ask if now he's going off on his own, and again I get the unfunny laugh. Well, I'm glad to be a source of such amusement.

Now I ask him who the present's for. Tells me it's for his wife. 'Nice,' I say. 'Is it her birthday?' 'No,' he says. Ahhh, that's sweet, I think. The man's getting his wife a present and it isn't even her birthday. 'Special occasion?' I ask. 'Yes,' he says. He seems to like that. He repeats it. 'Special occasion.' Only there's something not right about the way he says it. All this time he's fiddling with the little knot in the ribbon round the box, wrapping the stray ends round and round his little finger. Of course now I'm dying of curiosity. 'So what's in the box?' I ask.

Look at that. That's lovely that is. The sky all pink and flowery over the office blocks. That's poetry. That's the benefit of night shifts, watching the dawn. That and the empty roads. You get a lot more time to think. Not like day time. Day time's all argy bargy, effing and blinding, parping and hooting. Night time you make progress.

So, yeah, where was I? Right, Mr Nervous. Well he tells me in this box of his he has a blender. 'That's a lovely present,' I tell him. 'What make is it?' I ask. 'It's the best,' he says. 'I give her a lot,' he says. 'I give her everything. You understand? Everything. She's never wanted for anything. She wants a dress, I get her a dress. She wants a dog, I give her a dog.'

Now at this point I glance across and I notice there's this little dark stain on the wrapping paper around the bottom corner of the box. I point it out. He tells me it must have got wet at some point, and it's no bother. Only I'm sure this stain wasn't there when he got in. He lets go of the ribbon and it springs back. He starts wrapping it around his finger again, this time tighter. Well I start rabbiting at him, as is my wont sometimes, rubbish about all the things you can do with a liquidiser. Then I look across again and see that this stain has grown a little bigger. Well it's blindingly obvious to me what is happening. His box is leaking. So I interrupt my flow and make my observation. But Mr Fidget, he denies it. 'Oh no,' he says. 'That's not coming out of my box.' So what am I going to do? I leave it. I'm not going to make an issue out of it. What do I care about his box?

And I would have left it there, and I tell you I wish I had. I'm doing Italian eating habits, but now I'm keeping a wary eye on his present. We're going through Brockley – I'm taking him the back way – and I see that the stain is creeping around the bottom. 'Look,' I tell him, 'I'm not trying to be funny, but your box is definitely leaking.' And of course I'm thinking this is a bit odd. Blenders don't have any fluid in them, do they, not as far as I know.

Well now he changes his story. He tells me, get this, he tells me that he blended up some tomatoes in the blender before he packaged it up. The blended tomatoes must be seeping out. Well, hello. What rubbish is he talking now? He's telling me his blender, the present for his wife, has accidentally been left full of purée. What insanity is this?

Obviously I start to wonder if his lift goes to the top floor. Nothing unusual there. Some nights it feels like every other ride's a frothing loony. I've had bearded depressives moaning about killing themselves, psychos begging me to jump lights, and bog-eyed schizos asking to be taken to heaven. But this one doesn't feel like an out and out case, and believe me, you learn to spot them.

'Well,' I tell him. 'We want to stop. I mean, it's a shame. You don't want your wife to open your lovely present and this brand new spanking blender is icky with goop. That's a bit of a disappointment for the woman isn't it?'

'No no no,' he says. 'It'll be alright,' and he turns the box right over so the stained corner is at the top. There's a thump from inside the box, as whatever it is that's in there shifts position. I ask him if he still has the receipt for it. He reckons he has. I tell him to give it to her, with the guarantee, in a sealed envelope. That way, if the functions of the blender have been in any way impaired, she can open the envelope and take it down the shop. If it's all fine in there, she won't have to open the envelope and she won't find out how much it cost. He doesn't respond, and we cruise in silence to Lewisham. It's as I'm heading up the hill to Blackheath that I notice . . .

There. You see that? Fox. See the way he trots along the pavement like he owns it. Did you see that? No? You don't look like you're bothered. Me, I love animals. Love them. You know that *Animal Hospital* on TV? I'm not ashamed to say it. I'm a regular viewer. And sometimes, the things those animals have to go through, it brings a lump to my throat.

Anyway, Blackheath. Now I see there's more liquid leaking out the new bottom corners of the box. It's a mess. It's got to be making his trousers damp. 'Look mate,' I tell him. 'You should do something about this. Take it out, see what the damage is. We'll go to an all-night garage, open the box, empty the tomatoes out of the blender, buy some new wrapping paper, and re-wrap the present. Simple.' 'No,' he says. 'Just take me where I want to go. It's no problem. My wife will understand.' He's insistent. Says it won't matter. But by now, really, I'm no longer concerned about his present. I decide to get tough. 'Any of that goes on my seat, mate,' I tell him, 'And you're getting a cleaning bill. That's thirty-five quid.' 'Fine, fine,' he says.

Well what can you do? I tell Mr Impatient to grab an old newspaper from off the back seat and spread it over his knees. He does this, and he starts cleaning the box up, wiping the sides with a sheet of paper. Now he says that after he's dropped it off, he wants me to go to Heathrow.

Charlie's told me nothing about this airport trip, and I'm not too pleased. I just want to call it a night, get my breakfast and go to bed. Now I'm looking at an extra hour and a half. That's this job. Unpredictable. Long hours. But I figure at least I'll get a decent wedge out of the night.

'Going on holiday?' I ask. He nods his head. 'That's romantic,' I say, getting this picture in my head of this little guy giving this big gift to his wife and then spiriting her off to some exotic holiday destination. I start thinking that's not such a bad idea. Put a bit of romance back into your marriage. I see myself doing the same thing. Going home, tugging the wife out of bed, and whisking her off to Wales in the caravan. What the hell.

My little picture fades when Ears tells me he'll be going to the airport on his own. He explains that he's going to drop the box off at their house, that's the place in Eltham, and that I'm to wait for him. His plan, he says, is to go inside, leave the present in the hallway, sneak around, grab his stuff, and them come straight out. And I'm to park a little bit down the street. So as not to wake up his wife. He's very insistent on this point. His wife must not wake up. She'll get up in the morning, and she'll go downstairs, and there'll be the present, waiting in the hallway, and what a nice surprise that'll be. 'Lovely,' I say. 'That'll be a lovely surprise. I'm sure she deserves it.' 'Oh yes,' he says, 'she deserves it.'

Suddenly he screws up the paper and hurls it at the windscreen. He's in a bit of an emotional state, see? And now it's all boiling over. 'The dirty whore,' he spits out. I assure him it'll all look better in the morning. 'Leave them a minute,' continues Mr Misogyny, 'and they're wrapping their legs around someone else's shoulders.' I'm watching him out the corner of my eye. He's leaning forward, and he's got his hands held up, like this, fingers curled round, yeah? Like he's squeezing something. I'm accelerating down Lee High Road, and now I'm somewhat anxious to get this one out of my car. 'They can't help it,' he says. 'It's just what they're like.' He grips the sides of the box. His voice goes quiet and slow, and now I turn and look into his gnashing mouth. 'No,' he says, 'the people I blame . . .'

What with all this I'm not paying proper attention to what's happening in the road. I almost don't see it until it's too late. A cat, in the middle of my lane, trailing a back leg. It's lame, yeah? I get the feeling just for a moment that it's looking right into me, penetrating my innermost bits with its glowing eyes. Only animals can look at you like that.

So there's this cat caught right between the lights, and I slam on the brakes. I get a nasty jerk for my trouble, but the bugger next to me whacks forward. He sandwiches his box between himself and the dashboard and whacks his head into the windscreen. Boom. He's out cold.

This is all happening instantly, you understand? But it doesn't feel like it's instant. This bit feels like it goes on and on.

The box crumples, the wrapping paper rips and the nearest side flap pops open. Dark red gunk bursts out, all over the seat and the windscreen and the steering wheel and me. And you know what rolls out of the box and tumbles down between my feet? You know what I find myself staring down at, and what's staring back . . .

Oi! Oi! Get your head out the window. I'll pull up. Try and

keep it in, try and ... Not there, not there. Right, open the door. Open the door! Get it all out. Charlie, I'm going to be delayed for a while. Passenger had a little accident over my seats. You feel better? You realise I have to ask you for thirty-five quid now? Hang about, I've got some tissues somewhere.

J.J. Connolly

'KNOW YOUR ENEMY'

J.J. Connolly lives in London, and is currently writing a novel and a screenplay about the cocaine business in the Capital.

There was me, Tony and Roy and we're sitting round Roy's place waiting for Spanish Angie, Angelo. We've just taken delivery of a nice fat kilo of Charlie. We had it checked out with chemicals but Roy always likes to double-check, the human touch if you like. Although he's quite a player in the trade he don't really know if anything's any good or not, hence the Spanish Nose, connoisseur coke-taster to the court of King Roy. He knows how to move it, how to get paid for it, what to do if he ain't getting paid for it on time, the ins and outs of stock control, who gets a bit of bail and who gets jogged on sharpish. Roy is well cut out for the wholesale cocaine business. He has all the right connections, even if he does lack a certain diplomacy. He's a product of the nineties, a fuckin' mover, shifting with the market, using all the latest technical gadgetry and the occasional clump, well more than the occasional clump truth be told. Roy, not being much of a user, don't really know the good, the bad or the ugly when it comes to powder. He does know that the good goes quicker and so is more profitable than the ugly and the good can be cut to increase the profit all round.

Roy has a 'tell'. Everybody, you, me, got a 'tell'. A tell is something where you can tell if somebody's a little bit worried, a bit nervous, a bit anxious. It's like if something's gone in under the radar system and rounded the defences and scored a direct hit. I always like to find out what people's 'tell' is. Sometimes you have to deliberately put them off balance, not that anyone would like to upset Roy cos he's walking on red hot coals ninety per cent of the time anyway. He can't fuckin' relax. So anyways when people get thrown they show it in different ways, they may start fuckin' with a ring or scratch their arse or their nose, run their fingers through their hair, fold their arms, unfold their arms, maybe they drum their fingers. Roy's completely involuntary 'tell' centred on his left eye. On condition orange the actual eyelid started to twitch. When the emergency got upgraded to condition red the whole side of his face would start doing a mad fuckin' mamba and if things got to condition black, the ultimate one, you wouldn't need no fuckin' 'tells' cos it was a state of war. Some poor fucker would be getting thrown out of a window or getting his head banged off the concrete or the cozzers would be turning up with the sirens going full blast.

On this particular Saturday afternoon it was condition twitchy, so when the bell rings he sends Tony off to get the door thinking as you would that it was the Spaniard rendezvousing as arranged, but it turns out to be this fuckin' pizza kid trying to deliver a couple of fuckin' pizzas. Roy's antenna sparks up and he's off down the hall towards the door double lively. The kid is sure he's got the right address.

'No, no, no,' says Tony. 'This is 39 Gunter Road. You want 39 Gunter Street, two streets up.'

'Oh fuck, sorry mate, you're right,' says the pizza kid. 'I've got the wrong address, sorry to bother you.'

He's just about to go when Roy arrives on the scene.

'Them pizzas, I want them fuckin' pizzas. What was my order?'

The kid is smug for a moment.

'Bollocks. You said it wasn't yours.'

He must be new on the job I'm thinking. I'm walking down the hall myself. Roy's taken a quick step towards the kid.

'Don't be fuckin' smart with me you little cunt.'

He grabs him by the lapel. Roy's eye is going crazy.

'What's the fuckin' pizza you little cunt?'

The kid's crumbled and is hardly able to talk.

'Well, you had fuckin' balls a minute ago. What's the pizza?'

'Black olive and anchovies,' says the kid.

'My fuckin' favourite,' says Roy.

He goes in his pocket and pulls out a tenner and puts it in the kid's hand, he takes the boxes and hands them to Tony. The kid is totally bewildered and dazed. He could easily have shit himself. He's wearing those big fuckin' waterproofs and it hasn't rained in weeks so there's no way of knowing if he has or not. He's frozen solid, rooted to the spot. He looks like he's going to cry. Roy don't give a fuckin' monkey's. He drags us both back inside.

Straightaway Roy's got Tony by the throat and pinned him up against the wall.

'I didn't know it wasn't Angie.'

'Don't you look through the fuckin' spy-hole first?'

'I thought it was fuckin' Angie, Roy.'

'Don't ever answer the fuckin' door without lookin' through the fuckin' spy-hole first, okay? Ever.'

'Okay, okay.'

'Why do you think I had the fuckin' thing put in the fuckin' door in the first place for?'

'Okay Roy, for fuck's sake.'

Roy let go of Tony's throat

'He could have got us in right trouble. He could have been old bill.'

'Roy he was a fuckin' spotty herbert student for fuck's sake.'

'Oh right, you think the law will come with blue flashing lights on their hats do yer. He could have been a fuckin' plant.'

I'm looking out the front window and the pizza kid's looking exactly like a pot plant cos he's still rigid, unable to move.

'The old bill use kids like that, the old "Sorry mate wrong address" number. They wanna check out what's happening, who's at home. They use kids like that to do a little recce for 'em.'

I ain't convinced. I think that's just pure paranoia but I'm keeping schtum to keep the peace.

'We've got a fuckin' load of stock on the premise re-fuckin-member. Where's them fuckin' pizzas?'

Roy's pulling the pizzas apart now, and surprise surprise they're black olive and anchovy, thin crust. I don't know what he expected to find, bugs or what, but they taste very good, no doubt about it, very good indeed.

Roy's pacing, twitching, shouting, screaming. He's delivering a lecture on the black arts of spying, intelligence, surveillance, misinformation, counter-intelligence. It's his favourite lecture. Conclusion: vigilance at all times, always be guarded, don't trust anybody cos nothing is as it seems, don't ever talk on the phone or even in a room where there's a phone plugged in cos it can operate as a microphone and pick up any conversations and on and on and on he goes while me and Tone tuck in to the grub. We've sat through it before and know just to shut the fuck up, let Roy loose off and not ask any questions. It was a fuckin' good job that Roy wasn't one for getting high on the supply, cos the old Charlie can make you very, very paranoid in no time at all and Roy was already top of the world ma in the paranoia stakes. On and on he goes. Don't have a routine, don't have too many habits, alter your routes day to day, the old bill got spotter planes circling day and night, they got fuckin' satellites, they can read a newspaper in your backyard from outer space, The New York Organised Crime Task Force bugged John Gotti's motor, bugged his crews walking on the fuckin' street, on the fuckin' street you hear, you wanna be alert at all times, things ain't what they appear to be. Cozzers he's saying, I can fuckin' smell 'em on the fuckin' wind. You can't beat old fashioned animal instinct.

Turn it in Roy for fuck's sake, I'm thinking. You're givin' me fuckin' indigestion.

Luckily the doorbell's gone and it's Angie this time. I've looked through the spy-hole and seen him and the pizza kid who's still rooted to the spot. I've let him in and he's pointed over his shoulder quizzically with his thumb.

'Don't ask,' I've said and brought him into the back kitchen.

'Morning everybody,' says Angie, well stoned. It's about three in the afternoon.

'Have you been smokin'? I told you not to smoke, I want you clear-headed, I fuckin' told you.'

'It's about as clear-headed as you're gonna get him,' says Tony.

'Okay okay. Let's get on anyway.'

Roy's taken a small sample out of the main stash and he chops two fat lines out on to the mirror. It looks good, the chemicals say it's good but that don't mean fuck all. The Spanish nose takes one big hit up one nostril and one up the other one, one straight after the other. He immediately goes fuckin' ballistic. He's twitching and clapping his hands.

'Ahhhhh! Baby, yes yes yes.'

'Is it any good?' says Roy.

Angie's up and he's shadow boxing round the gaff. He's taking punches as well as giving them out.

'For fuck's sake, Is it any good?'

Angelo's doing a dance now, a kind of matador and bull thing, he's up on his tippy-toes.

'Look I don't pay you to . . .'

'You don't pay him at all,' says Tony.

'You shut the fuck up, you're gettin' on my fuckin' nerves. And you, Spanish, is it any good?'

Angie's starting to re-enter the world's orbit now. He's putting a thumb over each nostril and snorting like fuckin' mad to drag up any stray powder that's hangin' around. He's wet his finger and is dabbing up the bits and pieces that are left on the mirror and rubbing them into his gums. He talks at last.

'That stuff,' he points, 'is fuckin' good, excellent, isa so fuckin' good isa frightening.'

'Good,' says Roy. 'How much can we cut it by?'

Don't fuck about Roy, gets to the point.

'We canna go a long way with this.'

'Okay, let's get busy.'

Roy carefully rolls up the rug. He gets down on his hands and knees and slowly starts to work loose two bits of floorboard in the corner of the room. He places them to one side. He leans into the gap that's left and finds the brick strut supporting the floor. He pushes at two of the centre bricks, they bounce back into his hand leaving a perfectly square hole. He places the cover to one side and reaches in and comes out with a small strong-box. Roy puts it on the table and opens it and takes out a parcel of very white powder. The powder has been wrapped inside three or four bags. It is exactly the same size as the bags of sugar you buy in the shops, one kilo. The bag of sugar costs what? Fifty pence? Thirty pence? I don't fuckin' know I don't buy the fuckin' stuff, it's very bad for you. This bag cost me, Roy and Tony, me and Tone being the junior partners, twenty-seven and a half grand. Tonight we've arranged to sell a kilo across town for thirty-four dead, a drop above the going rate but we've got it kind of cheap cos Roy's got the right connections through his family.

By the time it's gone up people's hooters it will have cost somewhere in the region of sixty to seventy grand in one gram deals. It'll have the shit pounded out of it and it'll be good, but it won't make anyone's bell ring like it did old Angelo's. We'll get it cut about by Angie so we get another quarter kilo out of the first kilo. He'll take that to a geezer he knows who's making crack big time, and can't get enough good quality supplies. He'll weigh him on cash straightaway, won't turn him over hopefully, cos it ain't in his interest to do so, and Angelo will return to us sometime on Monday, after takin' his cut, ten large. He hasn't gone through with our money yet but there's always a first time and that's the chance you take in this business. Between Saturday morning and Monday midday we stand to make approximately sixteen and a half grand on our investment. This gets split between me, Roy and Tone, the fattest share going to the major shareholder and chairman of the board, Roy. We deal on reputation so we can't be going overboard and take the piss or people will start going some place else for their supplies. We're like any big reputable firm, we got to look on things in the long term rather than just make the quick killing. Also all the good people down the food chain need to chop the stuff about to keep their profits up, so if it's just shite by the time they get it and they get comebacks they ain't going to be happy with us. It's simply good business not to be greedy.

Spanish goes into his naff cowboy boot and pulls out a plastic bag that's already mixed with baby laxative and vitamin C powder. He pours the kilo of Charlie on to the big bathroom mirror that's laid out on the kitchen table and begins his work. He goes about it with skill and love, using two picture cards from a fresh deck so he looks like a magician doing sleight of hand tricks. He pushes the powder away from him and then pulls it back, chopping and cutting the whole time, calling it his baby, his little coochy coo, asking it to 'Come to Daddy,' telling the powder that 'Daddy loves you best'. He's tooting little lines of the gear to check as he goes along, doing a bit of quality control. He treats every tiny speck like it's important and precious, like it's fuckin' gold dust. He's swaying and dancing as he moves the powder across the shiny surface. He's like a blackjack dealer you'd see in the movies. Roy hovers over his shoulder watching like a fuckin' hawk, pushing and cajoling him to cut it finer and finer, but the Spaniard very calmly reins him back.

'Let's not tear the arse out of a good thing, eh Roy.'

From under the floorboards Roy produces an electronic scale, the type you use for weighing gold and diamonds and Angie starts to cobble together a kilo. Roy's pacing and clicking his fingers, his eyelids twitching. Me and Tony are happily slumped around watching the early evening drivel on the portable TV Roy's got rigged up on top of the fridge.

I got bored and wandered into the front room and noticed out the window that the pizza kid's still rooted to the spot.

He looks like a kid who hasn't been collected from school, like he's waiting for his mummy to take him home. He's been stood there fuck knows how long. I called Roy and Tony in. I thought it was funny.

'Look he's still fuckin' there, maybe he's shit his pants.'

Me and Tone laughed but Roy was back through the hall and out the door in a fuckin' rage, with me and Tony after him.

'Fuck off. Go on fuck off. What you hangin' about for? Go on, fuck off I said.'

Roy's aimed a kick into the kid's leg, once, twice in quick succession. Bang! Bang! The kid's buckled, stepped back and jumped over the wall as Roy's kickin' him up the arse, slapstick style. Roy's laughin' now and still shoutin' after the kid.

'Go on, sling your fuckin' hook, you're fuckin weird you cunt.'

The kid's in the middle of the street, pointing demonically at Roy, silent with a grim determined look on his face. All a bit spooky really like he's putting a jinx on Roy, a drop of the old voodoo. He's got long hair, purple and green, plaited with elastic bands so he looks a bit like an urban warlock. Now he's standing on one leg and is waving his bony fingers in a small circle like he's weavin' a spell. Roy don't like this. He's about to go over the wall when me and Tone have pulled him back and tried to calm him down. It's all turned into a bit of a push and a shove between me, Roy and Tone.

'Don't fuckin' tell me to fuckin' calm down. I've fuckin' told you two before about that, just fuck off okay, get your fuckin' hands off me.'

After a bit more pulling and shoving we've turned round and the pizza kid's gone, vanished, goneski, but his moped's still parked up at the kerb. Spooky.

We've got Roy back inside and Angelo's askin' what all the noise is about. I've just looked at the ceiling and said again, 'Don't ask.' Roy's fuckin' alight now, pacing and kicking chairs about, snapping at Angie, calling him a greedy Spanish cunt so Angie's got his shit together, struck a deal on the quarter we nicked out of the kilo and fucked off. Roy's plugged the kilo back in the hole, stuck the mirror and the scales in the dishwasher and sat me and Tony down to explain the workings of tonight's deal. This was a new customer, somebody we'd been working on for a few weeks. Roy's saying this is new business, good, clean business and this bird is fuckin' Numero Uno Quality Street. I'd met her very briefly in a wine bar over by Liverpool Street Station. She was a touch too coarse for my taste, but Roy was really taken with her. Denize with a zed. She wore all those Chanel power suits but had a diamond stud in her nose. She came across as being really uptight like you-know-who. She's got a voice like a fuckin' air raid siren, and steely eyes that say she don't give a fuck what anyone thinks of her. A bird in this game has to be as hard as fuckin' nails. After she had the kilo from us she was probably going to move it on in quarters to some of those city boys who like to deal part time for the thrill, the pocket money and the status trip it brought, but what she did with it after was her fuckin' business. Denize with a zed had heavily hinted that this could be a regular transaction.

For us it was fuckin' beautiful. A simple bit of cross town traffic. Take delivery in the morning and have it moved and paid for by the evening after cutting it and moving the surplus as well. Roy wanted everything to be sweet, and for us to look like a serious outfit. He wanted everything to run smooth. He wanted to impress this bird.

'She lives in this apartment block in Docklands, an old converted spice warehouse,' Roy's telling us.

'You know porters, security cameras, underground parkin', carpets in the hallways, the whole fuckin' number. She's a class fuckin' act.'

'Bit of you Roy? You fancy her don't you,' says Tony laughing.

It was the closest I've ever come to seeing Roy blush and look like clumping somebody at the very same time.

'Maybe I fuckin' do, but I don't mix business and pleasure, that's just plain sloppy. And don't take the fuckin' piss out of me Tone, just don't okay?'

Roy was never one for being pussy whipped by birds but he was obviously quite taken by Denize with a zed. It was a side of his nature he kept well hidden but it was nice to catch a fleeting glimpse. Bless him.

'Listen Roy, me and Tony can cut out after we've done the deal and leave you and this Denize on your own.'

If he realised I was taking the piss he didn't show it

'Fuck off, and another thing, you Tony, you stay downstairs in the motor while us two go upstairs and do the trade. She don't want no crowd scenes upstairs. She's double cautious Denize, which I like. It shows breeding.'

'What time's this happening Roy?' I ask.

'Eight-thirty. The meet's at eight-thirty.'

He had a little slip of paper with the address on it. I thought he was going to get us to read it, memorise it, and then eat it, but he left it on the table with a bottle of Tabasco sauce on top.

The door bell rings.

'Who the fuck's that?' says Roy.

'Not another pizza,' says Tony, moving down the hall. 'You expecting anyone Roy?'

There's always the chance of being turned over by some lawless hounds who have found out somehow that we're holding the goods.

'Check the fuckin' spy-hole this time Tony,' shouts Roy down the hall, but Tone's back in the kitchen in a state of high anxiety, panting and darting about.

'It's the law! Three uniforms.'

The bell rings again, but it's still a polite ring not like the old bill at all. The three of us creep up the hall and first Roy then me look through the spy-hole. There's a constable and a sergeant through the fish-eye lens, shifting from one foot to another, looking on their best behaviour, and behind the wall there's a cozzer who's obviously of high rank cos he's got a shitload of silver piping on his hat and his shoulders.

'Just keep calm,' I says.

'Don't fuckin' tell me to keep calm you cunt. Let me see.'

'Hang about Roy, if this was the Drug Squad they'd be in here now, and in the back as well,' I says.

'It could be a trap.'

'Then we're trapped all right, cos they'd have covered the back.'

'It could be some cunts trying to turn us over.'

'They've got a couple of police cars parked across the street.'

'Don't fuckin' answer it.'

Right on cue the bell rings again, but louder and longer this time.

'Okay, okay,' says Roy, but he don't make a move to answer it.

The constable goes to look in the letter box and I've pushed Roy and Tony up against the walls. We've scrambled up like mice. Plod stops looking and I look through the hole again and spot, you fuckin' guessed it, the fuckin' pizza kid.

'It's that fuckin' kid.'

'Not the fuckin' pizza kid.'

'Yeah. He must have called the law.'

'That's a fuckin' result then,' says Tony. 'It ain't about the stock.'

True, I'm thinking, but if they don't get a body they'll come tumbling back with the heavy mob and warrant after posting sentries. The pizza kid's got the black waterproof suit off now He's dressed in old tie-dyes and army surplus, and he looks like something out of one of those peace convoys, all grungy and soapy. He's got a guy standing behind him with his hand on his shoulder, like comforting, like, no they can't be, like a father and son. The older guy's got a really fuckin' naff golf sweater on, like what naff old TV personalities wear and on one hand he's wearing what looks like a golf driving glove. This guy seems to be telling everybody what to do, even the top cozzer. He's telling the sergeant to go and look through the front windows and he goes to it. Next he'll be sending them round the back I'm thinking. They ain't taking no for an answer. The top cozzer's through the gate now and is ringing the bell himself, long and hard.

'Roy, this may seem a bit drastic but I reckon we should open the door,' I says.

'You shit cunt.'

'No listen, this isn't about the gear, this is about you and the pizza kid. If they come crashing in here they may find it anyway.'

'They wouldn't find it, never.'

'But this is fuckin' double suspect, Roy. The cozzers are gonna start wondering what we're hiding.'

'He's right,' says Tony. 'The kid may just accept an apology, a few quid even.'

I'm looking back through the spy-hole. The sergeant's going on his radio, it could be for back-up.

'What's happening out there,' says Roy.

'I think they could be whistling up more troops.'

'Listen Roy,' says Tony. 'We tell 'em you've just split with the missus, miss the chavvis like fuck and all that, you're well wound up, having a bad day. You're very very sorry, flash the cash, give him enough for a good bit of the old wacky baccy and who knows.'

'You give 'em a false name if you're nicked, eat a bit of humble pie, head down, very sorry to have wasted the court's time, fifty pound fine,' I says.

'Who do we know who's dead recently? With no form? Jimmy Dixon. Tell 'em you're Jimmy Dixon. He wouldn't mind I'm sure.'

A few neighbours have stopped to watch. Mister golf sweater is getting them at it now.

'I'll be Terry Watson and you Tone you be Davy Higgs.'

'No,' says Roy, 'I don't fancy it, let's sit it out.'

'He only wants to see you brought down a bit, he's got his old man out there. He looks like his old man.'

'Come on Roy, it's the fuckin' smart move,' says Tony.

'Okay but you two fuckin' better be right.'

'It'll be cool Roy, don't worry,' I says.

I fuckin' hoped it would be. I opened the door and we walked outside.

'That's him, that's the one Dad,' says the pizza kid pointing at Roy.

So I was right, it was a father and son act.

'Nobody assaults my son and gets away with it, nobody you hear. I want him arrested right now and I mean now Chief Inspector. Common assault, that's the law.'

The golf sweater goes into one and fuck me the chief inspector's givin' it yes Sir, no Sir, can I tongue your arse please Sir.

Whoever the golf sweater is he's got rank over a fuckin' chief fuckin' inspector. He's got, I can see now, the golfing slacks and two-tone golfing shoes with freshly cut grass up the sides. The spikes are crunching on the pavement, like he left the course in a hurry. The pizza kid and his dad have got matching mobile phones, so the story's starting to hang together. I'm starting to think that maybe we should have stayed inside and maybe hid in the attic.

The chief inspector nods at the sergeant.

'I'm arresting you for common assault. You do not have to say anything blah, blah, blah.'

Roy looked for a second like he might try and leg it, but he just gave me and Tony a fuckin' filthy look.

'What about these two?' says golf sweater to the pizza kid, pointing at us two.

'Oh no Dad. They stopped me from being killed.'

Laying it on a bit thick ain't you son I'm thinking. He does look a bit crazy in that silent, darting, creepy, my-computer-is-my-only-friend kind of way.

'We'll be needing statements from you two,' says the cozzer.

'I'll be pleading guilty, don't be worrying those two,' says Roy.

The sergeant shrugged his shoulders and the chief inspector give him the nod. Roy was led to the police car across the street. He shot me a parting look to say 'you know what's expected of you, don't you.'

I replied with a look that said 'I'll be seeing Denize with a zed eight-thirty sharp and I'll be sending her your love Roy.' I gave him a little wink to keep his morale up but he just glared back. His twitchy eye was doing overtime.

Me and Tony sat around until half past seven. Then we got the kilo out of its hiding place and put it into an airtight plastic box that went into an old battered sports bag in among a load of dirty, sweaty training kit. I got the keys to Roy's BMW and the slip of paper with the address on it and off we went. We drove round in circles for a while. Tony was looking to see if we were being followed. We shot down tiny little streets. We parked up to see what suspect traffic went past us, if any, and then we went back the way we came. We went round roundabouts five and six times to see if anyone was doing the same. We stopped to fill the car up with petrol in spite of the fact that the tank was over half full. Me and Tony calmly looked up and down the street to see if anyone was about. When I was as happy as I was gonna be I reversed out up the one way street, turned the motor around, hit the gas and was away, over towards East London.

Roy used to play the music in his motor up real loud, like fuckin' deafening, cos he was so fuckin' para about being bugged in the BM. 'Remember John Gotti' he'd say, and everything got played so the speakers were rattling out of their boxes. He'd have to get in the back, regular, with a screwdriver and tighten everything up. Roy's such a fuckin' nut about all that bugging and shit, all that snooping and spying, that it's not beyond him to go down Tottenham Court Road and buy all the fuckin' gear needed to bug his own motor. Or come to that his own fuckin' flat. Me and Tony had driven in silence while we checked if we were being followed cos all that paranoia is very infectious. We would only talk with the sounds on. I'm driving fast but not fast enough to get a pull but anything following us would stick out. I'm throwing the BMW round a few corners. We drive through the park, it's summer, it's warm, it's Saturday evening, we're dressed like fuckin' princes and we're holding the folding to back it up. The sun's going down behind us but we've got the shades on and we're out to collect a nice bita wedginald from snake face so life is better than good. Tony pushes the cassette that's hanging half in, half out into the tape player and it's that Oasis gang. It really fuckin' hits the spot. I'm laughing. We look so fuckin' suspect, the sounds, the motor, the shades. We look like a fuckin' decoy.

'Fuckin' Roy, what's he like, eh Tone? Fuckin' headcase or what.'

'Yeah, fuckin' right. All that business with that fuckin' kid was totally out of order, completely unnecessary. He's always banging on about security and being vigilant and all that bollocks and then he goes around clumping innocent civilians.'

'Fuck only knows who the geezer in the golfing get up was.'

'He was obviously a Boss of Bosses from someplace. That fuckin' top cozzer was disappearing right up his fuckin' arse.'

He lit a fag.

'But if Roy's in the shit he can fuckin' get himself out of it on his fuckin' jack, or he can fuckin' stew in it if he wants. Fuck 'im.'

'I'm starting to lose fuckin' patience with him,' I says.

'Lose patience, not many benny. He'll end up going completely fuckin' mad will Roy, seeing fuckin' cozzers every fuckin' where.'

Tony was shaking his head.

'You've got to be in the wide awake club, on your toes like, but Roy's just too fuckin' much.'

I swung the motor into the Euston Road.

'Listen Tone, you know that business we've always talked about, getting out of this game, getting a bar someplace, some place fuckin' warm. We should start thinkin' very fuckin' seriously about it. London's fuckin' great when it's like this, summertime, but come fuckin' winter it's all fuckin' slush, and miserable, depressing fuckin' grey faces.'

He laughed.

'I think about it all the time. We could be anywhere, Spain, the West Indies, Africa, the Gambia. Now there's a fuckin' thought mate, people are starting to hop over there on package deals. I'm up for any fuckin' place so long as it's hot, hot, hot.'

'We've both got a nice few quid tucked away, We should start making plans before silly bollocks gets us well and truly fuckin' nicked.'

'You wouldn't call him that to his face,' laughed Tony.

'Too fuckin' right I wouldn't. The guy's a fuckin' lunatic. He's always been a very good money maker but he's a fuckin' loon.'

Tony again.

'Yeah, a nice little beach bar somewhere and a pukka fuckin' apartment nearby, fifty-fifty, no fuckin' about, no screaming and shouting ...'

'... And no fuckin' Roy trying to strangle you morning, noon and night,' I says.

'All the birds come to you, you don't even have to try, you're the host with the most, the top fuckin' kiddie.'

'All those birds come away on holiday to get pissed up ...'

'... And get a good fuckin' seeing to.'

'A drop of the old debauchery.'

'Which we will be happy to provide.'

'Sounds good doesn't it.'

'It sounds very fuckin' good,' agreed Tony.

'We want to get this done and give him a ring. We'll try and arrange a meet for tomorrow. I'll say it's a bit too fuckin' risky tonight. We'll stash the loot at your gaff and go and have a few lagers somewhere, maybe down by the river. He'll be out on bail, no danger, by the time we get through.'

'That sounds like a plan.'

'If he insists I'll go over and drop the motor by his and get a cab back. I ain't in the mood for Roy tonight.'

'Me fuckin' neither.'

We're driving through King's Cross.

'Oh fuck, shit,' says Tony, trying to lower himself further down into the seat.

'What?'

'Old bill!'

'Where?' I'm panicking but I'm trying to keep cool.

'They're good, they're fuckin' good but I ain't fuckin' convinced.'

'Where for fuck's sake!'

'By the dustcart,' says Tony, really straight faced. 'Those dustmen ain't fuckin' dustmen at all they're fuckin' old bill, we're fuckin' tumbled, it's on fuckin' top me old son.'

Tony's pissing himself. He can't keep it together any longer.

'For fuck's sake Tone, don't be fuckin' stupid. You had me right fuckin' going then. Don't fuck about. Be serious. I thought we had fuckin' Roy on board for a minute.'

My turn now.

'Look at that beggar, he's obviously a cozzer in some deep cover operation.'

There was an old beat-up tramp with his hand out by the steps to the tube station. I'm winding the window down and shouting.

'You ain't fooling anyone you old cunt, you definitely ain't fooling me Plod. I hope that money's going to the widows and orphans' fund pal.'

'They must think we're really fuckin' stupid.'

He's pointing at every fucker, laughing.

'Look at those old bill pretending to be German tourists. Look at the look on their faces, like totally fuckin' clueless, look at all the luggage, look at the big boots, let's face it they've gone the whole way with it, a lot of people would be convinced but not me I'm afraid.'

'Maybe they're Interpol.'

'On special assignment over here.'

'Tony, have a look at them spunk rockers, got the bottles of cider and every fuckin' thing. Good, very good but I ain't fuckin' sold sunshine.'

'Here, look at those fuckin' dudes man,' says Tony, pointing at a posse of black kids bowling across the width of the pavement. 'Look at 'em. Fuckin' police cadets, every single one of them. Shit man they're every fuckin' where, maybe we should just put our hands up and go quietly mate.'

We're pissing ourselves now and pointing all over the gaff. Him, cozzer, her, old bill, American tourists, FBI more like but you ain't fooling me. You might fool some poor mugs but you ain't fooling me Mister Gather. I know your fuckin' game pal. We're weeping with laughter and I fuckin' hoped Roy's ears were burning.

I'm driving up and through the Angel. I've stopped at a zebra crossing on the City Road to let this goth bird cross the street. She's all white face, spiky purple hair, black lacy coat, black eyes and lips. In fact I'm surprised to see her out and about in daylight. She starts to cross the road. She looks at the BMW and sees me and Tony doubled up laughing and assumes that we're laughing at her and her halloween costume. She starts shouting and screaming into the motor.

'Fuck you! Fuck you, you pair of cunts.'

'Turn it in Officer,' says Tony. He's a funny bastard Tony.

'We've tumbled you, don't fuckin' strong it.'

We're pissing ourselves even more, and the more we're laughing the more the bride of Frankenstein is taking offence.

'Come on Officer, back to the station with you, don't be driving the public mad, why don't you chase a burglar or something.'

She's pure stone-faced and all of a sudden she starts to maniacally kick Roy's motor. Roy would have shot her in the head if he was there but he wasn't, so me and Tony laughed even more cos the jam jar was the only thing Roy had ever shown any kind of affection for. We've got tears rolling down our faces, we're helpless, arms holding our guts, it's starting to hurt now. The goth sees all this and is shaking with rage. Her face is glowing red so much that you can see it under the white schlep. She takes off her boot with the pointed heel and starts to rain it down on the bonnet, over and over, making little holes on the shiny surface. I had to drive on, slowly pushing her out of the way cos soon she looked like she was going to start on the windows.

'What's your number?' Tony's shouting out the window. 'WPC what? I'm going to report you for damaging public property whilst on duty.'

She's giving us the finger. She's stood on the crossing with one shoe on and one shoe in her hand, shaking it at us and screaming up the street in hysteria, like a fuckin' madwoman.

Round Old Street roundabout, Shoreditch High Street and down into Commercial Street, the whole place fuckin' teeming with old bill in every kind of get up that it's possible to dream up. Street sweepers, ice cream vendors, backpackers, old Indian geezers with those baggy strides and turbans, all undercover gathers, trying to box clever to catch us boys going about our work.

'Do they think we're mugs or what?' says Tony.

The gaff was, as Roy said, a class arrangement. You buzzed the intercom from the car and the porter buzzed upstairs to see if you were expected. We sat tight for a minute while this got done and then we were admitted into the underground car park.

'Please could you come to the concierge station Sir, after you've parked. Please use the lift to your right. Please use one of the parking spaces marked "guest".'

We got the lift up to the porter's desk. It was a huge old converted warehouse with carpeted floors and sandblasted walls. The bare bricks had been varnished. It was deadly quiet on account of the heavy fire doors every ten feet or so. We came out of the lift and the porter was right in front of us. He was young to be in the job, those guys are usually fuckin' ancient.

'He is definitely, one hundred per cent, dot on the card, no fuckin' question old fuckin' bill,' whispered Tony, grinning all over his face.

'Shut the fuck up for fuck's sake, be serious, what's needed is a drop of composure here.'

'You're expected Sir, third floor and left out of the lift and three eleven is straight down the hall, Sir,' says the porter.

'Thanks,' I says and up we go, Tony holding the bag with the goods in it. I buzzed the door and Denize with a zed appeared, looking up and down the hall, looking double suspect, double fuckin' edgy.

'Quick, come in.'

'You okay?' I said.

She's looking at Tony, who she's never met before. He's hovering by the door.

'Who the fuck's he?'

'Oh he's my pal Tony. He's okay.'

'Where the fuck's Roy?'

'Listen, Roy's been held up but everything's cool. The stuff's in the bag.'

'No you fuckin' listen, you come in here without Roy and with some guy I don't know from the hole in my arse ...'

I fuckin' hate crude women.

'... and try and tell me everything's fuckin' cool.'

'He got held up, don't worry he'll be here next time. I can get him to meet you and explain.'

'It ain't going down, no Roy.'

'The stuff's in the bag right there, I'm here, you're here. Let's do the fuckin' trade so me and my pal Anthony can be on our way.'

'It ain't going down, no Roy.'

'For fuck's sake lady don't be a fuckin' ball-breaker on me now, don't fuck me about.'

'It ain't going down. No Roy Burns.'

She says it real slow. Hang on, she ain't talking to me anymore either. And she's called Roy by his surname. Roy wouldn't give his surname to fuckin' anyone. It took me years to find out, and then only by accident. So who the fuck's she talking to? I've spotted it in her face a split second before it's all gone haywire, a little hint of frustration, like nobody was listening to her. She put her head down and spoke to the space between her tits.

'Forget it. It ain't going down today. I'm sorry but I'll only deal with ...'

This is the bit in the movie where it all goes into slow motion.

Crash! I'm hit by a fuckin, great rhino charge. I'm totally clattered by this huge fucker wearing one of those baseball caps with chessboard sides that the Squad wear on raids. He was fuckin' quiet for such a big geezer cos I didn't hear a fuckin' sound until he put me up in the air. I'm winded and he sits on my back, the fat cunt, and ties my wrists with one of those heavy plastic clips. I'm looking along the floor into a very convincing loft apartment. There's about twenty fuckin' gathers running around the gaff now, some of them have got shooters, the radios are going mental, there's a lot of fuckin' noise, shouting, like fuckin' war-cries. Tony's got his hands up in the air cos three old bill have got guns pointed at his head. The law pull him down and tie his wrists in a moment, like they've been practising all their lives. He looks sick. I know how he feels. The old canister is totally spun. I'm fuckin' sick to the guts, bewildered and confused. I feel like somebody's upped me right between the ribs. I'm thinking what now?

The woman formerly known as Denize is having a fuckin' huge row with her governor.

'I fuckin' tried to abort the arrest, didn't you lot fuckin' hear me?'

'We decided to go ahead anyway.'

'With respect Sir, you're a wanker. Okay.'

'Listen. You don't talk to me like I'm a cunt. Not in front of other coppers, and certainly not in front of prisoners.'

So that's what I am now, a prisoner.

'You fucked up. I heard you giving the "Go" over my ear-piece.'

'I made a decision. And another thing, you ain't talking to your wanker of a boyfriend now. Okay?'

I felt a wave of sympathy for Denize's boyfriend. So she was all wired up, they could hear her and she could hear them. I feel like saying that's not very fair is it?

'Fuck off. I've worked very fuckin' hard on this operation. It's Burns I wanted and you came waltzing in after the graft's done looking for collars and nick these two pricks.'

'So where is Roy Stanley Burns then Officer?'

'I don't know.'

'We'll get him yet. Get him up, that one, either one, both of them.'

The fat bloke pulled me up. The governor stood with his face about a foot from mine.

'Where is Roy Burns?'

No comment. I didn't say a word.

'I'll ask you again. Where is Roy Burns?'

'I told you we should have plotted up outside Burns's drum,' says Denize.

'You said he was going to be here.'

'I thought he was going to be here.'

'But he ain't fuckin' here, is he Officer. I'll ask you again. Where is Roy Burns?'

No comment. Still not a peep.

'Bring him through here,' says the chief cozzer and they dragged me into the kitchen and stood me up against the wall.

'Look pal, this is how I see it. I don't really want you. You're just a make-weight, sure I'll nick you because I have to, because you're here with the goods with intent to supply. You're bang to rights as we say in our end of the business. But listen pal, I can always sort you out a deal on a lesser charge. You, you're just the fuckin' gofer anyway son. You're only the Joey as they say at your end of the business.'

I'm on every word.

'What's Roy done here? He's left you holding the baby, got you and Tony to test the water first and now the shit's hit, he's well out of it. So where is Roy Burns?'

No comment. I was mute. He looked at me like I was being totally defiant. He slowly shook his head.

'He'll be fuckin' laughing at you two now. He'll be thinking you're a right pair of cunts.'

He lit a small cigar.

'This is very very serious. You're looking at eight years, ten maybe, twelve if the judge had a row with the wife that morning. That's long time to do out of misplaced loyalty, twelve fuckin' years.'

It wasn't defiance, misplaced loyalty, fear of what Roy would do if he found out I bubbled him up, or anything like that that made me keep quiet. The real reason was I knew that if I opened my mouth to talk I was going to throw up all over the head man. I couldn't have talked even if I wanted to, not without throwing up black olive and anchovy thin crust pizza all over this guy, and the way he was talking it could mean another five years on my sentence. I kept my mouth shut. I didn't believe that shit about doing a twelve but I knew I was in shit up to my neck. I was sick on top of sick. He knew my name, he knew Roy's fuckin' middle name, Stanley, which we would never have got out of him in a million fuckin' years. They knew all about us. 'We should have plotted up outside Burns's drum', that's what that bitch had said. But hang on, maybe they don't know everything. They've got Roy booked as the Mister Big and me and Tony as just simple, dumb runners, the Joeys as the top lawman had called us. They didn't realise that it was some of my property in the bag and I for one wasn't going to tell him any different, no fuckin' way. It was in my interests to let them go on thinking exactly as they were.

'Where is Roy Burns?'

No comment.

'Bring in those photos, let him see how photogenic he is. You take a lovely snap mate, really good, I'll get some copies for your mother shall I?'

He starts throwing down photo after photo on to the worktop, all with a typed caption of the exact time, date and place stuck in the bottom right hand corner. Me, Tony and Roy leaving Roy's gaff yesterday afternoon. Me and Roy having a meet with Spanish Angie in a bar in one of those hotels in Bayswater, I forget which one but it's there on the caption. Fuck me, that was about five or six months ago. There's smudges of us doing really fuckin' everyday sorta shit, going to the gym, going to the café in the market. There's one of Roy coming out of a blow job shop on the Cally Road. There's one of Roy coming out of the Credit Swiss in Knightsbridge about three months ago. How long have they had us under obs? Weeks? Months? Years? So much for Roy's 'Cozzers I can smell them on the wind' routine. He was all ready to get loved up with one. Tonight they were going to claim the prize but they simply ran out of luck.

'Do yourself a mighty big favour and save yourself a lot of grief; just tell me exactly where Roy Burns is right now.'

At that exact moment Roy was being bailed at the little local nick. The timing was fuckin' uncanny. Under the name James Dixon he was due to appear at the Magistrates' Court charged with common assault. He asked the desk sergeant what did he think he would get, bearing in mind he had never been in trouble with the police before. He reckoned nothing more severe than being bound over to keep the peace or maybe, worst ways, if the beak's piles are playing up he'd get a fifty pound fine. He would have turned up as well just to keep everything sweet and not have any messy warrants out for the dear departed Jimmy Dixon. Don't ask me how I know all this but I do. From the old bill's records, from papers that ended up with our defence team, from the guy who drove Roy about that night and ended up in here over something else. From a guy who was deported back from where Roy lives now who thinks the sun shines out of Roy's arse and who was a sidekick for him. From bits and pieces I picked up on the grapevine. I even got word from Roy himself, thanking me for not lollying him up and giving him time to vanish. He says don't worry and to come and see him when I get out. He keeps me well supplied with funds cos all mine were seized after the trial. He's old school is Roy.

After he got released that night, he got a cab back home but as luck would have it he needed a packet of snout cos he'd done all his in in the nick, had little young offenders poncing them as well, no doubt. He had the cab drop him on the corner. He got his fags and was just strolling up the street when he looked up to see a fuckin' huge team of cozzers in the chequered baseball caps backed up by the heavy mob in the black overalls with assault rifles crushing the door in. They were no doubt howling like fuckin' Red Indians and screaming 'Attack! Attack! Attack!', cos now it was personal with Roy. A crowd gathered so Roy blended in and watched for a couple of minutes. The Squad, realising he wasn't in, put the door back on as best they could, tidied up the mess and plotted up and waited for Roy to come home. Five minutes either way and Roy would have been home to greet the Squad or the Squad would've been home to greet Roy. A uniformed cozzer came up the street to remove the blue and white tape and disperse the crowd cos they would be a fuckin' right give away so Roy took his cue to leave. He shrugged his shoulders, turned round and walked away. He left behind a few bits of furniture, a top of the range hi-fi, TV and video, a few clothes, a couple of grand in cash that he always kept hanging around, a very dodgy mortgage and a black BMW with a slightly pock-marked bonnet that was impounded as evidence across town anyway.

Roy rang an old pal from a phone box and the guy came and picked him up. He took a chance and had a swerve past his mother's place to tell her he was going away for a while and not to worry. He couldn't leave without saying goodbye to Mum. Roy took a couple of keepsakes and photos out of the room that his mum kept as a shrine to him, kissed her goodbye, told her not to worry, that some people may come and say bad things about him but they were not true and she was not to believe them. They got in the motor and headed out towards the MI.

They drove up the motorway until they reached a big service station. Roy got out and went and bought a spade and a load of very naff beachwear, shirts and shorts all covered with day-glow parrots and tropical sunsets in the most horrendous fuckin' colours, all oranges and reds, purples and yellows. The most conspicuous shit you could ever wear. He also bought a big fuckin' bag to put all the stuff in. They got back on the motorway for about another ten miles and came off again near Watford. Roy started to direct the driver down narrow lanes until they reached an isolated wood. He had the motor pull up, he got out and walked into the trees, telling the guy he would be back in about five minutes, all being well. He found his bearings from a big, old oak tree, marched out into the undergrowth exactly ten paces and started to dig a hole with his brand new spade. Roy worked for about three or four minutes until he found what he was looking for. Down about two and a half feet he made contact with a watertight plastic box that had once been used as a catering pack for ice-cream; it was wrapped in a heavy clear plastic bag. He pulled it up, brushed it down and opened it.

Rolled up in tight wads, with elastic bands, were three different currencies, sterling, dollars and Swiss francs. He took out about half of each and replaced the rest in the box. They were all in high denomination notes. Also in the stash was a Luger pistol, a .22 with a home-made silencer, some ammo, bits and pieces of gold, a bottle of supermarket brandy and three passports. He took one and put the rest back. He put the brandy into the bag. He got changed into his nutty seaside attire, dropped his GA outfit down the hole, got his spade and backfilled it. He threw dust and dirt around and pulled back the brambles so nobody would ever suspect there was a hole there at all. Roy went back to the car and put the spade in the boot and the two boys drove across land to Luton Airport. He thanked his mate and gave him a few hundred from the wad of sterling. He gargled with the brandy and rubbed himself down with it so he had the aroma of the stuff on him.

Going into the airport he mingled with all the Here-We-Go's and Yahoos until he found what he wanted, a gang of Geordie birds going on their holidays. He shamelessly fired into them using a heavy Brummy accent, found out where they were going and bought a ticket to Malaga. They drunk all his brandy and did in his duty-frees as well. They thought he was a right cunt and took the piss relentlessly. Roy told them his name was Derek which they seemed to find hilarious but they served their purpose to give Roy a bit of cover. They landed in Malaga at eleven-fifteen and they simply waved Roy through without even looking at his passport, which pissed him off cos he'd always paid that little bit extra for the deluxe model snide passport. He was very tempted to ring his own number to tell the boys of the Squad not to wait up cos he wouldn't be home, but he resisted the temptation. He wanted to give the Geordie birds a volley of abuse but he just shot away to find some decent new clothes. A joke's a fuckin' joke he thought. The next day he hired a car and drove inland to look up some old acquaintances.

A contingency plan. Always have an escape route planned out. Roy said it time and time again and we used to take the right piss out of him, and knowing Roy he's probably got treasure buried west, east and south of London just waiting for him to creep back and pick it up. After a while the Squad will stop looking for him and start chasing the guy who's been promoted from the ranks to replace Roy and so it will go on. If he keeps his head down in sunny Spain they won't drive him too mad; who knows he may even slip back here soon.

The kid who got sent back from over there tells me that Roy's gone a bit funny.

'Like how?' I says.

'He's gone all weird on us,' the kid says. 'He was telling me all about fate and if your number's up your number's up and how if it's meant to be it's meant to be and if it ain't then it ain't and how it's all in the fuckin' stars. Now you know and I know that's all total fuckin' bollocks. He was tapping the side of his nose and winking he was. He was saying there's no such thing as luck only fate. Fuckin' weird it was and he hadn't had a smoke or nuffin'.'

'Is he still as twitchy as fuck?'

'Twitchy?'

'Yeah, he used to have a right bad twitch.'

'I've never noticed it. He's a really fuckin' calm geezer is Roy.'

I'll go see for myself when I get out of here. I pulled a seven but I'll probably end up doing about four if I keep my head down and do my bird quietly. I've done two, so I've got about another two to do and then I'll go see Roy. He's got one of those bar-cum-disco affairs down on the Islands. It's called 'The Olive and Anchovy' which is cute, and I do think Roy may have a point about fate and that. After all, Roy got the bar by the sea and me and Tony got the seven years apiece.

Some nights after I've been banged up for the night and maybe I've had a little puff, I lie back and look at the ceiling in my cell, and I can see his smug fuckin' face and I wish it was me who'd given that little cunt of a pizza kid a clip round the ear and a kick up the arse. It would have saved me a whole load of grief.

Jane Graham

'KITCHEN SINK'

Jane Graham publishes a zine entitled *Shag-Stamp*. A collection of her short stories, *Floozy*, is published by Slab-O-Concrete.

'My son's lying dead in co-op coz a you!'

She screamed it, hurled it out into the street at him, a final, crushing, heart-felt accusation. Yet though it left a chill running through us, suddenly trying to suppress our tactless, ill-timed anger, it seemed to touch no chord with the man it was aimed at; he simply ignored her, got back into his car, and, revving the engine more than was necessary, drove away.

She was white, late thirties perhaps, although she had the kind of drawn out face which is hardened more by generations of poverty and tough-living than by simple middle age. He was younger, more gauche and smartly dressed, typical of twenty-something Anglo-Asian males. She was in dressing gown and slippers, distressed, hysterical even, laying into him with anguished calls and threats. He seemed reluctant to enter into it all. Why had he come here, to this woman he'd done wrong to, and now seemed in no hurry to make amends? She was all working class public emotion, making a scene, as he just stood there, untouchable, until with the final, most terrible and mysterious accusation he stepped back into his flash red boy racer affair of a car, put the keys he had been playing with back in the ignition and sped away from the scene. The woman gave us all a *what-the-hell-are-you-looking-at?* face and went back inside, slamming the door behind her.

Four a.m., 12 August, on a grey, red-bricked inner city Derby street. Across the road from the woman with the dead son, a small group of oddballs were having a street party. The sofa had been moved from out of the front room and on to the pavement. The few who were left by this time, being kept from sleep by unnatural means, were offering anyone else who happened to be up at such an hour to come in for a cup of coffee.

I was part of this party. It would be hard to explain why. Where do you want me to start? I'd arrived in Derby late afternoon the day before; a friend had talked me into it and then met some guy she was 'kind of seeing' on the train to Leeds, where we were headed to start hitching. I'd originally been planning on going to Wales for a festival. It was her that'd wanted to go to this thing in Derby instead. So those two had gone to the goth nightclub which opened Saturday afternoons and I, little seventeen-year-old me, thought, I don't need them, I'll go on my own.

It took a long time to find the people I knew, sat drinking cider in the park, and then it started pissing it down so we went to someone's house, I didn't know them, and then we ended up in the pub.

When it reached kicking out time news of a party circulated and it seemed as though everyone was up for going. By the time the bar staff were putting chairs on tables and sweeping up around our feet a big group of us finally swayed outside. I was with an acquaintance, but he'd been diverted and had his arm around the shoulder of a young lady. I'd been trying to keep close to him, not lose him completely, but out of tact to their flirting and privacy I struck up a conversation with a friendly guy whose pace had mirrored mine. Five minutes' walk later, we were drunken buddies. The couple had disappeared into the night and when I turned around I realised most of the group had drifted away too. So me and my new friend followed the last remaining handful through the unknown streets of Derby, on a magical mystery tour. I had been drinking since I'd arrived in the city, and my stomach sloshed with cider.

Outside the house, there was the sofa sitting there on the pavement. Before I had a chance to go inside, I was sidetracked.

'Would you like some coffee?'

A friendly, smiling man was asking me a question, a shiny blue coffee pot in one hand and a couple of chipped enamel mugs in the other. Coffee at a punk party seemed kind of strange but I *was* feeling a little tired.

'Yeah, that'd be great, thanks.' I took a mug from him and held it as he filled it for me from the pot. Then I sat down on the sofa and thought how nice and civilised this all seemed after all that drinking.

I took a mouthful of the coffee, not noticing if it had any strange taste to it. I was down to the last little bit when the conversation to the right of me started to tune itself into focus.

'Yeah, they're not bad at all. We've had 'em frozen since last year's season. Really good mushroom season, last year. Musta picked nearly a thousand. There's only about two hundred in here, that's the last of 'em. But it's almost come round again. I reckon the season'll start in three or four weeks, it might be early this year what with all this rain.'

Mushrooms. In the coffee. I'd never even thought. Shit. I didn't say owt, didn't let on my mistake, just sat there, thinking, *Oh well, I've never done mushrooms before, I'll just have to see what happens.* I was now planted firmly on the sofa with no real thought of moving or of seeing what was going on inside the house. Didn't sound like much was going on in there. I'd just assumed a lot of the people from the pub had gone on ahead. The guy I'd arrived with had disappeared. Which way had we come from? I'd not thought to notice.

I started talking to this woman who came and sat down next to me. She had long, loose, dyed red hair and was smoking a cigarette with blue nail varnish on her fingers. Her name was Julie and I'm sure she said she lived here, her and her husband, who was the guy with the coffee pot. I stopped worrying about the mushrooms, they weren't really doing anything, I thought, as I wittered on like a wound-up toy. We were having a real good chat, and she seemed real nice and friendly and all. We were talking about school careers advisors and how they expected you to all have this and that worked out, and I'd told mine I was gonna be a film star, and Julie said, 'Well, I told him straight I was gonna leave school, sign on and be a junkie, and here I am,' and I laughed a lot, coz I thought that was a good one. For some reason she thought I was hilarious. Everything I said seemed to crack her up, but I thought that was good, we were getting along fine.

I'd almost forgotten about the mushrooms when I had to go inside and find the bog to take a piss. I was sat there doing my business when I started seeing snakes slithering through the dirty laundry scattered over the bathroom floor on the other side of the room from me. I pulled my pants up, pulled the flush and they were gone. I left the room and went back downstairs and outside. The house was pretty quiet. The guy I'd arrived with was crashed out in an armchair in the front room, his head lolling over the arm, his mouth hanging open.

The first thing I saw when I walked out was this fat, balding guy, a huge, disgusting beer belly spreading over a stained T-shirt, standing in the street talking to Julie. She introduced me to him, saying he was their neighbour. She laughed again, like he was their funny neighbour. I shook his hand, which was pudgy and slimy, like lard. He gave me an unpleasant, lascivious look. He sat down on the sofa next to Julie and I sat on the pavement without thinking much about it because there was no room left on the sofa with his fat arse there. He started coming on to me almost straightaway, and if you'd have been asked to make a caricature of a dodgy dirty bastard there's a good chance you'd have come up with him. He was lecherous, slimy and unpleasant. 'Janey Baby,' he kept slavering, his face close to mine, spitting in my ear, with his slab of lard hand rubbing over my leg, kneading at my knee.

In reply, I just started rolling around on the pavement, taking the piss in the most abusive way possible, giggling maniacally. He seemed so ludicrous to me, tripped out as I was. What a dumb bastard, I thought. Julie by this time was acting like I was a complete star, which encouraged me to be more abusive.

I really could not give a fuck about this dirty bastard and his dirty hands.

Then I got distracted by more snakes. It was certainly snakes that had caught my imagination and were slowly crawling up the red-bricked walls across the road. I ignored the neighbour and watched the walls of the houses for some minutes. The drainpipes were moving, slithering slowly upwards.

And sometime shortly after, the red car pulled up quickly outside the house across the road. When that odd couple enacted their scene for us it was theatre for our drugged selves, hilarious, mysterious, a jigsaw puzzle, a soap opera unfolding here and now. It was also the end. The mention of death kind of did our heads in, it was something more than a couple having a domestic. It slowly began to bring us down, as soberly we went back inside. The man I'd arrived with had woken up and was doing the ironing with a contented smile on his face, an insane, lanky, hunched sort of housewife with a matted, limp mohican of indeterminate colour. Julie was laughing again; 'Nice one, he's doing the housework,' she joked. 'He should come round here more often.' Except the cord was hanging loose on the floor, leaving the plug feet away from the socket.

I came down to Jobfinder (Central region). The best job offered was probably with the Forestry Commission. We'd moved the sofa back into the front room, and I was still on it. I began to feel unwell as the sun rose, and thought if I didn't get some sleep real soon my violently throbbing head might explode.

Although it had been morning for some time, I awoke from an unsatisfactory doze to consider this Sunday. Facing the TV, which had never been switched off, I sat there, being brought cups of instant coffee and pieces of toast by a guy in a blue check shirt who I couldn't remember seeing last night. I took them gratefully. I thought about how I was supposed to be going to Wales. I was too scared to hitch on my own right now. I looked through my coat pockets and discovered I had less than a pound to play with. Drinking the coffee, some more facts began to dawn on me. I was in a strange house in a strange town full of strangers. The man I had somehow considered I knew seemed odd, a bit mad, and anyway I didn't really know him at all. My head was fucked. As in really fried. I wanted to be home. I wanted to be Dorothy with Toto and just be able to tap my shoes, want hard enough and I'd be there. I wanted my bed, things I knew, people I knew. But I had no money and would have to spend some more time on that sofa before I could get my head round the practicalities of hitching back.

The guy I'd met on my way here, the lunatic housewife, left to hitch back to Manchester early afternoon. I should've joined him, but I just didn't have my act together. I told him I'd come and see him sometime in Manchester.

Julie came down later that afternoon, a syringe in her hand, said a quick hello, pottered about in the kitchen for a while before going back upstairs for the rest of my stay. She was in a dark blue dressing gown and her face looked pale without its make-up. I thought, 'Oh God, I'm staying with junkies,' in jumbled panic, a kaleidoscope of public information images accompanying the thought; danger seemed imminent with my inability to rationalise.

The man who made me coffee and toast was called Dave, he told me. He was just staying there for a few weeks. He was nice to me that day, waiting on me like I was a convalescent. Towards evening he fried up a big pile of chips, which we shared. A few hours later, Dave and Julie's husband, the mushroom man whose name I didn't know, told me to budge up and joined me on the sofa to watch a film on the TV. I watched the opening credits, heard everyone tell me it was a really good movie, then fell asleep and opened my eyes just as the end titles were disappearing slowly off the top of the screen. Soon after, stretching their arms, the people who lived there stood up and disappeared out of the room to bed.

I put my legs back up on the sofa and stretched out, ready to go back to sleep. Dave had switched off most of the lights and I thought he'd gone somewhere to sleep, too. Then I felt the presence of someone hovering near me, followed by the light touch of a hand on my shoulder. I realised he'd been stood there, watching me, for some minutes. I moved my body away, said clearly I wasn't interested, and he backed off. But I felt freaked out, heart in my mouth, a look in my eyes like that of a cornered animal. It was nothing like the come-ons of fat neighbour, but my nerves were shot to shit.

I began to feel completely trapped, in that house, on that sofa. I wanted so bad to leave but I couldn't find the strength. I felt like the woman's son, lying there in the co-op, because there was nowhere else to put him. It all seemed horribly symbolic now. Everything seemed to be falling apart.

As soon as I noticed daylight the next morning I left. I somehow felt I had to do it before anyone else got up, without having to face them. I found a pen and a scrap of paper and wrote a quick thank you note before quietly leaving. Once out the door, the daylight seemed bright and I had no idea which direction to go to find the motorway.

Eventually, after asking a few people and getting on a bus I found the motorway and stuck out that thumb, the only resource I had left, and felt myself moving. Moving towards something concrete and tangible, my real life, like this was some crazy dream I had been trapped in. But then the elation of seeing the miles slip away on the road signs turned wrong again as my lift, about to drop me off as he left the motorway at his exit, still with his eyes facing the road asked in the most matter of fact way whether I'd like to earn some money by having sex with him, and the normal reality I was trying so hard to believe still existed some miles up the M1 spiraled away from me again, leaving me there in the cold at that junction with the cars speeding by, and I couldn't catch any of them. Trapped, isolated, standing there.

I don't want to be here anymore. I want to go home.

Of course I carried on hitching because it was the only thing to do and I got a nice lift and was back in Leeds with its familiar streets and everything would have ended there but, wanting to share my experiences with another, I decided to stay in Leeds, call on a sometimes boyfriend, perhaps he'd offer me sympathy, intimacy, pliant flesh to bury myself in. But as soon as I got there I sensed it was all wrong, yet again, what's happening to me with these guys? He didn't want to know me. There was another woman there, and an atmosphere of tense silence fell on the house, fell on us all as I hovered, unable to commit myself to either staying or leaving. Finally he told me he had a band practice shortly and escorted me to the door. Of course I should have left the minute I arrived, but sat there in his room, I felt buried alive by the multiplication of headfucks, not moving or leaving but stuck there like a record in that screaming silence. The silence of a corpse in the co-op, a male of indeterminate age, perhaps an illegitimate, mixed race baby, left to waste away through neglect and lying, waiting in the co-op funeral parlour until someone would foot the bill. Pure kitchen sink melodrama. But that scene had been so funny at the time, as we laughed hysterically at another's misfortune, crawling on the pavement with a hand over my gob so the poor woman wouldn't hear me.

Karline Smith

'PROMISE'

Karline Smith is the author of *Moss Side Massive* (X Press). Her short story, 'Letters to Andy Cole', is published in *City Life Magazine Short Stories* (Penguin). Two further novels, *Balancing Acts* and *Ghetto Flava*, are forthcoming. Karline Smith lives in Manchester and has received support for her writing from the North West Arts Board.

She sat upright in the huge, king-size bed, silk sheets gently resting below her full naked breasts. Just fifteen minutes ago Daimo Palmer had enjoyed them, biting and sucking her cocked nipples as they made love ravishingly.

He watched her snorting the thin line of cocaine. Falling short of getting down on his knees, he had begged her endlessly to ease off from the stuff. For one, she couldn't think straight when she was buzzing. And two, the more money he gave her, the more gear she bought.

She offered him some, innocently, like a child offering him sweets. He shook his head fiercely. No, none of that shit for him. He had tried it occasionally, but the only thing guaranteed to give him a thrill was freaky, hard-core sex. Besides, he was no fool. As a top Manchester basketball player he'd never risk it. Cigarettes were the only weed he was semi-addicted to.

She screeched with pleasure. The skag was kicking in. Leaning her head back against the pillow, she closed her eyes in rapture. Her shiny light-brown hair fell against the pillow and seemed to form around her head like a soft halo. A poem that he had learned at school came to mind suddenly. He thought it fitting to share it with her.

> *This creature who lies tenderly*
> *With beauty blessed yet full of sin,*

As mortal night doth o'er us fly
till Phoebus shews himself again.
When in my arms she'll wake and then
her beauty will entire begin.'

She *was* beautiful. Beautiful, but lacking in the brains department. Her mother had given her the name Promise. Promise thought talent was something you could buy with money. Daimo paid for her singing and dancing lessons and paid her agent just to keep her on his books.

However, there were three things that made her stand out from the rest. Her astounding beauty, arresting figure, and her erotic voyeurism. She was thrilled to share him with other bedmates.

Her dynamic looks were the key to the plan and she used that beautiful asset expertly to snare the bait.

The plan was so easy even a blind monkey could have done it. A simple case of blackmail. She was a model aspiring to be an actress and singer. He held the key to her future, promising her a high profile career in return (said he had lots of TV contacts) if she could swing it. Of course, he wouldn't be doing anything for her if there was nothing in it for him; he couldn't hang it without her. But she couldn't swing jackshit, especially with skag slowly killing the three barely functioning brain cells in her moronic head.

She had flawless, smooth to the touch, honey-silk, tan-brown skin. Her eyes were an unusual shade of green with an everlasting miscreant twinkle in them. Her lips were oval shaped, pink, full, pouting, kissable. The shape of her face was also elliptical, her cheekbones high, and her nose rectilinear. Her hair was long. It was a shiny shade of brown. Unlike many of her black contemporaries in the modelling industry, her hair was all hers and not a weave.

She started to laugh.

'What's so fuckin' funny?' he asked. She continued to heave and hic, the laughter swelling to a hysterical agrarian crescendo. 'Promise, what's the joke, heh?'

Her laughter subsided slightly, just enough for her to say, through fits of laughter, 'You. You and your stupid poetry.' He was a basketball player who liked poetry but he knew that wasn't something to crack up about. 'And your boat-race,' she continued, 'when I said he wasn't prepared to pay. But I haven't told you he won't pay half a mint never mind a half a mil.'

She thought his extortion plan backfiring was so fuckin' hilarious did she? She wouldn't be laughing if she knew how badly he needed the swift injection of finance to boost his economic deficiency. His six months to collate this money was just about to run out. Layton had sent Pitbull, the glass-eyed dick-head round to pass the message on. And pass it on he did, by tearing Daimo's apartment to bits. Daimo had gambling debts. Blackmailing another high profile and so-called happily married sportsman who had just slept and snorted skag with Promise was the answer to his problem, he thought. He had the photographic evidence, a bit like an insurance policy but which he now could not cash in.

As he looked around the posh Manchester hotel room, with Promise's cackle resonating in his ears, he was reminded of the last time he saw Pitbull. He wasn't called Pitbull for nothing. Even the way Pit earned his nickname sent cold shivers down his spine. It was common knowledge that Pit had bitten off nose, ears, hands, feet and penis in a gruesome, savage attack, which left his victim badly mutilated. Pit had been sent by his master to deliver a message to him. You just don't mess with people like them and here she was laughing like it was all just some big joke. Stupid, stupid bitch.

His *whole* life, his career was at risk here. She didn't have *anything* to lose. A horrific thought hit him like a hurricane. Maybe Promise was laughing because she'd taken the payoff instead, pocketing the five hundred grand. Maybe she'd double-crossed him and here he was thinking she was just some pretty but sub-intelligent bitch. After all, nobody was not going to pay up after seeing photographs of themselves snorting charlie in bed with a woman who was not his wife, and your career could be in shit street if these photos were leaked to the press. It didn't make sense. Yeah, maybe she was really laughing at his gullibility. Suddenly he felt a massive revulsion. He reacted in a split second, bringing his right hand forward and pushing his anger into a force that swept her clean out of the bed.

Promise was out before she knew what hit her. She fell awkwardly, her head connecting with the side of the nearby bedside cabinet, her neck snapping with an audible crack.

For a moment his actions stunned him. He looked at her sprawled undignified, naked on the carpet next to the bed. White dust scattered around her like scattered cremated ashes, a trickle of blood flowing from some place on her face. He didn't know where.

Bending down, touching her, he couldn't detect any signs of life. Her eyes were wide open, staring vacuously.

He felt weirdly sedate.

Whistling to a boom-tune on Kiss FM, he dressed slowly, admiring himself in a full-length mirror. He was handsome with a tall, lean but slightly muscular physique. His skin colour was light brown, like *café au lait*. His hair was neatly and purposely cut close, his jaw smooth and movie-star defined. He was considering growing his hair in baby dreads like Lennox Lewis. He pretended to box his reflection and smiled.

Once dressed, he sat on the edge of the bed and looked at Promise. He had to leave her. To be seen anywhere near the scene of a conspicuous death would tarnish his immaculate reputation. And that's all he cared about, his rep. She had nothing to worry about now, he thought, as he left two fifty pound notes on the bed. No one could trace him back to her. They had signed into the hotel as Mr and Mrs Smith, paid with cash instead of credit card. Whoever found her would conclude that she was just a high-class whore, scoring her last hit.

Two years later he was still seeing her in his dreams, always trying to say something that he didn't understand. He never thought of himself as a person who had dreams, even from childhood, and could never recall any. The dreams became more powerful and vivid. Most of the time she was laughing, just like on the night of her death and he would wake up in a cold wet sweat, with the sound of her laughter resonating eerily inside his head.

To dream less of Promise he found himself in the aortic veins of Manchester, passing through clubs and bars that would take him through to dawn. The police had decided not to investigate Promise's death. An unfortunate tragic accident brought on by a huge drug binge, they stated in the press. Only he knew different. And he was trying desperately to forget. The various sexual encounters with men and women, who pleasured his body and took his thoughts to psychedelic dimensions, seemed to work for a while in helping him to disremember. Then he became bored and longed for that one-to-one relationship which he mastered and controlled.

On November the fifth he met her. A dark and rainy northern night that quickly dampened the fervent tradition. She was sitting by the bar in the Haçienda; a new local band called Oasis was playing. The place was crammed with sweaty, gyrating bodies. As the hypnotic beat and the words of the singer poured through him, he saw her. He knew it was she. Definitely maybe. He had found *his* oasis in the middle of a desert. As soon as he saw her he wanted her. Her presence was causing a sensational stir amongst the people around her. Daimo pushed his way through the small crowd at the bar, ordered and was about to pay for his drink when the barman told him his drink was taken care of, nodding in the woman's direction.

Drinking a small neat brandy, long legs elegantly crossed on a bar stool, she watched him, smiling. He returned the smile. She was a honey bronze, brown-skinned, attractive young woman. Her hair was cut short and stylish, which suited her small elfin face. Her hair was brown with a beautiful, healthy shine. A pair of onyx and silver drop-earrings hung from her ears, glinting in the subtle light cast by the bar. She had small, heart-defined lips, painted a deep cherry red. Her nose was slim, her face egg-shaped. Her eyebrows were neatly shaped in two arches and her round, long-lashed, brown eyes watched him unwaveringly as he approached.

He thought he recognised those deeply eye-linered eyes but he couldn't be sure. Her face wasn't one of the regular ones, yet familiar. He hoped to God he didn't have to talk to her for five minutes or so before asking who she was. She stood up as he got nearer. She was riveting, dressed in a striking designer green, navy and red plaid jacket, with a matching short circular skirt. She was wearing black patterned stockings and the suspenders on each long leg were clearly visible. Somehow, she managed not to look cheap, carrying the image well, like a professional fashion model. Keeping her eyes on him she took off her jacket slowly. The body shirt she was wearing beneath it was made of a flimsy black material. The entire upper half of her body was on display. There was no sign of a bra. Her breasts were voluptuous for such a willowy shape, very round and bouncing freely as she started to walk towards him. Almost everyone around them watched as she embraced him, kissing him fully on the mouth. Her breasts rubbed against him; her perfume set his pulse racing. Taken completely by surprise, he felt himself go stiff with excitement. She kissed him on his lips. Hers tasted like satin cushions.

'Thank you for the drink,' he muttered awkwardly, clearing his throat.

'My pleasure, Daimo. You're looking good.' Her voice was deep and husky.

Surprised by her open affection he pulled back and looked into her eyes. He couldn't hide his frown. She giggled girlishly. He was captivated yet disturbed. Then thought, why spoil the fun? If she knew him and he obviously didn't know her, what did it matter? Anyway, he was a famous sportsman, most people knew him.

Looking down at her chest then back up to her face quickly, he asked, 'Aren't you feeling a little bit cold?'

'No, not at all. Perhaps we can go somewhere private, Daimo?' she suggested.

*　　*　　*

Looking around admiringly, she sat on his cast-iron four-poster bed in his apartment bedroom, tossing her high-heeled sandals across the floor. 'My feet are killing me,' she said, rubbing her toes. 'So what do you do for a living?' she asked, opening a bottle of red wine and pouring it into two glasses.

Was she messing? If she knew his name surely she knew he was a basketballer for the Manchester Leopards, although his career hadn't been going too well lately. His move to the USA to play for the Indiana Pacers had fallen through. Injuries and illness had plagued him for two seasons.

'I play basketball.'

'Really?' she asked, handing him his glass and snuggling up to him. 'I'm sorry, I'm not into basketball. I don't know one side of a pitch from the other. Call it female ignorance.'

He laughed, taking a huge drink of his wine. 'Court. It's court not pitch. Footballers use a pitch. Anyway, enough of that, let's get down to what we really came here for.' Putting his drink down, he took off his shirt and started to unzip his trousers.

'Sure Daimo. I'm all for that,' she said, looking at him salaciously.

She let him do whatever he wanted to do with her, between more bottles of red wine. He had never felt a sensation like this before in all his years of making love. He felt like he was waking after a long sleep. He felt vibrant and as soon as he stopped he felt energised and would start again. She told him she loved him. In the late hours of the morning, she lay peacefully asleep while he sat up, alone with his erratic thoughts, smoking. This was the woman he was prepared to spend the rest of his life with. Suddenly, just like that. He just knew it. And he was going to propose to her, in the next few hours. He got up, went to the bathroom and urinated. Suddenly he felt weak. A whooshing sound rushed in his ears. He held on to the sink, steadying himself. He inhaled and exhaled slowly. The dizzy spell passed quickly. Daimo put it down to the excess of drink last night. When he came back she was awake, sat up in his bed, smiling. He climbed in next to her. She poured him some more wine, left over from a third bottle last night.

'You're so beautiful,' he said, drinking quickly. She smiled, her eyes twinkling like diamonds.

'Daimo, do you believe in reincarnation, the supernatural and all that?'

He was stunned by her topic of conversation. He laughed suddenly. 'You mean old wives' tales an' all that?'

'No, I mean people coming back from the dead in another body.' He laughed lackadaisically. He began to stroke her neck, then kiss it slowly. He had a strong desire to take her from behind and ram this crap-talk out of her until she was fully submissive.

'No it's all crap.'

'Ever had your fortune told?' He was halfway down her body when he stopped briefly. He'd met a gypsy fortune-teller once, but when she started to read his palm she suddenly stopped and would not continue. Daimo told her he had never had his fortune told. He suddenly felt cold. He didn't even know who he was talking to.

'I didn't quite catch your name,' he said, feeling inept.

'I didn't throw it.' She laughed. 'Cherish.'

Cherish? He wanted to fuck Cherish again but instead felt compelled to ask her if *she* believed in the supernatural.

She was confident. He saw her eyes shine suddenly like glass. This hocus-pocus stuff obviously excited her, aroused her like an aphrodisiac. She began to caress him.

'Yes, I believe in obeah, voodoo, black magic whatever you want to call it. Things unseen. I believe we can take any form we want.' Daimo had heard his grandparents talk of ghosts or 'duppies' as they were known back home in Jamaica where they came from. When he was a young boy, on holiday in Jamaica, a neighbour had died after a long illness. The local people believed her niece, whom she had thrown out seven months' pregnant and who later died in childbirth, had killed and tormented her from the grave. Daimo thought it was just fantasy and hearsay. He was no doctor but believed that old Dulcie Gray had simply died a natural death. He laughed spasmodically, humming the tune from the twilight zone.

'Yeah right!' he said emphatically, with mock exasperation. She looked at him seriously, withdrawing her hand. His dick was bone-hard and she was stopping. He laughed. 'Aww, that's bullshit. When you're dead you're dead that's it. There's no heaven no hell. Fuck all.'

'Dulcie Gray wouldn't have said that.' Cherish looked directly at him.

Daimo felt his heart wire up a vicious heavy bass tempo. Felt oppressive. Now she was commanding his attention, unnerving him slightly.

'What?' How could she know about Dulcie Gray? Maybe Dulcie Gray was a folktale that she'd heard.

'Dulcie Gray had a soul. Each one of us has a soul. Some souls live inside bodies, impounded by blood and flesh. Some roam boundless and free. There are souls around this room, watching us right now.' Daimo took a long sip of his wine. This girl was a sicko. No, this girl was a McDonalds double-wacko meal with irregular fries. He wanted her to leave right now. How could he have ever thought she was right for him? He found his eyes wandering around his apartment as the warm red wine poured into his body. He felt warm. Sedate. Then he saw them, his beloved deceased grandmother Melvena, his dead cousin Benito tragically killed in a car crash when he was seventeen. He saw other recognisable dead faces staring at him, their eyes locking into his mind ghoulishly. He choked on his drink.

He opened his eyes wide, closed them tightly, but they were still there. He felt himself getting weaker and weaker. The faces began to spin. His blood was tingling; sharp sensations like hot needles. There was a strange foul smell and a dampness. It was a few seconds before he realised he was shitting loose stools. The air around him felt as if it was being vacuumed out of his room. He couldn't breathe. It felt like he was in a hot dryer spinning wildly. Suddenly it stopped and darkness seemed to be filling the room. Through the darkness he saw Cherish's lithe brown body slipping gracefully into her clothes. She was smiling. Bending over, she kissed him on his hot wet forehead as he gasped for air.

It suddenly occurred to him. She had put something in his drink. *Who the hell was she?* He tried to focus on one of the half-empty bottles of red wine. He tried to get up but felt as if a thousand pairs of strong hands were holding him down on the bed. *Who the hell was she?* Through a strange haze he saw that it was darker than any red wine he had drunk before, but intoxicated by a sexual stupor he had failed to notice. *Why was she doing this to him?* It had tasted sweeter than any wine he had tasted before too.

His head was swelling, felt like it was going to explode as the realisation of her identity hit him like a heavy projectile.

'First the paralysis will creep up to your chest then lungs,' she began in a cold tone. 'The medical profession will conclude through an autopsy that you had a stroke brought on by stress. The headlines tomorrow will read "Basketball Player Dead From Heart Attack"; you died in tragic circumstances, alone in your apartment.' Her voice started to break with high emotion. 'Promise, she still talks to me a lot. She was the type of girl that enjoyed thrills, but then you knew that, didn't you Daimo? But I bet you didn't know Promise was into other things to fulfil her craving for total freedom from the body. No, you wouldn't have noticed. Too damned wrapped up in yourself. My sister and I practised every spirit art, Ouija boards, tarot cards. If you had taken any notice of our second name you would have known we were related to the talented Phala D'Souza, High Sorceress of the Dark Mystics, our generations spreading far and wide throughout the smaller islands of the Caribbean. But shit, I forgot, you don't *believe* in all that crap. That's why you were careless with the people you used and slept with, not noticing they were collecting a little bit of you all the time. Hair, skin, fingernails, toenails, pubic hair, saliva, and semen.

'Mixed with goat's blood, fowl feathers and exhumed bones we got a good result, wouldn't you say? She wanted you to suffer. She wanted your life to go downhill. You couldn't find any satisfaction in the relationships you had. Your career has suffered; no big American basketball deal like you had hoped. It was all down to her. You thought you were the one that chose her but Promise chose you. She chose you to join her eternally.' In his last dying seconds, Daimo found that he was terrified beyond all control. 'So you see, soul brother, Promise is making sure you won't escape her, not now, not never, not ever.' She bent forward and whispered, hot breath against a cold ear:

> 'This creature who lies tenderly
> With beauty blessed yet full of sin,
> As mortal night doth o'er us fly
> till Phoebus shews himself again.
> When in my arms she'll wake and then
> her beauty will entire begin.'

Tim Etchells

'TAXI DRIVER: A STRANGE TALE FROM ENDLAND (SIC)'

Tim Etchells is a writer and artist best known for his work leading Forced Entertainment, 'Britain's most brilliant experimental theatre company' (*The Guardian*). *Certain Fragments* (Routledge) is a collection of Tim Etchells' critical and theoretical writings about performance. Tim wrote a short story called 'About Lisa, a Short Bad Story in Twelve Good Parts', for Piece of Paper Press, which went on to form the basis for *Endland Stories: or Bad Lives*, a fiction collection published by Pulp Books.

There once was an obstreperous Greek taxi driver called Antagonistes.

He was a man who lived in the dark of Endland (sic) and was known to drink first and ask questions later. That bloke had piss stains on his trousers and bean gravy on his shirt. He wore his hair loose in one of them flamenco type hair-cuts and his belt had a buckle what looked like a skull and cross bones. He often went down discos at the Roxy but of dancing he did not care to do much only The Head Butt and The Stairwell. The Bouncers feared and 'respected him as an equal' © and if Taggy (short for Antagonistes) got in a fight they always stood back and let him bloody well get on with it.

It was in 1973, just after the winter, and just before the troops came back and killed everyone they hadn't killed the first time they came around.

One nite Taggy (short for Antagonistes) were working a late-shift in the taxi and at 3 in the morning things were too quiet for him my friend and he stopped off at Kev's Kebab Kastle near the fountain and had one kebab.

It all looked like it was going to pass off without incident when a couple of leggy blonde girls turned up and were the object of A's attention including dropping his mustard squirter, wolf-whistles and various unnecessary comments about their body-parts.

Before long a crowd had gathered and our Greek friend was

soon in deep deep shit with a bunch of lads from Doncaster who bundled him into their Maestro and drove him away.

When Antagonistes woke up he was chained to a rock behind Ladbrokes at Meadowhead, with his tummy exposed and a couple of eagles were eating his liver out. Each morning his liver re-grew and each nite the bastard eagles came to eat it out again. The pain was excruciating and all Taggy's cries for help were to no avail.

Several blokes what claimed to be mates of Taggy's were aware of his fate but none of them lifted a finger. Boris from the Rehab Unit couldn't give a fuck, Twig from the pub couldn't give a fuck and Calita this girl he was shagging sometimes couldn't give a fuck either. Only his step brother John John was concerned enough to try and help the bastard.

John John dragged Calita down there to help him get Taggy out of bother but the bolt-cutters what they'd borrowed from a bloke that worked on the railways would not cut through the chains and were soon all bended and twisted out of shape. Eagles were swooping at John John while he worked and Taggy was laughing so much and he cunt take it seriously and he kept farting and making that music from the Damnbusters and trying to persuade Calita to give him a blow job.

At 4 a.m. JJ and Calita left, leaving Taggy to his fate and them eagles to their late supper.

John John was a dumb bloke but at least he was loyal. Once his best mate at school had died and John John had sat in the mud with him until the coppers arrived. Another time he had told several lies to stop Taggy getting in trouble with his mum and still another time he had married a girl what he didn't even love cos he thought it were the right thing to do.

John John's IQ was not bigger than his European shoe size and he worked nites at an old factory where they made many plastic joke novelty items. If anyone asked he would say to them with fool's pride that the manufacture of glow in the dark skellingtons, rotating realistic looking plonkers and human skulls with them red flashing eyes was his trade.

After six weeks on the rock Taggy was getting right fed up.

1) His mobile was not charged up so he could not make calls.
2) He was getting 'bed' sores on his back and
3) Them eagles were still pecking his liver out every fucking night.

It was, as the poets say, a bloody big pain in the arse situation.

John John on the nite shift, the vast hall of the factory deserted but for a few sad blokes like him, many of them curled up and snoring like pigs in grime under desks as they try to get some kip. The 'thundering' machines stamping out the fruit of their wombs: rubber bones, jelly dicks, inflatable tits, rotatory eyeballs, the chattering teeth of vampires, 'speaking wounds', clockwork joke hands what grab a pauper's penny, etc.

At various times the sirens went off and a power shut-down plunged the hangar into 'silence and darkness' ©. Suddenly the dark seemed more dark than wer ever possible before and bombers flew overhead as part of the long full-scale showcase re-enactment of World War Two in which all European nations was currently co-operating. Bombs fell outside with a terrifying crash, troops were mobilised, the hole thing a supposed trophy to international good co-trade-development and joint-venture capitalism. John John muttered:

'Fucking Battle of Britain.'

Then he waited out the re-enacted air raid til the all-clear was sounded, his head nodding in near sleep, the room illuminated only by the glow of them skellingtons and other items, his fat face awash in a faint green hue.

And in the near dark John John had a 'brilliant idea'©.

After work he went down the local and talked to Reg the

barman. Reg the barman talked to this other bloke who sometimes went in that pub and who worked at an embalmer's and he in turn talked to another regular, — one of the fearsome chief canteen staff in the local prison (an evil mismanaged institution on a hill known as Doncatraz).

Before long they had a 'big mixer' going on out in the back yard of the pub, creating a whole wheeliebin half full of evil potion. Landlord pours the slops in there, the woman from the nick tips in three sacks full of old runny mash potatoes and boiled to death greens and sundry leftovers and the embalmer chucks in a few bits and bobs of skin and formaldehyde. And then to cement the mixture they get this old bloke from the pub to do a shit in there, holding him over the bin shrieking, with his crusty old 'before the war' trousers flapping round his ankles and his nylon shirt pulled up on his skinny tattooed belly. The stuff smelled fucking awful and even John John (who had no sense of smell whatsoever) had to have a big wooden clothes peg on his nose to stir the fucking shit.

When all the mixture was prepared John John nipped back to the factory and gathered together sundry items of its produce.

Up behind Ladbrokes where Taggy were lain upon the rock, things had certainly changed. First off he had made a friend in some dumb little glue-sniffer called Lampton. Lampton was a well known half-wit with Bostick often running off his nose but he did not mind running a few errands for Taggy as he lay there on the rock. First it was the booze run, then the fag run, then the dirty mag run and then day after day Taggy got the lad to bring him a paper so he could study the racing form and other sundry words of golden wisdom. All this costed Taggy a few bob but he didn't give a shit – one day at mid-day he sent Lampton off to Ladbrokes to place 50 quid each way on a nag called WORST CASE SCENARIO at 33–1. Of course the horse came in like a hero and Taggy was laughing.

* * *

From that point on it was party time at the rock pretty well day and nite and Taggy was forever surrounded by fawning associates and ex-biker types drinking GUN CIDER and Alcopops. A few Asian lads that were like the Pakistani equivalent of white trash started coming round too and brought a load of bad dope with them, and Marty from the boxing club started bringing his pitbulls down to try and scare off the eagles.

The nightly appearance of them eagles were soon proved to be a major piss-head attraction and the landlord of the local pub put up a whole load of plastic tables and chairs out near the rock and a few strings of festoon-type coloured lights stringed up between the streetlamps and that razor wire fencing out the back of Bar-B-Q to create an impromptu Bier Garten. Hot dog stands arrived, und with them das usual catering scum of kebab vans, tea stalls und das chip vans. At 2 or 3 in the morning when the eagles arrived, swooping and diving, there were screams of delight and terror from the crowd and sobs of terror from the many over-tired kids that were wandering around in bare feet.

Into this context did John John arrive one fateful night with a reluctant Calita in tow and a wheel-barrow full of stuff from the factory hidden under a pile of old sacks. While Wurlitzer-style music played out from tinny loudspeakers and good-for-nothing kids ran in circles squirting tomato ketchup at each other, Taggy lay on his bed of rocks, sheltered from the light rain by a gaudy golfing umbrella what bore the slogan: Bad Trouble In Paradise.

Taggy laughing, Taggy lain right there in the centre of the chaos like the whole of it emanated somehow from him.

John John and Calita made their way towards Taggy's rock, pushing through the crowd, to the strip of more empty ground that was closest to him. As they got near to people they all started moving off 'cos the smell from that wheelbarrow was really fuckin terrible. About 1.30 John John unpeeled the sacks off the barrow and started to take stuff off it. There were murmurs from the crowd. Calita sat perched on the rock next to Taggy and a couple of chronic pill-heads, making small talk.

What the fuck's he doin now asked Taggy.

I dunno, some daft plan said Calita.

Give us a blow job said Taggy.

Give yerself one said Calita, and laughed when Taggy strained against the chains what were holding him down, his mouth making the desperate shape of an 'O'.

John John pushed the wheel-barrow round the dead trodden grass, stopping it on occasion to scatter stuff out of his barrow. By the time he had finished Taggy was surrounded by a wreckage of bad stinking novelties: jelly cocks leaking fluids, chattering teeth spewing offal, fake fruits and false tits all pumped up with beer dregs and effluents, all items soaked and stuffed with the foul mixer of badness from the pub. The crowd backed off to a safe distance.

When the eagles arrived both the 'moon' and satellites was low in the sky. They came diving down twds Taggy but soon saw all that glow in the dark crap scattered all around him. They dived on the skeletons, the snatching hands, the talking wounds and all the rest of it, clawing at all, pecking and devouring.

Taggy cunt believe his luck. The dumb birds ate all the plastic shit and were soon drooping around in some dance of death, hopping, retching, lying down and stumbling.

When it looked like the birds wer really dazed and confused John John set about them with a tennis racket for a bludgeon. It was a right laugh to see him mashing and smashing and whacking with blood and 'lovely feathers' © going everywhere until the birds were pounded into the ground and a great sullen cheer went up from the crowd.

John John was hoisted on the shoulders of many of the great lads of that area – Pointy and Kev Filty and Dobbo and Two Eyes – and he was carried around the neighbourhood in triumphal procession, little kids scampering round and beating on impromptu drums made of dustbins and hub caps.

It was a night to remember. There were fireworks. Romances started. Romances ended. A bloke got killed. A baby got born in that skip at the side of Texas Homebase.

And as the crowd moved off in search of new excitements, cheering and singing, Taggy somehow got left alone.

In fact with the eagles well and truly pounded no one seemed to bother too much about the cunt.

For a few nights there were visitors. People curious to see if new eagles would show up or something or if the old ones would come back to life, re-composing thereselves out of the bloody earth like in an horror film. But when they didn't folks kinda forgot about him and after a few days the landlord took the chairs back to the pub where they had been before and people ate their chips there in the yard in hot air of the extractor fan like they always had before.

Things quietened down on the rock. Sometimes one of the old timers going into Ladbrokes would tip his cap to Taggy, or Lampton would sit by him, tears of glue welling up in his eyes, shaking with cold, in silence while Taggy talked.

Calita gev him his blow job of course. But after a time even she cunt see the point of having sex with a bloke who was a kind of ex-tourist attraction and a blast from the past and in any case who was chained up all the time.

John John always meant to go back and cut off the chains but he somehow never got round to it, so puffed up with the pride of slaughtering the eagles and everything. He was, as the poets say, 'easy distracted' by his new-found fortunes and had plenty of girls and went out drinking on alternate Fridays with Two Eyes and the rest.

One day in May he did stop by and sit a while with Taggy but they cunt seem to find much to talk about. Taggy was a changed bloke – he dint have the same interests anymore and John John was changed too. John John had a life, people at work were friendly to him now but Taggy just had the rock. He just wanted to talk about what he could see from where he was lying – problems, the universe, philosophy of isolation, creation of lies.

When John John left it wasn't even closing time but he made his excuses. Taggy was talking about Greece. How he wished he'd found time to go back there once, how he sometimes remembered the days of his childhood, not memories so much as flashes, strange pictures of another life.

Taggy's taxi went rusty. Some kids broke into it and drove it around for a few days, smashed up the steering column, scraped it down the sides. Week later they crashed it into a lampost at Wards Corner. It stayed there. After a month (I month) some dosser started sleeping in it. Soon the thing stank of piss. Kids burned the car. The dosser died.

Taggy grew old on the rock. Some nights he just used to stare up at the stars and wonder what went wrong with his life.

Stewart Home

'SEX KICK'

Stewart Home has been quick, clean and efficient since 1962. He is the author of fourteen books, including the novels *Blow Job*, *Slow Death* and *Come Before Christ and Murder Love* (all Serpent's Tail). His numerous volumes of cultural commentary include *Cranked Up Really High* and *Confusion Incorporated* (both CodeX). He is also the editor of three anthologies including *Suspect Device* and *Mind Invaders* (both Serpent's Tail). When he is not re-inventing world culture in its entirety, Stewart Home divides his time between drinking Islay Single Malts and Adnams Suffolk Ales.

The Strand

Cameramen and reporters were hanging around outside the Law Courts on The Strand. Most of the media jackals were wearing raincoats and needed a shave. Mark One stood out among the crowd; he looked more subcultural than the rest and held a Hi-8 video camera in his hand. Mark One was also known as Juan, Motorway and The Mexican.

'How come nobody is allowed into the court,' Motorway demanded.

'They've got some terrorists in there,' a reporter informed the alternative media operator. 'The cops are worried someone will attempt to spring them. There's a child killer in court two, people have been making threats, saying they are gonna end the cunt's life. Anyway, what difference does it make whether people are allowed in or not, you'd never get past security with that camera you're carrying.'

'I wanted to film Howard Clark during the product defamation case against him,' Mark told the journalist.

'I hate appropriation art,' the reporter snarled. 'Clark made an installation of Sweetimes Choco Bars in which the snacks protruded from fibre-glass cunts and were left to melt under the gallery lights. He clearly intended to slander Sweetimes.'

'Howard Clark is a genius. Here he is, I'm off,' Juan announced, grateful for an excuse to get away.

The Mexican set the white balance on his camera, then aimed the lens at Clark.

'Mr Clark, how did it go?' Juan enquired.

'Bad,' Howard exhaled darkly, 'real bad. Sweetimes got the ten million they were demanding, I'm bankrupt.'

'What you gonna do?' One demanded.

'I'm through with the art world,' Clark raged. 'No one offered me any real support. Maybe I'll start making movies. I'm certainly gonna have a lot of sex. I can pull any bird I want!'

'You're not what's considered conventionally attractive,' Motorway ventured tepidly.

'I don't need to be,' Howard proclaimed. 'Women aren't attracted by looks, what they like is socially dominant men!'

'Most working class babes wouldn't know who you are,' the Mexican objected. 'Even if they did, they'd probably find you a little strange.'

'I'm not interested in CIs, C2s, Ds or Es,' was Clark's rejoinder. 'I go for art snatch. I just love the sound of a bird with a posh accent bellowing obscenities as I batter her twat with my love truncheon.'

'Have you ever thought of starring in skin flicks,' the sound rushed out of Mark's mouth as if it was water babbling over pebbles. 'I've made a few, there's good money in that line of work.'

'I'll make porno with you,' Howard hedged, 'if we can use the profits to finance the musical I've always dreamt of creating. It's about a female soul singer whose career has been ruined by a sex and drugs scandal but who makes a massively successful come back with a skinhead band.'

'Are you sure this idea has legs?' The Mexican wasn't convinced it would perambulate.

'In the hands of a good scriptwriter anything will walk,' the bankrupt observed laconically. 'We've simply gotta hire the best talent going.'

*　　*　　*

'Sex Kick'

James Green turned the volume up on the in-car stereo as he swooped into Toxteth. The windows of his Fiesta were wound down and he didn't give a shit about whether his Frankie Goes To Hollywood tape was disturbing pig citizens. He wasn't just driving an automobile, it was an urban assault vehicle. Jim pulled up outside a dilapidated terrace and beeped his horn. Gary McMara, the band's secret weapon, emerged from his mother's house carrying a four pack of beer and a toothbrush.

'Oi, Gordon, get out! I wanna sit up front!' McMara sneered as he sped round to the front passenger seat.

'We're taking turns for the best seat and I'm first,' Gordon Bennet announced.

Gary was completely unfazed by his request for the front seat being flatly refused. He dived into the back of the Fiesta and farted loudly. Four of the hatchback's five doors flew open and the band leapt out. Meanwhile, their secret weapon clambered into the front passenger seat. Having got what he wanted, McMara opened a can of super strength lager. Gary rarely bathed or changed his clothes and was able to get himself a seat on the most crowded of buses because his mere presence tended to empty them. He was dressed in a dirty ill-fitting wool suit, which he'd adorned with a red arm band on which a celtic cross had been emblazoned over a white circle. Unruly hair, untied shoe-laces and a huge gut added to the former school teacher's dishevelled appearance. Gazza's attire contrasted sharply with the all black para-military threads and Hitler youth style hair-cuts sported by the Anal Exciters.

'You've stolen my seat!' Gordon Bennet complained as he leant on the front passenger door.

'Property is theft!' McMara shot back, making good use of the only phrase he knew from the voluminous works of the nineteenth-century anti-semite Pierre-Joseph Proudhon.

The smell of McMara's fart was dissipating and Gordon earnestly desired his seat back. He understood that the only way to dislodge Gazza was by appealing to the self-interest of his fellow musicians.

'If we throw Gazza in the boot, we can nick his beers and get lagered up!'

On hearing this suggestion, Michael Rake and Victor Vile grabbed hold of McMara and wrestled him out of the car. Simultaneously, Gordon snatched the keys from the ignition and used them to open the boot. Gary was then unceremoniously thrown into the luggage compartment. Immediately afterwards, the boot was slammed shut. The Anal Exciters got back into the Fiesta and broke open McMara's beers before speeding south down the M6.

City of London

Although the Worshipful Company of Arts Administrators were having a daytime meeting, the curtains of the boardroom had been drawn and they were fogged in a gloomy half-light. The leadership of this patrician guild were seated around a table. They were all wearing T-shirts with a print of a Constable painting on the front. Wagner's *Ride of the Valkyries* was tinkling away in the background as a shadowy figure known simply as Aries spoke.

'Art will be autonomous or it will not be at all,' Aries rasped, taking his cue from Adorno. 'We must use culture to instil moral values! And it is for this very reason that I have plagued Howard Clark! The leading representative of anti-culture, a man who has the audacity to present the public with unfinished daubs, must be reduced to the level of a laughing stock. That's why I've had so many attractive young wimmin brainwashed to pester Clark sexually. I want to distract the bastard from the creation of anti-culture and simultaneously drag his name through the mud as the gossip columnists set to work on their assigned task of character assassination. This is why I've had my men burn down Clark's exhibitions and physically attack his works. It's why I've paid critics not to review Clark's shows and am, at this very moment, bringing financial ruin upon the number one enemy of decorum and good taste!'

The men and women present made a series of satanic salutes, the index and little fingers of their right hands extended, the other two fingers formed into a fist shape with the thumb pressed against them.

'At the cross-roads! At the cross-roads!' roared the assembled throng.

'Organising the Sweetimes Choco Bars product defamation case against Howard Clark,' Aries whooped, 'was simply my first move in a new campaign that will destroy our most dangerous opponent! Clark is an avowed enemy of our cultural traditions and so I hired a reporter to keep an eye on him. Come in boy, and tell us what's just happened at the court.'

'Clark was fined ten million for product defamation,' the reporter gushed. 'Bribing the judge worked wonders. Clark is completely bankrupt, so he shouldn't be causing us any further problems. Nevertheless, I'll be keeping an eye on the malcontent, to make sure he doesn't get up to any of his dirty tricks.'

Berwick Street

The Anal Exciters were cock-a-hoop upon arriving in Soho. Jim parked his Ford Fiesta and the band got out of the car. Green walked around to the back of the motor and opened the boot. McMara sprang out and accused Jim of being an Everton supporter. The singer was not going to take that kind of thing lying down. He took a switch from the hatch-back and ordered the rest of the band to throw McMara over the bonnet of the Fiesta. He tucked Gazza's shirt up and began to apply the rod, and as he was angry with him, he laid on the cuts smartly, raising long red weals all over the surface of his yellow skin. McMara wriggled, writhed and jerked his hips from side to side, half turning over for a moment, so that Jimmy saw the front part of Gazza's naked body. What Jim saw paralysed him with astonishment. In that momentary glimpse, the singer caught sight of a little pink-lipped cunt, shaded at the upper part with a slight growth of mouse down. The missing years of McMara's life were suddenly accounted for. Gary had undergone a sex change in her twenties and later, regretting the decision, stopped taking hormones so that she lost her tits. For years, McMara had been living as a man although she was dickless!

Carpenter's Road, E15

'So what about it?' Juan discoursed. 'Do you wanna go to this gig tonight? The band are pretty hot. Maybe we could use them in our movie. I reckon they'd get their hair cropped if we asked them nicely. Perhaps we could shoot some porno footage in the toilets. I'm sure you could pull a bird or two and there's a big market for videos of rock chicks getting randy in seedy situations.'

'Hi, I'm Julie,' a girl who was standing outside Howard's studio announced. 'I just love your work, Mr Clark. I was so sorry about the court case. I was going to go down and support you when you were in the dock but I couldn't get the morning off work. Do you think I could come up and see your etchings?'

'Sure,' the Mexican replied. 'Howard will let you visit his studio, but only if you'll allow me to video him sniffing your arse.'

'Groovy!' Julie replied.

Clark pulled a set of keys from a pocket and opened the door to the warehouse, then led the way in. As the door slammed shut behind Julie and Juan, a girl called Judy Jones ran up and banged her fists against the wood.

'Howard, Howard, let me in! It's Judy, Judy Jones, don't you wanna see me?'

Piccadilly

The Anal Exciters had heard many strange and wondrous stories about London and since this was their first visit they still believed that around every corner was a street full of famous pop celebrities. The band had wandered down through Soho to Piccadilly Circus and were standing beneath the statue of Eros pointing at things and laughing.

'If you've got the money you can get anything you want here,' Jim observed. 'Maybe Gary could buy herself a new prick and pay a surgeon to sew it on.'

'Go on Gazza,' the rest of the group chanted in unison, 'show us your cunt!'

'I've heard there's loads of hookers working this area!' McMara undulated, hoping that by quickly changing the subject he'd avoid further embarrassment.

'Cunt, cunt, cunt!' the boys chanted.

'Look at that!' McMara howled, pointing at a nun in black stockings and stilettos.

'Cunt, cunt, cunt!' the rest of the Exciters hollered.

'What's the damage for a session?' Gazza shouted at the nun as she passed by, hoping this gambit might spare him further blushes.

'That depends upon whether you want oral or anal,' the nun replied in a deep masculine voice.

'Fuck me, it's a bloke!' McMara retched as she hit her forehead with the palm of her right hand.

'Spank my friend!' Jimmy shouted at the nun while simultaneously waving a twenty pound note at the male prostitute.

The nun lost no time but at once laid McMara across his knee and tucked up the transsexual's shirt. So coolly and methodically was this done, it was plain the transvestite was a professional flagellant. The Anal Exciters laughed loudly at the rent boy's deliberate way of setting about his strange task. McMara had a fat flabby bottom which the nun looked at for several seconds, a flash of disgust passing over his face. After this the punk used his right hand to stroke and squeeze Gazza's flesh and at the same time put his other hand under the hermaphrodite's belly, his fingers feeling their way around McMara's strange asexual cunt.

Gary didn't move and after a couple of minutes the rent boy was satisfied that the hole was a medical fake which wouldn't self-lubricate. The nun put his left hand over McMara's loins to pin his victim down and began to spank the she-creature. Gazza licked her lips and put her hands behind her arse. The nun stopped his ministrations for a moment, seized Gary's wrists and put his right leg over the she-creature's calves, then went on spanking McMara despite her yells and struggles, until her bottom was crimson. Then the nun let the masochist roll off his lap and on to the concrete pavement, where McMara lay on her face with her knickers around her ankles and her scarlet bottom bare. McMara's backside must have been smarting considerably, she was thoroughly frightened and sobbed and cried, vowing that she would write a pamphlet about the rent boy exposing him as an asset of the secret state.

Carpenter's Road, E15

Howard Clark's studio was decorated with hundreds of gaudy posters of female pop stars. Otherwise, the space was pretty bare. Howard walked over to an answer phone and pressed the playback button.

'Howard, it's Christine, I wanna suck your cock.'

As Clark filled a kettle with water and switched it on, Juan picked up a music paper and flicked through the pages. Julie was looking around wide eyed; she'd never been invited into the studio of a famous artist before

'Hi, Bhavna here, I want you to fuck my brains out,' the answer phone was still relaying its messages.

Julie picked up a dildo and began to examine it.

'Rose calling. It's eleven on Monday morning, I guess you must be in court. Hope it went well. My pussy is dripping, come over here and do something about it,' the answer phone was still relaying messages from Clark's many female fans.

'The usual crap,' Howard ranted after mentally processing the messages. 'Why doesn't anyone ever ring up to tell me they've won the lottery and want to take me on an all-expenses-paid trip to the Caribbean?'

'Stop whining and make the fucking tea,' the Mexican jeered. 'Once we've had a brew we can shoot this arse sniffing feature with Julie.'

'Julie, come over here and make the tea,' Howard barked. 'I want you to get into your role, you're a submissive.'

'Howard, it's Judy, speak to me! Speak to me! I know you're monitoring this call! Pick up the phone, I want you to fuck me! I'll kill myself unless you agree to have sex with me at least once a month!'

'That chick is a fuckin' psychopath, she won't leave me alone!' Howard announced as he jerked his thumb at the answer phone. Then added as the doorbell rang: 'Who can that be calling on me now? Julie, answer it!'

'Hello,' Julie purred after picking up the intercom.

'It's Judy, I've come to see Howard,' a disembodied voice announced.

'I'm not in,' Clark hissed at Julie.

'He's not here,' Julie sidled.

'I know you're lying,' the disembodied voice of Judy Jones wailed. 'I know Howard wants to see me really! You're jealous of our love for each other and want to keep us apart! It won't work because I'm going to sit on the doorstep until Howard comes out.'

Julie switched off the intercom, tossed her blonde hair back over her shoulder and bared her teeth.

'We'll have to sneak out the back way when we leave. That chick is a bleedin' nut,' Howard snarled.

'I'm sick of fucking around, let's get on with the action,' the Mexican tumbled as he picked up his camera.

Howard sat on a stool and Julie bent over his knee. Clark hitched up the girl's skirt, then eased his fingers under the elasticated waistband of her panties.

'What do you think you're doing?' Julie demanded.

'I'm pulling down your knickers,' Howard hated having to explain the obvious.

'You can't do that, not on camera, I'm shy! I'm not getting naked until we're alone!' Julie was no exhibitionist.

'For fuck's sake,' Clark swore.

'Don't fret about it,' Juan put in. 'The punters into this sort of muck don't much care whether or not they get to ogle a girl's naked arse. All they want is a bit of nasal action. Just get on with it.'

Clark yawned. He hitched the girl's dress up. Coloured smoke billowed up from under her white panties. Howard sniffed it and liked the effect, so he began inhaling great gulps of the stuff. After about ten minutes, Julie's arse stopped smoking, so Howard let her skirt drop back over her derrière.

101 Snack Bar

The 101 Snack Bar on Charing X Road clung to the edge of Soho like a tight red top stretched across silicon enhanced cleavage, and that's where the Anal Exciters were drinking tea and chatting.

'Do you think Blur will come to our gig at Blow Up?' Gordon asked rhetorically.

'Of course they fucking will, they hang out at Blow Up, it's a really cool club!' McMara insisted.

'Sure,' Jimmy acquiesced, 'but did you know that Blur drink in a pub called the Good Mixer. It's in Camden, so maybe we should go there for a beer.'

'Who cares?' Victor sneered. 'Let's have some more fun and games with Gazza, let's give her another drubbing.'

Hearing this, the she-creature leapt up from her stool and legged it down the street. The band chased McMara east up Shaftesbury Avenue, then caught up with the transsexual after she cut left into the little park behind St Giles in the Fields. The rest of the band crowded round their secret weapon while Jimmy fashioned a slender piece of birch into a rod.

'Let down your trousers and lie across the end of that bench,' the singer instructed.

'Oh, oh, oh!' Gazza cried. 'I know I deserve to be punished, I shouldn't have spread all those lies about people I don't like being fascists and working for the secret state. But please don't birch me. Punish me any other way than that. I'll suck everybody's dick.'

'I will not punish you in any other way!' Jim announced sternly. 'Let down your trousers at once and don't be such a coward.'

Gary turned half aside, and with trembling fingers unfastened her braces, then let her trousers down to her knees. She laid herself across the end of the bench, with her hands resting on the seat and the tips of her toes on the other side, thus bringing her body into a curve with her arse raised well up. Standing at the end of the bench, Jimmy rolled up the tail of McMara's shirt. The singer bared Gazza's bottom and as he did so, the transsexual uttered a choking sob. McMara received eight strokes, not very severe ones, but nevertheless the colour of her buttocks went from sickly yellow to a revolting deep red.

Cat Flap Club Jill

In the Cat Flap Club ladies' loo lots of girls were standing around gossiping, doing their make-up, snorting drugs and complaining about their parents. An unconscious and semi-naked boy was handcuffed to the bowl of a toilet. The door to his cubicle was half open. Mark One walked unselfconsciously into the Jill.

'Hey, what are you, some kinda pervert? Get outta here, this ain't no place for geezers!' a Rock Chick growled.

'Chill out, I'm making a movie!' Juan counselled as he held up his camera.

'I wanna be a star,' the dame chirped. 'I'm real talented you know. I can act and my boyfriend is gonna teach me how to play the bass.'

'How about letting me shoot a famous artist giving you a shrimp job?' the Mexican leered.

'If all you're interested in is my feet, you can forget it. I wanna see my beautiful face in this movie,' the girl was getting all suspicious.

'There'll be shots of your face, all you gotta do is fake an orgasm as your toes get licked,' Mark smarmed.

'Okay,' the chick was up for it.

'Let's pull a prank on the male lead before he comes in. Dip your foot in one of the toilets!' another girl suggested.

'Who do you think you are, the bleedin' director?' the Mexican complained.

'Nah, just a foot fetishist with a sense of humour!' the second Rock Chick rounded. 'Why don't you run this scene the way I suggest? If you do, I guarantee your skin flick will become a cult classic!'

There was applause from every corner of the Jill as the plucky young actress dipped her foot into one of the toilet bowls. The Mexican opened the main door and hollered out to Howard Clark who was standing in the corridor:

'Get on in here, you know what to do.'

Mark One filmed Clark entering the bog. Anyone who hadn't known this was set up would have imagined they were watching a classic piece of cinema verity. The first Rock Chick ran her hands over Howard's body and then announced:

'My, you're a good looking man, why don't you give me a shrimp job?'

'I just love the look of your feet.' The melody Clark put into the sentence made it sound like an aria.

Howard got down on his knees and licked the Rock Chick's tootsies. The actress getting the shrimp managed to keep a straight face but all the other gulls present burst into peals of laughter. Clark just couldn't work it out, so he focused his thoughts on what he was doing with his tongue.

Cat Flap Club Dance Hall

Howard Clark and Mark One may have made their way to the

Cat Flap Club with the intention of checking out rock talent, but standing by the bar drinking Rolling Rock straight from the bottle is a much more attractive proposition to fully grown men. The Worshipful Company of Arts Administrators' snoop was standing beside the zeroes eavesdropping on their conversation, when Kurt Cobain walked up to Mark One and greeted him.

'Hi, Mark, how's tricks,' Kurt had lost his familiar Seattle drawl. Anyone who didn't know better would have thought he was a jolly cockney geezer trying to pass himself off as a yank.

'Everything's fine,' the Mexican jammed. 'This is Howard Clark, I'm gonna be making a film with him.'

'Hi.' Howard wasn't really interested in the walking corpse.

'What you up to Kurt?' Juan put in smoothly. He was used to dealing with the living dead.

'Raising hell and looking for a starring role in a movie that needs an actress who's man enough to be a woman. You know just how much I love wearing women's underwear y'all.'

'So word is out that we're making a film and it's brought you all the way from the Kingdom of the Undead! You could be what we need, but before we make any decisions, we've gotta talk to the money men.'

Mark winked at Cobain, who winked back before walking away.

'You can't be serious!' Howard objected. 'Kurt's a cult figure and I don't even like his music, the only things he's got that we want are a penchant for cross dressing and the fact that he's dead.'

'A cult figure could be just what we need, Cobain would pull in fans of underground films.'

'No, no!' Clark was insistent. 'I want something really pop and mainstream. Resurrecting a fallen rock star would be suicide.'

'So who do you suggest?' the Mexican was buzzing.

'One of the birds out of Bucks Fizz, or Kim Wilde! My ideal candidate would be Divine. She's the Queen of Kitsch, a Pop Goddess and a talented singer to boot!'

'You seem to have forgotten that Divine is dead too!'

'No she's not, I saw her in the Kwik Save last week.'

'I still think Kurt Cobain would be excellent, and she's already told us that she wants the role. Do you think Cobain has really come back from the dead or was his suicide faked?'

'I don't care, I want Divine,' Howard was well pissed.

The reporter closed his notebook and walked out of the club. He couldn't believe that Clark and the Mexican could be so idiotic. While he had his doubts about whether Cobain was really dead, it was obvious the geezer in the Cat Flap Club was an impersonator. As for the idea of getting Divine, that was just daft. If he was looking for an actress who could sing, the snoop would have gone for Sinitta. Now there was a babe who'd be worth giving a couch test!

As the reporter took five, the Anal Exciters arrived in Greek Street. They were pushing their broken down Fiesta. The gig was over and everyone was leaving. It hadn't occurred to the band that the promoters wouldn't keep the place open until they turned up for their support slot. Just then, the guy who'd booked the Exciters emerged from the club.

'Eyeball! Eyeball! I see a band called the Anal Exciters! And where the fuck have you been?' the promoter yowled.

'Our car broke down!' the group caterwauled in unison.

'Well you'd better not fuck up the other gigs I've booked for you!' the rock entrepreneur shouted over his shoulder as he disappeared back into the club.

'So you're the Anal Exciters! I do a little talent scouting and I'd like you to come up to a rehearsal studio to perform for a few of my friends,' the Arts Administrators' snoop ingratiated.

Ingestre Place

Howard Clark and Mark One had been wandering through the streets of Soho for hours arguing. They walked down a back alley and into a punter getting a Bill Clinton from a hooker. Juan aimed

214

his camera at the coupled couple, not recognising the john in the Constable T-shirt as the bloke they'd been standing next to for half the night.

'What are you doing? Don't you know that children play down here?' Howard sprinted.

'What? What? Fuck off! I'm just enjoying myself.' The john's face was contorted, he didn't want to be interrupted.

'I recognise you from somewhere,' Clark persisted.

'This is no good!' The snoop was attempting to shield his face while speaking to the prostitute. 'I can't get off on it anymore! Stop it will ya!'

The hooker straightened up and smoothed down her dress. The snooper zipped himself up and legged it. While she wasn't in a hurry, the street walker was clearly preparing to leave.

'Hey, wait a minute Miss,' Clark was very interested in the tart. 'I'd like to talk to you. We're making a film, you could be a star.'

'A lot of my punters are more interested in having a chat than getting laid, but they pay me regardless of the service they're after.'

'Yeah, but your clients aren't asking you to tell the truth about your trade,' Howard vaulted. 'Come on now, I bet most of the punters don't cut it between the sheets!'

'You're right, but I ain't gonna stand here and discuss it with you unless you put a score in my hand.'

'I ain't got twenty quid,' Clark whined. 'I'm an undischarged bankrupt.'

'In that case, you can stuff it!'

The prostitute sloped off down the alley and from the way she walked and talked it, you could see she was one hell of a self-confident bitch.

City of London

The Worshipful Company of Arts Administrators had nothing

better to do than sit about in their meeting hall, so they were still fanned around a table plotting the future of the arts.

'I've just heard from one of our investigators that Howard Clark is moving into the film business,' Aries exuded stern manliness. 'He plans to use Divine as his lead. Is the actress signed to our management agency?'

'No,' Leo was solemn, some might say sullen, 'Divine is dead and not being an ongoing concern isn't signed up to an agency. However, we could approach Clark and his partner pretending that we represent the singer. Perhaps we should offer to buy the porno shorts our enemies are making to raise money for their skinhead musical! They're also interested in a band called the Anal Exciters, who appear willing to sign their lives away to us if we offer them a management deal.'

101 Snack Bar

The Anal Exciters were drinking tea in the 101 Snack Bar.

'If this geezer is interested in managing us, we should get a lawyer to look over the contract.' Victor Vile wasn't as stupid as his name implied.

'Don't be a twat, we haven't got enough dosh!' Michael put in.

'Michael's right, besides that's the sort of tactic that scares off top management,' was all Jim had to say on the subject.

'Do Blur take legal advice?' Gordon added theatrically. 'Did the Sex Pistols get a lawyer before they signed up with McLaren? Fuck no! We need a total shark for a manager and once he's overseen our meteoric rise to the top of the hit parade, we'll have the readies to sue his arse! That's what Johnny Rotten did!'

'Where's Gazza?' Michael was changing the subject.

'I left McMara in the car, she was a little upset,' Jim explained. 'I was annoyed with her for not sorting out breakdown cover after she'd promised to see to it, so I gave her a beating. I tucked her shirt up and began to apply the rod. I was so angry with her, I laid on the cuts smartly, raising long red weals all over the surface of her yellow hide. She wriggled, writhed and cried as the stinging strokes of the birch fell with a swishing sound on her flabby plump arse. I went a bit over the top and Gazza wasn't in a fit state to leave the car. She's such a baby she'll probably still be sobbing when I get back.'

A Flat in Chelsea

Mark One lived in Chelsea, something that his boyfriend Mark Two considered an impressive achievement. There were twin single beds in the Mexican's bedroom. M1 was shagging M2 on one bed while simultaneously holding a phone conversation. On the other bed, Howard Clark was fucking a woman up the arse.

'Okay, tomorrow lunch-time sounds great!' the Mexican barked into the dog as he humped. 'I can't wait to get over to the Big Time rehearsal studio to watch the Anal Exciters run through their set. It's good to know they've got professional management . . . Ciao.'

As Motorway put down the bone, he was still jacking his backside up and down.

'I don't see why those straights have to stay here tonight,' Two complained, his voice muffled because his face was buried in a pillow.

Howard Clark was beating out the primitive rhythm of the swamps. His grinding partner met his sexual ideal, she had big blonde hair, big tits and a remarkably high IQ. Howard loved intelligent wimmin because you didn't have to throw them out on to the street the minute you'd finished shagging them. He always enjoyed the inventive pillow talk of bright bitches.

'Stop moaning you slut!' the Mexican lashed his boyfriend, hoping Clark was too preoccupied to mentally process the bozo's complaints. 'I've already told you that Howard and I have a lot of business to sort out tomorrow. We're setting up a major feature film and we've gotta go all out to get the finance, then find a writer, director and stars!'

'That doesn't mean the cunt has to stay with us,' Two managed to splutter between orgasmic moans.

'Yes it does.' The Mexican was humping so hard he was very short of breath. 'For a start, Howard lives on the other side of town and we'd lose precious time if he had to waste an hour travelling over here in the morning. Secondly, there are still a number of details we need to sort out. If you'd only shut up, Howard and I might just be able to finish our discussion.'

'Oh, alright, but only if you'll fist me later,' the final syllable was pronounced several octaves higher than the first since Two was in the full throes of an orgasm.

'What about Kurt Cobain, Howard?' The Mexican was breathless. 'I think he'd be excellent in the lead role.'

'No way, I want Divine!' Clark was panting from his sexual exertions.

'You're obsessed!' Motorway gasped.

The chick Clark was fucking tossed her head back and screamed ecstatically as she thrilled to multiple orgasm after multiple orgasm. The DNA had seized control of her bulk and she was out on the mud flats of prehistory where million year old genetic codes were scrambled and unscrambled all over her well stacked form.

'Do you want me to call an ambulance?' Mark Two was addressing Howard. 'It sounds like your girlfriend is having an epileptic fit.'

Howard Clark's Dreams of Culture and Imperialism

Beneath the stern windows which lighted Howard's cabin lay a boat; he slid down the rope which held it to the ship. Then Clark undressed and plunged into the cool waves. After bathing he redressed and, reclining in the boat, he fell asleep. When Howard awoke it was dark and he was floating near the shore and HMS Venus on which he'd been a passenger was miles away.

Howard had no oars and dared not use the sails for fear the Moorish vessels in sight might discover him. He drifted towards a large building which was the only one to be seen, rising from the rocks near the water's edge. The keel of the boat soon grated on sand and Howard concealed it, for in his dream he believed he might be seized and sold into slavery.

Howard heard a whispered call from above. Two ladies were looking down on the artist. A rope of shawls was let down and he climbed up them. On clambering through a window, Clark found himself in the company of nine chicks. The winks and smiles of the harem led Howard to cheerfully submit while they disrobed him. Then the nine strangers entertained him with the dance of the seven veils. Once everyone was naked, Inez wrapped her soft arms round Clark and their lips met. With one hand the artist guided his shaft into her welcoming gusset. As Howard humped Inez, the other sluts gathered round and showered him with kisses.

Clark lay on his back with his head resting on Inez's breasts. Helene sat astride his loins with her face towards him, her little tapering fingers playing with his limber shaft. Once the member had stiffened, it penetrated the crevice poised above it. Helene undulated her loins until she and Howard enjoyed the glory of a simultaneous orgasm.

The artist inserted his forefinger between the lips which concealed Zuleika's maidenhead. His shaft became as rigid as a bone. Howard lay Zuleika on her back, spread her thighs wide open and entered her. Clark's whole being seemed to centre in his prick and he gushed into the black hole of a cunt before sinking back prostrate and exhausted.

A fat and charming Indian bird gently fondled Howard's genitals. Her large, round buttocks were elevated in the air and looked so temptingly smooth and soft that Clark climbed upon her in the way that a stallion would mount a mare. Howard kept pushing into the yielding mass without once drawing back till his shaft grew stiff with the delightful sensation, and his crest exchanged a wanton desire with her womb.

Clark parted the flaming red hair that concealed the fiery lips of another babe and commenced the onset. The delicious heat and moisture set the blood dancing in his veins. His love pole lingered a moment at the embouchement, then glided past into the clinging folds of her sheath. When he was completely entered, the cunt gave a convulsive contraction and the Circassian dissolved. At another plunge sperm gushed in consecutive jets.

Howard exchanged kisses with a pretty Portuguese girl and one of her companions. He felt his love muscle bathed in her melting shower. Clark drew out his rod and plunged it all dripping into a pretty Persian wanton. He was transported with a double rapture which his overwrought nerves could endure no more. He woke up to find the blonde with whom he was sharing the single bed, thrashing around in her dreams.

A Flat in Chelsea

Mark Juan, Howard Clark and Edward D. Wood Jr were seated in the Mexican's living room. MI and Howard had half drunk teas in front of them. Motorway poured Ed a cuppa from the pot. The Mexican and Clark had just got out of bed but looked stunning in comparison to Ed Wood, who'd recently arrived from the land of the living dead in his sister's underwear, which hadn't been washed since the tranny first wore it as a GI during WWII. Mark Two and the blonde were still asleep in the other room.

'I hope you don't mind me calling round so early,' the world famous trash movie maker coughed.

'No problem. You wouldn't have caught us in later on, we've got a lot to do today,' the Mexican assured him.

'I've come to talk to you about *Teenage Warning*.'

'You know about *Teenage Warning?*' Juan raised his eyebrows.

'That's what I've come round about. I think the lead would be ideal for me,' Wood enthused. 'I love the idea of a musical about a former night-club star who's recovering from a cancer operation and making a comeback with a gay skinhead band!'

'I think you'd be great.' The Mexican wanted to work with

Jess Franco but in the meantime Ed Wood Jr was acceptable as a substitute.

'I want all you skinheads out there to put your braces together,' Wood tugged, 'and your boots on your feet and give me some of that old moonstomping!'

Ed was demonstrating his skill at the grape crusher stomp. This was something of a mistake since several of his toes fell off during the routine. It wouldn't have been a problem if the stiff had been geared up in Docs, but shod as he was in sandals, the tootsies went flying across the room. Wood's flesh was badly decomposed and Clark considered the zombie's act highly distasteful.

'No, no, I want Divine!' Howard insisted.

The phone rang and as the Mexican answered it, Wood stuck his tongue out at Clark. The zombie put a little too much oomph into the gesture and his tongue fell to the floor with a soft plop. Howard viewed this as an even greater gaff than the earlier loss of toes. Wood was revolting and Clark knew intuitively that any movie featuring him as the lead was bound to stiff.

'What?' The Mexican was puzzled by the caller's patter. 'Your name is Napoleon? . . . Yes, yes, we've got some very interesting footage. It's not edited yet but you could see the rushes . . . How on earth have you seen our treatment . . . I see, someone put it up on the Internet . . . Okay, fax us your rewrite of the outline . . .'

'I'm going Mark, I'll see you soon,' Ed woofed before disappearing in a puff of smoke.

Howard, who hated the smell of fire and brimstone, flung the windows open, then proceeded to flap a newspaper about the room. After this, Clark scuttled around picking up the bits of Wood's corpse that had dropped off before pitching the rotten flesh out of the open window for the crows to eat.

Now they were alone, Juan explained to Howard that a bloke called Napoleon wanted to buy their porno shorts and was faxing through a rewrite of their film treatment. Pretty soon, paper was gushing out of the fax and the two men were reading the text in bemusement. It bore little resemblance to their proposed project.

Okay, so you had to make compromises to get film finance but this was ridiculous. Regardless, the Mexican had agreed to meet the man in Leicester Square.

St James's Park, Central London

Michael, Gordon and Victor of the Anal Exciters were stretched out on benches in St James's Park.

'Gordon, are you awake?' Vic enquired.

'Yeah.'

'How come Jim and Gazza got to sleep in the car? It's not bleedin' fair!'

'You're right,' Gordon agreed as he sat up. 'Let's play a trick on them to get our own back. Have you still got the management contract the geezer we met last night gave us to sign?'

'Yeah, why?' Vic raised himself from a horizontal position.

Gordon pulled some papers from a pocket and walked across to Vic. 'Let's swap the management contract for this hire purchase agreement I was going to sign to get a new TV. If Jim and Gazza fail to notice the switch before they give the contract back to the management team, they'll look like right fucking idiots!'

'Yeah, let's do it,' Michael put in, 'let's show them up as a proper pair of charlies. Then when we catch up with Gazza, let's give her arse a right paddling. She bloody deserves it, what's she ever done for the band? All she ever does is mouth off!'

Leicester Square

Mark One and Howard Clark wandered around Leicester Square approaching men carrying briefcases. Mark had a carrier bag filled with videos in his left hand.

'Are you Napoleon?' Clark asked a suit.

'No, I'm Jesus Christ, what's your name?'

'Howard, why?'

'You don't look like a Howard to me, you look more like a Josephine!'

'Are you Napoleon?' The Mexican's voice cut through the tourist ambience like a Stanley knife.

'Piss off.' The insult had undercover written all over it.

Howard and Mark were standing close to some phone boxes. A phone rang and was answered by a Worshipful Company of Arts Administrators' agent dressed in a shell suit.

'It's for you,' the conspirator exhaled as he held the phone out for Juan.

'Yes, yes,' the Mexican suspirated after taking the dog. 'It doesn't matter ... Okay.'

'Napoleon couldn't make it,' MI informed Clark after putting down the phone. 'We're to meet him outside the Law Courts in fifteen minutes.'

The City of London

The curtains were still drawn in the Worshipful Company of Arts Administrators' meeting hall. The leaders of this guild were still assembled around their table in a dimly lit room. They'd just refreshed themselves with mugs of strong coffee after sitting up all night.

'Our agents in the field are leading Howard Clark on a wild goose chase,' Aries screeched. 'Hopefully, he will soon be disenchanted with the movie business and retire for good.'

'Why don't we just kill the cunt?' Libra leered.

'Libra, are you mad?' Aries chewed the words up before spitting them out. 'Aren't you aware of the cults that form around dead artists? Clark is already enormously influential, if he died in mysterious circumstances, the fanatical devotion of his followers would pose a severe threat to traditional aesthetic values.'

'I hadn't thought of that!'

*   *   *

The Strand

Juan and Howard were standing on the steps of the Law Courts smiling at various men carrying briefcases.

'Perhaps you'd like to accompany me to my chamber, we could have some fun together,' a judge in a wig and carrying a suitcase suggested.

'I guess you're not Napoleon,' Juan batted.

'I've got all sorts of fantasy gear,' the judge assured the young man. 'Whips, leathers, the works. If you want, I can hire some Napoleonic outfits from a dress agency. I'd like it if you played Josephine.'

'Sorry mate, I've got other fish to fry.'

'Are you Napoleon?' Howard asked a guy wearing a Constable T-shirt and carrying a briefcase.

'Yep.'

'Over here, Mark!' Clark shouted at the Mexican

The Mexican shook hands with the old general. Both men's grips were firm but Juan was a little puzzled as to why Frenchie used the vigorous greeting as an excuse to press several of his knuckles with a thumb. Mark figured it must be some old fashioned sexual code for what were once quaintly called fruits. These days you could be upfront about being gay, so there was no need for such nonsense.

'Sorry about the problems meeting up,' Napoleon apologised. 'Dealing in porn, I have a lot of hassles with the cops. However, the bastards aren't likely to think of looking for me outside the Law Courts!'

'I've got some rushes of the stuff we're working on,' the Mexican grinned as he pulled a video cassette out of a carrier. 'You like young girls? I'll sell you my grandmother's arse, I guarantee you she's a virgin.'

'I'm not interested in your grandmother, your mother or your sister,' Napoleon was emphatic, 'not even as a package deal. What I'm desperate for are some foot fetish shorts and I need them delivered fast.'

'We can deliver anything you want,' and for good measure Juan handed Frenchie a couple of Ed Wood's rotting toes which he'd rescued after Howard threw them out for the crows.

'I'll call you at five.' After taking a nibble on the undead flesh Napoleon added: 'You're to wait outside the phone boxes at the very top of Charing X Road.'

'Can't you call me at home?' MI pleaded. 'You could even come around and I'll fix you up with a chick who's got a dick.'

'It's not safe to call you at home,' Frenchie was emphatic, 'the phone line might be tapped.'

'Supposing you want this chick I got for you,' the Mexican persisted, 'how do I let you know she's free?'

'You can't contact me,' Napoleon was glancing about nervously, 'it's not safe to give you a number before I've had my security boys check you out. Look, I've gotta go. You better be waiting for that call on Charing X Road at five.'

'Where to now?' Howard asked his friend.

'Let's go to the Big Time rehearsal studio in Camden,' Juan warbled after looking at his watch. 'The Anal Exciters should be there by now. We can start the auditions for the movie.'

Big Time Rehearsal Room 3

The Anal Exciters were dripping with sweat. The droog who'd booked them into the Big Time Rehearsal Studios didn't show much interest in the band, which the Anal Exciters mistakenly believed was proof of his professionalism.

'Right boys.' It wasn't clear whether the droog was rubbing his hands with glee or because he was suffering from pins and needles, 'I want you to run through your stuff again, but first, did you sign the contract?'

'Who's got the contract?' Jim was taking command of the situation. 'We'd better get it inked!'

Vic took Gordon's hire purchase agreement out of his pocket, opening it at the back page, so that everyone could put their name on the dotted line. Vic took a pen from his pocket and signed the contract before passing it on to Jimmy, who inked the papers without looking at them. After the signatures of all four band members had been collected, the droog pocketed the contract without looking at it.

'I've got to sign it, I've got to sign it.' McMara was jumping up and down like a three-year-old who needed the loo.

'Listen Adolf,' the droog machine-gunned as he simultaneously attempted to grab Gazza's nuts and was extremely surprised to find that there was nothing there, 'you're just a friend of the band, a secret weapon along for the ride, you don't play or sing so you don't sign on the dotted line or get any dosh. I don't like that stupid arm band you're wearing, or your smelly clothes, or your face, or your fat mouth, so just consider yourself lucky I'm prepared to let you hang around.'

'But I am the Anal Exciters!' the she-creature protested. 'The group are nothing without me.'

'Now you'll catch it,' the droog roared at McMara, 'don't ever speak to me like that again. I'll make your bottom smart, you horrid, smelly slithering piece of shit. James, if you value your management contract, you'll take this miscreant over your shoulders and hold him there so that I can flog him soundly!'

At twenty-three, James was a tall broad-shouldered Scouser, as strong as two men and given his proclivities for para-military uniforms and camouflage gear, not a bit averse to violence. Besides, the fact that McMara was old enough to be Green's mum had never prevented the singer from canning the old cow. Jim seized the she-creature's wrists, turned half round, and swung the big girlie easily up on to his broad back. Then, slightly separating his feet and leaning well forward, Green brought Gazza's body into a curved position, with her bottom thrown well out.

The droog stepped forward and pulled down McMara's pants and trousers, then rolled up her shirt and jacket. This was quite an unpleasant task since Gazza's clothes were not only soaked with sweat but also liberally splattered with urine and shit. Gary was now naked from her waist to the tops of her ankle socks. Even for someone middle-aged, McMara was remarkably fat and flabby, with her broad bottom hanging off her in a peculiarly repulsive fashion. There was plenty of flesh for the birch to play on.

The droog rolled up his sleeves, revealing muscular arms. Taking up a rod that was lying conveniently on a guitar amp, he lightly touched the she-creature's bottom with the switch while observing to the Anal Exciters that this poor specimen was clearly a masochist whose very sanity was to be doubted. Not the sort of person they should be hanging around with unless they enjoyed poking fun at the mentally retarded. Gary moved uneasily on her horse's back. Despite being a complete moron, she still had sufficient wit to understand that she was about to learn the meaning of pain.

Raising the rod high in the air, the droog laid on the first cut with considerable force. Again and again the stinging rod swept through the air, falling with a loud crack on the she-creature's smarting derrière. The sharp pain seemed to take Gazza's breath away. She gasped and made a gurgling noise, clenching her teeth so tightly that the outline of her jaw could be seen beneath her heavy jowls. McMara's eyes streamed with tears and she screamed long and loud. The rod fell slowly and relentlessly and the girlie's shrieks became piercing. McMara struggled hard, kicking vigorously, and a few small drops of blood appeared on her scarlet bottom. Thwack! The last stroke fell on the quivering flesh of the shrieking thing Gazza had become around the time of her sex change. The droog put down the rod and wiped his brow with his forearm. Jimmy let go of the victim's wrists and she fell to the floor sobbing.

'Right lads,' the droog was returning his full attention to the band, 'run through your stuff! You've not got long to practise before some movie people arrive.'

Big Time Rehearsal Studio Reception

Howard Clark and Mark One were standing in front of the receptionist's desk at the Big Time rehearsal studio. Julian Smith

had his feet up and was reading a copy of *Hottest Asian Babes*. He
threw down the mag and looked up at Howard and Juan.

'I'm booked up for the rest of the week.' Julian just couldn't
be fucked to deal with anyone.

'We didn't want a rehearsal, we're here to look over a few of
the bands.'

'Are you from a record company?' Smith was suddenly so
interested by the strangers that he took his feet off the desk,
an almost unknown occurrence.

'Nah, we ain't company dorks,' Howard snapped, 'we're looking
for a group to use in a film. I want a band with a few chicks in
the line-up.'

'We've got quite a few bird musicians in today,' Julian whispered
conspiratorially. 'You gonna give any of 'em the couch test?'

'I'm interested in the Anal Exciters but they're much too laddish
to let me give them an arse shagging,' the Mexican burbled ruefully.
'However, I hear Girl Boy Revolution are here and they're very
open to homoeroticism.'

'I'm not having any bum banditry in my rehearsal studio!'
Smith erupted. 'But I bet I could pull one of the Girl Boy
Revolution birds.'

'I'll give you a hundred and fifty quid if you can fix it so that
I can secretly film the encounter,' Juan said as he pulled a camera
from his bag and held it up. 'Three hundred if you shag one of
the Girl Boy Revolution wimmin up the arse!'

'You're on,' Julian said as he scratched his balls.

'It's a bet, but make sure the lights stay on because I can't film
anything in the dark,' the Mexican instructed.

Big Time Rehearsal Room 3

Having wandered in and out of a few rehearsal rooms, Howard
and Juan found the Anal Exciters strutting their stuff. Following
on from her thrashing, McMara was howling lustily in a corner,
but fortunately the band's two-chord thud masked this pathetic

blubbing and it only became irritating when they stopped for a break. The droog hadn't been paying much attention but he perked up when Clark and the Mexican looked in. The band launched into 'Mindless Aggression', their best number, and like the rest of their songs it was anything but subtle.

> *Mindless aggression, mindless aggression*
> *You're gonna get your fuckin' head kicked in.'*

The band chanted the introductory chorus and then stopped; something wasn't quite right. They checked the tuning on the bass and guitar. Gordon's top three strings were out. No one in the Exciters had a particularly good ear for pitch but they'd a little machine to help them get in tune. Unfortunately, the batteries had run down. Without this aid, it took Bennet nearly ten minutes to get a reasonably healthy sound out of his axe. The band skipped the introductory chorus and went straight into the first verse.

> *Down the disco you pull some bird*
> *She gives you oral in the bog*
> *Next thing you know her ex comes up*
> *And smacks you in the gob*

Then it was back to the terrace chant chorus and on into another unbelievably dumb verse.

> *Down the High Street on Saturday night*
> *Vandalising some litter bins*
> *Coppers say they don't like your face*
> *So you get your head kicked in*

When it came to lyric writing, Jim was determined to prove that his university education hadn't blunted his aesthetic sensibilities and transformed him into a sissy. The D to C chord progression, which dropped a fifth for the chorus, made few concessions to intellectuality. Nevertheless, by the time he left the Mexican was convinced that the Anal Exciters were exactly what was needed to make *Teenage Warning* a box office hit.

Big Time Rehearsal Studios Reception

Back in the Big Time reception, Julian pulled an aerosol can from his desk. It was labelled SEX HORMONES: GUARANTEED TO DRIVE WOMEN CRAZY! Julian sprayed the aerosol all over himself. He'd ordered the sex aid from the classified section at the back of a wank mag. He'd been a little frightened to make use of it in case it drove old ladies into a frenzy and they attempted to rape him. However, now that the arse shagging challenge was on with the Mexican, nothing could stop Julian making good use of this little gimmick.

'Jesus, what's that smell?' the guitarist with Road Plan complained as he walked into the reception.

'It fucking stinks in here!' Road Plan's bassist added superfluously.

'You know which studio you use, just get through there and pay me afterwards.' Julian may have been short tempered with Road Plan but he was relieved these effeminate prog rockers simply disappeared into rehearsal studio 4 and that they hadn't held him down and gang raped him, since he'd been worried that the pig hormones might arouse benders as well as grannies.

Big Time Rehearsal Room 7

Girl Boy Revolution were running through a song in the rehearsal room they'd rented. Howard and Mark wandered into the practice. Girl Boy Revolution wanted to experiment artistically and were working on a new song with a mournful tempo and occult lyrics. 'The One and the Many' was a million miles away from the Anal Exciters brash sound.

'Sex Kick'

'I have sought, I have found, I have joined, I will divide

There are two roads to destruction
In Moscow bodies were swallowed
The bloody sacrifice of many
In Washington minds are swallowed
The bloodless sacrifice of all

I have sought, I have found, I have joined, I will divide

A wolf and dog are in the field
Both descended from the same stock
The wolf comes from the East
The dog comes from the West
Fury, rage and madness

I have sought, I have found, I have joined, I will divide

Baal, Osiris, Hermes, Seth
Baal, Osiris, Hermes, Seth
Baal, Osiris, Hermes, Seth
Baal, Osiris, Hermes, Seth

I have sought, I have found, I have joined, I will divide

The aeon makes the cosmos
The cosmos makes time
And time makes coming to be
Time is in the cosmos
And coming to be is in time

I have sought, I have found, I have joined, I will divide

By the spirit of eternal love
Light and water are joined
Light, air and water together
The four-fold alteration
Fire, air, water and earth

I have sought, I have found, I have joined, I will divide
I have sought, I have found, I have joined, I will divide.'

Howard was introduced to everyone. The band were familiar with his art works and singer Mick Sick, in particular, was very excited to meet him. Mick, along with bassist Jill Power and rhythm guitarist Fiona Bear, represented the outgoing public face of the group. Drummer Sandra Soot and lead guitarist Martin Drop were the quiet, supposedly thoughtful members of the band who preferred to remain in the background. The Mexican enticed Mick and Jill across to the other side of the room. He'd soon embroiled them in his plan to humiliate Julian, the Big Time receptionist.

Big Time Rehearsal Studios Reception

The Mexican walked through to the reception. He sniffed the air and then pulled a face. Julian had his feet up on the desk and his dick in his right hand. His attention was focused on a particularly fetching Bengali girl whose private parts were spread all over the latest issue of *Hottest Asian Babes*. After looking up guiltily and clocking Juan, the receptionist threw the wank mag down and adjusted his clothing.

'Jill is gonna come through from the rehearsal studio any minute now,' Motorway gibbered. 'Where can I hide to film the sexual action without being seen?'

'Behind that rubbish sack,' Julian pointed at a bulging bin liner and the Mexican crouched down next to it.

'God, Julian, you look gorgeous,' Jill announced as she came through the door.

'Let me make love to you,' Julian used his best chat-up line as he rose from his chair.

'What's that smell?' Power was sniffing the air.

'What smell? I can't smell anything!'

'You must have a cold,' Jill cackled, 'it fucking stinks in 'ere!'

'Let me make love to you,' Julian's seduction routine was becoming monotonous.

'What? In here? I can't, someone might walk in!' There was an anxious note in the bassist's voice.

'We could lock all the doors,' Julian held out a key as proof of this statement.

'Give me the key!' Power snatched it from the receptionist's hand. 'I'll lock the doors, I wanna make sure no one catches us fucking! Where's the light switch? I wanna turn the lights off too!'

'You can't do that! Mark can't film in the ... I mean, you can't do that, you can't!'

'Why?'

'The lights will fuse! They have to be left on! There's a terrible fault with the electrics. It's being fixed tomorrow.'

'If I can't switch the lights off, I'll have to blindfold you.'

'What? Why? Don't you think I'm irresistible?'

'I'm very shy,' Jill explained as she took a scarf from her pocket and slipped it over Julian's eyes. 'I don't let blokes see my body the first time they screw me! But I love being fucked up the arse, I just love it! Will you bum fuck me?'

'Yeah, sure. I get more money for ... I mean, a lot of girls don't like that but I do, I love it!'

Jill led Julian into the centre of the reception and left him there, then she opened a door, so that Mick Sick could creep into the room.

'What are you doing?' Julian was puzzled.

'I was just checking that no one was in the corridor.'

Power then proceeded to lock the doors that opened on to the reception. Mick dropped his trousers and bent over Julian's desk. Jill positioned herself just to the side of her fellow band member. Now that all the players were in place for a classic piece of sexual deception, the Mexican stood up and set the white balance on his camera.

'Come over here and fuck my arse,' Power squealed at Julian.

'I'm bent over your desk. I'm just aching for you to fill my bum hole with a big manly cock!'

Julian stumbled forwards. He had his hands in front of him like a sleepwalker. He touched Mick's back, dropped his trousers and slipped his arms around the singer's chest.

'You're somewhat lacking in the knocker department!' Julian's confidence was increasing by the second. Thanks to the pig hormones he no longer felt sexually inadequate and was convinced he was gonna get laid on a regular basis.

'Don't say things like that,' Jill tutted from behind the desk, 'it's the kind of insensitive comment that made me shy!'

'Sorry babe!'

'Forget it, just grease my arse and give me some anal action!'

Julian was so excited that he didn't notice the bassist's voice wasn't coming from underneath him. Mick handed Julian a tube of KY. Julian made liberal use of the lubricant and then began humping his sex partner. The Mexican moved around the desk filming the two blokes having sex. Jill stood behind them looking very bored as she faked orgasmic moans.

As Julian hammered away at Mick Sick's arse, Howard Clark and the three members of Girl Boy Revolution who'd hung behind in the rehearsal room began banging on a door, demanding to be let into the reception area.

'What's going on? Let us out! We wanna go home and you've locked us in!' Fiona, Sandra, Martin and Howard heckled.

Jill walked across the reception and unlocked the door, letting everyone in. There were catcalls and jeers as the pranksters took in the scene. Seeing the homophobic Julian giving it to Mick Sick up the arse in the mistaken belief that the singer was a girl, caused the musicians to double up with mirth.

Cork Street

Howard Clark and Mark One were standing at the north end of Cork Street.

'I don't mind shooting more porno but I think we should be doing something about tracking down Divine,' Howard hurdled. 'We desperately need to get in touch with her. The film we're gonna make is a star vehicle – and unless we secure Divine's services, we're wasting our time getting the money together.'

'Stop whingeing and I'll let you fuck my cousin, young girl, virgin!' The Mexican was beginning to believe his own act and had forgotten that he'd actually been born and bred in Raynes Park. The conversation was interrupted when a woman in her mid-thirties approached Clark.

'Hi, Howard, I'm so sorry you lost the court case yesterday. If there's anything I can do to help let me know.' Hannah Deserts exuded self-confidence.

'Do I know you?'

'No, I'm just a fan of appropriation art, as well as your beautiful body!' Hannah extolled.

'Would you like Howard to give you a shrimp job?' the Mexican enquired.

'Yes!'

Having got down on his hands and knees, Howard proceeded to remove Hannah's left shoe and sock. Juan handed his lead a carton of live yoghurt which was immediately poured over Hannah's toes. The foreplay over, Clark licked the health food from the foot. Deserts was in ecstasy, her head thrown back and mouth open as Howard sucked her pinkies. Once the foot was spotlessly clean, Clark replaced the babe's sock and shoe.

'Oh, that was lovely, lovely. Before I go, let me give you my details,' Deserts announced as she handed Howard her card.

'You're a banker?' Clark said incredulously after looking at this prize.

'Yes, that's my business number.' Hannah hated people thinking she was square because of her well paid career.

'Have you ever financed a film?'

'I've financed several.'

'I wanna make a movie, maybe you could come up with the dosh.'

'For you Howard, anything! Just work out the budget and then visit me at my office. I'll put it through on the nod.'

Deserts waved at Clark, blew him a kiss and then left.

'We can forget about Napoleon and this porno lark,' Clark was triumphant as he addressed the Mexican.

'No way, we want to secure as many avenues of finance as possible. Don't count your chickens and all that,' Juan teetered. 'So we'd better split, we've a phone call to catch.'

Charing X Road

Howard Clark and Mark One raced up to the phones on the corner of Charing X Road and Oxford Street. Mark glanced at his watch, then grinned at Clark. The booths were occupied by blokes wearing Constable T-shirts and none of them looked like they were in any hurry to get off the dog and bone.

Moments later, one of these geezers finished his call and hung up. The phone immediately rang and the bloke held the receiver out for Juan.

'It's for you!' The droog sounded like he was auditioning for a b-movie.

'Hello,' then after a pause the Mexican finished with a curt, 'Okay, we'll be there.'

'We've got eight minutes to get to the phones in Charing X Station, where we'll get a message telling us when to meet Napoleon,' Motorway informed Howard after handing the phone back to the droog.

Mark One immediately began lapping south down Charing X Road. Howard followed. They bumped into people as they barged through the early evening crowds. The street was really busy and when they eventually got to Charing X Station they were totally out of breath. As this odd couple ran towards the ticket office, a phone was ringing. Clark raced up to it.

'Hello,' Howard mumbled as he picked up the phone. 'Yes ... Okay!'

'Where to now?' Motorway held his stomach as he stood up.

'Battistas at the top of Charing X Road.'

'What a bastard, we've just come from up there!'

Battistas Café

Howard Clark and Mark One were drinking coffee. They took no notice of the two men wearing Constable T-shirts who were seated at the next table. Only Napoleon interested them and he was nowhere to be seen.

Clark wanted to sit back and relax but the conversation at the next table kept breaking into his thoughts

'Look, I'm only interested in one of your clients,' the first lackey droned intrusively, 'so don't waste my time with a sales spiel about any of the losers you've taken on. The reason my night-clubs are successful is because I'll only book star talent. The only act you've got that fulfils this criteria is Divine.'

Howard looked across at the two men.

'There's an enormous demand for Divine's services,' the second lackey countered, 'and since she died she's found her relentless touring schedule particularly punishing. However, I'll have a word with her about the possibility of some lunch-time or late night dates.'

'Can't I have a few evening performances?' Lackey One demanded.

'Not for at least a year,' was the terse reply. 'Divine is all booked up. I'm doing you a real favour attempting to fit anything in.'

'Just give me any times and dates you can, I'm desperate to get a performer of Divine's stature! However, I'm also in a rush to get to another meeting! Bell me about Divine as soon as you can.'

Lackey One disappeared. As Lackey Two downed a mouthful of coffee, Howard Clark slid from his table and seated himself opposite the droog.

'Hi, I hope you don't think I'm being rude but I couldn't help overhearing your conversation. Are you Divine's manager?'

'That's right! Don't I recognise you from somewhere?'

'I'm Howard Clark, the famous artist.'

'Wow, I knew that I'd seen your face before! Divine is a big fan of yours, she's always wanted to meet you!'

'That's nice, because I'm a fan of Divine's and I'd like to offer her the principal role in a film I'm making.'

'I'm sure she'd be most interested. My agency has numerous acts who might be of use to you. However, I've gotta go and check out some fresh talent,' Lackey Two announced as he checked his watch. 'Here's my card, ring me at my office around nine o'clock this evening.'

'Will do.'

Lackey Two got up, shook Clark's hand and left. Howard sat back down with the Mexican.

'Where the fuck is Napoleon?' Juan wanted to know.

'What does it matter, it looks like we've secured Divine's services for the film!'

'We can't secure Divine's services until we've organised the necessary funding. Besides, I'm more interested in the Anal Exciters, you saw how good they were at the rehearsal this morning!'

A third Worshipful Company of Arts Administrators' lackey entered the café. He walked briskly towards Clark and the Mexican.

'Your instructions are to wait for a phone call in Leicester Square at nine o'clock this evening,' Lackey Three was about as mysterious as a dose of the shits. 'Napoleon is very pleased with the footage you've given him and will advance you a considerable sum of money if everything proceeds satisfactorily.'

Lackey Three turned on his heel and left.

'What a bummer, we'll have to miss the Anal Exciters gig at Blow Up if we're to make the meeting with Napoleon.' The Mexican was pained at the thought of this.

Leicester Square

Howard Clark and Mark One were standing together in Leicester Square. A girl wearing a Constable T-shirt approached Clark and put her arm around his waist.

'Hi, I'm Eve.'

'Hi, I'm Howard and this is my friend Mark.'

'We're a minute or two early,' Mark was looking at his watch.

'We won't have to wait long,' Howard assured his friend. 'I'd better phone Divine's manager, he wanted to hear from me at nine.'

'Don't forget to ask him about the Anal Exciters!' the Mexican hectored. 'Find out if he's involved with them.'

Howard jumped into a phone booth. As the artist did this, the phone next to him rang and Mark One picked up the receiver.

'Hi, it's Howard.'

'Hello,' the Mexican burped.

'Okay, no problem.' Clark used a deep voice which he thought came across as highly serious.

'Sure, I'll be there,' Juan affirmed.

The two men concluded their calls and moved back towards Eve.

'We've gotta get to Waterloo Station within the next ten minutes,' Mark announced.

'My instructions are to rendezvous at the Café Espana on Old Compton Street around nine fifteen,' Howard strutted.

'We haven't enough time to get to both places! What are we gonna do?' the Mexican reverberated.

'We'll have to split up,' Clark wheezed.

'Okay, we'll meet back at my pad,' Juan cried tearfully.

Waterloo Station

Mark One and Napoleon shook hands on the steps of Waterloo Station.

'Greetings,' Napoleon pronounced the word as though it was a death sentence.

'Hi!' Juan's voice was playful.

'Sorry if you've had to run around a bit,' Napoleon didn't really give a shit, 'but you know how it is. The cops have been trying to bust me for years. I'm very security conscious.'

'That's okay.'

'I really liked your rushes. I'll pay you a hundred thousand for sixteen hours of properly edited foot fetish material if you can supply it within the next seven days.'

'You're wanting a very fast turn around, I'll have to work day and night to get it done!'

'I'm offering you a lot of money. Is it a deal?'

'Okay, I guess I'll just have to buy a lot of whizz to keep myself going!'

Café Espana

Howard Clark was sitting with Eve and Lackey Two in the Café Espana.

'Divine is very interested in working with you, but what she needs is a script,' Lackey Two coughed discreetly. 'My client has just received a number of highly lucrative offers and we've got to get back to the blokes waving contracts at us within a matter of days. If you can get a script to me tomorrow, or the day after at the very latest, we might be in business.'

'But we haven't even hired someone to write the script yet! All we've got is an outline!'

'If you're serious about working with Divine, you'd better find someone who can write the thing overnight. After all, its not everyone who gets to work on a film project with one of the living dead!'

'I know someone who'll do the script!' Eve put in helpfully. 'Stewart Home, he's a great writer. We can give him a ring in a minute. I think he charges five grand, cash on delivery, for running something up overnight.'

'I'll sort the money.'

Blow Up Club

There had been quite a crowd before the Anal Exciters hit the stage, but the numbers dwindled as Gary McMara made his way around the Blow Up Club handing out poorly typed leaflets in which he made ridiculous accusations about the drugs baron Howard Marks being a neo-Nazi, as well as unbelievable claims that boxing star Frank Bruno worked for the secret state. Anyone who failed to vocally acknowledge that McMara was a genius for making these 'revelations' was subjected to verbal abuse followed by a sexual assault from the crazed she-creature. After Gazza had 'exposed' each and every one of the kids present as a fascist provocateur serving the repressive agenda of a reactionary police state and then hounded them from the hall, the audience consisted of a dog plus a few record company executives who were standing around the bar. McMara didn't dare accuse the industry types of being neo-Nazis, since that might fuck up the Anal Exciters chances of making it big.

The Anal Exciters hit the stage but after the first number they were less than pleased by the reaction of the dog that was watching them play. Obviously, it would have been unrealistic to expect any response from the record company bores propping up the bar. But not even McMara's idiot dancing had won applause from the lone mutt.

'It is my fancy to be treated as a naughty girl and spanked senseless,' Gazza minced into the microphone, seizing the initiative from Jimmy Green.

As the band ground out 'Rim Job', Jim threw McMara over an amp. The singer turned up Gazza's pretty, blue satin skirt, rumpling and creasing it a great deal. Then, to broaden out the spectacle, he slowly rolled up, one after the other, her lavender-scented, lace-flounced, snowy petticoats, and her delicate silk chemise. After this, James stopped and gazed in disbelief at McMara's ugly, coarse, pimpled arse, which was only partially hidden by dainty lace-frilled panties of the finest linen. Thanks to the way in which Gazza lay across the amplifier, the thin garment clung closely to the hemisphere of podgy flesh. Unfastening the drawers, the singer pulled them entirely off McMara's legs, which looked absurd in tightly-fitting pearl-grey silk stockings. Her garters were of dark blue satin, and her over-sized feet were cased in high-heeled maroon-coloured shoes purchased by mail order from a firm catering to the transvestite market.

Jim had taken care when turning up the undergarments to push them well above Gary's waist. Everything being ready, the singer began to spank McMara severely. Jim took his time, spanking slowly and Gazza winced at the hot slaps, every one of which printed a five-petalled red flower on her off-yellow pock-marked skin. As her bottom grew redder, McMara began to wriggle about in pain. The song finished and the effect of the spanking was rather spoiled by Gazza letting rip with a loud and very smelly fart. There was no applause. Neither the dog nor the record executives had any interest in the type of perversion they'd just witnessed.

A Flat in Chelsea

Mark One was filming Howard Clark sucking Eve's toes. Eve was sitting on the edge of one of the twin beds, stark naked and with a strap-on sticking up from her cunt. Clark was kneeling on the floor like some penitent monk who wished to mortify his flesh.

'Come on, come on Howard!' the Mexican encouraged. 'Pretend you've got a dick in your mouth! Eve looks great but you're faking it! Put some effort into it, you're supposed to be in ecstasy!'

'That feels so good, that feels so fucking good!' Eve moaned generically. 'You're making me feel like a real woman for the first time since I joined the Worshipful Company of Arts Administrators.'

'What? What? What are you talking about?' the toe-sucking artist ejaculated as he sat up.

'Oh, nothing, silly me! Don't stop sucking my toes!' Eve parried.

'Give the bitch more shrimp, this is gonna be a foot fetish classic!' Juan tensed.

Clark bent over Eve's foot and licked it. He was anything but convincing as a foot fetishist. What Howard wanted to do was suck the chick's clit.

'Oh God! That feels so good!' The girl meant it. 'Don't stop. You make me wanna do things to please you, like letting you know that Divine's doing a personal appearance at the Rough Trade shop tomorrow!'

'What? Is this true?' Things were looking up for Howard as he gazed down at that alabaster foot.

'Yes, yes! But don't stop licking my toes!' Eve squealed.

'Give her more shrimp!' Motorway belched. 'I'm getting perfect shots on my camcorder! Get sucking, you can ask her about Divine afterwards!'

The Mexican's Dream

After drinking eight Harvey Wallbangers with chasers, Jayne F. Dean drove the car at 120 mph through the deserted streets of Paris. As she entered a tunnel, one end of the long stole that was wrapped around her neck was thrown out of an open window by a man wearing a black two-piece suit. The three tramps on the grassy knoll raised their bowler hats as the scarf caught in the back wheel of the Mercedes. Cut to stock footage of Dean's Satanist boyfriend accidentally decapitating a photograph of the actress as he clips a story about black magic from a newspaper. Clenched teeth and cries of 'Leviathan' from the chorus.

The Mercedes emerged on the north side of the Blackwall

Tunnel with a coffin strapped to the roof rack. Crowds lined the streets throwing rotten tomatoes at the car and waving red flags. Rioting broke out on the Teviot estate. The lid of the coffin creaked open and the actress sat upright, took her head in her hands and placed it back on her shoulders. Rapturous applause. As the streets emptied and the car headed along the North Circular towards the MI, a naked male rose from the coffin. The fiend unfolded a collapsing seat. He settled down on it and after picking up a rod, ordered Dean to place herself over his knee.

The fury began to birch and though the rod was but a toy, the birching was no child's play. Swinging the switch high above his head for each stroke, the demon laid on the cuts slowly, with graceful sweeps of his round red arm and with such force that his body shook and the muscles of his bottom quivered each time he struck a blow.

The little be-ribboned birch rod hissed as it swept through the air and it made a sharp swishing noise as it fell on the rotten flesh encasing a well irrigated arse. The creamy skin reddened rapidly, and small weals rose in all directions on the broad, plump cheeks. Dean had winced sharply on receiving the first cut, the pain evidently being greater than she had expected; then she stiffened herself, clenched her fingers in the palms of her hands, causing several of them to drop off, and lay perfectly still. Nevertheless, her foul flesh quivered involuntarily at each stinging cut of the little rod.

A Flat in Chelsea

Howard Clark and Mark One were sitting drinking tea in the Mexican's living room with Eve and Stewart Home. Eve was still wearing her Constable T-shirt, Home was geared up in a hooded top emblazoned with the word 'PLAGIARISM'. At the author's feet there was a carrier bag stuffed with a number of thick A4 envelopes.

'Show me the film script!' Clark demanded seconds after Home plonked himself down on a chair.

'I'll need to see the colour of your money first.' At five feet nine Stewart was every inch the consummate professional.

'Will a cheque do?' Juan hiccuped.

'Wot?' Home was getting mad. 'Do you think I was born yesterday? Next you'll be telling me your production set up is registered for legal purposes as the Vulcanised Rubber Company.'

'Are you saying we're the Dambusters of the movie world?' The Mexican didn't like being insulted.

'Yes I am.' Stewart was determined to press home his advantage. 'Your films always bomb and your cheques always bounce.'

'Cool it.' Howard was determined to take possession of the film script the hot-headed young writer had knocked up overnight.

'Look,' Home had only been establishing a negotiating position, 'show me a few bank statements and I'll consider part payment by cheque.'

Since Clark was an undischarged bankrupt, that left Juan's Nat West account as all that could be used as a basis on which to assess the duo's assets. This was a little embarrassing since the Mexican's cash reserves rarely hit the three figure mark and had never got anywhere near four digits in the ten years he'd had the account.

'Okay,' Motorway was trying to sound casual, 'we haven't actually got five thousand pounds but we could come to some arrangement where we pay you so much every week.'

'Stuff that, I'm not taking payment on the never never. Just tell me exactly how much you've got.'

'Sixty three quid and ninety seven pence,' Mark admitted candidly, 'however, we can only afford fifty nicker since we need a few bob for bus fares and shit.'

'Well,' Home hedged, 'I can't let you have the script I knocked up last night for fifty quid. I'll flog that off elsewhere. However, I do have an experimental piece I'll sell you cheap. Give me the money and you'll get something quite unusual.'

'Here you go,' Juan said as he counted out five crumpled tenners.

Home pulled an envelope from his carrier and as he attempted to give it to the Mexican, Howard snatched it from his hand. The artist pulled out a wad of xeroxes and began to flip through them. As he did this, the smile on his face was quickly transformed into a frown.

'This is rubbish,' Clark complained. 'We can't do anything with this, it's just a load of photocopied gas bills and shopping lists!'

'Give us our money back!' Motorway demanded.

'Hold on a minute,' Home was supremely confident, 'and let me explain. This is an experimental film script. It works like the instructions for a Fluxus performance and related avant-garde art works. The actor and actresses read a section and it suggests things to them. Like all scripts, mine require interpretation and the looseness of the plotting serves to free up the reader's imagination. It's amazing what a randy actress will draw out of an experimental work.'

'Well, what does this suggest to you?' Howard demanded as he passed over a copy of an ancient electricity bill.

'Let me see,' Stewart was an old hand at this game. 'The bill is for £11.13. Numerologically that is one and one, which is two. Then you've got another one, taking you up to three. Finally, there's the three, so two times three equals six. That sounds pretty much like sex. It reminds me of an indie band I was once in. The singer was taking a sociology degree and writing her dissertation on the sex industry. As a piece of participant observation, she decided to work as a stripper and topless go-go dancer. She was living in Soho and doing this nude dancing, twenty minutes on, then rushing back to her bedsit for forty minutes off. So you have this character called the Jumble Sale Queen, who's not got that great a voice but she likes to get her kit off. She's back at her place between strips and across the way there are a couple into group sex. The bloke is in his early thirties and his teenage girlfriend and another seventeen-year-old are shagging him as the Jumble Sale Queen and one of her many admirers watch.'

'This is good,' Clark admitted, 'but I need more insight into the Jumble Sale Queen's character.'

'The Jumble Sale Queen,' Home didn't need to ad lib because this was all based on his experience of being a monumentally unsuccessful rock musician, 'had a huge wardrobe of highly fashionable secondhand clothes but because her flat was damp, they'd all got mildewed. One of her quirkier characteristics was that she always wore her jumpers inside out when she was at home. This is something her mother taught her to do because then if she spilt egg down the front, she could turn the sweater the right way out and no one would know what a mess it was in.'

'Okay, okay,' Howard interrupted, 'you've convinced me the script is worth fifty quid.'

After Stewart and Eve split, Howard and Juan discussed every avenue they could follow up for film finance. While both now considered the fifty quid a good investment for a completed Stewart Home script, the name on it was clearly more important than the actual writing. Financial backers want to know there is a script, they don't necessarily need to read it.

'Let's shift our arses, I wanna get out of here and up to Rough Trade!' Howard was agitated.

'Keep your hair on! It's not even eleven and your idol isn't scheduled to show before noon,' the Mexican sulked. 'I think your attitude towards Divine borders on obsession.'

'I don't wanna be late, this is one of the few chances we're ever gonna have to get close to Divine. Although we've made contact with her management company, there's no guarantee they'll present our proposal to her in a favourable light. The personal touch is the best way to deal with stars of Divine's calibre.'

The conversation was interrupted by a knock at the door. Juan got up and padded out of the room. Clark pulled a picture of Divine from his pocket and kissed it. Judy Jones made her way into the room followed by Motorway.

'I didn't let her in, she pushed past me,' Juan stumbled.

'How the fuck did you know where to find me?' Howard attempted to put Judy in her place with a withering glare.

'I dropped a homing device into your coat pocket. I bought

a dozen of them from a mail order firm who advertise in *Private Eye*.'

'Is this it?' Clark demanded after rummaging in his jacket and pulling out a piece of metal.

'Yes.'

'Have it back!' The artist handed his obsessive fan the bug. 'Look Judy, I've got a lot on today. I'll have sex with you and then you'll have to go.'

'You treat me like a prostitute!'

'I wasn't offering to pay you, but if you wanna turn tricks, I'm quite happy to take a cut of the profits.'

Howard and Juan put their coats on. Judy Jones watched; eventually it dawned on her that the men were about to leave. She considered her position, weighing and judging the evidence of her eyes before announcing:

'I'm coming with you.'

'Oh no you're not!' Clark contradicted as he picked up a length of rope from among the sex toys that lay scattered across the Mexican's living room floor.

Juan rushed to Howard's assistance as the artist pushed Jones into a wooden chair. They tied the girl to the seat and gagged her. The Mexican removed one of Judy's boots and filled it with custard. He then put the DM back on Judy's foot, while Clark removed the other boot and filled it with slop. Once they'd done this, the two men walked to the door from where they waved at Judy.

'We'll see you later,' Howard giggled.

Seeing Judy tied to a chair with her feet dipped in custard made Clark realise how sad and pathetic this young woman's life had been. Nevertheless, humiliating her had become a thrill the artist would find it hard to live without.

Talbot Road

After the Anal Exciters had set up their gear at the Rough Trade shop, Jim drove them a few blocks down the road so that they could sort out some personal matters in private. Green had just discovered that Gary McMara was lobbying the musicians in the band to sack him. Gazza wanted to take over as frontperson; being the group's secret weapon no longer satisfied her huge ego. Fortunately, the band had rejected McMara's suggestion out of hand since she could neither sing nor drive. For Jimmy, humiliating and punishing Gazza had become a pressing necessity. McMara was bundled out of the car and shoved around to the boot. She was bent over the hatchback while her wrists were strapped to the roof rack. The girl had never before been tied up for a whipping and she became dreadfully frightened and started to whimper.

Jimmy began the spanking. The smacks sounded loudly as they fell in slow succession on the flabby flesh and at each smack the marks of Green's fingers were printed in red on the slack, yellow-grey skin. McMara bore two or three slaps pretty quietly, then she burst into a loud fit of crying and winced at each smack After this, the singer picked up a rod and the birching began. Each cut extracted a loud, shrill squeal from McMara, making her twist about in anguish, while small purple weals rose in all directions on the red skin. Gazza writhed and cried, plunged and begged abjectly for mercy. Jimmy was mad as hell and gave no quarter.

Portobello Road

Howard Clark and Mark One strode down Portobello Road towards Rough Trade.

'Something's wrong! There should be crowds of young men milling about in the street!' Clark felt a sinking feeling in his guts as he dashed into Talbot Road with Mark One trotting along behind him.

'Where's Divine?' Howard raged at a Rough Trade shop assistant.

'Divine isn't doing a personal appearance here, you'll find her at our other shop in Covent Garden. The Anal Exciters are playing here today.'

'Fuck it!' Clark swore, then turning to the Mexican added: 'Come on, let's get outta here, we've gotta get across town double quick.'

'Why don't you stay?' the shop assistant suggested. 'The Anal Exciters will be playing in a couple of minutes, while Divine won't be dropping in to our other store until one o'clock.'

'Yeah, let's stay or we'll never see the Anal Exciters play in front of an audience!' Juan put in.

Jim Green led his backing band into the shop and after picking up the gear that had already been set up, they began grooving. Suddenly the place was full of kids, with everyone getting down to the vibe. Gary McMara had been left trussed up in the band's car.

A Flat in Chelsea

Judy Jones was still tied to a chair, struggling vainly and giving out muffled moans. Every time she moved, the custard in her boots squelched and as a result she had an orgasm. Judy rocked violently and the chair she was tied to tipped over. She wriggled across to the phone – which was sitting on the floor – and knocked the receiver off the hook with her chin. Judy then punched out a number using her nose against the push buttons. This took an extraordinary amount of effort.

'I'm sorry, the number you have dialled is not available,' a telephonist's voice announced.

Judy frowned and attempted to push down the phone hook with her forehead. Custard splashed down her legs and she let out a muffled moan of pleasure.

Talbot Road

The Anal Exciters were socialising with their fans after a twenty-minute performance. Jimmy recognised Howard Clark who was arguing with Mark One. The singer immediately walked over to the artist and film-maker.

'We've got to go now or we'll miss Divine,' Clark stropped.

'We've got enough time to say hello to the Anal Exciters, I promise you we won't miss Divine.'

'Hello Howard,' Jim Green was determined to make a good impression. 'It's great of you to come and see us today, and so soon after checking out one of our rehearsals. I can give you a lift to Covent Garden, since me and the rest of the boys are determined to catch this rare personal appearance by Divine. It'll be a bit cramped in the car but at least we'll get to know each other intimately, and we can natter about this film deal as we travel.'

Soon everything was agreed and Howard, the Mexican and the four members of the Anal Exciters were out on the street. The band were heartily sick of their secret weapon's huge ego and decided to dump her semi-naked on to the pavement. When McMara realised what was going on, she began to accuse each of them in turn of working for the secret state. Spanking no longer seemed like a harsh enough humiliation for Gazza and the Exciters quickly hit upon the idea of paying a crackhead to fuck her up the arse. They soon found a boy prepared to perform this odious deed for a tenner but he had trouble getting it up. After an abortive attempt at buggery, Motorway dropped on his knees in front of the druggie and to everyone's astonishment, took the teenager's tool in his hand and began manipulating it with a skilful touch.

'Oh how miserable and flabby it looks, but I'll soon make it stiff,' Juan announced.

Then bending down his head, the Mexican took the drooping prick into his mouth and tickled the tip of it with his hot tongue. Drawing the foreskin backwards and forwards over the nut with his lips, soon brought the member to full erection. McMara lay spread-eagled and trussed-up in the middle of the road, the crackhead walked across to the she-creature and immediately battered into the crepe-tissue of her arsehole. The Anal Exciters clapped loudly and wolf-whistled. However, their amusement was short-lived since a van careered around the corner and ran over the copulating couple, killing them instantly. The survivors leapt into Jimmy's car and sped eastwards.

Neal's Yard

Howard Clark, Mark One and the Anal Exciters dashed up to the Covent Garden Rough Trade shop and stopped outside it. There were no crowds milling around the doors, so it was obvious that Divine must be elsewhere.

'Fuck it! We're too late! We've missed her!' Howard tugged at his hair as he said this.

Split seconds later, Divine walked into Neal's Yard with her entourage, clocked Clark, then walked up to him and threw her arms around his neck before kissing him on the cheek. Bits of her flesh were falling off, she'd lost several fingers, all her teeth and a hell of a lot of weight. Being dead had clearly fucked the cult figure's health but she was still unmistakably Divine.

'Howard Clark! I don't believe it!' Divine boomed. 'We could have so easily missed each other, it got so crowded in the shop that we took all the fans wanting autographs to a larger venue around the corner. I only came back to thank the Rough Trade staff for their hard work on my behalf!'

'I'm a big fan of your music!' Clark felt like a blushing schoolboy having his first crush.

'And I absolutely love your art work!' Divine enthused. 'I'm organising a boycott of Sweetimes Choco Bars because of the way those bastards have persecuted you!'

'God, you look even better in death than you do in photographs! You're delicious!' Howard spluttered almost incoherently as he stood back and gave his idol the once-over.

'Thanks.' As she said it Divine winked, and since the eyelid wouldn't reopen, she had to tear it off with her right hand and throw the rotting piece of flesh in a conveniently placed garbage can. 'You don't look bad yourself. Unfortunately, I've gotta rush off in a minute, I'm supposed to be doing a secret gig at the Acklam Hall with a backing band whose flight from Rome has been cancelled. I've got to round up some replacements!'

'Let me introduce you to my friends the Anal Exciters! I'm sure they'd be very happy to help you out!' Clark gesticulated.

'We'd love to help you, it would be an honour!' the Exciters sang out together.

'Wow, I'm flattered, I read in the music press that you are the future of rock 'n' roll!' Divine croaked before turning to Clark and saying: 'Okay, before I take the Anal Exciters away for a quick rehearsal and sound check, there's some stuff you should know. When I told the devil how much I admired your art, he confessed to working for this organisation called the Worshipful Company of Arts Administrators who have been conspiring against you. The blighters have been giving you the run around. There's a bloke called Napoleon pretending he's gonna buy a load of films from you, but be warned, he'll never pay up. Some other geezer is impersonating my manager and although I wanna star in your movie, this bloke can't arrange it for you. The cads have also signed the Anal Exciters to some tacky management deal, so you boys better be careful!'

'Luckily I substituted my HP agreement for the management contract, so we're only obliged to pay off the cost of a colour TV,' Gordon crowed.

'Your what?' Jim railed as he slapped the guitarist across the cheek.

'He's saved your career, you should be thanking him!' Divine announced as she pulled the singer away from the guitarist. Then she turned towards an assistant who'd been lurking in the background. 'Charlie, over here, I want you to tell Howard all about the Worshipful Company of Arts Administrators.'

After kissing Howard Clark, Divine made tracks with the Anal Exciters. Howard had strict instructions to get backstage at the

Acklam Hall before the gig started. In the meantime, Charlie would tell him everything he needed to know.

101 Snack Bar

Howard Clark and Mark One were drinking tea in the 101 Snack Bar. Customers came and went, buying fags and snacks. There was a steady take out trade from people working in the Charing X Road area but not much room in the caff for people who wanted a seat.

'What's the next move?' the Mexican demanded.

'I should go and see that banker bird we met yesterday,' Clark chattered. 'I've got her card in my pocket. I wanna sort out the finance for our movie before we meet up with Divine again. We've gotta look professional, have everything properly prepared before we discuss the film with our star. After I've sorted out the money, I'm gonna call on some old mates in the East End. I know a few squatters who'll help me put an end to the evil operations of the Worshipful Company of Arts Administrators.'

'That sounds good!' the Mexican retorted. 'I'd better go and free the chick who's tied up in my flat. We can't leave her there forever. Hopefully, she'll have learnt her lesson about harassing blokes. I'll meet you at Finches at five o'clock, that way we'll have time for a pint before we pop down the road to catch the secret Divine show at the Acklam Hall.'

'Before you split, we'd better work out a rough budget for the movie. That banker chick said once we'd come up with the figures, she'd put the finance through on the nod.'

'I've got a pen, have you got a piece of paper?'

'Nah, but we can use this!' Clark handed Juan a napkin.

'We'll need cameras and a crew but we won't be able to pay most of the cast.'

'We'll have to pay Divine, she's the star, her fee should be the biggest single item in the budget.'

'How much do you think she should get?'

'Let's work out the budget and give her thirty per cent on top of that!'

A Bank in Central London

Howard Clark was sitting in the clients' chair, Hannah Deserts was in total command of the situation. The room was painted a tasteful canary yellow and decorated with full colour photographic prints of cattle mutilations.

'Here you are, three hundred thousand pounds in used notes, you can count it if you like.' Hannah grinned as she opened a suitcase full of money and slid it across her desk.

'It's okay, I trust you.' Howard closed the suitcase before placing it between his legs.

'I thought it would be better giving you cash, that way you can hire a lot of people cut price on the black.'

'You're so thoughtful.'

'That's because I like you a lot. In fact, you make me feel kind of submissive. Usually, I'm a top. I have a lot of fun coming on sexually with the small businessmen who approach me for loans. I drive a lot of them crazy! They can't follow through on the sexual signals I send out for fear that they're misinterpreting the vibes I'm giving off! I come on very offended if they give me any innuendo. The bastards are like putty in my hands, desperate to fuck me but also terrified I won't give them a loan!'

'Power corrupts, absolute power corrupts absolutely.'

'That's what I liked about your art work, you've never been afraid to use clichés! Now throw me over a piece of furniture and sniff my beautifully formed behind!'

Howard got up, walked around the desk and hauled the bank manageress out of her chair. He threw her over an overstuffed sofa and lifted her skirt up. She was wearing black stockings held up by suspenders but no knickers. She had a fake tiger tail hanging from the base of her spine. The tail shot up as Clark bent forward and sniffed her bottom.

'Arses smell so much nicer than feet!' Howard could feel a grin spreading across his face as he said it.

A Flat in Chelsea

Judy Jones was still tied to the chair, punching out a number on the telephone, using her nose against the push buttons. This took an extraordinary amount of effort because her attention was endlessly distracted. She was sexually aroused by the custard squelching in her boots every time she shifted her weight.

'I'm sorry, the number you have dialled is not available,' a telephonist's voice announced.

Judy frowned, then attempted to push down the phone hook with her chin as Mark One entered the room.

'What the fuck are you doing?' the Mexican snarled.

Motorway strode over to Judy and untied the gag that bound her mouth, then replaced the receiver.

'What are you gonna do to me, you beautiful bastard? God, I feel so horny, no one has ever made me feel like this before! That custard squelching in my boots has really turned me on,' Judy's frail grip on reality had completely snapped.

'Who were you trying to call?' Juan inhaled.

'Pour a can of spaghetti over me and I might tell you!' Judy's voice rose an octave as she spoke.

'Just tell me!' The Mexican was doing his hard man act.

'God, you're so manly, I'm gonna have to obey your commands!'

'Spit it out, who were you trying to call?'

'My friend Jane. Last time I spoke to her she said she was having trouble paying the phone bills, I guess she must have been cut off.'

'Why didn't you try to call the cops?'

'Because you've taught me something very fundamental about myself. Until this morning, I hadn't realised I was a food fetishist! Now, for God's sake, get a tin of something from the kitchen and pour it down the front of my dress! Forcing me to wait so long for consummation after such yummy foreplay has made me unbelievably horny! Unless you splatter me with food very soon, I think I'll go mad!'

'You're already mad and I'm not gonna splash tinned spaghetti over your tits.'

'Why not?'

'I'm not doing it,' the Mexican swished as he untied the girl.

'I'll give you a blow job!' she offered.

'You don't understand.'

'What don't I understand?'

'I'm gay, I'm not interested in getting oral from a girl!'

'Oh, come on! Don't be so pathetic! Be a man! Once freed from the fetters of social convention, we're all polymorphous perverts!'

'But I like men!'

'What about if I offered to pour a tin of baked beans into your knickers?'

Judy took Mark's hand and dragged him into the kitchen. They threw open a cupboard and begin pulling items from it.

'Ooohhh, ooohhh, tinned spaghetti, I just love tinned spaghetti!' Judy was holding this prize against her breast.

'It's my favourite, I just love Daddy's.' Motorway closed his eyes as he clutched the brown sauce.

'Quick, get a tin opener!' Judy interpolated.

'I'll get the tin opener once you've poured this bottle of brown sauce into my briefs.'

Judy took the bottle from Mark's outstretched hand, undid his flies and poured the sauce into his knickers. The Mexican took an opener from a drawer, wrenched it around the spaghetti tin and splattered the contents over Judy's top. Then the two perverts fell to the floor moaning mechanically.

Beck Road

Howard Clark was banging on the portal of a squat. A crusty called

Nick opened the door. He was dressed up in a white bunny outfit and had a tube of smarties in his left hand.

'Yo Nick!' Clark greeted his friend.

'Yo Howard!' Nick echoed. 'Come in!'

'I haven't got time, get the crew out, we've gotta go on a blitzkrieg! There's some folk who've been pissing me about and I wanna pay them back in their own coin.'

'Okay, I'll get the boys.'

'Hey fellas, get on out here, Howard needs some help fucking over a bunch of bad men!' Nick had turned around and was leaning back into the hallway as he shouted.

In single file, lots of youths, dressed up in all sorts of animal costumes, trooped out of the squat and into the street. It didn't take long to march on the City of London. The mob assembled in the street outside the Worshipful Company of Arts Administrators' HQ. They had anger in their hearts and Molotov cocktails with lit fuses in their hands.

'Now!' Howard Clark yelled.

Everyone present hurled their petrol bomb. This was followed by a stock shot of a building exploding. Cut to shot of people running down the street. Flames, burning, smoke, sound of sirens.

Finches Pub

Howard Clark was standing at the bar drinking a pint. He looked at his watch and scowled. Moments later, Mark One and Judy Jones walked into Finches. Howard stared in disbelief at Mark and his companion.

'You're late and what the fuck is she doing with you?' Howard was on the verge of throwing a tantrum.

'It's a long story. I told Judy she couldn't come with me but she insisted. She's a very persuasive woman.' The Mexican looked sheepish.

'Save it, we'd better get a move on, it's nearly five-thirty, I don't wanna be late for Divine!'

Having said this, Clark stepped back from the bar. Mark One and Judy Jones turned to follow him.

'Hold on a minute, you're not coming with us!' Howard stabbed a finger at Judy.

'Yes I am!' The girl stamped her foot to add emphasis to the statement.

'Hold out your hands!' Clark grimaced.

Judy did as she was told. Howard grabbed her wrists and dragged her to a pillar running up from the counter to the ceiling. He forced one arm either side of the post.

'I love it when you treat me rough!' Judy moaned mock sarcastically.

'There's a pair of handcuffs in my pocket, take them out and 'cuff her wrists.' Clark was addressing the Mexican.

Mark took the restraints out of Howard's poke and secured Judy to the pillar.

'I love it when I'm made to wait for sex!' Judy was getting excited, her knickers were wet.

'Hello doll, what are you drinkin'?' an ageing rocker leered at Judy as Howard and Juan made their way out of the pub.

Acklam Hall

Divine was on stage with the Anal Exciters rocking out behind her. The place was packed with both ordinary punters and rock journalists who considered this the hottest double act since Anthony and Cleopatra. Besides, it wasn't every day that a major star made a comeback from the dead.

'And now I'd like to introduce you all to the man who made this concert possible by suggesting the Anal Exciters act as my backing band,' Divine announced. 'I'm gonna be making a movie with this diamond geezer over the next couple of months, but right now what we're gonna do is sing a duet. This is Howard Clark, the famous artist, who's becoming an increasingly close friend of mine!'

Howard bounced out into the centre of the stage. He hugged and kissed Divine, holding the undead singer against him so tightly that one of the drag queen's arms fell off with a soft plopping sound. However, a roadie quickly fixed the arm back on to Divine's torso with some gaffer tape and the crowd went wild during an unworldly version of 'I've Got You Babe'. After the duet, the Anal Exciters launched into an up tempo number. The top flight rock managers Ron Rush and Derek Dosh were standing in front of the stage waving fat contracts at the musicians, both desperate to sign up the Anal Exciters before the A&R men who were crowding the bar got in on the act.

Credits unroll

Jenny Knight

'STUPID'

Jenny Knight is in her early twenties and a musician in the loosest sense of the word. She is not as stupid as she once was, but not entirely bright either. 'Schering PC4: a Love Story' was published in the *Typical Girls* anthology (Sceptre); her forthcoming novel is called *Lady Muck*.

You can snorkel for hours and not reach the other side. There are hundreds of rare, tropical strains of hair, dead skin and semen to be found. Personally, I always drop half a cigarette in, as the combined furriness of the bubbles and the smokeables cause my muscles to relax.

This is my first Jacuzzi, a murmuring marble monster squatting in the building site of the bathroom, brand new and sparkling seductively. It is as big as a truck, with special knobs and dials that some sly hand can twiddle, to make great whooshes of streams whoosh out into unsuspecting orifices, and a bubble-maker with all different settings that goes *bbbbrrrrrrrr*, frighteningly loud, so that you're up to your ears in foam in minutes. Daddy says one day he'll make the whole room water-tight, and we'll froth it up right to the ceiling! Soon! But for now, the Jacuzzi has leaked down to the floor below and the floor below that, which is the last straw for the tenants downstairs, who are already pissed off about the banging and the drilling and the phantoms outside that throw coins and cans up at the windows, and the girls with screaming babies on their scrawny hips always stalking poor Daddy, and the crazed hooker who periodically kicks the front door in. They vocalise all this in a fierce letter. Daddy puts it up on the pinboard, next to all the final demands.

'Once my bathroom is finished, I'll get in and never come out,'

Daddy tells me with his sad smile. 'Nobody will ever see me. They'll say: 'Where is he?'

'"Oh, he's in the Jacuzzi."

'And I'll get smaller and smaller like a shrivelled little prune until I disappear.'

I call him Daddy, so you don't need to know his real name. I'm not a pervert or anything. I'm just a little confused. I play the part. Some people hate that – hate stupid little girls with their saccharine 'wuv me' vulnerability trip – and I will too when I'm older. Will slap my head and roll my eyes. But some people go for it. So right now if you want me to be your stupid little girl, I will be. Get me while I'm young, Daddy, get me while I'm young. Just tell me what to do. Just call me Stupid. It's an unspoken agreement we have.

At eighteen, I am still precocious and coltish enough to pull off the whole knock-kneed Natalie Imbruglia / abused Bosnian orphan / pee-trickling-down-thin-thigh sort of look. My voice is calculatedly pitched in squeaky naiveté.

> *Wipe the smile off my face.*
> *Take the spring out of my step.*
> *I'm a bubble begging to be burst.*
> *Questions, questions! I'm so full of questions!*
> *And Daddy has all the answers.*

'You look beautiful tonight,' he says. And I do. We admire my legs, stretched out in front of me. I am his 'terrible teenage temptress'; I lead him astray I do! I'm a wicked girl I am! I must have been here forever. I am supposed to be at school, but I keep forgetting. In fact, I can't remember a fucking thing. Daddy has taught me to blot out everything. Blot out all the unpleasantness that most people have to deal with. He says I am unhappy, so I am. His heart bleeds for me. The last precious drops before it runs dry for good.

*   *   *

I lower myself into the warmth of the purring Jacuzzi, go slitty-eyed, watching my pebble-dash flesh turn pink. The builders have put in a little marbled ledge above the main arm rest. It officially acts as a soap dish, but Daddy has put a Coke bottle there. Resourceful Daddy! From where I float, I can load it up with smooth white pebbles and smoke with the most minimal of movements. The water closes in around my neck, comforting, pacifying, stupifying. It is deliberately warm, to lull me into a false sense of security. It is a malevolent mother. It seems to resent me. When I press the bubble-jet button with my big toe, a million little farts rise up at me in an impudent symphony. But I just laugh at them.

Daddy says he'll join me.

Soon.

Says it hourly, but then gets distracted and disappears. And here I am, waiting in the chilly water, trying to look shiveringly seductive. Eyeing up the Coke bottle and the soggy rocks. He shouts from downstairs: 'Soon!'

I spitefully sweep the drugs into the water.

'Soon' we will go on a proper date. Snap out of this. Show them all. This is apparently just a brief, weak interlude in the Life of Daddy. But I hope it never ends. If he snaps out of it, I will lose him. What grown man would want a stupid little girl?

I'm easily confused. He finds that endearing. I am especially confused when abandoned on a crack come-down, all wired and tired and terrible. He finds that tedious. Daddy keeps leaving me. He keeps wandering off to different parts of the house and doing things without me. He gets tired of me following him around. I sit on my bit of carpet with my can of beer and try to look attractive and like great company, but sometimes he is gone for hours. I bite my nails and clean between my toes distractedly. I can't remember what we've been arguing about, but I'm sure it's something. He will argue about nothing when he is like this. He seems unforgiving and stony and is pretending I'm not here. I try taking off more clothes. No dice.

Daddy has been smoking in the Jacuzzi for four hours. He has shut the door behind him. I sit on the other side of it and wait for him to come back. While I am waiting, I screech silently and claw at my face and pummel the air in front of me. He is two metres and a million miles away. I picture him, eyes shut, head back, mouth slack, red prick poking through the bubbles. His skin is now so stretched that his belly-button protrudes, the middle-age spread gone up in smoke. He says you should always listen to your body – it's a hell of a lot smarter than your mind. I can hear him exhaling a thick lungful. He is busy obeying his body; oblivious to me. Very quietly, I whine and scratch at the door. Finally he lets me in, and I gratefully envelop my puny nakedness with scummy bubbles. His ardour has cooled with the water. He shuts his eyes against me. I watch the jets carry him off . . .

. . . And then Daddy comes back to me, and here he is and here we go, and he grins and ruffles my hair and makes everything good again. I feel like wagging my tail and jumping up and licking his face, but I remain expressionless because I am eighteen and stupid and unsure. He crouches down and gives me all of his attention.

'Hello there, what have you been doing?'

Dying.

'Shall we get something to drink? Would you like that?'

Oh yes. I am dispatched to the offie with a fifty pound note, bursting with happiness.

Outside, outside the flat, the cosy bubble bursts and the world roars in. I am bombarded with badness. Bad people, bad business, bad area. Bad vibes, *maaaan*. The journey to the off licence is fraught with danger. I fight my way there like my life depends on it, all elbows and snarls, and return with our booty, half-hysterical.

Papa Bear always says: 'You don't have to leave. Why would you want to leave?'

And I can never remember.

'You're safe here. Everything's alright now, isn't it?'

Yes.

But three days later, when I don't know who I am anymore, he will decide it is now time for me to leave, and I won't know where it is I am supposed to be going, and I will wish that I would die, or that some jealous crackhead would kill me on my behalf.

But right now, I'm safe. Daddy coos sympathetically at the state I'm in. Undresses me attentively and puts a beer in my hand. Runs the water. All better now. I lie back on him and he turns the bubbles on gently and holds my head and puts the biro in my mouth. I close my eyes and suck on it like a good girl and he takes it away again. He says, 'You don't have to go home yet. You can go whenever you want to. Don't you worry about a thing.'

I mumble some weak-willed protestations about school, family, addiction, whatever, and then sink back and allow the water to swallow my neck and silence me. When I start to float off the seat with the bubble-jets, he secures me in a strangle-hold.

Secures me in a strangle-hold.

No one will ever love you like this again.

No.

No.

There isn't much of a courtship. We coyly float nearer and nearer towards each other until Daddy takes advantage of an unexpected jet to propel himself on top of me, and soon we are ricocheting around the tub, bouncing off one stream after another, and snogging for dear life. I start to panic as I keep going under, so I grab hold of Daddy's hair and he stops poking about long enough to spin me around and secure me in the traditional life-saving hold. It seems that this may be a satisfactory solution until Daddy starts spluttering and slipping too, so we decide to call it quits and swim for dry land. Daddy wraps me up in a big dust-sheet and puts on his jeans. They hang off him, and his curls bob wetly over his Mutley-grin.

'That was fun, wasn't it?'

Yes! We tread the iron spiral stairs carefully under our pink, tender feet. Back downstairs, Daddy falls asleep on the burnt carpet in front of *Knots Landing*, with his head collapsing on to my stomach and his elbow denting my budding tit. This is very uncomfortable for me, but it is all I ever wanted. I fling out an arm and sift through the carpet fibres, lay my ash on the foil and reverently light a lump. I feel scared, like I'm doing something I shouldn't be. Somebody stop me! Nobody does, and as I am just an irresponsible JD, of course I go ahead and do it. My mouth goes numb, and so do I.

I don't think I'll ever sleep again. I am slack-jawed and still, in front of MTV. Daddy is snoring softly, oblivious. I tiptoe around and steal things. Coins, fags, photos, letters. Slip them into my clothes as quiet as a mouse and as dirty as a rat. I have always been a thief, pocketing little tokens and prizes and pieces of people wherever I go. To trap a part of them forever.

But back to the matter in hand.

I have made a miscalculation. I turn hot and cold and hot again and I feel like I'm gonna puke. Not happy. The stillness of the early hours always makes me feel uneasy. Daddy has gone to sleep and left me on my own. He promised he wouldn't. He always falls asleep with the blink of an eye at unexpected times and in unexpected places. I am envious. I sit and look at the back of his head for a long time, unable to do anything else. I am abandoned. I need reassurance. I need attention. I need a drink. Wanker. I am wide-eyed and grinding, hunched up so tight I might implode. Things keep flashing before my eyes, too fast for me to discern. Strange things creeping up on me like they're trying to tell me something. I say nothing.

I don't think I'll ever sleep again.

I wake up in Daddy's slumbering arms. Outside it is sickeningly light, and the market palaver is at a steady midday pitch. I don't know what day it is, but it won't go away. Whatever it is, it is insistent that it is time for Daddy to wake up and leave me. I can't do anything about this. I am filled with doom, and my teeth are aching. My head is mashed against the pillow where I left it, and the pillow is sodden with drool. If I swing my eyes as high as they will go, I can see MTV. It is the same video I fell asleep to, on heavy rotation. The sound is muted, but its repetitive hook plays insistently through my head over and over and over until it's all I know and have ever known. My mouth tastes horrible. If I swing my eyes as low as they will go, I can see my tongue is thickly coated with a heavy beige mucus. I don't know what to do about it. I put it back in my mouth for safe keeping. My left nostril itches unbearably. I am extremely uncomfortable, but I don't dare move for fear of waking Daddy. If Daddy wakes, he will more than likely get up and leave. My left nostril screams at me. I whimper back at it. I make a minute, ineffectual wiping motion on the pillow with my head in an effort to placate it. Ordinarily, I realise, when I am all lonely and cracking up, actual blows to the head will not wake Daddy, so it is highly unlikely that a small finger up my own nose will. But I cannot risk that. So I lie here very quiet for more than fifteen minutes before the phone rings. Daddy starts and jumps up. Seems bewildered to find an admirable pair of legs entwined with his. His nostrils are a mesh of snot. His hair is standing on end. He does his crinkly-eyed beam.

'Whah, eh? Oh, hello! What are you doing there?'

I look mournfully and meaningfully at him as he squints a smile and reaches for the phone.

Another thief, stealing him from me. The Bringer of Drugs. He is pleased.

He is gone again.

Daddy doesn't have to light me – I can light myself – but I think we both get a kick out of it. I sit between his legs, and he carefully picks out one big round cream rock and two little ones from the piles along the bidet. Encircles me and the pipe in his arms.

'Just a teeny one. That's huge!' I say, feebly.

'It looks huge, but it's flat,' says Daddy, placing a rounded monster on the foil.

He lights them thoroughly, tenderly holding my hair from my face and watching me as I suck hard. I eye the melting rocks carefully to be sure I have every last drop, then put the pipe down and squeeze my nose, holding it all in 'til I'm about to bust. The fun bit is over. I watch the grey smoke oozing out to make sure I really got it good, and the strong taste of ether fills my mouth as I exhale. I go '*boof*' in distaste as the last bit comes out, and Daddy repeats '*boof*' after me, still watching. I feel the old dumb doubtfulness wash over me, the fear that I am maybe stupid, that I can't shake off. My mouth quickly goes numb and I champ on my tongue experimentally. I can no longer feel my ulcers. I am now high.

Then Daddy lights himself. I watch him very closely.

'Can it kill you?'

'No, no,' he wheezes.

He can't hold it in as long as me, and he starts to choke and *hack hack hack*.

'It's probably not that good for your lungs,' he eventually admits.

Feeling sick and miserable in the Jacuzzi. The sweet stench of burning plastic takes advantage of my passive state and plugs my nostrils like cruel fingers. A thin layer of scum coats the froth closing in around my neck. So sick.

'Poor baby,' Daddy says sympathetically and tries to blow the smoke away from me. He still smells. The room smells, the water smells, everything. It makes me ill. I decide I have classically conditioned myself against the drug and I will never be able to bear it again whether I want to or not.

I'm such a liar.

I'm so stupid.

Daddy sits between my legs and I wash his hair. His eyes are shut and his mouth caves open. He clutches the pipe like a security blanket, and I have to keep stopping shampooing so that he can smoke. I'm not enough. Needs smoke too. How does that make you feel? You're not enough. I fiddle with the grey hairs on his chest and finger the mole on his back. I listen to his breathing grow deeper, falling deeper into despair with it. Please wake up. He always wakes up with strange and exotic hairstyles, and doesn't notice for hours until one of the circling wolves is allowed in and compliments the chignon. I guard him jealously.

He likes going outside even less than me. Hasn't been out in months. Perhaps I am stronger than him. Remember that terrible moment of realisation as a child when you realise Daddy doesn't have all the answers after all?

We call a cab to bring us cigarettes. My brand, his treat. They deliver them to the door. I have to go down to the door to fetch them, though, with one of his fifty pound notes. Right now, I am not too young to feel the rapid deterioration of my lungs, but far too young to care. Each ragged gasp placates me. Reassures me I'm still here and someone is moving me through the motions. Right now, I have just become an adult, but I can still get away with pre-pubescent behaviour in certain circles, with certain men. Girls hate me. I hate girls. Daddy likes me, I think. He is kind enough to pretend he does, at least. I am training him to start hitting me. Be a disciplinarian Daddy. Smack me about proper. I nag him constantly.

Pleee-aasee.

He takes a sighing lungful. 'Soon,' he promises with a vague pat.

'Soon.'

But soon it will suck me under. I'm trying to be strong, but I don't know how ... or what the hell for. Maybe it would be better if I drowned. Pulled under the dirty water and eaten away like acid. My clean, bleached bones will float to the surface and be lovingly boxed by my grieving parents, as beautiful remnants of my former self. Aw, it's fucking tragic. I'm such a sentimentalist. Box my ears, not my bones. Teach me a lesson. Before it's too late. I am so tired. Would you just please ... HIT me.

For now I must carry on working on my studies – that is becoming as bad as bad can be. And only then can I redeem myself and learn to be good for the first time in my life. I am a keen, attentive student. I am so busy learning and floating in my womb-like Jacuzzi that I forget about outside and school and the distant world over the Westway. Still, I have never been cleaner. Thanks to my useless Svengali.

Ruin me!

Harder!

Harder!

Maybe it's wrong. Maybe he's a bad man. But he can only ruin someone who allows themselves to be ruined. Same with anybody, any situation.

Later I will hate. Hate. Hate.

Now I will just lie back. Shut up. Be good.

I'm his girl. He says so. All his old girls line up outside at night and whimper and howl his name. He has cut them out like cancer, unmoved. He turns up MTV when they throw stones at the window, and disconnects his phone when they hit re-dial over and over. Chuckles at my troubled lower lip and gives me a stroke. Loads me up. Pulls me to him. And I let him. But I know someday he will suddenly cut me off for good, without notice, with nothing. Abandon me. Leave me in the thick of it. Leave me for dead. And then what will I do?

I don't care.

There are people I could turn to, centres I could go to. But I won't. I won't care. I don't know why. But I do know that I will be cut off.

Soon.

I don't blame him.
I knew from the start.

The excitement of the Jacuzzi has worn off somewhat. Even when he remembers to run it, he forgets to get in it, and never quite gets round to joining me when I do. I don't like it on my own. The rumble of the jet flows is suddenly threatening, and the mounting bubbles ... ominous. Something is ending.

Of course, I suck it up. It's so romantic. He's going to die. I love it. My imagination runs wild. I will play the grieving girlfriend to the max and follow him down to my own tragic demise. What more could I ask for?

Daddy is lying on top of me in the Jacuzzi, dozing and drooling slightly. I've held him this way for hours. When he is fast asleep, I like to play with him. Interfere with his dreams. I scratch his stubble. Stick my fingers up his nose and watch his lips vibrate. Lift his eyelids so that the whites of his eyes gaze blankly at the ceiling. I examine every line and pore, and trace them tenderly. He looks exhausted. Poor thing probably hasn't slept properly in a week. Poor Daddy. I stroke his hair and take a handful of curls and consider plunging him under. It's for your own good, my sweet. There, there, Daddy, go to sleep. I place my hands on his head and gently duck him until the water reaches his upper lip. He splutters in his sleep. I let him bob up again. Like an anorexic, he bruises on contact. His back is a black and blue ordinance survey map of furniture. I squeeze his arm between mean finger and thumb and bruise him some more. He doesn't care. I don't care. There are people that care, but I've gone and forgotten them. I will care one day, when I grow up. Grow up to be appalled at all this nasty business.

What a *bastard!*
What a *stupid little girl!*
Etc.

Daddy will never grow up. No one will let him. They all need him. They all need him passive and pliant and pathetic.

A child. They will sit on his chest and keep him there, until he dies.

Soon.

Billy Childish

'BERNADETTE'

Billy Childish is a legendary figure in underground writing, painting and music. Born in Chatham, England in 1959 he left school at the age of sixteen, after being assured that he would amount to nothing. After working in Chatham's Naval Dockyard as an apprentice stone mason he enrolled for an unsatisfactory spell at art college, which ended with his expulsion. Diagnosed as dyslexic at the age of twenty-eight, Billy has published more than thirty poetry collections, and featured on over eighty LPs for a variety of independent record labels. He is the author of two novels, *My Fault* and *Notebooks of a Naked Youth* (both CodeX; Notebooks of a Naked Youth is published in the US by Sun Dog), and has exhibited his paintings all over the world. A major poetry collection, *i'd rather you lied: selected poems 1980–1998* is also published by CodeX. This story is an extract from his forthcoming novel, *Sex Crimes of the Future*.

'Ughh! Look at me, I'm coming! I mustn't, I must save it! Dear God, I swear on my mother's life never to wank myself off over the vile pornography of my fellow human beings ever again!' I look to the mirror and kiss it. 'On my honour! Ughh!' I'm on my knees, licking at the pages, the beautiful blonde hairs around Bernadette's noble arsehole. The paper goes damp, I see her little cunt peeping out at me from the next page, playing hide and seek with me, so to speak, tormenting me horribly.

'Ahh, Bernadette, such a lovely blonde arse, a real Nazi arse, an arse of the Third Reich!' When it comes to anal sex I really am what my mother calls 'a sodding bugger!' I dribble on the cheeks, biting at the quivering flesh. I stick my naughty little tongue in there as well, that's the sort of fellow I am – unabashed!

Bernadette's arse is not like my girlfriend Karima's arse – not in the least! Karima's arse is down in the cave, doing the hoovering or making some toast, I should think. 'Ha ha ha! ... Ahh – ohh – Jesus – fucking – Christ!' I really can't help pulling at myself Bernadette, but I mustn't!

Karima's arse isn't at all Nazi-ish, not in the least. Hers is a Turkish arse! A soft, dusky brown, an arse of the Ottoman Empire! A heavenly arse with a spray of dark fuzz just at the base of her spine.

There is very probably a camera in this toilet. I sit on the pan and turn the pages, the wallpaper is looking at me. It has flowers on it and inside the flowers are eyes and somebody's left the tap running. It really is as if someone is watching me. I have to stop myself from wanking, honestly, my cock's so hard it could spurt any second, without me even touching it!

Just now I said that Karima is probably doing the hoovering, which is a downright lie and I know it. Karima doesn't even own a Hoover. Actually, it was sarcasm, and then I smile to myself. That's what makes me so hateful – making up ridiculous, unfounded accusations about people and then laughing behind their backs without them even knowing about it. It's all the fault of my obnoxious nature.

'Oh, Bernadette, I love you, in my own special way, and your arse really is so pretty. I hold you to my lips and kiss you.'

I have a little bottle of whisky. I uncap it and lap at it like it's a teat, like it's one of her wonderful girl-like breasts. I take a hot swig and cough. I look down at myself, that's something I love to see – my cock swaying about like a bayonet ready to stab Bernadette's beautiful behind. I must mind that I don't split my foreskin again, it's fragile, it's too tight.

Back in her troll's cave, Karima fits it in for me. That's another sight I love to see, but in fact she can't manage it on account that my cock's too blunt. I have to ease it in there myself. Just fitting the knob in takes some manoeuvring but then it's held there like it's in a vice and she pumps up and down on it, her big arse cheeks shuddering as she goes into multiple orgasms.

'Just as soon as it goes in I start coming,' she says, and just hearing her talk that way makes my cock grow another inch. 'You can get it bigger than that,' she says, pulling on it, 'that's it, make it nice and thick!'

Her bed's so narrow that I can stand with one foot either side of it, put my hands on my hips and lower myself in there, my thighs and calves cramping. I spit on her arse and slap it. I really am like a porno star up there, riding away like a cowboy.

Karima looks over her shoulder, pulling at her arse cheeks. 'It's too big,' she says, 'I want more of it in there but it won't fit,' and I just keep staring at myself in disbelief, the veins swelling up. 'It's gonna come, where do you want it?'

'In my mouth!'

'Say please.'

'Please!'

Quickly, I pull the head out, step forward and squirting, feed it into her mouth. I'm on my tippy-toes, her little tongue flickering at the spunk hole as it leaps out of me, my thighs stuttering. It feels like the top of my skull is going to come off. I stagger and collapse on top of her. Karima rolls over, gurgling on it, then lies there smiling up at me like the cat that's got the cream and I kiss her, with her gob full of me.

Karima's half Turkish with tits like a pair of deflated Zeppelins!

'Ahh – ohh – ugh – ugh – ahh!' I rub my knob up and down the page of my Nazi girl's arse.

'Oh, how I love you Bernadette, if only we'd been in the SS together, with your black SS britches round your ankles, your lovely jackboots and a little Nazi dagger on your hip. Christ, I'll whip your muscular arse for you, you little BDM slut! You Nazi bitch! Ow! Your beautiful blonde arse. Bernadette, I want to spurt on it, to fuck it and come all over it, to drown it in spunk!'

Really, all my thoughts these days are sinful!

When I first saw you across the room, Bernadette, the scent of danger and sex filled my nostrils. I pretend not to be afraid of you yet all along I know that you could crush me under your heel at any moment, like as if I was nothing more than a poisonous insect. And so I took you home with me Bernadette, to hold you in my hands and conquer you. You must want me and desire me, Bernadette. I live through you, you hold my life in your masterful hands, will you give me sex, or will you reject me? Do I live or die? – Bernadette, you must decide.

I grin at her like a mad man. My SS princess. I glance fearfully at her hard face hoping for just a hint of a smile in her flint-like eyes.

I sit here shivering whispering to this sad girl until really I have to laugh at myself for pretending that I am a man at all. I whisper to the pages.

'It's true Bernadette, that I wish to conquer you, to pull you from your pedestal and drag you through the dirt, for you to hold me and desire me. For me to be your king. But I will be a merciful ruler, if you in turn will only be merciful with me: your eager slave. Let me be king of your body, Bernadette, let me mould you and put you on your knees before me.'

'Actually, I'm a poet, Bernadette, which is a scummy trade.' Really, I'm a painter, which is even worse. And I read you two of my poems, here in this toilet, two beautiful poems from my damaged heart. And you look out at me from beneath your insolent fringe and your eyes say I've heard all that stuff a hundred times before. Which only goes to prove that you are more than just a little bit stupid!

And I showed you my drawings, also in my notebook, and you raised your beautiful eyebrows and looked at me harshly. I lifted your face with my hand and tried to brush the hair from your eyes but you snapped at me, 'Don't do that!' You are German, or Polish, or possibly both, Bernadette, and can therefore be forgiven.

Turn to me, Bernadette and I'll bite your lips and spread your cherry-red lipstick right across your fucking mouth! Did anyone ever tell you that you look like Myra Hindley, Bernadette? Such a cold, hard face. I'll dribble you all over with goo and saliva, you beautiful, petulant child. And what lovely little teats you have, like naughty little puppy-dogs, like a twelve-year-old girl's tits, budding like rose buds, ready to be bitten and eaten.

Bernadette, I'm so full of pus and deceit! I'm drunk and my knob is going soft. Quick, Bernadette, turn around, stick your arse high in the air and let me lick at it again!

Suddenly the door handle turns and the man from across the landing tries to come in. I drop my book and lunge at the door, trying to hide my cock. 'There's someone in here!' I sob, pushing the door shut on his horrible leg. I kick at it and throw the bolt and stand there breathlessly with my trousers round my ankles, listening.

There's some rough out there and soon he will be banging the door down and treating me as if I have no rights to use the toilet at all, which I most certainly do! He is going to wake up the whole house banging around like that when I, as a paying tenant, have just as much right to use the facilities!

Well clear off you Nazi brute I'm fucking your women in here! And I start to sing Rule Britannia, Britannia rules the waves! I really sing it out, my knob being kissed and loved by her beautiful soft Nazi arsehole. 'Here's one from old Tommy, you Bosh wankers! Your hot little SS bitches like a length of English cock, so heil-bloody-Hitler!'

I sit and listen. I can hear him breathing on the other side of the door. He paces up and down then shouts at me to come out. I try to peek through the crack in the wood. Who is that berk out there, shouting his mouth off, German? German? 'Rule Britannia!' I look down and the sight of my fat cock in that undulating arse, it reminds me of my Turkish sweetheart. Ahhhh – ooooh – ahhhhhh – ooooh! – Karima! My legs trembling, stuffing my fat cock in there. I am beautiful, I am desired!

Is that a little piece of string I spy hanging from your cunt, Bernadette? And you reach between your legs, pull out that swab of blooded cotton and let it drop heavily into the open bog. Oh, so you're on, are you, you little SS slut?! You little Myra Hindley!

I raise the open whisky bottle to my lips and chug it back. The hot liquid is suddenly in my mouth. It surprises me, fighting its way up my nostrils until I snort like a bull.

Really, please, that I am so shy, that I blush, that I'm scared of the powerful race of women. But oh, how this one worships me! And I am a gentleman, I am a hero. Please, forgive me, God, for all my sins.

I lean over her pale back and kiss her hard mouth. So you've read poetry just like mine, Bernadette? And you've seen drawings just like mine, Bernadette? And now I'm fucking you in your soft little pussy – then in your wonderful arse – in your pussy – in your arse. And you're crying gently, biting the soft flesh in the crook of your arm.

Soon my book will be printed, Bernadette, it will have a spine and it will sit on the shelves of all the book shops of London town! And it will confound all those who dare to speak my name disrespectfully. William Loveday will not be made a mockery of again! All those who have damned me and wished me to amount to nothing. Mister Bennit and all my teachers who have hated me, and my parents whose eyes have never admired me, will be smashed from the field! And I will personally spit in the eye of every book shop owner who has said, 'Oh no Sir, our policy is that we can only display books on our shelves which have spines!' – Fine, you fork-tongued traitors of art, you illiterate geniuses, you want a spine? – then you shall have a spine! And you will crawl to me upon your bruised and damaged knees, Bernadette, and kiss my blood heavy cock, imploring me to read you my poems, which will fall like stones into your ice-cold heart.

'Bernadette! Uh – uh – uh – ahhh!' And I stagger, my thighs cramping. 'Achtung, I'ch comer!' and I pull my cock out and feed it spurting into Bernadette's upturned mouth. It covers her lips, it drips like glue, ruining the pages. So beautiful to see a cock spurting and to know that it is yours and to know that the tongue wants to love your spunk-hole and to drink it in torrents.

I fall broken to the floor, kissing her tears. 'Don't cry, my sweet Bernadette, my poor little SS princess.' And she smiles bravely up at me.

'Don't you cry when you come?' she speaks. 'I always cry when I come.' And I droop my head and kiss her teats, they have my spunk on them, like icing on two little cup cakes. I lick the cherries, collapsed there on that cold, tiled floor. Alone.

Suddenly there is a terrible rapping on the door. 'I have to go now, Bernadette, the Devil's running after me. Maybe there will be another sweetheart like you waiting for me in the next town, to help me to destroy my desperate heart and loneliness. But of course, she could never really replace you, Bernadette, for you are immaculate, you are alive, trembling with life. And you have given me everything so willingly. And besides, women hate me, Bernadette, and give me nothing. Can you believe that? Such a fine person as me, a young writer and an artist to boot, so capable of love, if only I was allowed to show it.'

'What the hell are you doing in there! I want to take a shit!'

Hurriedly I turn back the pages, trying to clean them with toilet paper. 'I'm scared that I might lose Karima, Bernadette, lose all the women and be left with nothing. Because there can never be enough women, Bernadette, to blot out the cold stare of my mother's disapproval.'

Bernadette pulls on her black stockings and we go to leave.

'Ouch! Look at your poor toe, it's almost hanging off! One of your poxy boyfriends tried to push you under a tram? Aw! it's black and blue. You should mind what arseholes you hang around with, Bernadette! Look after yourself, get yourself a nice fellow, an Englishman, like me.'

The man outside really does try to shoulder the door down like some kind of insane brute.

'Oh, if I could just stay and fuck you always, Bernadette, but no, the SS would be too fine a place for the likes of me. And besides, I am an Englishman and even though I despise my own race, I cannot deny my creed of moderation in all things.'

I look fearfully to the door. 'I must go now and leave this bathroom. I have to go back to England, Bernadette. And you must go back to wherever it is that you come from. I firstly am a painter, though of course I despise all painters. Secondly, I am a poet, though poets stink worse than the most villainous crooks.'

'Actually, to tell the honest truth, Bernadette, I only write out of boredom, to be adored – that's it! I do everything to be adored. But that doesn't necessarily mean that I worship success, Bernadette. In fact far from it. If somebody brought me success on a plate,

I would vomit on it before accepting so much as one stinking crumb of their humiliating charity!

'No, rather than be applauded for my genius, I will crawl under the floorboards and become a sucking louse, a pea-bug. Do you hear me, Bernadette?! I will become so small that nobody will ever find me! That's my ultimate ambition – to become a nothing! To become a zero! Because I'm afraid of my power and intellect, Bernadette.'

I go to open the door then turn back once more. 'Does that amuse you, Bernadette? Then good, because it was meant to be funny. Because I assure you that I will never be caught out or be surprised by anything. Because the only way to be truly safe is to never give anything away and to remain always closed. But that is also the way of the Devil, Bernadette, and to be a true artist I must do the exact opposite, I must open up every vein in my poor emaciated body, untangle every last nerve and be surprised by everything! Absolutely everything! Which I am not. Go ahead and mock me if you wish, Bernadette. I am, above all else, a contradiction and we artists are used to ridicule.'

Suddenly the door handle rattles most violently. 'What really seemed to annoy Mister Bennit the most was my complete lack of qualifications and the fact that I had no education. Also, that I lived in the provinces behaving cheekily and not believing in the seriousness of his position.'

'You see I am a rapscallion, Bernadette, a naughty little monkey.' I lift the pages to my mouth. 'Your tits taste of my spunk, Bernadette, you're naughty as well, aren't you, you little SS urchin! I will right my book, Bernadette. A book of beautiful poems, poems the like of which the world has never seen. Karima says that I should stop writing such filthy lies, but what she doesn't realise is that it is she who will get my book printed for me in her ridiculous art college!'

Bernadette pulls on her leather mini skirt, sticks her poor foot into her stilettos and hobbles out of the bathroom, me following.

There is a man standing in the hallway grimacing at me. He has such a dark look about his eyes that I have to look away out of decency. I push back my hair, light a hateful cigarette and walk past him. I wave my sweetheart goodbye. She's a tough one, stood there, all sex, pale broken and lost. A lovely one, one full of gonorrhoea and herpes.

Really, I have sinned against my own nature and humanity and I have only fooled myself. Puffing myself up in my own eyes with my devilish sex and this unknown woman. She has taken me into her mouth, her finger-tips have caressed me. I have been made alive by her, but by the same token she has killed me.

Really, her hand touched mine and already I was erect. I held my breath in my throat and looked down at myself, marvelling at her princesses' fingers stroking my rampant cock.

I am alive, I am loveable. The race of women accepts me as a man. I am William Loveday and I will humble them!

Darren Francis

'THE SPRAWL'

Darren Francis was born in London in 1969. He has appeared in several bands over the years and his fiction has been published in a number of publications and formats, including the collections *Skin* and *Technopagan* (Pulp Faction). 'The Sprawl' is excerpted from a novel in progress. For further information, details on other projects, readings etc., see: www.members.xoom.com/Akhenaten/

'Righty tighty,' Thurston says. 'We've got, oh, an hour and a half until boarding. Jisel, where did you put the coke?'

We're in the Gatwick departure lounge, already checked in, hand-luggage at our feet or over our shoulders: Thurston, Jisel, Wendall, Porn, Dennis, me.

'Thurston,' Porn says, 'I forbid you to take drugs on to that plane with you.'

'As my manager I'd expect nothing less of you. But it's okay. I'm not going to take them on with me. I'm not that stupid. We'll just do what we've got before we get on.'

'That's a good idea,' Jisel says, takes a phial of cocaine from her make-up bag. Her dress gleams like mother-of-pearl. I polish my sunglasses on my tee-shirt, belch in a flurry of repeating onions, feel almost healthy today.

'A damn fine idea.' Thurston itches eczema'd hands.

'Thurston,' Porn says, 'I want to make one thing categorically clear right now—'

'Yeah, sure, whatever, save it, grand-dad. Want a line, Jonah?'

Thurston bent over the toilet cistern, beating out cocaine lines on the bruised back of his filofax. I stand with my spine flat against the door, turn a cigarette in my fingers, feel sweat pulse on my temples.

'I always get stopped by customs, anyway.' Thurston so tall

he booms over every space he occupies. Immaculate KMFDM tee-shirt loose on his tight bones. 'It must be something in my face.'

'Or the fact that you normally can't walk past them in a straight line.'

'Yeah, it could be that too. I got strip-searched once, on the way back from Amsterdam. I ever tell you about that? What a weird old caper. Rubber gloves, the full monty. Had nothing on me, apart from some seriously hard-core porn, but they let me keep that. "A man needs a good and varied array of masturbatory material," I told them, "otherwise he can get too bored and frustrated, and what would happen then?" I think they understood. Pornography's cool. I admire its honesty. It doesn't claim to offer anything beyond the next hard-on. Anyway, I don't worry about customs anymore. Now I just stride right up to the fuckers and say, "I have nothing to declare except for my drunkenness". And Dennis was telling me that what he used to do ...'

He snorts the first line through a rolled-up five pound note, bangs cubicle walls, arms spread like Prometheus. 'Yeah ... What he used to do was tape wraps of speed inside the lining of his jacket. Apparently that fooled all but the most ardent searches.'

He snorts the second line, pockets the note, turns, smiles, hands me the coke.

'I'll meet you with the others,' he says. 'Don't take too long.'

I cut out and sniff a line, then piss with a shake and a flush before rejoining my friends.

'Madam, your carriage awaits,' Thurston says to Jisel, presenting the phial of coke on his out-stretched palm.

Jisel, thin as chicken wire, hair bleached blonde curls heaped forward, silver torque around each wrist, loose smile from a hundred magazine spreads. Ex-MTV face, a face in which you could crave the promise of anything, a face so architecturally perfect I can't believe she exists when I'm not looking at her.

'Can you please at least try to be discreet?' Porn says.

'I'm going for a pee,' Jisel says.

'I need to go too,' Dennis says. 'But I've got my own supply. I need to use it up before we get onboard.'

Dennis is an ex-Motorhead roadie who lives on Dunn's River Nourishment and mainline amphetamines, can't remember how he lost all his front teeth, and smells like he's been sleeping in Lemmy's cast-off leathers for the past three years. He roadies for us now.

'Sorry I was so long,' Jisel says on her return. 'I had to queue.'

'In an airport?' Thurston says.

'There was still a queue.'

'Isn't it quaint, the way chicks have to queue for the toilet? Right. Does anybody else need to go?'

'Don't talk about me like that,' Jisel says. 'You're not my father, so don't talk about me like that.'

'Sorry babes. Here comes Dennis. I reckon if we hurry we've got time for a swift pint or two.'

We leave the bar an hour later, barely make it before take off. Thurston has bought all of the seats two rows either side of us, so nobody can sit in them. The plane becomes a nightclub at 9,000 feet and rising. Thurston entertains us with tales of ne'er-do-wells, drunkenness, fisticuffs and villainy. I've heard most of them before in one shape or another. Like all of Thurston's stories I know they are not to be fully believed, that the kernel no doubt contains a truth but that the husk is repeated elaboration. In the toilet I mine a line of speed, didn't like to mention in front of Porn that a wrap lurked down my sock. Enough to synchronise equilibrium and altitude. Exhaustion closing around me like the fog of the world. I return to my friends, laugh and switch out from them, listen to Nick Cave on my Walkman, buoy through as the tape repeats over and over, 'Tender Prey' on one side and 'Kicking Against The Pricks' on the other.

JFK to Manhattan Island. It's every star you could wish upon. Songs and TV cop shows made New York as familiar as the London suburb I was birthed in. Coming here is like going home.

Tonight is still a young night; it has not snorted, copulated, inhaled, or fallen over drunken. We check into our hotel, dump bags in rooms that smell of bleach and starched cotton sheets. 'You may have read or seen it on TV that a man got shot in this room last week,' the bell-boy says as I drop my jacket on to the bed, 'but don't worry. We've cleaned it all up. You won't notice a thing.' Jisel and Thurston share one room, Wendall and me share another, Porn and Dennis each get a room to themselves. Nobody wants to share a room with Dennis.

'So, dude, have you worked out what's wrong with it yet?' Thurston says.

'Well, I'm not a technical man, but my initial assessment would have to be that it doesn't work.'

'We know it doesn't fucking work! That's why we're down here wasting time talking to you rather than standing up there and going through a few numbers. Now why doesn't it work?'

'Well as I say I'm not a technical man, but—'

'Will you please stop saying that? And how can you not be "a technical man"? You're a sound engineer, for Christ's sake!'

'Well I've yet to peak on my learning curve, so to speak . . .'

'Meaning you don't know what the fuck you're doing.'

'Well I wouldn't actually put it like that.'

'No? Then how would you put it? No, don't answer that. I know. You're not "a technical man". Look. Just get the motherfucker on its feet. I don't care how. Just do it. We'll be backstage. Give us a shout when you're done. And if it's not up and running by the time our manager arrives there'll be arses sore for miles around.'

We leave the sound engineer combing greasy nape-long hair with his fingers, tongue between lips as he reaches for his mobile. In the grotto of the dressing room I dine on a cigarette, watch Porn pace the floor and Dennis sat on a flight-case, disevering then tending the meat of his bong. Scrappy anaemic Wendall, smells of patchouli and pistachio nuts; palms flat on his knees, black dreads scurrying to his hips and stubble that never shifts. It's like any other skinny mirror-lined and black-walled dressing room I've seen, daubed with the names of bands never heard of since. Jisel has gone shopping.

'And the fucking beer's warm,' Thurston says. 'The rider was mighty early, I must say. Maybe the bar staff felt sorry for us. Porn, can you do me a favour?'

'What's that?' Porn says. Gunmetal silk suit. Scrotal heft of neck. Splodge of mishealed broken nose. Grey hairs stretching to the back of his head.

'Will you go and find me some drugs?' Thurston says.

'No, I won't. And you know me, Thurston. Am I the kind of man who would refuse you anything?'

'But you have to.'

'Thurston, come on, don't mess this up. The band are in the States, there's a lot of people out here very excited, a lot of people who want to see and hear the new material. And I should also remind you that we don't as yet have a US record deal. Speaking of which, there are some people over here I want you to meet. This is a big thing for you guys, now please, don't mess it up.'

'Porn, believe me, I've no intention of doing any such thing, and neither should you. Now I'll ask you one more time. Pretty please, just be a good boy, fuck off and don't come back until you have procured me some chemicals.'

'You can't talk to me like that!'

'The hell I can't!'

Porn looks at each of us, one at a time: Thurston, Wendall, Me, Dennis, Thurston.

'Then I quit!' he says, and turns to leave.

'You can't quit,' Thurston says, 'because you're fired.'

'No,' Porn says, 'I have quit. And I shall be calling the press tomorrow to explain the situation.'

'Yeah, right,' Thurston says, 'as if anybody could give a toss. Just fuck off. I don't want to see your face around these parts again.'

'Children, children ...' Wendall says. 'Aren't we forgetting something?'

'What's that?' splinters Thurston.

'We're here for a reason. We have a job to do.'

'We do?'

'The band. The tour. Remember?'

'Oh yeah,' Thurston says. 'That's right. Now let's start to be a bit more fucking professional about this, shall we? Or it won't be Porn that quits.'

'No problem,' Dennis says. 'Classic OOBE.'

'Pardon?' Quadraphonic.

'Out Of Band Experience. Happens to the best of them.'

'Thank you, Dennis,' Porn says. 'Thurston, I'll make a deal with you. No drugs until after the gig. After the gig you can do whatever you want. That's your time, not band time.'

'At least let the dog see the rabbit ...'

'Thurston.'

'Oh come on ... Music without drugs? I'd rather have a day job.'

'Thurston, we've just had this conversation. I don't want to have it again. I trust this is the last we shall hear on the matter.'

'It's certainly the last you'll hear from me.'

'Good. I trust we both know where we stand. Now I'm going to talk to that sound engineer, then I need to make some calls and see a few people.'

When Porn has departed Thurston steps up to Dennis, gives him a wodge of hundred dollar bills. As usual Dennis has only washed areas of skin that might be exposed in public.

'Dennis, could you go and find me some drugs, please?'

'Sure my friend, what do you want?'

'Some coke. Maybe a bit of acid, too. Some speed for later. Grass, but only if it's good, no shit, and it has to be grass, not resin. Whatever pills you can find, and ... oh, who cares. A nice pick 'n' mix. You get what you can. You know my tastes.'

'I know just the man to satisfy your needs.'

'Yeah? Does he do fire-arms too?'

'You name the figure and I'll see what I can do.'

'Only the best, the cost is no object.'

'I'll let you know.' Twists a Cuban heel on his cigarette butt. 'Be about an hour, okay?'

'Cheers, dude. And keep the change. Oh, and ... Dennis? Do us all another favour, too, would you?'

'What's that, friend?'

Thurston tucks a five dollar bill into the breast pocket of Dennis's jacket. 'Go and buy yourself a fucking deodorant.'

'Always remember,' Thurston says when Dennis has departed. 'If you want drugs ask a roadie. Never ask a manager. Because, as they say, it's not in their fucking contract. We know it is, of course. Keeping their fucking bands happy is their job, after all. Pure and simple. How are you doing, Jonah?'

'Fagged and shagged. A little nap would be nice.'

We console ourselves with the rider. Dennis returns fifty-five minutes later, dribbling whisky bottle askew in his right hand, dressed in a brown paper bag.

'Cheers, Dennis,' Thurston says, 'you're a god damn national hero. Maybe you should be managing this fucking band. What have you got for us?'

'All kinds of stuff.' Dennis produces a plastic bag from the inside pocket of his jacket. 'Grass, coke, acid, a few Es, various pills ... There's some speed, too. Lots of speed, in fact. The dealer's an old friend of mine and he owes me a few. He said we could have the speed for free because it's so crap. He's been trying to shift it for weeks and nobody wants to buy it, and he's too kind-hearted to rip people off. Said you needed to snort three or four lines to your normal one.'

'My kind of poetry,' Thurston says. 'Any luck with the other little business?'

'I'll let you know.'

'Cheers, dude. What about our friendly neighbourhood sound engineer? Has he got that fucking PA sorted out, yet?'

'I don't think so. It didn't look like it to me.'

'Dennis, I don't want to take the piss, but can I please ask you another favour? Can you do the sound for us tonight?'

'I don't know the first thing about sound engineering.'

'Yes you do. I know you do. Anyway, you know more than that dumb fuck out front. I don't trust him. At least you know what we should sound like.'

'Sure.' Dennis tosses aside a half-smoked cigarette and lights another. 'Okay. No problem. It's like Lemmy always used to say—'

'Another time. Jesus, just wait until Porn talks to that engineer, he'll make sure the fucker never works in this town again. Right. Let's get charleyed up.'

Soundcheck time is always the same. An hour or so of standing on stage, bass slung across my body, chain-smoking as Wendall presses buttons and Thurston yells down the mic at the sound engineer; Dennis, in tonight's case. I stand at the side of the stage and thrum the bassline to 'Street Hassle'. These venues look so queer and out of joint when fully lit and empty. Thurston always seems to want it over with as seamlessly as he can. A quick asphyxiation of guitar and then he's done. Eventually we're allowed to run some songs through. Just want a cosy bed to sleep in. Could happily miss the gig for that.

'Any other problems so far?'

We finish soundcheck at seven, two hours until showtime so we return to the hotel. Get stoned, exchange swift coke-lines and play chess, Wendall and me against Thurston and Jisel. Wendall and I win three games straight. The drugs are sneaking ahead of Thurston and making his moves before he can. And they are chiefly Thurston's moves. Jisel eyeing the shopping bags slabbed beside the door; she hasn't opened them since she got back. Regardless of us the clock is patient. Porn by now no doubt bordello-driven. Dennis stayed at the venue, exchanging tales of difficult bands and amphetamine psychosis and methane with their crew.

'And on the seventh day God rolled a spliff and chilled out,' Thurston says. 'I think when we get back from the tour we should have a party.'

'Any particular reason?' Jisel says.

'Nobody needs a reason for having a party. Besides, there are a thousand reasons you could give.'

'Like a wedding anniversary?'

'Yeah, like a wedding anniversary. I want a classic party, you know, where everybody either gets into a fight, gets laid, or passes out in a pool of vomit.'

'Or all three, in your case,' Wendall says.

'Yeah, or all three. I must say, this coke's the fucking bollocks. It's really kicking in now. I feel great. I want some music. Does anybody have any music?'

But the only tape I can find, apart from Sprawl stuff and Dennis's Motorhead and Biohazard collection, is one of mine with *White Light/White Heat* on one side and the first Suicide album on the other. Sure I've got some more somewhere, squirrelled amongst tee-shirts and paperbacks and notebooks.

'You could have bought some fucking tapes, too,' Thurston says to Jisel, stares at the cassette and CD player, a vacant possession on the bed.

'I'm going to the toilet,' Wendall says. 'Has anybody got any porn mags?'

'Nada,' Thurston says. 'Remind me tomorrow.'

'Think I've got a Lou Reed tape somewhere,' I say.

'Which album?' Wendall says.

'*Transformer*, and—'

'Yuk,' Wendall says.

'And *Berlin*.'

'That's a bit more like it.'

'I really don't want to listen to *Berlin*.' Thurston says. 'Much as I love it, much as I know it's a great album. I simply couldn't stomach it right now.'

'Iggy?' I say, still upending my bag.

'Which albums?'

'*The Idiot* and *Lust For Life*.'

'That's a bit more fucking like it,' Thurston says. 'Right. Whack the sweet babe and let's get loaded.'

Bigger crowd than I'd anticipated. Thurston is bouncing in sync to the beat before we start playing. 'I'm a super fucking nova,' he shouts, tosses the *Jaws* theme in ragged sheets of feedback. Someone shouts 'Trash'. Thurston says 'Fuck Trash. Fuck Bleak House. This is how it is.' I toss my hair over my face, hide there: Thurston starts to sing, kicks dumbly in the direction of his distortion pedal. I wanted to open with 'Nature Doesn't Care' but Thurston said he didn't feel sufficiently at ease with it yet so we start with 'Western Lands', then 'Snuff,' then 'Ice Age'. Takes me two or three songs to get into it. I close my eyes, focus on a blur near the apex where the beat is. Thurston slums lazy rhythm guitar, slurs rather than sings, rarely delivers the words like I wrote them to be sung. Guess it's called attitude. The dry ice clears a little. The audience – and I can only see the first few rows – wear Bleak House tee-shirts. Their eyes are hands on Thurston and me. Wendall still astray in the ice somewhere. Thurston forgets what he's supposed to be playing, lashes the same riff for fifteen minutes and through three different songs. We plan to end the set with 'An American Trilogy', receive a half dozen claps. 'Well you didn't like that one much, did you?' Thurston says, so we play 'We Gotta Get Out Of This Place', sung by me and segueing into 'Helter Skelter' after thirty-five minutes. 'This is a song U2 stole from Charles Manson,' I burr. 'We're stealing it back.' Safe within the stupidity of electric guitars. Strobes beat in my eyes and people shout silent and all I can hear is veins bursting in my temples.

*   *   *

Backstage jackknifed and snorting the end of the line. Cigarette in one grasp, hand-me-down beer in the other.

'Well, at least we did the gig,' Thurston says. 'Even if we sounded shit, at least we got up and played. Cheers, Dennis.'

'No problem,' Dennis says. 'I have a plan for the night. A cunning plan.'

'Has it anything to do with what Lemmy used to say?' Wendall says.

'No, not really.'

'Then shoot,' Thurston says.

'Okay. Let's go and find a chick with a dick. I've always wanted to shag a chick with a dick, just to see what it's like.'

'You mean, shag a bloke or a bird with a gender crisis?' Thurston says.

'Thurston, that's unfair,' Jisel says.

'But true,' Thurston says.

'You mean they're blokes?' Dennis says. 'I thought they were women born with dicks as well.'

'Sometimes,' Wendall says. 'But rarely.'

We leave the venue when the rider is drunk, and into the glitter and fizzle of bar-room air. Every shiny lattice of possibility mapped out for me by pharmaceuticals. I want to infect all places with me. 'We are Borg,' Thurston says.

'Allow me to buy you all a drink,' Porn says. The girl behind the bar has eyes the shape of teardrops. Porn unleashes his tie, gives her his Amex card, says 'charge all this party's drinks to this, please.' Wendall shreds beer coasters, piles them up like the potato-mountain Richard Dreyfuss sculpted on the kitchen table in *Close Encounters*. Jisel hooked on Thurston's arm; laughing so light, as always cherishing and loving only what, moment to moment, happens to fall before her. Dennis sags with sleeplack, grinds his cigarette out on the rim of the bar.

'I bet you're looking forward to Vegas, Thurston,' he says.

'How comes?'

'You mean to tell me you're not a gambling man?'

'No, not especially. That's Porn's vice.'

'Oh, I've been known to dabble on occasion,' Porn says.

'He's being modest,' Thurston says. 'As usual. He used to do it for a living. You drinking again, Wendall?'

'I think drinking is the only thing that's going to get me through this tour intact.'

'Excellent news. Welcome back to the land of those still living.'

'Were you telling me the other day about somebody freezing hamsters?' Jisel asks me.

'No, I don't think so.'

'Oh. It must have been somebody else, then.'

'For pet snakes, probably,' Dennis says.

'I was thinking of buying a bar when we get back home,' Thurston says.

'Why?' Jisel says.

'It'd be good to have your own bar. You could drink there whenever you wanted. You could have lock-ins and invite all your friends. You could play pinball and pool until six in the morning.'

'And you wouldn't get thrown out,' Wendall says.

'I suppose it'd be good,' Jisel says. 'And considering how much you spend in other people's bars we'd be saving money, most likely.'

'I need a smoke,' Dennis says. 'Anybody got a smoke?'

'We need to talk about tonight's show at some point,' Porn says. 'It was a fiasco.'

'Can it wait until tomorrow?' Thurston says. 'I'd rather not think about it right now.'

'Yes I expect it can.'

'Good. Let's have lunch and talk about it then.'

'So you guys are English?' says a man who resembles the face on the Turin Shroud.

'Yeah, that's right,' I say.

Muscles loll lazy neath his tee-shirt as he shifts posture.

I can't quite see the print from this angle but I think it's Oasis.

'You know, I can always tell,' he says. 'So what, are you on a vacation?'

'We're in a band,' I say.

'What kind of music do you play? I'm an REO Speedwagon man, myself. You guys ever check out REO Speedwagon? How about Todd Rundgren?'

'No, I can honestly say I've never had that pleasure,' Thurston says.

'Well if you ever get the chance you should check them out.'

'I'll remember that,' Thurston says.

'And you know something else?'

'What's that?'

'I'm a musician too.'

'No kidding,' Thurston says. 'Is that truly a fact?'

'Yeah. And do you know what I play?'

'I can't imagine.'

'I play the drums.'

'Never.'

'I do. So which one of you guys is the drummer?'

'Nobody.'

'So what sort of music do you play then?' He caresses the muffy fluff of his goatee. 'Are you some kind of fag band? I can't imagine a band without a drummer.'

'Gay,' I say. 'Nobody says "fag" anymore.'

'Whatever you wanna call it. A queer's still a queer. But I'm not sure where you guys are at. Run it by me one more time. I can't imagine a band without a drummer.'

'That's a shame,' Thurston says. Dennis beside me slumping further and further on his stool. 'I thought live drummers had long been exterminated from the musical food-chain. Besides, I don't believe in drummers. I believe in drum machines. They don't talk back for one thing. They also don't get too pissed to keep the rhythm, snort all your drugs, want a cut of the wonga or try to shag your wife.'

'Hey, no problem.' He glances at his shoes. 'I respect you, you respect me, be cool.'

Thurston grabs him by the scruff of his tee-shirt, says 'don't you ever turn away from me when I'm talking to you! Don't you break that eye contact. Fucking listen when I'm talking or I'll break your face open.'

'I think I'm going to leave right now.'

'God's teeth!' Thurston says as we watch the man empty his glass and head doorward.

'Thurston, I don't think you were very nice to that man,' Jisel says.

'Never work with children, animals or live drummers, that's what I always say. I don't think I was unnecessarily cruel. Was I unnecessarily cruel?'

'Yes you were,' Jisel says.

'It's not like you to worry about something like that, Thurston,' Wendall says.

'I ought to remember, though,' Thurston says. 'It's not like back home. Back there you can have a good, honest, down to earth bar-room brawl. Over here, they're more likely to just shoot you stone dead then and there for spilling their pint or something.'

'I fancy a hot dog,' Jisel says, saliva-wets her finger, scrubs a wine stain that has befallen her skirt. 'Oh look what I've done.'

'Why?' I ask.

'Why did I spill wine on my skirt?'

'No, why do you fancy a hot dog?'

'I don't know. You know when you just think, hmmm, I know what I fancy, and what I fancy right now is a hot dog. I wish my nose was more curvy. Jonah, don't you wish my nose was curvy? Curvy noses are so much more sexy, don't you think?'

I wonder at it a while, have seldom considered that desire or no can be defined by a piece of anatomy so nonchalant as a nose. Curvy or straight or turvy or otherwise, I have to concede to the notion.

'Jesus,' Thurston says, 'what is it with you two? Every time I look up from my pint you're huddled together, whispering into each other's ears. Why don't you just jump into the sack and get it over and done with?'

'If only you meant it ...' Jisel laughs.

I mince to the toilet. Men are always dicks out before they open the door. These days every second is valid. Compound smell of KY, come and condoms. 'I can always tell who is English,' a German woman told me in a bar in Cologne. 'Englishmen take their drinks into the toilet with them.' Sick of stranger men that follow me into latrines. Sick of sprawling over urinals, forehead against moist concrete, last year's singles looping my mind as I wait for piss to happen. Need a pissing mantra, an advert to my bladder, the correct tempo of voice and iteration that tells my innards 'Mercy. This is the time and the place, now submit, it is my will.'

Into a cubicle. Seat fouled with urine and pubic hair. It's like confession with voices murmuring from the other side of the wall. Who will I go home with tonight? It's seldom a question of desire. Out of the cubicle and into a girlish boy. Snakeskin flicker of his arms. Anticipate Krisco kisses. He smiles and speaks but I can't understand a word. Barely recollectable from first impression, not what I'm seeking in a bedmate right now but I'm prepared to give him a whirl.

'Who's the Chinese kid?' Thurston says to me when I rejoin my friends.

'He's Japanese.'

'Yeah, whatever. Who the hell is he?'

'I have no idea. His English is barely better than my Japanese. I think his name's Kyoko.'

'So what are you planning to do with him?'

'No idea.'

'Haven't thought about it yet?'

'Exactly.'

'You villain.'

I light a cigarette. Know this is one of those times when you are so drunk that every action and every thought poses imminent danger. Kyoko so arch and pinched, stroking his stomach and limbs as if admiring how skinny he is.

'Let's go,' Thurston says. 'You can bring the Jap if you want.'

The world is out of focus again, a bad reproduction that flickers at the edges. Every event is just a location I'm passing through. Piss a Jackson Pollock against a wall. We move on to hot million-eyed streets, follow the meander of Broadway on to Fifth Avenue. Ghost so happy to make me the machine. Monsters of love bred from the siesta of reason. Jisel on one arm, Kyoko's antique jabbering on the other. The sky bends down to touch us. I look up at Cassiopeia and Cassiopeia seems calm for me. Keys to the kingdom dropped down a drainage grille. Thurston sharks ahead of us, flips his jacket off and plays matador with the traffic, sings to the tune of 'Firestarter'; 'I'm a lager zombie! Twisted lager zombie!' The street curls around us, loose threads tugging at my every step. It's astonishing how drunk you can get when you really dedicate yourself to it.

We taxi to the hotel: Thurston, Jisel and Porn in one car, Wendall, Kyoko and Dennis and me in another.

'Don't forget we need to pick the van up tomorrow,' Porn says as he departs to his room and to cable TV serendipity.

'Why the fuck can't we get flights?' Thurston says. 'How comes we have to drive everywhere? Nobody drives around America on tour anymore.'

'Porn reckons it makes us more of a proper band,' Wendall says. 'A band should be on the road, honing their craft. Literally on the road, he reckons.'

We retire to the room I'm sharing with Wendall. I light a cigarette, suck up familiar nicotine, shake the match which refuses to out itself. Pencils of cocaine. A night in this hotel with breakfast costs more than my flat for two weeks. I need some music, consider Suicide but think anew. You have to be very careful with that album. It's dangerous. It can tilt the fragile or too tightly wired into irredeemable psychosis. Wish

I had Psychedelic Furs' *Talk Talk Talk*; it would be an ideal soundtrack.

'Good God,' Thurston says, 'I do believe you're drunk as a lord.'

I nod, don't really care if I have another drink or another line. Know I can do it all again tomorrow. As pornography, this band is hard to beat.

'I don't do the expensive stuff, just the cheap stuff,' Thurston is saying, holding a beer bottle to the sweating swathes of his temples, each in turn. 'The expensive stuff fucks with your head too much.'

Ghostrider. Kyoko shouts and cries in the corner, suddenly fluent in English, downloading to any receiver. Can't hear a word of it. Trousers at ankles, pallid slender penis flapping for all the world. 'Shut the fuck up!' Thurston shouts in his face. 'Shut the fuck up or I'll shoot you!'

'Yeah?' Wendall says, 'and what are you gonna do that with?'

'This,' Thurston says, pulling out the largest handgun I've ever seen, even in films.

'Thurston, where in hell did you get that?' Jisel says. 'Give it to me now!' And he does.

'Well excuse me all to hell,' he laughs.

I swoosh beer on to flames suddenly jetting from the ashtray. All motor functions redundant. No sense of touch or of the placement of objects. Nothing like Sister Ray says. Kyoko screaming, eyes jutting, ripping at his clothes. 'There was a fire,' I say, 'but it's okay now. I put it out.' I stagger from side to side of the room, my boots arguing with my patient feet and the hands that seek to separate the two of them. Sky beginning to blue again. Kneel before the toilet, hang my dick over the edge so my piss might reach the target. Think I'm gonna be sick. Think I can contain it. My face reaches for the floor and my body follows.

I open my eyes, peer over the edge of the duvet. Some nights are too deranged to submit to the cruel consideration of wisdom

the back of the van, where he lies in sleepless stupor until we pull up outside the next venue. Some gigs we put the bass on to DAT and I play guitar so Thurston can focus on his vocals. Mostly he'll remember the lyrics, occasionally to find that he's singing them in the wrong songs, but I don't think anybody notices apart from me and sometimes Wendall. If there's one thing I can say in favour of drugs, what makes them win out over people, it's that they always do what they promise to do. Back on the bus and to lines of light stripping past me. By the end of the first week I'm sick of every song. Drugs hold me vertical when alcohol fails. No more love songs.

Contact without feeling. You don't know me, but. Mind atwixt in perfect pitch and fingers bored with peeling condom wrappers. Another empty beer can. Anonymous. Even names can't identify. I need a face to put a person in place. Soft skin turns to a catalogue of numbers and nothing that matters much. 'I don't do this very often.' Whatever. A spiky neon-haired woman I don't remember seeing before, back from the delicatessen with orange juice and bagels, young sun at her heels. Woke up to the smell of coffee with my flaccid dick half inside her; 'Did I miss something?'

On my back in her stockings and skirt and Sprawl tee-shirt, her too-small boots tight on my toes, listening to the rush of the shower next door, her echoing voice sings a song I wrote x thousand miles away. Shower done and she comes in naked, squeezing her hair with an Elvis Presley towel.

'How comes I always sleep with men who want to wear my clothes?' she says, silver frames of spectacles, her flat-footed toes splaying with every step.

I sleep some, small and dreamless. Can't remember the last time I had a dream. She's gone when I wake up. Unmemorable. Rub sandalwood into the nape of my neck. Clean my teeth with a mentholated cigarette. My bag full of soft drinks and beers looted from the dregs of last night's rider. The surest hangover avoidance technique, I've learned, aside from not drinking or water before sleep, is to continue drinking. Have to soundcheck in six hours. I sit on the bed, sip beer and turn postcards I bought in New York a week and a half ago but haven't got round to posting yet. One for ex-Karen, one for current Polly, one for Whitney c/o The Goldsmith's, one for my parents. I don't think about my parents much, except sometimes when I'm sober. Hope Thurston's got some speed left, or I'll be on the floor by the time the gig is done.

Lying on the bed listening to Big Star on my Walkman. Feel like taking some mushrooms and going out to the desert. The door opens: Wendall.

'Jonah, get up. Quick.'

'What's going on?'

'It's Thurston. He's OD'd again, the stupid twat. He's in hospital. Jisel was screaming. Didn't it wake you up?'

'No. What happened?'

'He collapsed. His heart stopped beating.'

'Will he be okay?'

'I think so. The last news was good. Oh, he's conscious and everything, I think it's just his body saying "no more", after so many years of abuse.'

'What about ... the band, and stuff? The tour?'

'I have no idea. Porn's down at the hospital with Jisel. I guess we'll know when they get back. Stay here. I'm going to have a shower. We should hear from Porn soon. Fuck knows where Dennis is. Have you seen him?'

Wendall stumps into the bathroom and I lug through my bag, can't decide which of my plain black tee-shirts I want to wear today, settle on the one with pinhole burns on the belly. Dress, sit on the tip of the bed and churn my teeth, listen to the shower-beat of water on ceramic, peer through the window. The weather uncertain if it wants to be rain or sun. Don't want to go out there. You need a car to get from one side of the street to the other. My cigarette smoked too quickly, before I'm ready to stub it out, so I light another.

'Who's been in here?' Wendall, towel around waist, walking

across the room to his bag. 'There aren't any clean towels. It wasn't that woman from last night, was it?'

'Yeah. What the hell did we do last night?'

'Don't you remember?'

'Not really.'

'What's the last thing you do remember?'

'I really have no idea.'

'Do you remember doing tequila slammers with the Ministry roadcrew?' Wendall sat on the bed, his laptop screen a guff of colour and shape.

'No. When was that?'

'That was pretty early.'

He takes his clothes to the bathroom. I tug on my stinky boots. Sip cold coffee, a film of milk-fat drifting at the surface and scumming on my lips. Think, is it too soon to have another cigarette yet? Wendall comes back in, clothed now, sits by the window, touches his chin, fingers rasping over a patina of stubble, says, 'He doesn't actually overdose, I don't think. Literally, I mean. I think it's more that the sheer degree of different drugs and alcohol constantly sloshing around inside him gets too much sometimes and his body just throws in the towel.'

A knock on the door yields Porn.

'Where's Jisel?' I ask.

'She's with Thurston.'

'Will Thurston be okay?'

'Thurston is an asshole,' Wendall says.

'I've been speaking to the record company,' Porn says. 'They're not happy.'

'What do you mean, they're not happy?' I say. 'What about Thurston? I think it's Thurston we should be worried about.'

'Jonah, I know you're concerned about him,' Wendall says. 'We all are, but he'll be fine. Believe me. I've known him a lot longer than you have. He's pulled this trick more than once before.'

'So what do we do?' I stare first at Porn's shirt-cuffs with their attendant margins of grime and then at my chewed nails, where I pause and consider further chomping.

'The rest of the tour dates are on hold,' Porn says. 'The label want Thurston to go back into detox as soon as he gets out of hospital.'

'He'll be lucky if he doesn't get deported, I should think,' Wendall says.

'He won't get deported. I think we should all head back to New York. There's a clinic near there that Thurston will be moved into. It's one of the best. No expense spared. I've booked us a hotel there, too, while I formulate a gameplan. Jisel's offered to pay the hotel bill so that you guys can stay over here until you start recording the new album. Dennis will be going home, when I can find him. We don't need him here.'

'So that's it?' I ask. 'We just wait?'

New York slight return. Thirty-six hours since my head knew a pillow and I don't feel sleepy. When you're touring bodily functions become redundant. Eating, sleeping, shitting; even though we're no longer technically on tour the song remains the same. Hotel time never changes; there to be idled until the next combination of location and event is imminent.

I think it's early afternoon. I'm in my room, alone with my superlatives and listening to The B-52s. 'Planet Claire' and 'Song For A New Generation'. Knees banging at each other. Amphetamine transit. No longer seeing stegosaurs lurking in subway shadows. You soon learn to discard or sometimes cherish your hallucinations. Can accept seeing people you know are dead or on the other side of the world, or friends telling you they were mauled in the hallway by luminous tiger-striped sharks, them even still bleeding from the wounds, or being woken in the night by a noise that sounds like someone coming up the stairs with a chainsaw. I can get used to anything. Just present it as normal for long enough.

Swallowing orange juice to wash away the acid tab I basted on my tongue, I step on to the balcony of Jisel's hotel room and into the sun. Have no particular intentions. Nothing to do but sweat. Jisel is supine on a sun lounger, wears a tee-shirt cut to the bottom of her ribs, paperback in her wraithly hands. I can feel the drug drawing me into its singular dimensions. It starts at the intestines, diaphragm contracting, compacting itself to infinite density, pulling me in to that feeling beyond drunk, when you're going to vomit but it feels that not just your breakfast and your beer but your viscera in their massy entirety will spill out on to cool stone floor.

'Have you seen Wendall today?' I half-lotus myself on the ground next to her.

'Yes, he said he was going downtown to meet some old friends of his.' Jisel closes the book, keeps a finger in her place. 'But don't worry, Jonah. I'm here. You'll have to talk to me instead.'

I open a beer, sweat out a sewer through my skin. This is the worst weather for drinking. Every movement sends my pores agush some more. One of those lazy Fitzgerald Indian summer afternoons that never ends, a 'What shall we do?' that goes unanswered. The sky's that kind of blue you only see in films. Insects buzz like aircraft. The clouds are so 3D. I can't decide which cola I want to drink today. Every object fills my vision too soon, before the presence and implications of the previous object have registered.

'Did you sleep okay?' I ask.

'No. I always find sleeping such a chore. I lie awake wondering which direction I should be looking in after I've closed my eyes. Do you know what I mean, Jonah? Do you ever get that?'

'Yeah, sometimes. I normally just nod off straightaway. I'm normally too drunk to worry about anything except waking up again.'

She places the book on the floor. 'What am I going to do with Thurston?'

'Do you love him?'

'How the hell should I know? But I do know that I can't leave him. He's impossible to leave. What am I going to do? Jonah, tell me what I should do.'

'Jisel, I can't tell you what to do.'

'Well I haven't got a clue. Somebody has to decide for me. But you must really hate me. I mean, Thurston is your friend.' She stares and I watch a lizard of recognition scurry across her face. 'I've never told anybody about this before, but every now and again I used to get a call from Porn or someone, saying, "Jisel, it's Thurston, he's ..." and I'd think, right, this time it's the big one, but thankfully it never was.'

The heat turns the city to ribbons. I watch my hands shrink and pulse and pustulate. Gregorian chants echo to my left.

'Hello?' I turn and say. 'Do I know you?'

'Let me tell you a secret,' Jisel says. 'When Thurston gets unbearable I lock him in a room all by himself, with no drugs or alcohol, for forty-eight hours. When I let him out he's drenched in sweat, so humble, telling me how much he loves me and how much he needs me and begging for my forgiveness.'

'And do you?'

'What?'

'Forgive him.'

'Well it doesn't take much to say you're sorry these days, does it? Any idiot can say they're sorry, and hey presto, instant atonement.'

I nod, share a glance with the skyscrapers. The city has nothing to say. Another cigarette gone and I need more, something else to take up the purpose of my hands, to say to them, 'this is where you should be, this is what you should be doing.' Brief surges of space. Need actions that replicate the fuzz inside my head. Want to listen to The Great Dominions. Jisel rests on a further thought, the words hiding under her tongue.

'Oh, dear,' Jisel says. 'But don't worry. Thurston will be out again soon and then everything will be just like it always was. Oh, fudge.'

'What?'

'Nothing. It doesn't matter.'

I turn my head to ragdoll hair, cinerous skin, spiderwebs painted on each cheek. Scissored leather jacket. Black and green hooped tights. Skirtful of flowers. Blue Converse All-Stars held together with safety pins. Vaguely cute.

'You're ... Jonah?' she says.

'Yeah. Who the hell are you?'

'Gee, I love your album.'

'Okay. How did you get up here?'

'Took me ages to find your room. Mind if I hang out with you guys?'

'Whatever. I mean, after all that effort ...'

'Excellent.'

'What's your name?'

'I'm Jane. Hello.'

'I hate being in love sometimes,' Jisel says, twisting tortoise-shell RayBans in her fingers. 'I really hate it. What about you, Jane? Jonah ... I'm not even going to ask you, because I know it can wait for a future day. But Jane, what do you think? What do you think about being in love?'

'Sorry ...' I say. 'Jane, this is Jisel. Jisel, Jane.'

'I know who you are.' Jane stares at the chipped purple sheen of her nail gloss. 'I've never been in love.'

'I don't think love exists, actually,' Jisel says. 'I think it's all just circumstance, the people one happens to come across.'

'Sure,' I say, can't think how to answer her so light a cigarette. Watch the fuzz and furl of Jisel and Jane but know I'm never here. This cannot be a fixed point. These people cannot be me. Their words no longer registering, just dictionary sounds with nothing to tether them to me. I stare at my left thumb-nail. Impossible trajectories. Infinite divisibles. Intervals too chasmic to calculate. How do I reconcile me? Where does me go? These can't be the voices in my head. The voices in my head would never speak phrases so trite.

'Can we please try to have these conversations one at a time?' I say.

'Which conversations?' Jisel says. 'I'm going back inside for awhile, I think. I need a shower.'

I intend and begin to mouth a reply but the beat of the sun distracts me. Instead I watch Jisel's legs as she scythes back into the room. Smile, turn to Jane. Her gaze fixed at me. Close my eyes and she's closer now.

'Do you like me?' Jane's upper lip doesn't move when she speaks.

'Well ... I have no idea. What do you want me to tell you?'

'I guess the truth.'

'The truth? Well I'd probably sleep with you, but I don't know if that means I fancy you.'

'You foolish old romantic,' Jane laughs, eyes shining like an amusement ride. 'It must be really excellent, being in a band and all.'

'No, not really.' I thrill to every hair that shivers on my legs, hark for further hallucinations. 'It's just what I do.'

'Of course it's excellent. Have you got a bent cock?'

'Er ... No. Why?'

'Oh, I usually only sleep with men with bent cocks. I prefer it. It feels better. But I do sometimes make exceptions.'

Her kiss tastes of nicotine and coffin-worms and strawberry bubblegum. Crescent moon of rings around each of her ears. With blue pressing in all around us it's like we're underwater.

'I have to take my clit-ring out,' she says, 'it'll tear the condom.'

'Have you got a condom?'

'Sure I do. Why, haven't you?'

'In my room I do, yeah.'

'I don't want to go to your room. I can't even be bothered to move.'

She says 'I want to fuck now,' so we do, and laugh, a passable shag but hardly O Fortuna, smoke a cigarette, listen to an airplane clipping off somewhere while the sky burns out around us. Condom's smug smile at my boots. Signals from the sun. Baby crocodiles scurry along the concrete floor. Music seems the most inane of pastimes to crave. Tiny hairs curled at the tops of her thighs. I scratch the black beetle of a cigarette burn on the back of her hand.

'Ouch,' she says, 'that hurts.'

'You don't really like sex, do you?'

'No, I don't like it at all.' She chews purple nails. 'I guess it has it's uses, but ... I always wonder if I'm missing out, wonder if the next one is gonna be really good. I didn't particularly want to fuck you, anyway. I just needed somebody that wasn't my boyfriend.'

I listen to my cigarette burn down, watch the disk of the sun change from yellow to gold to copper. Clouds stuffed full and making us sweat. I want to hear 'Heroes'. Hate the way songs rove out of control in my head. New York has been repainted by Max Ernst. We drop glasses and pot-plants into the swimming pool six floors down, chart ripples that shine like fishskin. I reach for her skirt and pull it on.

'Are you cold?' she says.

'No, not really. We're going to a party later. You can come if you want to.'

'No. I don't go to parties anymore. I just hate that sudden moment when you realise you've slept with everybody in the room. That's one of the reasons I don't want to stay around here anymore. America sucks. You know how I see America? It's like looking at a long line of stillframes, stillframes of everything you dreamed of but know you'll never have. Did you see *Independence Day*?'

'Yeah.'

'Well that's what I want to do to America. What those alien guys did, that's what I want to do.' Wind turning her hair into flames. 'I want to be abducted by aliens. Don't you? But they only take people who don't want to be taken. If you want it they leave you alone. Do you think that means they're only after non-believers?'

'Like any good evangelist.'

Jane does up her buttons. Veins run fine as fresh scars. Jisel oscillates down the corridor singing 'Kinky Boots', presents her pinched face to the balcony and the wisdom of the sun. Applies lipstick then presses her lips together.

'Remind me to have a word with room service,' she says, watches me light a cigarette. 'The tiles in that bathroom simply aren't straight. They're all over the place. Jonah, why are you wearing a skirt?'

'Sometimes these things just have to be done.'

'Oh. Okay. I fancy going for a walk. Jonah, do you fancy going for a walk? Come for a walk with me, Jonah. You can bring your new friend.'

'Yeah, okay . . .' I say from behind a drape of hair.

'Only, one thing, please.' Jisel pencils her eyebrows in a palm-size mirror. 'Yes, could you please put your trousers back on? Not that I have a problem with transvestites, it's just . . .'

She hugs me, rubs her hip against mine before she passes back into the room. Her neck smells of sun and wine. In the toilet I stand unable to remember if I've pissed or not. 'Little Fluffy Clouds' is playing in my head, follows me back to the balcony and Jane where a line of speed stills my dervishing synapses.

'Where the hell did I put my shoes?' Jisel whoops. 'Any of them?'

'Can we swap e-mail addresses?' Jane says.

I tell her I don't have one; she laughs, says 'Guess a telephone number will have to do, then.' I invent a string of digits and we share a microdot between us. Her face smudged like a Francis Bacon. Just as an experiment it would be interesting to see how long I can carry this on for, before mind and body dissolve to ectoplasmic slush and the boundaries split then relocate themselves. This is what I need to know.

We step out on to pavements, into a Lovecraftian city of impossible non-Euclidean dimensions. Jane doesn't walk, she dances, in steps of muted excitement. Stoops for smalltalk with a cat on stucco steps. We're pursued by the flapping manta rays of newsprint sheets. Listen to cars collide with brittle-bodied insects.

'I forgot how much I loved acid,' Jane says. 'It's cool. It's like Disneyland.'

In Central Park it rains. We buy balloons, let them go, watch until they are specks. Jane spits without parting her lips. The rain is soft on our skins. The World Trade Centre melts into twin pools that well and merge and swallow Wall Street. Ants crawl over me. Let them crawl. I don't much care for the fights the sunsets have amongst themselves.

China Miéville

'DIFFERENT SKIES'

China Miéville was born in 1972, and is currently studying for a PhD in International Relations at the London School of Economics. He has worked as a writer and illustrator for magazines and fanzines. His novel *King Rat* is published by Macmillan, and he has had short fiction published in *Neonlit: The Time Out Book of New Writing Volume 1* (Quartet).

2 October

Seventy-one and melancholy.

I suppose it should be no surprise. It was not like this last year, though. End of my biblical quotient, should have been hugely traumatic, but the big not-very-secret shindig Charlie et al organised for me rather took the sting out of it. I didn't think much about the age itself until later. This year, though, I woke up and straightaway felt as old and dry as kindling.

Physically I'm weak but no weaker than yesterday. I still feel as if this fatigue were some interloper. It doesn't bother me as much as it might because I cannot take it seriously. It is so absurd that I should be out of breath after a flight of stairs that I feel I must be victim to some trick. It is not so much the effect as the simple fact of being past seventy that sticks in my craw. It frightens me. I do not believe it.

No visitors this year, and no great welter of presents. Last year must have exhausted budgets and indulgences. I am down to a couple of handsome books from Charlie (there are other trinkets of course but not worth mentioning). People my age have no money, and I think the younger ones resent buying something which will be ownerless again so soon.

I am being morbid. I am hardly at the end. I know that if I were frail, or made a great deal out of birthdays, or was lonely, that I would have visitors. But as I am not and do not, I have subsisted – happily enough – on cards and telephone calls.

I had an extended lunch with Sam at the café, that he gave me gratis when he learnt it was my birthday. Then I came home to supervise the installation of my present to myself.

It is a whimsical thing, which has been a monumental faddle to organise, but as I sit here looking at it, I really can't say I regret it.

I've bought myself a window.

I saw it a fortnight ago at Portobello Market. It was in one of the antique shops up near the top, by Notting Hill. I can't say why it appeals – it's hardly fine art. But there is something about it which is awfully compelling.

It's about a foot and a half high by two wide. In the centre is a lozenge of deep red glass. Surrounding it in radial sections like slices of pie are eight triangles of what I think was intended to be more-or-less clear glass – to my spoilt late-twentieth-century eyes it looks green or blue, dirty and discoloured. The segments are held together and separated by a framework of thin black lead.

It is a rude piece. Each pane is streaked with knotholes that warp the world behind them. Little scabs of clotted glass. The colours are not pure and the paint on the pane is at the point of flaking. But still, there is something in it I can't ignore.

The second time I saw it, I realised I was relieved it was still there. So I thought 'This is ridiculous, I don't have to wait for my pocket money', and I bought it. It sat around for a week without being unwrapped. Today I paid a man from the hardware centre to pop round, remove the top central pane from my study window and replace it with my new – old – window.

I'm sitting at my desk as I write and I can see it above me. It is fractionally smaller than the other panes, and the man made some wooden frame to fit it tight in the space. He's smoothed the edges down until the frame is totally unobtrusive. He's warned me not to touch the glass for a day until the putty dries.

It sticks out, I suppose, surrounded by five other, cleaner panes – one to either side and the three below which can be swung open a crack. They are probably half its age, and consequently much purer, flatter glass. But I like the look of the odd thing.

It is at about head height. From up here on the fifth floor, my view over West London is enviable, over half an acre of grassland and then the ranks of lower houses. When I sit at the desk the old window rises to hang suspended over the roofs beyond like a heavy star.

The evening light comes right through the middle piece, the red lump. I suppose it is a sun itself, rising or setting. It is an odd colour for the sun, that dark scarlet. It sends extraordinary coloured rays on to the wall behind me. It is like a fat glass spider in a metal web.

I will resist the temptation to write forlornly 'Happy Birthday to me'. I do not know what is coming over me. I am going to bed, where I will read one of Charlie's books. A nice day, really. I must put a lid on this mawkish forlorn-old-man thing that I seem to have going.

4 October

I have finished one book and moved on to the other. I 'phoned Charlie today to tell him how much I was enjoying them (a small lie, as regards the second book – it is not nearly so good). He was pleased but slightly bemused to hear from me, I think. After all, we spoke only three days ago.

This morning I went for a walk long enough to make me ache (not a Herculean feat, of course). I had a chat with Sam on the way back, then got home to this armchair. I will admit to being slightly aghast at the relief it was to sit down.

That was when I spoke to Charlie, and I must admit that it was not the best conversation. Nothing was *wrong*, of course. I am not angry and nor was he. I was just made aware (not deliberately – he was raised too well for that, I like to think) that he does not know

what to make of me these days. I am in a halfway house. We have
never been close as friends are close, we do not trade intimacies (his
choice, and one I have respected since he was a lad). He is much
too old to need me, and I am not yet old enough to need him.

Perhaps he is biding his time until then. Then our affection can
come into its own, then roles will become clear and he can wipe
up my drool and cut up my supper for me, and wheel me over to
the window to enjoy the view.

Since that 'phone conversation I have sat dumb for a fair
old while.

I found myself – I sort of *came to*, I suppose – gazing at the
window over my desk.

It is a splendid thing. It is very good to stare at.

I was thinking of it while I walked. All the obvious, idle thoughts
– Who could have made it? When? Why? Over what did it look?
And so on and on. When I walk into the little study into its light,
those questions do not dissipate but return in strength. When I
look at that strange glass it makes me think of all the other old
windows that have been lost.

It comes to life at this time, in the gloaming. When the light
deepens and seems to send spears directly at it.

Although … it is not right to say that it comes to life. That
is not right.

'Life' has never, I think, been its attraction. It is too still
for that.

I know it very well, by now. I have spent some time over the
last days looking at the eight evenly spaced triangles around the
central stone. Each is stained with its own impurities, each is a
unique colour. Counting clockwise from the top, my favourite is
the sixth, the slice between west and south-west. It is a little bluer
than the others and the ruby at its apex makes that blue shine.

I have reread the words above with amusement and discomfort. For
goodness' sake, am I turning into some sort of mystic? I knew I was
smitten with the thing – I cannot remember being so thrilled with

ownership of anything material. But I am perturbed by what I have written; I sound like an obsessive.

The fact is, I have read today, and walked and chatted and all of that, but I have been thinking always of my window.

All manner of whimsies enter my head. The sun has gone, now. The darkening sky is moiling pointlessly with cloud cover. Perhaps the window is not a sun but an asterisk, interrupting the grammar of the sky, with me sitting below it like a footnote.

This is not healthy at all. The low(ish) spirits that settled on me on my birthday must have taken deeper root than I had thought. I think I must be lonely. I will make some phone calls. I think I will go out tonight.

Later

Well how terribly deflating.

My good intentions to snap out of this reverie have been stymied. I do not know anyone who is alive, local, and up for a meal, a drink, or anything else. Flicking through my address book was depressing and led to a meagre list – a pathetic list – of possibilities. And none of them wanted to come out to play.

It is night, now, very quiet, and I feel awfully bloody deserted.

5 October

I was not going to write today, as nothing of any note had happened by the evening (I will not dutifully record the tedium of shopping and television and more bloody reading). But then the oddest thing happened.

It is late and my sitting room is cold and dark. I am still trembling slightly, nearly half an hour after the event.

I came into the study at about 10 p.m. to fetch a book. I did not bother with the light; I could see what I was after on the desk quite clearly in the light from the hall.

As I bent over for it, I felt a tingling on my neck, less than a breath but much more than the vague sense one sometimes has of being watched.

I straightened quickly, in some alarm.

It was dark outside. Not a clear, starlit dark either, but a dismal cloudy shadow. It was a drab night. Desultory sodium-light from the streetlamps before and below me, that was all. No moon.

But the red glass at the centre of my window was shining.

It sent icy scarlet light on to the desk below, and on to me. I swear that was the source of the raised hair on my neck.

I gaped up at it. My mouth must have been slack. All the impurities and the scratches on the inside of that central panel were etched sharp and vivid. It seemed to have a hundred shapes, all of a sudden, to look momentarily like a huddled embryo and a red whirlpool and a bloodshot eye.

I must have been staring at it for no more than three or four seconds when it stopped.

I did not see it happen. I was not conscious of any light going out, anywhere. Perhaps it was extinguished as I blinked. All I know is that one moment it shone and then it did not.

My retinas retained no afterimage.

Perhaps it was an isolated light from some aeroplane or some such, that happened to shine directly and strangely through my window. I am thinking much more clearly now than when I started to write, and that seems the only possibility. Looked at like that, I do not know why I bothered to record this. Except that when the room was lit up with that light, something felt very strange in the air. Very wrong. It was only three seconds but I swear it made me cold, deep down.

8 October (Night. Small hours)

There is something beyond the window.

I am afraid.

I am no longer bemused or concerned or intrigued but truly afraid.

I must write this quickly.

When I came home in the evening (having thought all day about what happened last night, even when I denied that that was what I was doing) I felt a peculiar disinclination to enter my study. When I finally conquered it, of course, there was nothing untoward in there.

I looked nonchalantly enough up at the window and saw the sky through it, just as I should. Pitted and cracked by the old glass, but there was nothing out of place.

I dismissed my nerves and pottered around for a few hours, but I never relaxed. I think I was mulling over the odd light of the previous evening. I was waiting for something. That was not quite clear to me at first, but as the evening grew older and the sunlight was smothered, I found myself looking up more and more through the sitting room windows. I was thinking of what to do.

Eventually, when the day was quite gone, I decided to go into the study again. Just to read, of course. That's what I told myself, in my head, loudly. In case, I suppose, anything was listening.

I settled down in the armchair and leafed through Charlie's tedious book, that I am labouring to finish.

I glanced up at the window, now and then, and it behaved as glass should. I had turned off the main light, was reading by a little lamp to reduce the reflections. Beyond the window I could make out the occasional intermittent lights of some aeroplane passing from the left-hand window-pane through that central, much older one, and out again. They ballooned briefly as they slid behind old bubbles in the red glass.

I read and watched for at least an hour, and then I must have fallen asleep.

I woke suddenly, very cold. I could only just make out my watch – it was a little after two in the morning.

I was huddled like some pathetic child in the armchair, in darkness. The bulb of the lamp must have blown, I remember thinking. I stood shakily and heard the book fall from my lap. I looked around, confused and shivering.

I think the constant white noise of rain was what woke me. It was coming down hard. I saw the dull shine of the streetlights glint and move slightly through the slick of water on the window panes. I fumbled, trying to gather myself, and saw the room by red moonlight passing through that central pane. As I turned, I saw the moon briefly.

I stopped suddenly.

My throat caught. I looked back at the window.

The old pane was dry.

Dirty rain was pounding against its neighbours, but not a drop spattered against it.

The moon was shining full in my face through the glass, distorted by its impurities. I was quite still.

After a moment I walked closer to the old window. All around me was the low, mindless sound of rain. I stopped just in front of the desk and looked up at that moon. As far as I could see through the buckled glass, it was in a clear, dark sky. I could see stars around it.

The sky visible through the rain in the other windows was a mass of cloud.

I moved my head slowly to one side, watching the moon. It moved slowly out of the old starburst window and past the dividing frame. It did not appear in the right-hand pane. When I moved my head quickly back, it returned, to vanish again on the opposite side.

The new panes and the old looked out over different skies.

I pulled the desk quickly out of my path and stood directly in front of the intricate frame. I put my hands to it, trembling, and brought my face up to it, and looked out.

I stared through the glass and the moonlight and then with a flash of fear that made me sick, I saw the top of a wall. Through the greenish glass below the red centrepiece, in the light of some ghost moon, I saw old bricks and crumbling mortar only a few feet before me, topped with broken glass.

Beyond that wall there was a low, angled roof sloping away into the darkness. I looked right, pressing my face against glass which was colder than the other panes. The wall stretched off as far as I could make out.

I fumbled behind me for the desk chair, pulled it over and stood on it carefully without taking my eyes from the view. I looked down through the old window, tracing the black bricks below me. And there, perhaps six feet below the glass, was the ground.

I rocked with disorientation. Sure enough, to either side of me, the window-panes still looked out over the London night, over the stretch of scrub and the dark slates fifty feet below.

But the patterned glass in the centre overlooked an alley, only a little way from the pavement. Scraps of rubbish skittered soundless across the cement.

With my ear pressed against the old glass, the silence that seeped through was greater than the pathetic puttering of the rain. My heart was beating so hard it shook me. I took in the dim sight in front of me with a numb foreboding that grew worse every second.

It became terror when I turned my head slowly, and saw that I was watched.

I saw them for less than half a second, the clutch of dark figures that stood motionless in the entrance to the alley. But in that moment I knew that their glowering unlit eyes were all on me.

I cried out and stumbled, tottering and falling.

I landed heavily and fell, then writhed until I could stand, and then I ran for the door, moaning, and I slapped the light-switch and turned and the moon had gone.

The old window admitted the same view as all the others. Like its fellows, it was wet with rain.

It is nearly morning, now, and I do not know what to do.

I thought at first of telling somebody: Charlie, or Sam, or someone. But then I hear the same story told to me by a seventy-one-year-old and I know what I would think. Alzheimer's, old-timers'. Or madness. Or blindness. Or a simple lie.

At best I would think I was being told a story in that irritatingly fey metaphorical register that some people adopt in their dotage (in which 'I think often of my long-dead husband' becomes 'I have lovely chats with your father').

I could only tell someone if they would come and see it. And it might not happen again, or not while they were there, and then I would be left with their pity. I will not have that.

10 October

They are children.

They are taunting me.

That other city came back last night. I have avoided the study for two days, and I do not know what happened beyond that window. Let it come and go, I thought. Like tides changing outside a seaside house. No need for me to care.

I woke in the night, at some unspecified dark hour. I lay for a long time in bed, trying to work out what had disturbed me.

Eventually I heard it. A faint hiss. A whispering.

A voice was coming through the wall. From the study.

I lay there numb and cold with my eyes open. It came irregularly, furtive and insistent. I sat up and pulled the top cover around me like a cloak. Mute and fearful I shuffled from my room and stood outside the study door. The sound was louder here, sliding insidiously through the wood. I knew that I would not sleep again. I set my jaw, reached out and opened the door.

The room was bathed again in that ghastly moonlight. It made my books and shelves look ancient and insubstantial. Everything was motionless, basking with the stillness of a dead thing. The moonlight extended from the old pane in a canal of dusty luminescence.

Through the rest of the window I saw scudding clouds, but it was a clear night in that other city. And as I stood there on the threshold of that freezing room, I heard that voice again.

OI MISTER.

It was a child's voice.

It was whispered, but it filled the room with ease. It resonated in weird dimensions.

I heard a thin tittering and a shushing noise.

There was cold outside me and inside me.

OI MISTER.

I heard it again. I inched forward into that terrible dark room. The desk was where I had left it. There was nothing between me and the coldly shining window.

There was another sound, a sharp tapping on the glass. I heard it again, and this time I saw a handful of little dark shapes appear from nowhere in the bottom of the old pane and rattle against it.

Someone, I realised, was throwing *stones.*

I crossed the floor in slow, tiny steps and picked up the chair, which lay where it had fallen. I mounted it and looked down as steeply as I could.

There was a quick, furtive motion in the shadows of the alley. Fear chilled me and blurred my eyes. I could see almost nothing in that great trench of darkness, but I made out the shapes of figures pushing themselves quickly flat against the wall directly below me, so that I could not see them.

And one of them spoke again.

OI MISTER YOU OLD CUNT, and there was a chorus of malignant giggles.

Another stone was thrown, much harder this time. I felt it through the glass, and stumbled back. I kept my footing. I screamed at them in my fear.

'What d'you want? Leave me alone!' I shouted, and was greeted with raucous and stifled laughter.

One by one little shapes pulled themselves from the wall and emerged into my line of sight. They were little more than shadows in that profound darkness. But I could see that they were children. Unbelieving, I pulled myself down for a moment to stare through one of my other windows, but nothing had changed. I was fifty feet up, and the only wakeful thing this side of the horizon. I was staring out over little urban hillocks and clots of grass moving fitfully in the wind, and the endless maze of hunched houses all unlit and silent.

But up there in the other nightland that uncanny gang was hurling stones at my window, and hissing vicious abuse in spectral voices, and calling me old man, old man.

Quite suddenly I truly realised what was happening, for the first time that night I was fully aware that I was being taunted by *phantoms*, by *delinquent ghosts*. I seemed to wake, to feel the chill air and hear the rat-tat-tat of stones and the cruel words from a pack of children who *could not be there*. And I stepped off the chair as horror clotted in my gorge and I felt my legs nearly fold, and I walked as steadily as I could to the light and turned it on and when that did nothing to stem the flow of vitriol from the ghost city I slammed the door three times.

And when I turned back, thank God, thank God, it had all gone.

I do not know if the children fled in fear or if they are still there, waiting wherever the city has gone.

11 October

I went back to the shop from where the window came.

As I foresaw, the woman knew nothing, remembered nothing,

could tell me nothing. She had had the window for months, part of a lot from somewhere she did not recall.

She looked at me, concerned by my manner. She asked if there was something wrong. I could not stop a fleeting, hysterical laugh at that, an incredulous grin. It must have been the most horrible rictus.

I was possessed by some unclear, nebulous emotions that I cannot define. A sense of urgency and isolation. A deep feeling that the past was done, that it was the present that should concern me.

What is the nature of that place?

I think of it in so many ways.

The window remembers what it used to see. That is clear. I do not know where I look out or when, but it must be the older view from that cracked pane (more cracked now, I realise, after last night's little broadside).

So am I living in a window's memory? Is this nothing but a repeat of the pointless brutality directed at some old man like me, who first lived behind that sunburst window? Perhaps this window looks out on to some imbecilic, repetitive Hades like a stuck record.

Or perhaps this time it is different.

Perhaps those little roughnecks want to finish something off.

13 October

The little tykes. Ragamuffins. I imagine fat boys smoking and thin-faced girls. Dead eyes. Little ruffians.

The little terrors.

The *terrors*.

They will not leave me. They croon at me and mock my shuffling old-man walk. They scribble obscenities on the wall opposite, and on the bricks of my house, my other house that I cannot see.

They piss and hurl stones.

I do not leave the study now. I am learning what I need to know for my defence. I wait for the ghost city to wax back to me, and when it comes I investigate it to the limits of my vision.

There is a drainpipe by my window, on my other wall, my ghost wall.

I have heard them scrabbling a short way up it, scraping the rust and mortar. I have listened to them whispering, daring each other to climb it. Calling me names, gearing each other up with hatred and poison to break my window and *scare me to death*.

I do not know what I have done or what he did, the man who lived in that other house. Perhaps he was just old and funny and stupid and lived where no one could hear him scream and beg.

I will not call them evil. They are not evil. But I am afraid that they are capable of it.

14 October

I sat in the study and waited all day and they came at last at night, and I cried for them to stop and stood on the chair with my pyjamas flapping idiotic around my ankles. I watched as one pulled chalk from its trousers and began to scrawl on the wall opposite my window.

It was too dark to see. But when they had made me cry they fled, and the ghost city stayed beyond my window until just before dawn, long enough for me to read what had been written for me.

YOUR DEAD OLD MAN.

15 October

I have gone out and looked around and everywhere, in all the parts of the city, wherever I have been, youth seems to fill London.

I have heard animated swearing from girls and boys on bicycles and buses. I have seen signs that read 'Only two children at a time' on the doors of small grocers. As if that were a defence. I have wandered the streets in a strange state, staring around me at the little monsters that surround us.

For the first time in my life I see people look at me and glance away embarrassed. Perhaps I have not showered recently enough – I have been preoccupied. Perhaps it is just my broken walk. They could not know that I am newly like this. I was not this derelict thing until a week ago when the children came.

I am afraid of all these unchecked, unbridled younglings. *None of them are human.* They are all like the ones who come to torment me at night.

I cannot look at them, at any of them, without this horrible fear, but also with a jealousy. A longing. I thought at first that this was new, that it had come through the window with that alien moonlight. But when I look at other adults looking at children, I know that I am not alone. This is an old feeling.

I have prepared myself.

I returned to the hardware shop where the man who fixed my window in place did not remember or perhaps recognise me. I bought what I will need for tonight.

I have spent this day, this perhaps last day, walking slowly around with my hands behind my back (they sought out that old-man grip to go with my old-man limp). And when I saw that it would soon be time, that the afternoon was nearing its end, I shambled home again.

I am ready. I am writing this as the light wanes. So far the old pane, the haunted pane, shows the same sky as its siblings.

I am sitting just below the window with my walking-stick by my feet and my new hammer across my lap.

Why me? I have pondered. I was not especially cruel I do not think, in any measured or repulsive way. I have had little to do with children.

During the night visitations, I have seen glimpses of flapping, ridiculous shorts half a century out of date, and discerned the old-fashioned, clipped voices of my merciless besiegers (the tone is not disguised even when sneering in wide-eyed sadism). And yes of course I have thought of the years when I was like them.

Perhaps it is as simple as that, that I look out at my own times running in those hordes. Is this to be that sort of banal morality tale? Am I my own abuser?

I do not remember. I can see myself running through rubble with others, and sifting for prizes and smoking vile things and torturing stray animals and all the rest, but I do not remember singling out some old man to be his personal harpy. Perhaps I deceive myself. Perhaps that *is* me, out there.

But I cannot believe that Hell is so trite.

I believe that I am just an old man, and that they have a game they have waited sixty years to finish. A game that makes them drunk with contravention. With wickedness.

I am watching and waiting. And when the sun has gone and the light behind that intricate pane flickers and changes, when I look down to see those spirits scamper to their stations with all that monstrous baleful energy, then we shall have a race.

Why not just break it now and have done? Shatter the damn thing.

I have thought of it a thousand times since this began. I have imagined hurling my shoes or books or self at that old glass and sending it into the sky in hundreds of pieces. Pattering down on to the grass so far below.

Or I could simply have it taken out again. I could replace it with a pane like all the others. I could return that glass trap to the bemused shopkeeper. I could leave it carefully in a skip for some other unsuspecting soul. I could sink it in the canal, a piece of disintegrating debris among so many, emitting its ghost light to the fishes.

But the children would still be waiting.

They are not *in* the window but beyond it. And they have not yet had blood. They have picked me. I do not know why, perhaps there is no reason, but they have picked me. They have me in their sights. I am to be the victim. They have been poised on the brink of this all my life.

Wherever I hide the window, they will be waiting. And if I break the glass into my own world, then nothing will have changed for them in theirs. They will stand in stasis in that hidden city and wait, and wait, and I am afraid of when and how they might find me.

They are just out to see how far they can go.

But if I watch, and strike at the right moment, if I am fast enough, I will take the fight to them. I will strike a blow for old men.

If I can shatter the glass when their alley waits beyond, if I can smash it into *their* city, then things might be a little different. It might be a way in.

I want to emerge from the ruins of that window and drop (a short drop if you hang from the rim) into the alley (into the ghostland, immersed in the dead city, but I will not think on that) and I will wave my stick and run for them.

Bloody little hooligans.

If please God I catch one I shall lay it over my knee and by God I shall give it a hiding, a bloody good hiding, I shall teach it a bloody lesson, I will, I will thrash it, and that will, it will put an end to *all this nonsense*. I can't run away. I have to put a *stop* to this. They need to be taught a *lesson*.

(Oh but even as I write that I feel so stupid, it is an idiot's plan. Insane. I catch a glimpse of the rucked skin on my old hand and I know that I can no more climb from the window and drop to the ground in that other city than I can leap mountains. What can I do? What can I do?)

I will try. I will do my damnedest.

Because the alternative is untenable.

I know what they are gearing up to. I know their plan. When

the window changes, I will look out once more over that dingy alley, and their message, their chalk threat, will still face me. And I must make it up and out and at them tonight because if I do *not*, if I hesitate or I am slow, if I fail, if they are faster, if I do not go *out* ...

They will come in.

Steve Beard

'THE LAST GOOD WAR'

Steve Beard was born in the M4 corridor in 1961. He has appeared at Pharmakon in 1992 and Virtual Futures: Datableed in 1996, and contributed to magazines as various as *i-D*, *Wired*, *Ray Gun* and *Skin Two*. The initial volume of his hackwork is available as *Logic Bomb: Transmissions from the Edge of Style Culture* (Serpent's Tail). Meanwhile, he has authored the surrealist book *Perfumed Head* (Book Works) and the ambient novel *Digital Leatherette* (CodeX) characterised by William Gibson as 'neo-Blakeian riff-collage'.

POWICK BRIDGE AND OTHER STRANGE ATTRACTORS

It begins with the looting of a convenience store by local residents of the Powick Bridge estate in Middle England. 'Asian Capitalist Fuck Off' is the slogan sprayed on the charred walls of the Stop N Shop franchise managed by Trevor Cholmondeley-Patel. His autobiography, *Refusal Often Offends: How I Started the Northwest European Middle Intensity Conflict*, is later filmed as an interactive movie starring Bruce Willis. He eventually becomes a dollar millionaire and emigrates to Florida.

THE DRIFT TO EDGEHILL

Copycat rioting spreads to the Edgehill estate as local media nets webcast the news of the Powick Bridge incident to the rest of Middle England. Land vehicles are overturned and set alight at the edge of the estate by stoned juveniles who taunt the huddled data vendors and digicam stalkers. By the time the Crown mafia decides to send in troops to contain the situation, members of the para-political action group Underground English Resistance have already moved in to barricade the estate.

THE DISTURBANCE AT EDGEHILL

Babylon TV Commentator #1: In an attempt to batter the Edgehill rioters into submission, the Crown mafia has been deafening them with sonic blasts of heritage rock played at high amplification. The rioters have responded by setting up their own sound system on the roof of C Block and hammering out shock waves of nosebleed techno. Who will win the struggle for hearts and minds, Reggie?

Babylon TV Commentator #2: The side with the biggest amps, Ron.

BRENTFORD AND TURNHAM GREEN

The tightly organised cells of UER begin to mobilise in South England as a call to arms is posted on the MicroNet. They unearth caches of weapons – power drills, encryption software, ex-Irish War service revolvers – and conscript local gangs of carjackers and joyriders to storm designated Crown bunkers such as weather centres, orbital prisons, research and training centres and military bases.

HOPTON HEATH, SEACROFT MOOR AND LICHFIELD

Networked rioting spreads to the fenced territories of North England. The Crown mafia mobilises all active army units to put down the mass insurrection with water cannon and rubber bullets. Babylon TV choppers scramble to cover the events from rooftop helipads all over Ukania.

THE SOUTHWEST AND THE DISTURBANCE AT STRATTON

Excerpt from Underground English Resistance political flier: How to Make a Petrol Bomb. Step One: Liberate vehicle. Step Two: Drive vehicle to designated target. Step Three: Remove vehicle's petroltank cap. Step Four: Insert lit box of matches. Step Five: Scram.

RIPPLE FIELD AND CHEWTON MENDIP

The Crown mafia issues a D Notice to the Ukanian gatekeepers of Time Warner, Disney, Viacom, News Corp, Sony, Seagram and all relevant global media nets proscribing the filming of what they refer to as 'the local difficulties'. The pocket cable station Babylon TV sidesteps the ban by renting time from a Korean fatsat whose footprint covers Northwest Europe. Other datavendors form a syndicate to buy pooled footage at graded rates and agree to let Babylon TV front for them in any future legal action.

THE DISTURBANCE AT CHALGROVE FIELD
Roberta Lockyear emerges as the chief spokesperson for UER on the MicroNet. Her polyvalent body stylings and enigmatic facial scarifications are what attracted the sponsors of Babylon TV to her live vid feed on the Fuck The World telethon. It is as if she has been selected as the phobic object of choice by a resurgent Europe preparing for immolation. Urban Decay offer her a modelling contract.

THE DISTURBANCES AT LANDSDOWN AND ROUNDWAY DOWN
Urban Decay meta-media sample: Shot of Roberta Lockyear crawling across a quicktime billboard. Ethnocentric Afro-Saxon fetishes orbit her head and her contacts flash red with the cross of St George. She sighs as a downtrodden icon of the Palace of Westminster morphs into the Kremlin and through a moebius involution seems to spit her out whole. 'Ukanian Troops Out Of England' unfurls in a banner strap beneath the logo of the cosmetics industry sponsor.

THE PHASE SHIFTING OF BRISTOL 1.0
Excerpt from Deutsche Telekom inter-office memo [translation]: This doesn't make it as atrocity footage. Tanks and rolled cars in the street? It's too Prague '68, too Tiananmen Square. English guerrilla forces have a political settlement as their military objective. They don't need to make war. Instead they're playing a waiting game using ritual elements – stalking, hiding, simulating –

borrowed from hunt sab campaigns. Where's the sense of threat? It's all too tame.

THE ATTRACTOR AT ADWALTON MOOR

Charles 3 decides to take personal command of the political situation in Middle England. He appears on the *Lite Lunch* chatshow on Pearson TV and declares a state of national emergency as he pats his grandchild on the head. The invited studio audience laughs dutifully. He appears withdrawn, psychotic and old. His webcast is picked up by US datacarriers and rolls across the North American heartland spliced with archive footage of Hirohito and Saddam – an electronic cloud swollen with premonitions of war.

THE ATTRACTOR AT GAINSBOROUGH

The Palace of Westminster is shut down and a Ministry Of Defence situation room established in a Whitehall bunker. Domestic propaganda bulletins on the old UBC nets code the members of UER as toxic waste elements, genetic regressives and mutant human livestock. The international corporate credit of the Crown mafia's original D Notice expires and US datacarriers mobilise in Ukania. Carefully targeted Babylon TV voxpop subliminals flirt with the idea of ecocide.

THE SOUTHWEST AND TORRINGTON

UBC propaganda tape splice: Close-up of the surgically enhanced features of a Sloane Warrior, her mouth taut with the shock of the Torrington Offensive. 'We can't fight these scum with rubber and water. I blame Europe. We need to implement a mass culling. Otherwise it's all over.' Cut to the zip of a Ukanian Army body-bag.

THE CONTAINMENT OF GLOUCESTER AND ALDBOURNE CHASE

Realtime TV czar Larry King persuades Charles 3 and Roberta Lockyear to share satellite time on his CNN chatshow and accept his mediation of their dispute. The old King is visibly anxious, the youth rebel cool and indifferent. Nothing is resolved and the ratings take a dip. The satellite feed is taped by the Anti-Federal Reservists and shows the two white guys discussing their drug habits while the credits roll. The soundbyte is sampled by the Real Fake Messiahs and becomes a crossover hip-hop hit on the East Coast.

THE FIRST DISTURBANCE OF NEWBURY 1.0
The RAF unloads surplus Cold War smartbombs into the evacuated treehouses, bashes and shanty dwellings surrounding the motorway by-pass at Newbury. Operation Excalibur (a name picked at random by an MOD computer) is designated a success by Crown spin doctors.

THE FIRST DISTURBANCE OF NEWBURY 2.0
The RAF nosecone footage from Operation Excalibur is sold to Sony licensee Mudwrestler and becomes the basis of the cult vidgame War Porn.

ATTRACTORS AT WINCEBY AND HULL
Operation Excalibur reschedules tolerance limits in the suburbs of Middle England so that the emergency Crown rhetoric of 'strategic social withdrawal' is now accepted as routine. Old US Army bases are rezoned as housing estates (inhabitants are advised to bring their own tents), housing estates as prisons (time-coded smartcards are issued to all inmates), prisons as gulags (the writ of habeas corpus is abolished). Refugee columns appear on the hard shoulders of the motorways.

STRANGE ATTRACTORS IN THE SOUTH AND WEST
Babylon TV in-car traffic analysis vox pop: These people should be made to pay road tax. Fucking peds.

THE ATTRACTORS OF BASING HOUSE AND ARUNDEL

The civilian dead at Newbury are designated UER and bulldozed straight into the ground by Crown military engineers. Babylon TV switches attention to the Whitehall soaps, where an army general's driver has come out as a transsexual. Nude pictures are posted on the MicroNet. Roberta Lockyear's celebrity is eclipsed.

ATTRACTORS AT NANTWICH AND NEWARK

Underground English Resistance opens a new semiofront in the conflict by specifying out-of-town hypermarkets, logistics industry sheds, motorway service stations and other autonomous commercial zones as legitimate military targets. They announce that an old Soviet briefcase bomb has come into their possession and threaten to detonate it high above London. The FTSE 100 index takes a dive. The Crown mafia puts out a wake-up call to its sleeping partner.

STRANGE ATTRACTORS IN THE SOUTH

The Corporation of London mobilises its occult forces of cryptoanalysts, games theorists, remote viewers and meta-mathematicians. Crown territory is recoded as a 3D killzone sited along multiple electromagnetic wavelengths. The concept of 'civil society' is understood by all networked players to be suspended for the duration of the conflict.

THE DISTURBANCE AT CHERITON

The Crown's psy ops forces secretly firebomb a Texaco 24-hour hypermarket. The UBC datafeed nudges Babylon TV into labelling the incident as a terrorist action. UER deflects the spin by accepting the designation.

ATTRACTORS BEFORE CROPREDY BRIDGE

Time Warner databyte: Hand-held vidcam footage of a skin-graft op taking place in a mobile burns unit plugged into the remnants of a motorway bridge. The medical technicians wear Kappa. The patient is conscious. The VO is making a pitch for medico-military donations on behalf of 'a tiny island kingdom racing to beat the nuclear clock'.

THE PHASE SHIFTING OF CROPREDY BRIDGE
Reuters' financial systems analysis report: The Ukania crisis zone no longer a productive field for the investment of virtual seed capital. Growth cycles encouraged to propagate elsewhere. Tip: South Africa.

THE DRIFT TO MARSTON MOOR
The Corporation of London rouses itself from its digital mantras and shifts into the atavistic shape of the Walking City. Clumps of fibre-optic cable are wrenched from the earth. The sun blinks.

THE DISTURBANCE AT MARSTON MOOR 1.0
Radio transmission from strategic North England target site: shhhzzz fuck oh fuck oh fuck oh fuck oh fuck oh fuck oh fuck ohshhhzzz ...

THE DISTURBANCE AT MARSTON MOOR 2.0
Babylon TV Commentator #1: The resistant cells of the body politic invader have been totally recuperated by the molecular genetic code of London's Walking City. The immunisation process is complete.
Babylon TV Commentator #2: Who's gonna clean up the mess, though, Ron?

THE GHOST DANCE IN THE SOUTHWEST
Straggling UER survivors from the Marston Moor ecocide campaign filter into the Southwest along one of the old motorway corridors. Cornish insurgents who have set up their own tribal moot in the peninsula hook up to join them upon the advice of their data prophets. A promiscuous seepage of hybrid bodies, split memes, army surplus drugs and intra-Atlantic rhythms begins to

assemble itself around an emergency call. Cornish remote viewers plug the whole mix into the Tintagel data hoard and invoke the terrible loas of Merlin. There is a brief interval of calm.

THE DISTURBANCE AT LOSTWITHIEL

US datacarriers resort to the old imperial paradigm of Otherness to characterise the modernised bardic warfare taking place in Ukania. Folk memories of the US Army's own exterminist campaigns – against the Seminole, the Vietcong, the Amish – bleed into the delirious footage of tattooed warrior-monks and cyborg berserkers.

LOSTWITHIEL TO NEWBURY

Surfpunk combatant diary: Man, we were amped up to the max on those GlaxoWellcome beanies. Patched right into the event as it crashed over our heads. Rode it all the way down into the cognitive dreamtime. Hit the zone and the songlines opened right up. Merlin jumped me and let me take out five, six levels of enemy intention in a coupla pico-seconds. Punkass London gameboys. That Walking City turned out to be a real scissors-and-paste job.

THE SECOND PHASE SHIFTING OF NEWBURY 1.0

The peripheral weakening of the Corporation of London's cognitive immune system leads to a sudden collapse of international confidence in its core black bank network. Capital takes flight. The cyberspace map of the world's financial markets tilts in the direction of the occult data havens of the Caribbean.

THE SECOND PHASE SHIFTING OF NEWBURY 2.0

London throws off the ruined shell of notional Crown symbolic determination and puts the shout out to its imperial codemasters in Washington DC. The Cornish surfpunks go home. Underground English Resistance dissolves into a wash of sectarian factions – the Sovereign Mobsters, New Edge Levellers, Atomic Saxon Warriors, Overground English Assemblage, etc.

MON/ROSE'S FIRST GHOST DANCE: TIPPERMUIR
London's call is intercepted by the Edinburgh posse who see their chance to extend fractional caste hegemony over the disputed territories of North England and beyond. A summons is issued to the celebrated event programmer and occult data runner Our Lady of the Holy Mon/Rose. Her remit: Redeem Scotland. She exits retirement and sets up her Orpheus spook engine under Eildon Hill. People get scared.

MON/ROSE'S FIRST GHOST DANCE: ABERDEEN
Babylon TV Commentator #1: The Hibernians are quitting the reservations. Taking to the highlands and tearing up the roads. What's going on?
Babylon TV Commentator #2: It's just another mass rave, Ron.

MON/ROSE'S SECOND GHOST DANCE: FYVIE CASTLE AND INVERLOCHY
Mon/Rose sifts through the wreckage of received national myths and begins to build a simulacrum of Albion under Eildon Hill. She peels back the antique landscape fittings of Walter Scott and discovers that beneath the tales of selkies and peasant charms lies the unsoothing reality of aristocratic inter-alliance and Ukanian dynastic sovereignty. The French Revolution is judged a missed opportunity. The American Revolution is invoked.

FIRST OPERATIONS OF THE BENIGN INTERVENTION FORCE
Washington DC returns London's call and receives the signal to move in and secure its off-shore Northwest European database. The Defence Space Council calls up its classified Ukanian air-space intelligence programmes from distributed milsat sensors – Lacrosse, Vortex, Parcae – and compiles a map of ammunition dumps, high relief targets and airfields. US medico-military intervention carries a United Nations brand name and organises

itself according to a warcrime prevention mandate. The electronic ether hums.

MON/ROSE'S THIRD GHOST DANCE: DUNDEE
Mon/Rose floats into the Jacobite dreamtime hitched between the escape of the American Revolution and the compromise of Ukania's 1688 constitutional coup. She taps out the counter-myth of saviours-in-hiding over the loas of Bonnie Prince Charlie and James 7 until she makes the connection with the sleeping totem of Arthur and slides all the way back to the Caledonian suicide bomber Calgacus. There is serial tumult.

MON/ROSE'S FOURTH GHOST DANCE: AULDEARN
Mon/Rose sounds out her anti-imperial catechism. 'Ukanians Go Home. Anglo-Saxons Go Home. Romans Go Home.' She invents a psychic double to cope with the stress of handling such a massive disturbance and it ravishes the bound and gagged loa of the primal hunk Gogmagog. 'Trojans Go Home.' Mon/Rose exceeds her Scotch remit.

THE DRIFT TO NASEBY
Fort Knox DISSIMNET remote viewing unit random surveillance printout: interrupt the, er, the domestic electronic transmissions with our own version of . . . with an accurate picture of the situation using, yuhknow, digital simulation and voice synthesis and [static] . . . like, er, yuhknow, like in Guatemala and so on.

THE DISTURBANCE AT NASEBY 1.0
General Mercedes Fairfax St Clair of the UN Benign Intervention Force models her invasion of Ukania as a police action designed to stop the human rights abuses of warlords and bandits while establishing the minimum necessary conditions for a rapid transfer of humanitarian aid. Washington DC sponsors secret Dublin peace talks between the Crown mafia, English Overground Assemblage and the Edinburgh posse. Mon/Rose is cut off.

THE DISTURBANCE AT NASEBY 2.0
UNBIF Unmanned Aerial Vehicles disable strategic Ukanian targets using a wide range of non-lethal weapons. Operation Aircraft Carrier One in the end yields three North American casualties – all from friendly fire. Other non-US military dead are officially discounted.

THE ATTRACTOR AT LANGPORT
Radio transmission from Stealth aircraft electromagnetic pulse operator state monitoring system: Cold, cold smoked the bitch!

THE DISTURBANCE AT ALFORD
UNBIF Operation Aircraft Carrier One corporate sponsor credits: Thanks to Bolt Beranek & Newman, Evans & Sutherland, General Dynamics, General Electric, Grumnan, Hughes, IBM, Lockheed, Loral, Martin Marietta, McDonnell Douglas, Motorola, Rockwell, Silicon Graphics. Party on, guys!

THE DISTURBANCE AT KILSYTH
Forensic sample from approved Dublin list of indigenous London war dead: A 17.5 per cent match for names included in the Central London Residential UT phonebook.

THE PHASE SHIFTING OF BRISTOL 2.0
The UNBIF enters the most politically sensitive phase of its operation – deployment of specific human resources. US military personnel are bulked up in Kevlar frag vests and airtight fatigues. They are equipped with optical munitions, neuro-chemicals, acoustic weapons and superadhesives. It looks good on the live satellite feed. They play like maternal cyborg relief workers.

THE DISTURBANCE AT PHILIPHAUGH
Time Warner databyte: Massive African-American techno-warrior blinking in the thin light. Off-screen VO: 'What are you doing

here?' Peripheral attack of hand-held low-energy lasers. 'It sure beats McDonald's, know wha I'm sayin.'

THE SWARMING OF ROWTON HEATH
Fag Hag Lad Mag double-page fashion spread: Mil tech babes doing catwalk turns on a model of the Ukanian landmass photoshopped to resemble a phantasmic aircraft carrier with a steep white prow. Headline: Arcadian Shoot-'Em-Up. Strapline: Haute couture combat gear goes wild in the country.

THE FINAL SWARMING IN THE SOUTHWEST
Babylon TV Commentator #1: Members of the UN Benign Intervention Force are being mobbed by hordes of weeping people wherever they go. Mon/Rose and her tartan army of recalcitrants have no real popular support.
Babylon TV Commentator #2: This just in, Ron ... General Fairfax St Clair has called off the final assault in time for the ad break.

THE LAST MINUTES OF THE FIRST MIDDLE INTENSITY CONFLICT
The US Department of Defense sells the licence for the official version of the Northwest European MIC to the National Football League. The sim for the sports arena uses much of the original footage.

THE SECOND MIDDLE INTENSITY CONFLICT
Time Warner soundbyte of the war as delivered by General Fairfax St Clair: We have no further use for enemy production.

MON/ROSE'S LAST GHOST DANCE
Mon/Rose is locked tight with her massive stacked up under Eildon Hill. She takes a deep breath and reels in her psychic double. The Orpheus engine spits fire from its wheels as the bonds of spacetime dissolve and the loas of Gogmagog begin to shove their

way up through the earth. Mon/Rose has prophesied the vitrified duns and brochs of Albion as the elevated docking stations for interstellar contact. She awaits deliverance of a messianic crannog redeemed by the leakage of sanctified positroniums. She thinks she can take the heat.

THE DRIFT TO DUNBAR

Fort Knox DISSIMNET remote viewing float tank readout of realtime intercept drone pilot: uh huh yeah yeah baby you lissen to me now thass right here I come nice n slo lemme in now thass it you know you be wantin it you called me up girl and here I all am *request dropzone coordinates* no no no never never doubt that I am here for you never stop believin I am whatever avatar you want me to be just keep those eyes closed nice n tight *enemy defences neutralised* uh huh uh huh come on now thass it UGH *intercept over* I am the fuck outta here.

THE DISTURBANCE AT DUNBAR AND ITS AFTER-IMAGE

General Fairfax St Clair becomes the temporary lord protector of the Ukanian state apparatus as the Dublin peace talks stagger towards a conclusion. She fills the interregnum with a Westminster victory parade which uses Mon/Rose's corpse as its principal symbolic component. Artists and craftspeople from London's mystery cults construct an effigy of the vanquished data runner and set it in a mobile crinoline fashioned from her broken bones. The most devoted of her followers form a mass suicide cult and hurl themselves in the path of the fatal juggernaut as it rolls down the Mall. The remainder content themselves with offering their sacrificed mistress a tribute of soft toys, cellophane-wrapped flowers, helium balloons and other mortuary goods. Burial is at sea.

THE LINKS TO WORCESTER

Time Warner defining moment of the war: Massed ranks of

Hibernian dervishers – decked out in warpaint, jewels and bones – prostrate themselves before the descending shape of a UNBIF UAV as it is received by the ecstatic figure of Our Lady of the Holy Mon/Rose on Eildon Hill.

THE DISTURBANCE AT WORCESTER AND THE LINE OF FLIGHT OF CHARLES 3

The UNBIF gets on with the mundane business of disarming combatants, maintaining ceasefire boundaries, arresting war criminals and stage-managing elections as power is transferred from General Fairfax St Clair to the new regional assemblies in Westminster, London and Edinburgh. The Ukanian state apparatus is dismantled and airlifted to the island of Jersey where an embittered Charles 3 sets up a government-in-exile without bothering to unpack. The old Palace of Westminister is condemned and pulled down.

Tony White

'AO'

Tony White is the editor of *britpulp!* and the author of cult pulp novel *Road Rage!* published by Low Life Books in 1997. He has worked in a variety of occupations including a spell on the 'Bukowski Shift' in the Royal Mail's North London sorting office, and is currently Literary Editor for *The Idler* magazine. Tony White's novel *CHARLIEUNCLENORFOLKTANGO* ('your standard, violent, stream of sentience, alien-abduction cop novel') is published by CodeX. His forthcoming novel, *Satan! Satan! Satan!* is published by Attack! Tony lives in the East End of London.

Every school child knows the last words of Harry Klein: 'Wolfgang! Get my ruler! I'm gonna measure the Book of Judgement!'

Not quite so well known though is the story of a little orphan called Hans who was born the only child of a simple tradesman's family in Bremen, Germany, in 1884. No-one really knows what caused the fire which killed both of his parents. Like the late Hermann Kumpfmüller in his flawed but near exhaustive biography *Klein's Größenmaß* (Schriftenreihe der Akademie, 1967)[1] we must rely upon conjecture. Perhaps, as Kumpfmüller suggests, one dark winter's night little Hans was awakened by fearful noises and crept down to his father's workshop. Perhaps he did gaze in terror on a primal scene lit only by a flickering oil lamp: that of two sweating bodies, half naked, rolling in the sawdust and seemingly intent on killing each other. Perhaps his father caught sight of him and bellowed at Hans in animal rage. Perhaps little Hans then ran from the workshop in terror, knocking over the oil lamp. Perhaps too he heard his mother's cries of pleasure turn to screams of terror and death. What is documented though, is that with both parents dead little Hans was sent to the orphanage: his sole possession being a small steel ruler that he rescued from the ashes of his father's workshop.

[1] See also *Measure for Measure: The Klein Story*, H. Kumpfmüller, trans. Quintin Pontalis (Chicago Univ. Press, 1975)

Aside from the annual bill for his and all the other orphans' upkeep in the parish records, little is known of those years. Was the orphanage a happy place full of laughter and games, or was it presided over by some grim tyrant whose only thought was for the pleasures that he might take from his pathetic charges? No documentation remains. Even Kumpfmüller himself is somewhat vague about the identity of the sadist whose lascivious presence casts such a shadow over the early chapters of his study.

What *is* known is that some years later a well dressed man was walking through the poorer district of Bremen, reading aloud to his companions from a letter, when suddenly a young urchin ran out from the shadows brandishing a metallic object. Mistaking it for a weapon of some kind, and fearful for his life, the man's escorts seized the boy, and were about to beat him soundly, but seeing that his 'attacker' was merely a scruffy little child, he bade them to stop, and asked:

'*Was gibt es so Wichtiges, junger Mann, daß Sie meine Begleiter deratig erschrecken müssen?*'[1]

'*Verzeihung gnädiger Herr,*' said the urchin, '*darf ich diesen Brief ausmessen?*'[2]

'*Wie heißt du, Junge?*'[3] he asked.

'*Hans, gnädiger Herr,*'[4] said the boy proudly.

This man of course was Klein, 'der Wolf', one of the nation's leading industrialists and a friend of the Kaiser. So captivated was he with little Hans's pluck and curiosity that, on discovering he was a poor orphan and being childless himself, he adopted little Hans as his own son and gave him the best education that money could buy.

Little Hans Klein's school days are so well documented in Kumpfmüller's biography that I do not need to repeat them here.

[1] 'What is so important, young man, that you should wish to frighten my companions so?'

[2] 'Please sir, may I measure that letter?'

[3] 'What is your name, child?'

[4] 'Hans, Sir!'

One crucial episode though, demands clarification. Coming home
from school for the summer holidays, Kumpfmüller tells us that
Hans (who was now a tall and handsome young man) encountered
a group of older boys who were playing with paper darts and
loudly cursing their poor performance. He boldly approached the
boys and asked if he might measure their darts: perhaps they were
made from incorrectly proportioned pieces of paper. But the bullies
grabbed his rule and beat him, before forcing him to tearfully eat
the paper darts.

'*Iß sie,*' they commanded, '*und wir werden morgen früh deinen Haufen
ausmessen!*'[1]

Then, laughing, they ripped his trousers off and took turns to
bugger him. So severe was the beating Hans received – with his
own ruler – that the numerals and increments were to be graven on
the soft skin of his thighs and buttocks for weeks afterwards. Brutal
though this episode may seem, recent research has questioned not
only its central position in Kumpfmüller's study, but also its
basis in fact.

In March of 1904 Hans met, and was instantly captivated by,
a young girl out walking with her governess. That they became
the greatest of friends is well documented in the letters that he
sent her from university. Perhaps Kumpfmüller is correct when
he suggests that Hans fell in love with Anna Meyer at this time.
And perhaps they did discover that true love can be a tender thing
full of wonder and joy, far removed from the brutality of the
orphanage or the gang rape. Who could fail to have been moved
by Kumpfmüller's account of their reunion upon Hans's return
from Berlin (although more attentive readers will know that the
episode where the young lovers are disturbed was removed from
later editions of Kumpfmüller's biography after it was pointed out
in court that Anna's governess was an elderly woman at the time,
and confined to a bathchair).

The reader may forgive me for the abbreviated nature of these

---

[1] 'Eat them and we'll measure your turds in the morning!'

notes. The story of Klein's rapid ascendency in his adoptive father's company is well documented, and his marriage to Anna Meyer was the social event of 1910. Kumpfmüller's account of their wedding night is based solely upon the testimony of a maid (known only as 'Mathilde B') who was apparently driven by an insatiable sexual curiosity to secrete herself in the wardrobe of their bedchamber. And while that story – of beatings with a steel ruler, marked flesh and a congress unlikely to result in the conception of children – may have become a classic of post-war erotica in its own right, researchers have been unable to locate any 'Mathilde B,' in the employment records of the Klein household.

Anna died in childbirth one year after the wedding, survived by their son. Shortly after this tragedy the grieving Hans was entrusted with the task of establishing an office in the United States. Perhaps it was then, upon encountering the bewildering array of stationery in use in the New World (various European gauges, English Foolscap, Quarto and American Letter) that Hans's simple dream was forged: to harmonise the papers of the world. An ambition which can only have been accelerated by the turmoil of the Great War. And, as Kumpfmüller reminds us, the assassin Princip was himself a stationery clerk.

The 1920s and '30s were decades of discovery and intellectual ferment for 'Harry' Klein. The public renown that would follow his company's transformation of the machinery of the print and paper industries was preceded by years of private toil and domestic anguish, in a period that came to be immortalised by John Huston in his film *The Paper Man* (1961, Paramount Studios). Montgomery Clift's lead is held to be among the best performances of his career: he brings a kind of other-worldly grace to the role of Harry Klein. And who could forget the scene where a distraught Harry blames his son Wolfgang (played by a still fresh-faced Kenneth Anger) for the death of Anna. However the movie's most famous line, which warrants Klein's second entry in the Oxford Dictionary of Quotations: 'The pen may well be mightier than the sword, but it ain't worth a damn without paper,' is now known never to have actually been spoken by Klein. It came – rather – from the pen of veteran screenwriter Jerry Friel.

At 11.30 p.m., on 3 December 1938, after years of trial and error, Klein set his machine cutters for the ratio 7:10. The rest, as they say, is history.

In a letter to the then President Franklin D. Roosevelt, he described his joy at finding what he called, 'the ideal gauge for standardised paper production. I have discovered,' he continued, 'a ratio whereby the sheet can at the mid-point of its longer side be cut, with resulting sheets exactly the proportions of the original retaining – ad infinitum. I shall the mother sheet designate A0, and with each bisection thusly: A1, A2, A3, A4 and so on.'

Klein cannot have imagined that with his, 'and so on', he was laying down one of the most quixotic challenges of modern organic chemistry. Readers with a scientific 'bent' though, will doubtless have seen the widely syndicated electron micrographs of a two-molecule-thick wafer of crystalline Benzo-silicate being 'cut' by research students at MIT to produce a mind-bogglingly small A100 sheet.

Klein's death in 1940 came just a few weeks before a patent lawyer named Chester F. Carlson filed patent documents for a machine to duplicate patent documents: the first mimeostat. Sadly then, he never lived to see the development of the photocopier, and the subsequent adoption of his A gauge as the universal default standard for photocopier production.

In what is surely the most poignant part of his biography, Kumpfmüller tells us that Harry Klein chose the designation 'A' for his paper gauge in remembrance of his dead wife. My own researches have confirmed this. Indeed last year I visited the Smithsonian Institute, to whose care Klein's notes and letters, his ruler, and those first sheets of 7:10 paper were entrusted by Wolfgang Klein before his death in 1983. As we gazed upon its yellowing surface in the climate controlled vault constructed for its preservation by the Klein Foundation, the curator confided to me that Smithsonian staff refer to that Ur sheet of A0 paper simply as 'Anna.'

Jack Trevor Story

'RIDING BAREBACK (JACK'S LAST WORDS)'

Jack Trevor Story wrote *Live Now, Pay Later* — which was pretty much his own creed — and his early novel *The Trouble with Harry* was filmed by Hitchcock, who paid him one hundred pounds for it. Jack Trevor Story also wrote some of the best *Budgie* scripts for television, and *Postman's Knock* for Spike Milligan, while many remember him as an eccentric, charming columnist for *The Guardian*. In the late sixties, following publication of his masterpiece, *One Last Mad Embrace*, and after visiting Michael Moorcock one Boxing Day, he was arrested on a minor traffic issue and taken to Ladbroke Grove Police Station. Thereafter his career became increasingly erratic. In the last year of his life he experienced untypical bouts of paranoia. His publishers went bankrupt and his books went out of print. His only books still currently in print are published by Savoy, Manchester.

Jack spent his last years in a small flat attached to the farm museum in Milton Keynes. He died in 1991 having just completed his last, and possibly greatest, novel, *Shabby Weddings*. The pages reproduced here are those he wrote only moments before a fatal heart-attack at his typewriter: Jack's last words.

The Jack Trevor Story Memorial Prize is a literary award, the terms of which are that the recipient should spend the money within a fortnight and not have a thing to show for it.

Peter burst into my ear from the traffic around him at Tufnell Park tube — just now. I told him I've finished the book. He told me that no condoms has paid off with his Mexican girl, Sylvia (Sylvia?) with a dose of something or other. The Royal Free told her to round up her lovers and Pete got a needle stuck into his dick with a bit of cotton wool. Oh, fuck me! Dad! But they are both okay. Tell Berkhamstead and Carol.

'How do I get to Walthamstow from here?'

'Keep going east, cross Holloway Road into Seven Sisters and ask a policeman. Me and Ulla got married.'

'I'm just passing Holloway Prison.'

Well. Maybe it's the same thing. If I get any morsel of serious joy we shall actually do it. Somewhere quiet, the year's unnoticed event. We have our second-order state of bliss but it leaves me unprotected from the danger of unusual behaviour and Social Services. Also I kissed a new girl today in The Vaults pub at Stony. Lucy looks like Bimbo-land in her big Spanish Moss of blonde hair and leathers with a band-aid skirt — she is academic, her dad none other than Professor Bamwell of bio-chemistry, family home in the French Rhône river country. 'I would marry you tomorrow,' she said, when Chris had gone for the car. Lucy runs a high-tech author-servicing scam and plays drums.

'Here he comes.' Chris came in fast under the Bull Coaching arch and vanished for a minute before re-appearing facing Leicester and home. I asked Lucy to come and see me. Damn, she doesn't drive. 'I've got a group account for taxis – no problem,' she said. 'Bring your drums!'

'I love you.'

'I know.'

It's good because she knows about the umbrella; about the other side of my bed. She is reading this book right now. As you are. Yes, indeed. STOP PRESS: Good news time – Sylvia and Pete are expecting!

THE END

And I'm in Love!!